Sadie's Secret

**Center Point
Large Print**

Also by Kathleen Y'Barbo and available from Center Point Large Print:

Flora's Wish
Millie's Treasure

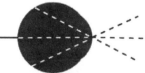

This Large Print Book carries the Seal of Approval of N.A.V.H.

KATHLEEN Y'BARBO

CENTER POINT LARGE PRINT
THORNDIKE, MAINE

The text of this Large Print edition is unabridged. In other aspects, this book may vary from the original edition. Printed in the United States of America on permanent paper. Set in 16-point Times New Roman type.

ISBN: 978-1-62899-516-9

Library of Congress Cataloging-in-Publication Data

Y'Barbo, Kathleen.
Sadie's secret / Kathleen Y'Barbo. — Center Point Large Print edition.
pages cm
Summary: "Sadie Callum is a master of disguise. Undercover agent William Jefferson Tucker is not looking for marriage—pretend or otherwise—but he needs the cover of a wife to clear his name and solve the art forgery case that has eluded him for years. But what will happen to his heart?"—Provided by publisher.
ISBN 978-1-62899-516-9 (library binding : alk. paper)
1. Large type books. I. Title.
PS3625.B37S33 2015
813'.6—dc23
2014050335

For Kay Malone
I miss you, friend.

"Do you particularly like the man?" he muttered, at his own image; "why should you particularly like a man who resembles you? There is nothing in you to like; you know that . . . Change places with him, and would you have been looked at by those blue eyes as he was . . . ?"
Charles Dickens
A Tale of Two Cities

The Lord said unto Cain, Where is Abel thy brother? And he said, I know not: Am I my brother's keeper?
Genesis 4:9

One

May 10, 1889
Louisiana State Penitentiary
Angola, Louisiana

Detective William Jefferson Tucker of the Criminal Investigations Division, London Metropolitan Police, stepped across the threshold of the sewer pit known as the Louisiana State Penitentiary at Angola with one purpose in mind. To see his brother, also named William.

William John Tucker.

His twin. His polar opposite.

With his first order of business being an explanation of exactly what John had done this time, he turned toward Major Samuel James's office. When in doubt, go to the top, that was his motto. And Major James was the top dog around here.

"Hold on there," someone called. Jefferson turned to see a uniformed guard coming toward him, one hand on his holster and the other pointing in his direction.

"Just paying a visit to the warden," he said with all the charm his mother had taught him. "Nothing to get upset about."

"We'll just see about that," the guard said as he

nodded toward the other end of the dimly lit hall. "Just come on back here and sign in, and then we will see if the warden's interested in visiting today."

Shaking his head, Jefferson tried not to show amusement at the man's pompous behavior. While he had seen the other side of a jail cell on many occasions, it had always been in the position of arresting officer and not prison guard. To spend day after day in this place would cause anyone to own an ill temper.

When the papers were produced, Jefferson signed them. "Anything else you need?" he asked as politely as he could manage.

"Any kind of proof you are who you say you are would be appreciated," he said in a tone that just barely toed the line between polite and sarcastic.

"Gladly."

"And I will be needing your weapon."

Routine procedure in prisons, and yet Jefferson hated it. Reluctantly, he removed his revolver and handed it to the guard.

"That all you got?" He gave Jefferson a sweeping look. "Nothing else you can hurt anybody with?"

"Just a folding knife."

"Hand that over too."

Jefferson offered up his knife and then reached for his identification, carefully selecting the papers that would not give away his current undercover role in London. Placing what he had on the rough slab of wood that served as a desk between them, he stood back and waited while the guard examined the documents.

"And what brings you here?" The guard took in an exaggerated breath and then pretended to cough. "Sure can't be the fresh air and sunshine."

Jefferson played along, pretending to find the gag amusing. "I am here to see my brother."

"Your brother?" The guard clutched the papers as he looked up at Jefferson. "And just who would your brother be?"

"John Tucker."

"John Tucker," the guard echoed as he opened an oversized leather book that sent a cloud of dust into the already rancid air.

The odd idea that this process was beginning to feel very much like checking into a hotel occurred. Jefferson decided he would keep that thought to himself.

"Don't see any John . . ."

"*William* John," he amended, irritated not for the first time that his father had insisted on giving both his sons the same first name and then calling them by their middle name.

The guard's grimy finger paused below a line of scribbling. "Tucker. Well, here we go. William J. Tucker." He looked up at Jefferson, his face now unreadable. "Wait here."

Without another word of explanation, he hurried off down the hall, Jefferson's credentials still clutched in his hand. A door shut somewhere off in the distance and then opened again.

"Initial for your property here," he said when he returned.

Jefferson noted the date and the items he had just surrendered and then placed his initials on the line beside them to indicate agreement.

"All right. Come with me, Mr. Tucker," the guard said, not quite making eye contact.

Detective Tucker, he almost said. Instead, Jefferson kept silent. Better not to make enemies of anyone in this place. "Yes, of course." He followed the guard past the warden's office and around the corner, stopping at an unmarked door.

"Right in there," the guard said as he used a key from his vest pocket to open the door.

The room was dark, but a lamp in the passage-way sent a weak shaft of light across what appeared to be a table and a bench. "I would be much obliged if you would turn on a light in here," Jefferson said, the last of his patience with the ridiculous situation disappearing fast.

"Just go on in and a light will come on."

He was about to protest when the guard shoved him inside and turned the lock.

"Open this door!" Jefferson demanded. "This is not funny. I demand to see either my brother or the warden immediately."

"You just wait right there, Tucker. You will see the warden for sure."

Jefferson felt along the edge of the wall, his fingers sliding across a combination of dirt and slime held together by something so foul smelling he refused to contemplate its source. A moment later he found the bench and managed to sit.

Outside the door footsteps approached and then halted. He heard voices arguing, their words indistinguishable through the thick walls.

Finally, the door opened and a man whose attire told Jefferson he might be the warden stepped inside. The guard shadowed Major James, as did another underling of some sort.

"Look," Jefferson said, "all I wanted was to see my brother. Is this how you treat all your visitors, Major?"

"The major isn't here today, but I am the man in charge. You can call me Butler. Won't need any name other than that. And as to your question, no. This is the way we treat those who belong inside a cell."

"Inside a cell? What are you talking about?"

Butler thumped Jefferson's credentials with his free hand. "These here papers say you are Jefferson Tucker. Is that correct?"

He gave the man a curt nod. "It is."

"So what you're saying is that you are indeed the man whose name you have given to the guard?"

"Yes," he said, this time with far less respect.

"And that you have a brother currently incarcerated in our fine facility." When Jefferson nodded, he continued. "And what is that inmate's name?"

"His name is John Tucker," Jefferson snapped as he sensed a shakedown of some sort in the offing. It was time to tell them who he really was. "William John Tucker. Look, I know how these things work, and I am not someone you can play around with. I have credentials that prove I am a detective with the London Metropolitan Police."

The man's eyes narrowed. "I'm not sure I would believe that. You certainly don't sound like no foreigner, so I suggest you change your tune and own up to the truth."

"Here's the truth for you. Either let me see my brother or the warden, or you can give me the reason why."

Butler chuckled. "Oh, we will do better than that." He nodded to the two men, who approached Jefferson. Though he tried to resist, they slapped handcuffs on him. "We are going to put you in his cell."

"What are you doing?" he demanded as the two men jerked him out into the passageway.

"Taking you to where you belong, Jefferson Tucker," said the guard who was still in possession of his revolver and the folding knife.

"I do not belong in a cell!" Jefferson protested

even as he was being dragged through the doors into a cellblock that smelled worse than it looked. And that was saying something.

Instantly a deafening noise began as prisoners shouted and banged whatever they could grab against the iron cell bars. The guard took out his pistol and fired one shot.

Silence quickly reigned.

Up ahead a door swung open. "Looky here, Tucker," the other guard sneered. "Your room is ready. Welcome home."

"Wait," the man in charge said. "Let's let these boys say their howdys first."

A prisoner stepped out of the cell. He was dressed in clothing so dirty that Jefferson could not discern a color or what kept it from shredding into rags. Legs shackled, the prisoner shuffled toward them. And then Jefferson knew him.

"John? Is that you?"

His brother heaved himself against Jefferson. Though the smell caused Jefferson's eyes to water, he stood his ground as John held him tight.

"What have you done, John?" he said to the man who, under different circumstances, would be nearly a mirror image of him.

"Just what I had to," was John's quiet reply. "I hope someday you will forgive me, Jeff, but I wasn't built for a place like this."

"Neither of us were. And rest assured Mother

has no idea her boy's in trouble. It would kill her if she knew."

"She always did see the good in me," John said. "She still does."

"Even though she never could see to give me Father's gold pocket watch when I asked for it first." John looked down at Jefferson's vest. "I see you're wearing it now."

He glanced over at the man calling the shots. It took Butler only a moment to reach down and rip the watch from Jefferson's pocket.

"Neither of you'll get it now."

"The major will hear about this," Jefferson said, earning him a punch in the gut that took his breath away.

The warden's underling fixed John with a glare that shut him up quick. "All right, Will Tucker," he said to Jefferson. "Are you verifying that this man is your brother, John Tucker? And that he is your twin?"

"I am," Jefferson said through the pain in his gut as he took in the sight of his always well-groomed brother with streaks of dirt on his face, his hair coated with grease and, from the look of this place, thick with lice.

"Well, I believe that is proof enough for me." Butler tapped John on the shoulder. "You were right in saying you were not Will Tucker, John. On behalf of the state of Louisiana, I hereby declare you to be a free man."

John grinned like a fool and then nudged the bully. "Does that mean I get the watch that is rightfully mine?"

"Don't press your luck, son. Just get yourself out of here while I am still in a mood to let you. Major James might insist on a trial to settle the facts, and you know how long those things take."

"I know when I've been bested, so you can keep the watch." John shuffled off behind the guards without so much as a backward glance.

A moment later, the cell door clanged shut behind Detective Jefferson Tucker of the London Metropolitan Police, leaving him once again in the middle of a mess his brother had created.

Two

April 1890
Chicago, Illinois

"Absolutely not." Pinkerton agent Sadie Callum shook her head, her mind made up. If only she could convince her supervisor.

"You're still the lead agent on the case," Henry Smith said. "And as such you are obligated to see this through to the end."

"But I *did* see it through, sir. Will Tucker is back in the Louisiana State Prison with an additional ten years added to his sentence thanks to his escape. End of story."

A nice speech, and yet one that had completely missed its mark. Henry's expression gave that much away.

Will Tucker. Nemesis to two other Pinkerton agents and now, unfortunately, it appeared he would reprise his performance with her as well.

Sadie thought of the man whose face she'd studied carefully during the hearings almost a year ago. They had been required to address his escape and subsequent additional crimes. Nothing in what she saw told her Will Tucker was a man given to crime.

Unsettling, and yet wasn't that what made him so good at what he did? Surely the women he duped had seen what she had: a man with some measure of culture and kind eyes of an interesting gray color that went green when the light was just so.

Tricks of the light, that shifting color, and yet Sadie would have given anything to paint him. Or capture him in a sketch.

But what emotion would she give to a man whose expression belied his personal behavior? A conundrum indeed, and the reason she was more a patron of the arts than a creator of them.

Henry shook his head, redirecting her thoughts. "Not so quick, Miss Callum. The story isn't quite at its end. There's been a complication."

She let out a long breath. "I fail to see what

sort of complication would require me to travel down to Louisiana and that awful prison again, especially when Mrs. Astor has asked for me personally."

And on a case that held her interest like none other had ever done. A case where art was at its center.

"Mrs. Astor will either have to wait or hire someone else to see to the cause of her Rembrandt." Henry removed his spectacles to pinch the bridge of his nose. "Simply put, our Mr. Tucker has continued to claim that the Pinkertons and the State of Louisiana have incarcerated the wrong man."

"Of course he has. If the prisons of the world opened their doors and released all the inmates who claimed to be wrongly accused, we would have no need of jails or jailors."

"Perhaps." He put his spectacles back into place and then pushed a folder across the desk toward her. "However, this communiqué from the Metropolitan Police in London tells quite a different tale. You should entertain yourself by reading it and then return tomorrow to discuss your thoughts on the matter."

Sadie looked down at the folder but made no move to accept it. Instead, she shook her head. "What does a London police agency have to do with an American jewel thief?"

"You have your reservations. I understand that. However, our agreement was that you would continue to represent the Pinkerton Agency in the Tucker matter until such a time as the case was closed."

"Reservations," she echoed. "Yes, sir, I do, and I think I've stated them clearly."

There was more, much more, to cause her to protest returning to Louisiana, though she would not state those reasons now. Instead, she met Henry's gaze across the piles of books and papers in a room very much like Daddy's office back in River Pointe, Louisiana.

There, her father and five brothers made decisions that affected lives, property, and the prosperity of the sugarcane enterprise and those in their employ. Here, Henry Smith did much the same.

He checked his wristwatch and then pushed back from his desk to stand. "Come back tomorrow at ten sharp and we'll talk about it." Before she could respond, he reached down to retrieve the file and handed it to her. "And read this, Miss Callum. Carefully and without prejudice."

In any other situation, Sadie would have bristled at the statement. This time the words were warranted.

Though she accepted the file, she offered no response. Instead, she allowed Henry to escort her downstairs, where he insisted on having his driver deliver her to her hotel.

"Lincoln Park Zoo," Sadie said when she was

certain Henry had returned to his office inside the building.

"But Mr. Smith said—"

"He said you were to deliver me to my hotel." She smiled and gave him a carefully practiced shrug. "And yet it's such a lovely day. I enjoy the zoo and have so few opportunities to visit."

She could tell he was struggling with the decision to comply with her request or obey his employer, but in the end her smile won out. A little while later she was at the zoo's entrance.

What she had told the driver was hardly the truth, for she found the place dirty and smelly and not much different from a walk around the barn back in River Pointe. Today the sea lions were loose—at least, that is what the newspaper boasted—and the place would be filled with folks trying to get a peek.

All the better to hide in plain sight. And perhaps keep her brothers off her trail. For if they continued to meddle in her life, continued to try to keep tabs on her comings and goings, her days as an undercover Pinkerton agent were numbered. Aaron had already ruined a perfectly good stakeout just last month by walking up to her and identifying her by name. He had refused to say what he was really doing in Denver.

"Considering an interest in a copper mine my left foot," she muttered as she pressed past the throng at the sea lion fountain.

More likely the eldest of the five rowdies she called brothers had drawn the short straw and was sent to find out just what their sister was up to. Her cover had been shredded, and Kyle Russell, the other agent on the case, had to complete the investigation on his own.

Something Henry had never upbraided her about. But then that was just how he was, kind to a fault when it came to those under his protection. But even Henry's kindness had it limits, and she suspected she had come close to reaching them.

Today's weather was mild for April, a sunny day with a bracing wind that thankfully did not originate off the frigid north of the lake. Though she missed few things about her life back in Louisiana, the mild winters were definitely at the top of the list. The impossibly hot and humid summers went all the way to the bottom of that same list.

Gathering her valise closer to her side to avoid pickpockets—a habit borne of her Pinkerton training rather than a necessity here—Sadie looked up to see the redbrick building that housed the primates. There she found Uncle Penn waiting.

Pennsylvania Monroe III rested his bones against the side of the building, not one to sit when standing would do. Though his attention was given over to a newspaper, she suspected he had already spied her and was watching her approach.

The instinct to courting covert activities had apparently been grafted into the family tree when Aunt Pearl married Uncle Penn with the War Between the States not yet a memory.

Daddy always said Uncle Penn had come to the South to spy for the Yankees and carried off his sister instead. In his defense, Penn would say nothing beyond the statement that good sense trumped any other business, and marrying Aunt Pearl was both good sense and good for business.

"What news is so fascinating this day, Uncle?" Sadie asked as she moved into place beside him, linking her arm with his as she offered a bright smile.

"I could ask the same." He nodded to the file under her arm. "And yet we both know I will not. So what say I escort a lovely lady on a walk? I know John and Victoria would love to see you again, and I've promised to stop in for tea."

"I am amenable to a walk, but I must beg off on the visit." She glanced at the file and then returned her attention to her uncle. "Duty calls."

"And not another trip to the Academy of Fine Arts?"

She thought fondly of the institute that had cultivated the love of art her boarding school education had begun. "I wish I could, Uncle, but not today."

"Then I shall enjoy our brief time together, and perhaps I will convince you of the need to leave duty behind in favor of dinner with an ancient relation."

Sadie laughed for the first time that day. "Dinner would be wonderful, but should I ever consider you ancient, please shake me back into good sense."

He shrugged. "And yet I am. Now, see that you do not lag behind, young lady. I'm keen to get where I'm going without further dawdling."

A short while later they walked past Newberry Library at Uncle Penn's usual rapid pace to pause at the front steps of John Thompson's lovely home on Dearborn Avenue. Whatever the connection between her uncle and the wealthy lawyer beyond their shared attendance at Amherst College before the war, Penn never elaborated, though he also never failed to pay a visit when he was in Chicago.

Grasping her hands in his, Uncle Penn indicated neither a willingness to release her nor any hurry in turning to climb the steps and see his old friend. Something in his countenance gave her cause to worry.

"What is it? You look troubled."

"Not nearly as much as you will be when your father's letter arrives." He shrugged. "It's likely waiting for you back at the hotel."

She let out a long breath. A missive from home was indeed overdue. Her father generally penned something abrasive and loving in equal measure and sent it within hours of her departure. Oddly, she'd been here almost a week and heard nothing from him or Mama.

Neither had any of her brothers pestered her, be it with telegrams or calls. Thus, she expected a Callum man to jump out from behind a tree trunk or other hiding place at any moment to announce his deep concern for her welfare.

Or to demand she accompany him back home where she belonged. A statement that rarely produced the desired effect.

She centered her concentration back on Uncle Penn. "Then perhaps you would be doing me a service in preparing me for whatever Daddy's planning to lecture me on this time."

"I ought to. Really I should."

He looked away as the lakeside breeze ruffled the ends of his graying hair. Once a redhead, his diminishing crown of glory, as he called his ginger curls, was fading and retreating faster than the Confederates at Pea Ridge. Only once had he made the statement in front of Daddy.

"No," he finally said, "I'll allow for the fact that Seamus Callum somehow came to his senses between the writing of my telegram and the sending of your letter." Steely eyes met her gaze. "And I'll leave it at that. Now, humor an old man and allow me to put you into a hansom cab. I'll not have you walking alone no matter the training you have, understand?"

He punctuated the statement with a wink that made it impossible for Sadie to argue. He kissed her on the cheek and then helped her into the cab. "Virginia Hotel, Ladies' Entrance," he told the driver. "We will meet again for dinner, yes?" he asked Sadie.

"Yes, Uncle," she said as she settled back for the short ride to Rush Street.

After paying the cabbie, Sadie cast a careful glance in all directions and then went inside. Striding down the gilded hall as quickly as she could manage and still project some air of respectability, she set her sights on the far end of the passageway. Stepping past the white marble statue of Nydia, the Blind Girl of Pompeii, she passed the guest elevators to stand at the broad semicircle of black marble that was the reception desk.

A few moments later, a packet of letters in hand, Sadie made her way up to her room with much less assurance, much less haste. For in the packet, addressed in the bold handwriting of her father, was a letter to Sarah Louise Callum.

The name he called her when no other name would suffice to contain his ire. Or, on far too many occasions, his disappointment.

Rather than wait, Sadie deposited the letters on the desk and settled herself in front of them. A woman of the world, she was, and a Pinkerton agent besides.

Sadie reminded herself of both things as she reached for her father's envelope. And yet as she tore open the seal and pulled out a single page of vellum purchased by Mama at the best stationers in New Orleans, her heart pounded as if she was a little child.

Home, he demanded. A word. A sentence. A threat.

Home.

He'd written other things. Something about a photograph in the *New Orleans Picayune* that was causing a stir. A postscript to request she report her travel itinerary forthwith.

She would have to ask Henry if he knew what sort of fuss Daddy meant. If the tempest was bigger than a teapot, it would be heard and reported back to Henry Smith, especially if it involved one of his agents.

More likely, her mother had read of some distant relation's wedding and decided it was time for Sadie to come back and find a husband.

Yes, that was it. Mama and her matrimonial machinations were most likely behind the letter. But Sadie had no husband in mind, nor did she intend to find one, not while she still had plenty to occupy her time. Mama would just have to wait, and thus so would Daddy.

Sadie set the letter aside and reached for the file Henry had insisted she read. Somehow, even Will Tucker's impossible case seemed less daunting than a brief letter from Daddy. Less worrisome. And certainly less taxing to what remained of her patience.

The dossier was brief but impactful. The London Metropolitan Police were in receipt of a missing persons report from one Honorable Eliza Tucker, who wished to follow up on the failure of her son, a detective in the employ of the police, to return from a business trip to the United States. They were also in receipt of letters from an inmate incarcerated in the Louisiana State Penitentiary claiming to be their missing detective.

Known next of kin for William Jefferson Tucker was his brother, last of Mobile, Alabama. The brother's name was William John Tucker.

His twin.

A third letter, from the warden of Louisiana State Penitentiary to the state prison board dated May 10, 1889, acknowledged the release of a prisoner and the incarceration of another. Wrongful imprisonment was the reason.

The name was Tucker. William Tucker.

No middle name declared.

Sadie sat back and tossed the last letter onto the desk. If there were two William Tuckers, then which one sat in prison?

Instinct told her the answer. Instinct also told her that, if she valued her freedom, the last place she needed to be right now was anywhere in the state of Louisiana.

Three

Sadie arrived at her supervisor's office at exactly ten o'clock the next morning. Unlike adhering to the fashionable lateness she had learned at her mother's knee, she was always prompt.

Determining that this was someone else's case, someone else's responsibility, she kept her suspicions to herself and tried to ignore the niggling voice that was her conscience. Or perhaps it was merely the enemy of her soul bent on sending her back down to the place where she least wanted to be.

Other agents could be moved to the Tucker case. Surely Henry would see that she should be helping Mrs. Astor with her art troubles. Who better to fit into the drawing rooms and salons of Fifth Avenue than she? Indeed, Sadie Callum was born to take on this role. A role she had assumed with great success during much of her career with the Pinkertons.

With each step toward the entrance of the agency's offices, Sadie bolstered her argument. Louisiana judges preferred to deal with detectives of the male variety, as witnessed by the grief she received when she climbed into the witness box to testify against Will Tucker during his resentencing hearing.

She sighed. Testimony that would have to be refuted if this Tucker were to be released. The judge would want to hear from her. Would probably require it.

And yet she did not want to go. With all she had in her, Sadie determined she would avoid the assignment at all costs, something she had never done before.

So, when Henry opened his door to usher her inside, she smiled with the confidence of a woman on a mission. A woman with an argument that would cause him to see the sense of sending someone else down to the Louisiana State Penitentiary to free the wrongly imprisoned Tucker. Because whoever freed that man would likely be sent to search for the other. She gave that a moment's thought as she stepped past Henry and settled in the spot where he'd delivered yesterday's ultimatum.

If only she could guarantee that Will Tucker wasn't spending his time within shouting distance of River Pointe, Louisiana. Or New Orleans, which he tended to favor with his presence on multiple occasions, according to the vast array of documents Pinkerton agents McMinn and Russell had compiled.

No, Tucker was a Southerner who tended to keep his activities and his location distinctly Southern in nature. And between Mama's people in New Orleans and beyond, and Daddy's plantation in River Pointe, there wasn't much of the area beneath the Mason-Dixon line that didn't contain a family member.

She sighed again. It was indeed a conundrum.

What was right would prevail, and she knew, at least in part, what that was. However, sending one Tucker back to freedom did not mean she wanted to arrest the other. And that argument had yet to be well developed.

Thoughts on the subject roiled and swirled but refused to find any solid and defendable form. Instead, the more she considered her words, the more she knew she would sound like a petulant child not wanting to do what her father asked. And yet, in some ways, she was exactly that.

Sadie busied herself with adjusting her sleeve and studying the view out the third-floor window as she waited for her boss to broach the subject.

"I take it you've read the file."

She sat up a little straighter and schooled her features to keep them neutral. "Yes, sir. I have."

"Then you've decided," he said as he sat down in his chair across the desk.

What to say? She chose silence in the hopes it would give her a moment to find one last solid reason to beg off the case.

Henry leaned back and steepled his hands, his gaze missing nothing as it swept her face. And then, slowly, he nodded.

He knew. Of course. That's why he was sitting on the other side of the desk, second only to the man whose name was on the sign outside.

All that remained was to give up the ghost and admit the truth. And yet the idea of stepping on the train to New York and Mrs. Astor was powerful incentive to try one last time to derail the situation.

"There were conflicting statements in the file," she said demurely. "And I believe the judge still thinks he is holding the correct Tucker behind bars."

"I didn't ask what the judge thinks." His eyes narrowed.

"Yet his opinion is the only one that counts, isn't it, sir?" A poor counter to Henry's statement. She was running out of time, and worse, running out of excuses.

"You're too good at this Pinkerton game to show it, but I know you have the instincts." He pressed his palms against the desk's top and leveled her a no-nonsense look. "Who does the state of Louisiana have locked up, our perpetrator or his twin brother?"

"His twin."

There it was. The truth. Two words that hung in the air between them.

"And what specifically has caused you to arrive at this decision?"

"There were numerous factors that indicated

the two men had been switched, but only one concrete piece of evidence," she said.

"What was that concrete piece of evidence?"

"Eye color." She hurried to explain as Henry's brows rose. "In every instance where victims of Will Tucker—that is, John Tucker—described the perpetrator, his eyes were either gray or green. Thus I am left to believe that John Tucker has gray eyes that can shift to green depending on the light."

"Go on."

"Yes, well, the man currently incarcerated has, according to documents provided by the London Metropolitan Police, eyes that are blue except under certain conditions."

"When they also appear gray."

"Exactly, sir."

"Then get him out." Henry held up his hand to stop any protest before it found voice. "Just do your job, Miss Callum," he said with a weariness that hadn't been evident moments before.

Just do your job.

"Yes, sir." She gathered up the file. "And Mrs. Astor?"

"She will understand."

A flicker of hope rose. "Are you saying my duties only extend to offering testimony as to the identity of the prisoner and then I will be released to take on the Astor case? The topic is well within my area of expertise, as you know, and Mamie and I have a shared history of friendship, although we are no longer close as we once were."

Henry sat back in his chair and picked up a pen from atop a stack of papers. For a moment he appeared to be more interested in writing instrument than the topic at hand.

Abruptly, he dropped the pen and it clattered to the floor. "You do not wish to continue as lead agent on the Tucker case, then."

A statement, not a question. And yet Sadie felt compelled to respond.

"I do not, sir."

"And would your reluctance to continue have anything to do with matters more personal than professional?" He paused only a second. "Has your father demanded your return?"

Startled, she met his gaze. "He mentioned something of the sort in his last letter."

That the Callum family had no idea of Sadie's true calling as a Pinkerton was common knowledge with Henry Smith. How much he knew beyond that basic fact was a mystery to Sadie. Uncle Penn had likely spoken in her defense, possibly even enlightened her employer as to the issues Sadie faced as the only daughter of an impossibly archaic father.

"Did he mention a photograph that appeared in the *New Orleans Picayune*?"

Of course Henry had known about it. "Yes, sir. He did."

"Would you like to see it?" He opened the topmost drawer of his desk and withdrew a folded newspaper. "I must say it's quite a good likeness of you and Agent Russell."

He slid the newspaper across the desk toward her and then waited silently for her to pick it up. Trembling fingers retrieved the paper and unfolded it to lie flat across the desk.

There, just below a heading touting the Society column and the byline of its author was a photograph of Senator Robert Davey taken at a reception held in his honor last fall. Sadie recalled assisting Kyle Russell in seeing that the senator slipped out the rear exit of the venue, eluding a possible threat on his life.

Unfortunately, they did not elude a cameraman from the *Picayune*. Odd that the photograph would be published now when nothing had appeared in the newspaper at the time.

She shrugged. "I fail to see why a photograph taken six months ago would cause any concern for my father."

"You didn't read the accompanying article. I suggest you give it a look."

Her attention went to the words beneath the photograph. The first sentence, phrased as a question, caught her breath in her throat and held it there.

Why would a man newly married to a veritable saint dedicated to the establishment of libraries and educational facilities cavort about New Orleans with this woman?

"Cavort?" Her mouth gave voice to the word, and yet it fell hollow into the silence. She saw her name a few lines down and was drawn back to the page.

Gently educated, well bred, and of a lineage that should have given her pause to be seen in public in such a manner, Miss Sarah Louise Callum escapes out the back exit and clutches at the arm of . . .

"Should have given her pause?" Sadie pushed the paper away. "Clutches at the arm? Kyle and I were providing security for the senator at his request. If I am clutching anything, it is the Remington pistol in my hand."

Henry's expression remained unreadable. "I recall the assignment as one that was arranged at the last minute when you were already in the vicinity, am I correct?"

"Yes. I was there for my mother's birthday. You asked me to come into the city for a few hours to provide assistance to Kyle, which I did." She shook her head. "I told you nothing good comes of my trying to work as a Pinkerton in Louisiana. It's just impossible."

Henry shrugged. "You might want to read the rest of it. She has included a statement from your father."

Sadie picked up the paper once more and

scanned the remainder of the article. *"I have no knowledge of my daughter's behavior on that evening, but you can rest assured this is not what it appears."* Again she set the newspaper aside. "Well, finally. The voice of reason. Of course it's not as it appears."

"Because it appears as though you were enjoying an evening at the Opera House with a married man, when in fact . . ."

"My father would have no knowledge of what I was actually doing there." She sighed. "Unless someone told him."

"I believe you and I have had this conversation on more than one occasion, Miss Callum. I respect your choice not to tell your family you're a Pinkerton agent. I would not be the one to compromise you to your family or, for that matter, to anyone else."

"Then either Uncle Penn told him . . ."

"Or he is defending his daughter in print when he has no idea why you would allow Kyle Russell to squire you to an evening at the Opera House."

The obvious answer. Again, she sighed.

"You understand there are two separate matters here that must be dealt with. The issue with your father and his understandable anger notwithstanding, I'm going to stick to how this affects your ability to do your job."

He swiveled to retrieve his pen. Sadie made

use of the unguarded moment to glance back down at the article.

One must wonder what Miss Callum's response to that same question might be. Sarah Louise, this writer welcomes an audience with you at your earliest convenience.

"Not likely," she muttered.

"I beg your pardon?"

Sadie glanced up at him. "Nothing. Sorry, sir. Please continue."

"I appreciate that you stated your reluctance to return to Louisiana before you knew of this situation brewing in New Orleans." He paused. "Under the circumstances, I fail to see how you could carry out your duties to any extent without scrutiny."

"So I'm to take on the Astor case after all?"

"No, Miss Callum," he said firmly. "You remain lead agent on this case for now."

"But, sir, I—"

"Hear me out," he said with a wave of his hand. "What that man sitting in prison needs is a Pinkerton who can write eloquently in his defense. That is your current assignment. Should the judge require your presence at any further hearings on the matter, then of course you will be in attendance."

She nodded. "But as to actually taking up the Tucker case?"

"Until the Louisiana State Penitentiary releases

that William J. Tucker, we have no reason to search for the other one. I'll speak to Mrs. Astor, but I see no problem in beginning to gather the facts of her case once you have completed the task of informing the judge of the agency's opinion as to whom they are holding. Seeing as this falls within your area of expertise, that is."

Sadie smiled. "Then I will leave you to begin work on this project." At his expression, she hesitated. "Unless there is something else?"

"There is, actually." He seemed to wrestle with his response. "Your uncle and I have been friends for many years. You know this."

"I do."

"And it was on his word that I took a chance on you." He smiled. "A chance I am very glad I took."

"Thank you, sir."

"I only wonder if the agency's gain is your loss."

"I don't understand."

Henry nodded to the paper. "A woman's virtuous reputation is her treasure. My mother used to say that. So I wonder . . ."

"If I've been robbed of my treasure?" She shrugged. "If that is so, then I suppose I will just have to hire a Pinkerton to find it. A pity Kyle is wishing to retire."

"I doubt your father is finding humor in the

situation. So there is one more thing I require of you before you take on the Astor case."

"What is that, sir?"

"Go home and make peace with him."

Four

Home. Where was that, exactly?

Jefferson Tucker had spent so much time wishing to be released that he hadn't given any thought as to where he would go when it happened.

His clothes hung in rags, and he hadn't shaved in almost a year. He'd been told those who left Angola went out with a suit of clothes and a bath. No amount of scrubbing, however, would remove the stink from his memory.

The judge, apparently called in on short notice, stared down from his place on the judicial bench as if expecting Jefferson to respond. With what? Thanks?

Hardly. Not when he had been incarcerated by the man's own hand and without hearing a single word to the contrary. The thought that false testimony was indeed the cause crossed his mind, but Jefferson resolutely pushed it away.

"Is there something else?" the judge asked.

"Yes, sir. I require my father's watch, my folding knife, and my revolver."

The words came out not in the meek tone of a prisoner but in the defiant voice of a man long scorned and forgotten. Still seated in the witness stand, the pretty blond Pinkerton agent's expression showed surprise.

The judge, however, was not amused. "I fail to understand your request."

"It is a demand, sir." Jefferson straightened his backbone and tamped down on his anger. "Not only was I wrongly imprisoned, as has been attested to in this court, but I was also robbed of my father's gold watch and the sidearm and folding knife I carried. I want them back."

"Do you now?" The judge looked down at the Pinkerton agent. "Miss Callum, you've studied the documents in this case, have you not?"

"I have, sir."

"And do you recall any such property list accompanying the prisoner upon his incarceration?"

"I do not. However—"

"See there, boy. No such property list exists and therefore no way to claim lost property." His smile held neither humor nor any sort of good feelings toward Jefferson. "So unless there is any other matter before the court, I—"

"Excuse me, sir."

All eyes went to the Pinkerton agent. What had the judge called her? Miss Collins? Carlson?

His grin faded. "Yes, Miss Callum? Have you something further to say?"

"I do, sir." She shuffled through the stack of documents until she arrived at the one that made her nod. "Yes, here it is. While there is no such incarceration list, I believe the fact has been established that Mr. Tucker was indeed jailed under extraordinary circumstances."

The judge cleared his throat. "Go on."

The woman's attention returned to the papers before her. "Before he was a prisoner, he was a visitor. And as such your deputy entered the man in question into the visitor's log on the tenth of May last year. In that note, he says the visitor was relieved of one revolver and a folding knife. I see that Mr. Tucker initialed the entry here."

The judge leaned over to retrieve the page from the Pinkerton agent and appeared to be studying it. Jefferson took the opportunity to study her.

Though she had obviously attempted to dress in a manner that would hide her beauty, the effort failed miserably. On any other woman the drab brown day dress that had been buttoned practically to her chin might have appeared matronly. Something a child's governess might wear back home in London.

On Miss Callum of the Pinkerton Detective Agency, the fit of the gown and the way she wore it defied any good reason to call the garment anything but stunning. And though she had scraped her blond hair back into a tight knot that was partially hidden beneath her matching plain brown hat, Jefferson found himself wondering what those flaxen strands might look like falling free around her shoulders.

What those lips might look like if they would only smile.

"Mr. Tucker?"

He tore his attention away to focus on the judge. His rambling thoughts, however, took a little longer to follow suit.

The judge's eyes had narrowed behind his spectacles. "It appears you have your documentation for your weapons. Should they prove impossible to find, I declare a like amount shall be paid to you. Do you understand and agree?"

Owing to the quality of both items, Jefferson doubted they remained anywhere that they might be found. "I do, sir."

"Now, as to the other matter. Have you any proof of the watch you claim is missing?"

"Of its ownership, yes. Of the fact it was taken from me almost exactly one year ago today by a man named Butler, yes."

"Butler, did you say?"

Jefferson nodded. "That is the name he gave me. And the proof of where the watch is now?"

The judge leaned back and offered an impassive look. "Yes?"

"Sir, I do not wish to cause any grief to this court, but I believe if you will look at the inside of the gold watch on your chain you will see an inscription that reads *To Harrison William Tucker from your Lizzie on the occasion of our wedding, 17 June 1866.*

The judge's face contorted in rage as he reached for his gavel. "Bailiff, take this man away. This hearing is at an end."

Rough hands grabbed the back of Jefferson's shirt and threw him toward the courtroom door he had entered what seemed like only moments ago. As the guard led him back to his cage, for to call the enclosure a jail cell would be too generous, those remaining behind bars began to shout his name and offer crude cries of welcome.

Anger propelled him, and even as the cell door clanged shut once again, his mind fed the white-hot emotion. Were he young and stupid, he might have punched the wall or cried out in anguish.

Instead, he sat on the pitiful pile of straw and rags that served as his bed and brought his rage down to a seething fury. He would leave this place, and when that happened he would exact his revenge.

And no nonsense about the plunder of an Egyptian's tomb or the wrath of a man whose trade in antiquities might be interrupted by the conclusion of Jefferson's investigation would deter him. It had not before his wrongful incarceration and it would not after.

Indeed, he remained set on accomplishing two things: his release from prison and the satisfying completion of his case on behalf of the British Museum.

Jefferson let out a long breath, sucked in fetid air, and then repeated the process. No, he forced himself to recall, revenge was for the Lord.

Revenge is Thine, not mine. The words his governess had insisted he and John repeat each time their disagreements escalated.

John.

He forced his thoughts away from his brother, the better to keep his temper manageable. Someday that wrong would be righted.

Either by him or the Lord. At this moment, Jefferson did not care which.

Two days later, Sadie sat very still, her thoughts centered on the argument she'd just lost with Henry. Though brief, their words were spiced with just enough vigor and irritation to cause her to need more than a moment to calm herself.

But a moment was all she had. The prisoner would be released any time now, and it was her job to see that he arrived safely at his destination.

Her job. To babysit a man perfectly capable of seeing himself back to Mobile, Alabama.

She allowed a quiet but inelegant snort. If the man were in possession of the credentials the London Metropolitan Police had claimed, then he well ought to be able to see himself onto some sort of public conveyance and find his way home.

Sadie sighed. For all the humor she might attempt, there really was nothing funny in the situation. Had this fellow not been so impertinent as to accuse a judge of receiving stolen property, he might have slept in his own bed in Mobile last night.

As it was, finding a means to have him released had taken a full two days. Two days of delay she could ill afford. Another sigh. At this point she would never get to New York City to solve Mamie Astor's Rembrandt problem.

Thanks to Uncle Penn, at least the issue of her father's demand that she immediately return home had been temporarily handled. How long Daddy would be put off by his brother-in-law's visit and the assurance that Sadie would be along shortly was anyone's guess.

So was the reason he would give for her delay. Sadie's only request was that her uncle not lie. Beyond that, she would trust his good sense and creative mind.

According to Henry, the plan was to transport Mr. Tucker by carriage to St. Francisville some twenty miles to the south. There, the new agent in charge of the Will Tucker case would make contact and take over.

While she fully expected Henry to make the attempt to lull either Lucas McMinn or Kyle Russell out of their retirements, she doubted he would meet with success. Other agents were fully capable and likely near enough to the vicinity to be of service. With the notes in her valise, he—or possibly she—would have no trouble taking up the case where Sadie left off.

Which meant she would then travel on to New Orleans and then to Callum Plantation in River Pointe to face Daddy.

The weather was chilly for the last day of April, and the sun's light barely showed through the thick clouds, although the hour was well past noon. Back home in River Pointe, these sorts of days gave over to fog and dampness that could soak a person to the bone. North of Baton Rouge, however, the gray morning was merely unpleasant.

The talk was of flooding up and down the Mississippi River. Levees were giving way and fields and roads inundated with water. That she would be traveling along that very river was not lost on Sadie. She prayed there would be no danger or delay.

A picnic basket Uncle Penn had provided before dawn sat at Sadie's feet untouched. Perhaps Mr. Tucker would make good use of it, for she had no desire to make the attempt. Reaching for the handkerchief soaked in Guerlain Lavande perfume, her current favorite, Sadie made yet another attempt to blot out the scent of the awful prison as it wafted through the open windows of the carriage. The effort failed miserably, so she reached to close the windows.

A jostling alerted her to the fact that the driver had climbed from his position, and the blur of a man in a dark suit hurrying toward the prison's main entrance told her where he'd gone.

Sadie steeled herself for the moment when the Tucker fellow would join her. There was more jostling as the driver apparently returned to his position. Then the carriage lurched into motion. Lowering the window, she called for him to stop.

A moment later the wheels ceased their motion and the driver jumped down to stand at the window. "Trouble of some kind, Miss Callum?"

"Have we forgotten Mr. Tucker, Sam?"

He glanced up and then back at Sadie. "Mr. Tucker prefers to ride with me, ma'am."

"I see. And why would that be?"

"Perhaps because he hasn't had a bath since this time last year. The fellow mentioned he'd welcome a nice rain shower to knock off some of the critters."

Critters. Sadie shuddered.

"Ah. Well, then," she said as she recalled the filthy but defiant prisoner she'd seen in the court-room two days ago. Indeed, that man was not one with whom she wished to spend any length of time in an enclosed space.

However, Henry's instructions were explicit. *"Shadow Mr. Tucker until you hand him off to the next agent. This man might not be the Tucker*

46

we're looking for, but he is our only link to him."

He could not be allowed to ride atop the carriage where he might easily jump off at the first stop or, worse, be set upon by his brother or others.

She met the driver's expectant gaze. "Tell him that is quite impossible."

"But, Miss Callum, he's a mite worse for wear, having been in that place long as he was."

"I understand that, but I'm afraid there's nothing I can do about it. I am charged with an assignment and I must fulfill the terms."

Sam nodded. "I'll let him know, then."

Sadie waited, handkerchief in hand, until the sound of men's voices rose outside. Sam Fenton was one of several drivers handpicked by the Pinkertons and on call for situations just like this. He was paid far too well to ignore an order, and thus a few minutes later, the door flew open.

"He gave me a mite of trouble, but I believe I explained it so he understood," Sam said. "He may have a headache when he wakes up, though."

A body wrapped in a blanket landed in a crumpled heap on the floor at her feet.

Five

The moment Sam pulled away the heavy fabric and tossed it behind him, the odor arose. And then so did the source, scrambling to his feet as the door slammed shut. Mr. Tucker's hand went to the latch, but Sadie got there first.

"I wouldn't advise that," she said as she tried not to gasp from the horrid smell. "My assignment is to keep you in sight, and unfortunately for both of us, that means you must ride in here with me."

The man ran a hand through tangled wet hair that promised to be a lovely shade of pale brown once the dirt was removed and sat down on the bench seat opposite her. "You're the Pinkerton agent."

Southern with an influence of something else she hadn't noticed during his courtroom testimony. British, from his dossier, by way of Mobile, Alabama. There should be a story in that, although Sadie didn't expect to be around him long enough to hear it.

His clothes had been well cut, the shoes, or what remained of them, more of a Western variety. A man of means, perhaps. Or had been.

"Agent Sadie Callum, Mr. Tucker," she managed before retreating behind her handkerchief. "I'm to escort you as far as St. Francisville, where another agent will take you the rest of the way to your home."

"And protect me from my brother?"

Indeed, there had been some discussion that the original Will Tucker might be provoked to act once word of his brother's release reached him. The potential threat was enough to have Henry send Sam, the biggest brute of the agency's drivers, to escort them on this leg of the journey.

"If necessary."

He did not look away. "It won't be."

A trickle of blood slid down his temple and into his ragged beard, staining the reddish hairs a darker crimson. Sadie made the difficult choice to give up her handkerchief.

"You've been injured by my driver," she said as she offered the delicate bit of cloth. "I'm terribly sorry."

"Not as sorry as you'll be if you don't lower those windows and let in some fresh air." He accepted the handkerchief and then swiped at the strings of hair hiding his face. "And for the record, he didn't hit me hard enough to do this. That happened during a disagreement with one of the guards before I left."

Her gaze collided with his as the carriage lurched into motion. "Oh."

Mr. Tucker lowered the window nearest him and then reached down to retrieve the blanket covering the food basket. "You'll be needing this," he said as he handed the blanket to her and then lowered the other window. "Especially when the rain hits, which I figure should happen soon."

Sadie accepted the blanket, not because she needed it to ward off the chill but because the layer of fabric just might make up for the loss of her handkerchief. If only she had access to the bottle of Lavande that was tucked into the trunk she'd given the driver this morning.

"Won't you eat?" she said to distract herself. "I'm sure you'll find something to your liking in the basket."

He eyed it for only a moment before nodding. "Anything without bugs or rot would suit me." He shook his head. "I'm sorry. That wasn't appropriate for a woman to hear."

"I assure you I've heard worse, Mr. Tucker," Sadie said as she lifted the basket onto the seat beside her companion. "Please, enjoy what my uncle has provided."

The man's neutral expression went slack when he spied the contents of the hamper. "You'll join me?"

"I assure you I've had my fill already." And she had, though not of the contents of the hamper. This morning's toast and jam would have to be sufficient until she could exit the carriage. With the stench, likely nothing else would stay down anyway.

"Please," she said again as she gestured to the

hamper and then reached inside to offer him a tin plate and a blue-checked napkin. "This is for you."

"Thank you." Somewhere between the fried chicken and biscuits and the jar of sweetened tea, he finally filled what must have been an extremely empty gut. "I haven't had food like that in a very long time," he said as he dabbed at his mouth.

Sadie's response was just a smile. As she certainly hadn't had the presence of mind to consider that the former prisoner might be hungry, she could take no credit.

Her traveling companion leaned back against the seat, his eyes falling shut as the carriage jolted along. Just when she thought he might have fallen asleep, he opened his eyes once more.

"It seems a year in prison has caused me to forget my manners. I owe you a debt of gratitude, Miss Callum."

"Honestly, you do not. The food was courtesy of my uncle. I will pass along your message when I see him next," she said as she tried not to think of how soon that would be.

"I wasn't referring to the chicken and biscuits, although that was a mighty fine meal." He paused. "You stood up to the judge when a lesser man—or rather, woman—wouldn't."

She hadn't expected that. "I was merely doing my job."

"A job you're apparently quite good at." He let

out a long breath. "I'm going to miss that revolver and folding knife, but I don't suppose I can complain about being compensated for them. The London Metropolitan might have a different idea about that since the weapons belonged to them."

"Yes," she said as she reached for her reticule, "but this belongs to you." Retrieving the pocket watch the judge had entrusted to her, Sadie placed it in Mr. Tucker's palm.

He smiled. "Should I ask how you got this?"

"Apparently his honor had no idea that he had purchased—or been gifted, as the story varies—a watch that might have been stolen."

"Might have been?"

Sadie shrugged. "Does it matter? You have your watch back, and the judge has his reputation intact. A satisfactory arrangement."

"A win for both of us," he said, sarcasm coloring the statement. "Are you part of this arrangement?"

"If you mean is having a Pinkerton agent assigned to you part of the agreement with the judge, it is not." She paused to toy with the edge of the blanket, resisting the urge to lift it to her nose. "However, our agency has a strong interest in seeing that your brother is captured and returned to jail—"

"As do I."

"Yes, I can imagine you would."

"No, Miss Callum. I do not think you can imagine."

His words held a quiet yet steely tone. He was correct. She could not imagine.

"And so the Pinkertons intend to use me to find my brother?" Mr. Tucker shrugged. "Best of luck with that. I doubt John will wish to keep company with me any time soon."

"John?"

"Yes, my brother." His smile did not quite reach his eyes. "Oh, I see. You don't know his full name, do you? I thought the Pinkertons knew everything."

The statement grated on her already fraying nerves. "There is no need to mock me, sir."

"You are correct. There is not. Do forgive me."

Whether he intended sincerity or sarcasm, Sadie could not tell. She elected to believe it was the latter.

"Your brother is John Tucker, not William Tucker?"

Her traveling companion shifted positions, resting his hand in his lap. The soiled napkin remained in his palm.

"He is both, as am I." He seemed to be studying the scenery as it passed before returning his attention again to Sadie. "Were you aware that my brother and I are twins?"

"I was."

"And did you also know that we are close enough to be considered virtually identical by most?"

"I had figured that much," she said, although any resemblance to the clean-cut Tucker she met last year was fleeting at best considering this man's scruffy appearance.

"Well, then, here's the rest of the story. "The firstborn son is given the middle name of his father as his first name. My grandfather's name was Richard Harrison Tucker. My father's name is Harrison William Tucker."

"And so you are William Tucker?"

"Yes. William Jefferson Tucker, to be precise."

"And you go by Jefferson."

He nodded. "The complication is that because the doctor could not tell my father which of us was born first, he insisted we both follow the naming tradition. Therefore, I am William Jefferson and my brother is William John."

"Interesting."

"Only in that it does complicate matters when the law is looking for William J. Tucker and there are two with the same birthdate and parents."

"Which is why you were incarcerated."

"That and the fact that my brother appears not to have inherited any sort of conscience." He sighed. "So while I commend the Pinkerton Agency for wishing to keep tabs on me, I cannot say it will mean you will somehow find John, though I wish it were so."

Sadie tried to think of what kind of man would allow his brother to take the fall for his own crimes. To see his brother jailed when he knew he was the one who should have been in prison.

"You're trying to imagine why my brother would switch places and leave me behind bars."

"How did you know?"

"It's a natural question, don't you think?" Mr. Tucker dabbed at his temple once more and then tucked the handkerchief into his coat pocket. "I'll be owing you a handkerchief too."

"No, please don't worry about that. Now, about your brother. Is there anything else you can tell me that might help us to capture him?"

He seemed to consider the question a moment. Slowly, however, he shook his head.

"Miss Callum, I ceased understanding my brother and his ways many years ago. I wish I could help, but I'm afraid I cannot."

She decided to try another way. "Perhaps you might have some insight into places he frequented before you lost contact with him. Maybe you know of family members who might shelter him?"

"Most of our family is in London, and I assure you none other than perhaps our mother would open the door should he knock."

"London." She paused to think on whether John Tucker might have somehow found his way back there. It was possible—anything was possible— and yet it didn't fit the pattern of behavior he had exhibited thus far.

"You and John were born in London?"

"We were." He regarded her impassively. "You're wondering why I don't sound as though I'm British?"

"I am curious, yes."

"Part of that is because I've made a concerted effort not to. Nothing shuts down a conversation faster than an accent that doesn't appear to be local, if you know what I mean. However, I am British on my mother's side and Southern thanks to my father."

"Alabama?"

"Mobile, yes. John and I divided our time between London and our grandfather's home in Mobile. The home came to me some years ago after Grandfather died, although my grand-mother is still in residence."

"Just you?"

"Yes, just me. As I said, our family has known of John and his ways for quite some time."

"I see. Now I am curious. What caused your father to marry a woman from England?"

"A romantic, are you?"

Sadie's chuckle held no humor. "Hardly."

"Soured on love at such a young age? A pity. I'm newly released from prison and in hopes of finding an adventure with a lovely lady to remind me of all that is good and pleasant in the world."

Again her temper flared. The man was teasing her, and not kindly.

"Romance does not always lead to happiness, Mr. Tucker."

"And yet it could." He was still teasing, but something in his tone, his expression . . .

Sadie pressed away thoughts of what sort of man might be hiding beneath the grime. "I believe you were going to tell me about your parents, sir."

"Yes, of course. My father sailed aboard a Confederate ship during the war. Their job was to run the Northern blockade and find safe port in England, where the cause of the Confederacy was appreciated. The ship would then load up with supplies and return to port somewhere in the South."

"Sounds dangerous."

"I suppose it was. And then one morning my father woke up in England as a man without a country. The South had surrendered. To return meant the vessel would be confiscated and he and his crew would be charged with a number of crimes, not the least of which being piracy. So he released the crew to do as they wished, turned the vessel over to the authorities, and applied for asylum, which was granted. Then he met my mother. They were married soon after."

As the carriage rolled on down the rutted road, Mr. Tucker seemed lost in thought. Sadie tried to think of what it must have been like for a man to have no home to return to. It must have been very sad indeed.

"I don't know what it is about you, Miss Callum. I've never told anyone that story."

"It's a story with a happy ending. There's nothing wrong with sharing that kind of tale."

"A happy ending, yes, mostly. John and I certainly enjoyed a good life in England, and we were allowed frequent visits to Alabama once my father's status as a former Confederate was resolved. Which makes it all the more difficult to understand . . ."

"Why he turned out so different from you?"

He met her gaze. "Why do you think John and I are so different?"

"Other than the obvious?"

"No, Miss Callum, we're very much alike, John and I. We have our loyalties. We only differ in what those loyalties are."

Six

What an interesting statement about differing loyalties between the Tucker brothers. Sadie took a moment to consider the British detective's words carefully. "That begs the question, then, Mr. Tucker. What are your brother's loyalties?"

He looked away. "John has only one, and that is to himself."

"And you?" she asked, and then wished she could take the question back. What did it matter what this man pledged allegiance to? He was not the suspect.

"God," was his simple answer. "And then a few others come after. Family and country would be tied for second."

"I see."

Not what she expected from a man who might have become embittered toward the God who had allowed him to rot in a filthy prison for a year.

Heavy clouds gave way to patches of fog and a drizzle of rain as the carriage continued south. Keeping the windows open on her side of the carriage proved impossible when the rain slanted in to dampen everything it touched.

Mr. Tucker had fallen asleep, his head resting against the leather seat in what appeared to be a most uncomfortable angle. Worse, raindrops pelted him, staining his coat a shade darker in places.

The air outside had turned cold, and Sadie was now grateful for her blanket. But Mr. Tucker had neither blanket nor any other protection from the weather.

She made the decision to reach beyond her traveling companion to slide his window up. Just as the glass clicked into place, Mr. Tucker's eyes flew open and he grabbed her. The world tilted, and she was flat on the floor of the carriage, a half-awake, foul-smelling madman looking down at her.

His fetid breath came in gasps, and then, slowly, he blinked. Fingers bruising her shoulders tightened their grip.

"Release me immediately," she said, her voice low and every bit as lethal as the Remington in her skirt pocket.

Realization must have hit him then, for he jumped back and scrubbed his face with his hands. Sadie seized the opportunity to scramble back to her seat.

For a moment he stared at her, his gaze wild and his breathing still ragged, and then he cleared his throat. "What happened?" he managed, his voice rough.

"You were being rained on, and I thought it prudent . . ." Words evaporated as the carriage hit a rut and tossed her against the door. When she returned her attention to Jefferson Tucker, he hadn't moved a muscle.

"I'm sorry. Instinct. Not an excuse, I know. Did I hurt you?"

He had, but not intentionally. The back of her head throbbed and she might have bruises where his hands had grasped her, but she would not tell him that. Instead, she elected to change the subject. "Have you any idea what you'll do when you arrive in Mobile?"

She could almost see the confusion dissolve as his thoughts appeared to center on her question. "My first priority is to retrieve the case notes I had delivered there before setting off on my visit with John. Some might say that not having those notes with me when I was falsely incarcerated was a lucky coincidence."

"But you do not believe in luck?"

He shook his head as his gaze met hers. "Nor do I believe in coincidence."

Sadie smiled. "Neither do I. Have you any plans to return to London?"

"I suppose that's up to my superiors."

"Oh?"

"I've been off the job for quite a while and away from London. I'm not certain I've been missed by anyone other than my mother."

Sadie had no good response to that, so she settled for a nod and then drew the blanket close. Mr. Tucker once again settled back against the seat but kept his eyes resolutely open.

At the appointed meeting place just north of Baton Rouge, the driver stopped beneath the sheltering arms of an ancient magnolia tree. The sound of a horse and then men's voices permeated the interior of the carriage.

"Expecting someone?" her companion asked.

"Yes. The Pinkerton agent who will be escorting you the rest of the way to Mobile."

Sadie waited for the door to open, only to find that the man had apparently moved on. "Perhaps he has elected to remain outside with the driver."

Mr. Tucker shook his head. "I'll have to

register my disappointment at the sad state of the Pinkerton agency and its employees."

"How so?"

"I had hoped I'd be sent someone who would be smart enough to come in out of the rain."

"You didn't want to." Again she wished to take back the words.

"Not exactly true." He looked down at the clothes he wore and then back at her. "A man has his pride."

"And I have trampled on it. Now it is my turn to apologize."

Sadie rode the remainder of the way in silence, the better to keep herself from owing the man across from her yet another apology. When the carriage drew to a halt in front of a hotel whose name she could not read through the rain-splattered windows, she gathered up her things and waited until Sam opened the door.

"This is where we part ways, Mr. Tucker."

He captured her gaze. "Then let me thank you one last time for the assistance you've given me in retrieving my watch and my freedom."

"Again, I was—"

"Just doing your job." He smiled. "Yes, I know. Now, if you don't mind, I'm going to see if I can find a place where I can get another set of clothes and then a bath and a shave."

"According to my instructions, there should be clothes waiting for you in your hotel room. And

I'm sure they will accommodate you here for a bath."

His hands rested on his knees, his fingers drumming a tune and making Jefferson Tucker look more like a nervous boy than a man who had only just been released from prison. "Then all that remains is a shave and a haircut."

"Sam will accompany you wherever you need to go. I'll see that your key is left at the front desk. I believe the rooms have been taken under the name of Callum."

"I won't forget that," he said. "Or you."

The driver jerked the door open and looked at him with a wary expression before turning to Sadie. "Ready, ma'am?"

"Yes, Sam. If you'll just help me get inside, I'll be fine. Mr. Tucker will be getting a shave and haircut. Will you please see to any other needs he may have?"

"For you, I will."

"Thank you." She turned her attention to the man sitting across from her. "Good day, Mr. Tucker."

Any response the former prisoner might have made was lost in the pounding of rain against the tin roof and the clatter of a wagon pulled by oxen rolling down the street. When Sadie had descended from the carriage and looked back, the door was shut tight, leaving her to assume Mr. Tucker was now dodging raindrops on his way to the barbershop with the replacement agent on his heels.

"Please enjoy whatever's left in the basket my uncle packed," she told Sam after he had bundled her inside the hotel with his overcoat draped above her head to keep her dry. "And share it with the other agent."

"That's awful kind, ma'am, but it's just me. That rider was just a messenger. He left a note for you and said for us to go on and get settled for the night. The agent will meet up with us at the hotel in the morning."

"That wasn't the plan."

"The fellow said levee breaks and flooding has our man delayed until morning, and that's all he knew. I figured the delivery of the message could wait until I got you inside and dry. He said we were fortunate to not be making the journey a week ago when most of the roads near the river were impassable."

"And yet I'm sure Mr. Tucker wishes the opposite."

"Yes, ma'am."

Sadie accepted the slightly damp envelope and then offered another word of thanks as she tucked it into her valise. A look around the tidy but humble reception room told her this was not the type of hotel she had enjoyed in Chicago.

It was, however, a place where any casual visitor to the city might walk past without realizing there were rooms to be had. Likely Henry chose the place for that very reason.

"I reckon Mr. Tucker knows where to find you when he's ready," Sam said. "Or should I go and make sure he comes back soon as he has his shave and haircut?"

"Oh, yes, please. Until the replacement agent arrives, he's under my care. I just assumed the other Pinkerton was with him. In any case, I will see that you're compensated if you'll just keep close to him until then."

He stepped away, and then she called him back. "Sam?"

"Yes, ma'am?"

Sadie chose her words carefully. "About Mr. Tucker. I was under the impression that the Pinkertons would furnish him with a decent suit of clothes. Do you know anything about that?"

"Ma'am, I reckon those clothes were decent once upon a time, but they sure aren't now."

"No, I mean a new set was to be provided."

"Not that I know of, though it's possible the fellow who's meeting us tomorrow may bring extra clothes with him."

To make the poor man wait until tomorrow for clean clothes seemed most inhumane. She frowned and then opened her reticule to retrieve a sufficient amount of cash to cover the items. "Would you see that he gets something suitable?"

"I will, ma'am," he said as he ducked back outside.

Within minutes the efficient staff had Sadie and her belongings in a comfortable but sparse room on the second floor overlooking the main road. Her first order of business was to open the envelope the driver had given her.

Floods prevented train from departing on time. Expect to arrive Baton Rouge late tonight. Will update if needed.

Jefferson ducked his head under the water again, holding his breath. He hadn't had a bath in so long he'd forgotten how good it felt to be clean. Intending to stay in the tub until the water was too cold to bear, he would get out no sooner than then.

Combined with a shave and a haircut, he felt like a new man. The knock on the door must mean his clothes were being delivered.

"Just put them on the bed," he called.

No response.

"Hello?" he said. Another knock was his answer.

Reluctantly he climbed out and wrapped a length of toweling around himself. Still dripping, he padded to the door just as someone knocked yet again.

"The bed would do just fine," he said as he opened the door.

Two men stepped in, neither of them carrying

clothes. And then the room tilted and the lights went out.

He awoke a few minutes later when someone slapped him. This time, Jefferson's instincts kicked in, and he landed a punch on the nearest thug's jaw.

Not waiting to see the results, he whirled around on the other man and waylaid him with a swift blow to the midsection that doubled him over. A quick look over his shoulder, and he spied the first man laid out on the floor, one hand cradling his face.

"What's going on in here?" The driver who had bundled him up and thrown him into the carriage outside the prison rushed into the room. The one who had shadowed him to the barber and back as if he were some sort of paid nursemaid.

"These two came to pay me a visit," he said as he surveyed the pair, both dark-haired and looking enough alike that they might be related. "Any idea who they are?"

"No," the driver said. "I've never seen these men. You want me to get rid of them for you?"

"I think they're able to get up and walk out on their own. Aren't you, boys?"

"Not going anywhere without her," the man on the floor said.

"Her?" Jefferson demanded.

"We're looking for Sarah Callum," the fellow with the sore jaw said as he gave Jefferson a look that might have held more danger had he been able to stand. "What have you done with her?"

"Sarah Callum?" Jefferson said as he recognized the name of the Pinkerton lady. "I think you boys have made a mistake. I am the only one staying in this room."

The man who had taken the blow to the midsection rose up on his hands and knees, his face still contorted with what was unmistakably pain. "There's no mistake. The clerk said this was her room."

"Well, the clerk is wrong." Jefferson looked to the driver for confirmation. "You want to let them know there's no one in this hotel by that name?"

And there wasn't. He'd spied the lovely lady slipping into the dress shop across the street while he was waiting for the bathtub to fill.

"He's right," the driver said. "Now, which one of you wants to explain to the law why you're breaking into a hotel room and causing a ruckus with an innocent man?"

"We didn't intend to cause any trouble," Sore Jaw said. "When she left the jail, we . . ."

So the pair had been following Sadie. "Go on," Jefferson demanded. "And while you're at it, you can explain why you were playing hide-and-seek with this Sarah woman."

"It wasn't like that," he protested. "See, we were just trying to keep her . . ."

"Keep her what? Frightened?"

"No," they said in unison.

"Then what?" He looked to the other fellow.

The men exchanged looks but said nothing.

Whatever the reason, these two obviously weren't keen on giving the cause of their interest in the pretty Pinkerton agent.

Jefferson adjusted his towel and then strode over to Sore Gut and helped him stand. Rather than speak, he glared.

"Looks like we made a mistake, mister," the stranger said. "We don't mean any trouble."

"Well, it's too late for that because you've troubled me plenty. And my guess is you must have been troubling that woman you mentioned as well. Not the kind of man I tend to tolerate."

Grabbing his arm, Jefferson guided the man to the door and threw him out into the hallway, where he landed on his behind. Sore Jaw followed of his own accord, although Jefferson gave him a solid push to send him hurrying out of the room.

"I'll forgive the error if you get out of town the same way you came in. If I see you again, I won't bother to take it easy on you next time. You'll be lucky if the law catches up to you before I do. And leave the spying to the professionals. Got it?"

Both men scrambled up and out in record time.

"Want I should follow them?" the driver asked. "I don't cotton to the idea of anyone looking for our Miss Callum, especially when there's two of them and only one of her."

Our Miss Callum.

"It wouldn't hurt to be sure they hightail it out of town like they said they would," Jefferson said. "Maybe you could just stand out front to see that they don't return to the hotel. With the train station just down the road, maybe they'll get the idea and leave without any further trouble."

The driver—hadn't Miss Callum called him Sam?—gave Jefferson a curt nod and then set off down the hall in the direction the pair had gone.

So much for enjoying my bath, Jefferson thought as he closed the door. Instead, he hurried into his new suit of clothes Sam had on his arm when he came in and did his best to comb his hair.

Those two hadn't argued about leaving, and yet Jefferson didn't feel any better about the lady being out alone. He'd find her and see that she was safe. It was his duty as a gentleman and the least he could do.

A gentleman without any sort of weapon. His anger flared. Then he saw his watch.

The Pinkerton lady had saved him, and he owed her. Snatching up his grandfather's prized possession, he set out to see what he could do to even the score by making a trade for the revolver he had spied in the shop next to the barber.

Whoever those two were, they wouldn't get past Jefferson Tucker again.

Seven

Sadie noticed the man shadowing her right away. He managed to keep his face mostly hidden as he walked a discreet distance behind her, but the cut of his clothes and the way he wore them on his muscular frame put her in mind of a pugilist she once saw on a New York street corner. While that man had been encouraging all comers to take notice of him, this one seemed determined to do the opposite.

The rain had ceased, leaving a sheen of dampness across everything the mud had not touched. With the purchase of a new dress for her return home, Sadie tired of the chase and was ready to return to the hotel and a hot meal before bed.

Tomorrow was a day she had put off far too long, as witnessed by the telegram given to her just before she left the hotel earlier. Uncle Penn, in his own cryptic way, had managed to send warning of Daddy's ire and his refusal to accept any further delay.

The package must arrive on time else the recipient will come looking for it.

She had not yet responded, although likely her uncle was anxiously awaiting confirmation of her arrival. He and Daddy weren't the best of friends on a good day owing to their conflicting allegiances during the war, so her father was most assuredly making Uncle Penn's life miserable.

"Shall I have this sent, miss?"

Sadie returned her attention to the clerk at Hattie's Dressmakers. "Yes, that would be lovely. I'm staying just across the street there."

She nodded toward the hotel and then spied the stranger in conversation with her driver. While the man's back was to her, she could see Sam nod and then gesture behind him.

By the time she picked her way across the muddy street, the man had disappeared. A glance told her the driver was watching. She smiled and then turned toward the telegraph office, located in the opposite direction from where Sam had pointed.

Likely she would not be followed there, not now that Sam had made his presence known. Making quick work of sending a response letting Uncle Penn know his package would be headed toward its destination in the morning, Sadie strolled back to the hotel at a leisurely pace.

For the first time all day, her stomach growled, reminding her of how little she had eaten. And while penny candy wasn't the best meal, right now Sadie couldn't think of anything that would taste any better.

Hurrying back across the street to Dupre's Mercantile, she just barely slipped inside before the shopkeeper closed the door for the evening.

The elderly Mr. Dupre met her apologetic expression with a smile.

"Considering the penny candy?" he asked.

"How did you know?"

"I know my customers, and you . . . well, I had you pegged for a candy girl from the minute you walked into my shop."

She moved toward the candy display, offering him only a quick glance before turning her attention to the delicacies displayed there. "You did?"

"Sweets for a sweet lady." Had he not been teetering dangerously toward at least eighty years of age, Sadie might have thought Mr. Dupre was flirting. When he tucked in two extra candies, she knew for certain he was.

"Thank you," she said as she retrieved enough money to pay for the candy she had requested as well as the two pieces she'd been gifted with. Then she waved away the old man's protests. "I insist."

Out of the corner of her eye, she again saw the man who had been following her. Somehow he had slipped into the mercantile and now appeared to find a keen interest in a horse collar over in the tack section.

"Thank you, Mr. Dupre." She tucked the bag of candy into her reticule and turned toward the tack department, only to find the man was no longer there.

Reaching down to press her palm against her loaded Remington pistol, Sadie put on a neutral expression and moved casually toward the door. Sam would be watching once she stepped outside, or at least he should be. If this man meant her harm, she would get the draw on him with the driver acting as backup.

Sensing a presence just behind her, before she reached the door Sadie whirled around to see the stranger. Only he was no stranger.

Her heart did a flip-flop as gray-blue eyes met hers. "Mr. Tucker?"

"Miss Callum," he said with a nod.

A sweeping glance told her that the London policeman had been shaved and shorn and scrubbed clean. His grin was broad, offering a pair of dimples as a nice added surprise. Indeed, now that she thought on it, the man did resemble the twin whose reputation had put him behind bars. And yet this Tucker . . . well, he was the kind of handsome that caused her breath to catch. Something she had never experienced in the presence of the other Tucker twin.

Somehow, though, his smile didn't exactly reach his eyes.

Looking beyond her, he seemed to be taking measure of something on the street. Or across the street.

"Thank you again," Mr. Dupre said, coming up to them and getting the door for her. "I'll have plenty of that candy here tomorrow should you wish for more."

She smiled. "I'm afraid I'll be leaving on the early train."

"That is a pity. Is there anything an old man can say to change your mind?"

"I'm afraid not." Sadie chuckled as she went through the opened door, only to have her breath catch when she noticed two very familiar faces standing across the street.

Brent and Cade. Her brothers.

She turned and slammed into Jefferson Tucker, who was walking out of the store behind her. Out of the corner of her eye, she saw Brent looking over in her direction, so she did the first thing that came to mind.

She kissed the Tucker fellow.

On the lips.

Right there on Main Street in front of anyone who might be looking. And this she did in front of her brothers. For one thing they knew about her was that she would never kiss a man on the street. She'd been raised to behave like a proper lady at all times.

And thus the woman they saw could not possibly be her. Only it was.

Acting against character was a classic diversionary tactic learned during Pinkerton training, and one that almost always worked. Thankfully, she had never had to kiss a stranger.

Until now.

She pulled back slightly and saw that the boys were still in view. So she lifted up on her toes and deepened the embrace, even moving one hand to run it through his hair.

Reluctantly, she broke off the kiss and then pushed him back inside the mercantile. Sadie slammed the door and rested her back against it. What were *they* doing here?

No doubt the pair, fraternal twins who rarely did anything separately, had been sent by her father to see just what sort of delay had kept Sadie away.

Leaning to the right, she lifted the flour sack curtain and looked out across the street. Indeed, Brent and Cade were standing outside the livery next to her hotel as if they hadn't a care in the world.

"Well, now," Mr. Dupre said. "May I interest you in some of what the lady is having, sir? Or are you in the market for some other purchase?"

Jefferson Tucker's grin returned full force as he turned to stand next to Sadie, casually linking arms with her. "We've kept you well past closing time, so we will just go out the back door with you," he said smoothly as he led Sadie toward the rear of the store.

"Back door?" the shopkeeper called after them. "But I'm not ready to leave. There are things yet to be done, and—"

"Then we will see ourselves out." Mr. Tucker picked up his pace, causing Sadie to scramble to catch up.

Whatever the reason, her companion apparently wasn't any more anxious to be seen in front of the mercantile than she was. Only when they stood in the alley, shadows gathering around them, did he pause.

"Please convey my thanks to the Pinkerton Agency for their diligence in seeing to my happiness," Mr. Tucker said.

She looked up, confused. "I'm sorry. Your happiness?"

"Well, Agent Callum, that kiss was the kind that would make a man smile."

"Oh." She shook her head. "You are incorrigible, sir. Did you not recognize that as a technique used for drawing attention away from my identity?"

His chuckle was maddening. "That's an interesting way to put it," he said slowly. "The only attention it drew far as I can tell was mine. And trust me, you had my full attention."

Sadie opened her mouth to say something and then thought better of it. As much as she wished to put him in his place and end his teasing, a more pressing matter needed to be attended to. She moved to the edge of the building and peered around. Unfortunately from this vantage point she could not see her brothers.

Jefferson Tucker tapped her on the shoulder, causing her to jump. Sadie whirled around, prepared to give him a lecture on protocol during stakeouts, for this was arguably a form of stake-out, when he leaned down and kissed her again.

"Mr. Tucker!" Sadie pressed both hands against his broad chest and used her considerable strength to move him backward. "What in the world possessed you to do that?"

"Me?" He looked down at her as if she were the lunatic instead of him. "You're the one who kissed me first. I was just returning the favor."

"Kissed you?" She shook her head. "As I said, that was an elementary diversionary tactic."

"Well, it worked," he said, grinning unrepentantly. "I've been completely diverted from thinking about anything else."

Cade came into view, and Sadie ducked back behind the wall. This was ridiculous. She certainly couldn't stand behind the mercantile for the remainder of the day.

And as nice as Jefferson Tucker's kisses were, she could not have him kissing her again. Not ever, but especially not now.

Mr. Tucker stepped in front of her, and she scooted out of the way. "Over here. They will see you."

"They?" He leaned out beyond the corner of the building and then looked back down at her. "I know those two."

"You do? How?"

"We became acquainted a little while ago back at the hotel. Want to tell me why two men would bust in on me while I'm taking the first bath I've had in almost a year? And before you say anything, you should know your name was mentioned."

She searched his face for evidence of ill treatment. While Brent was amiable by nature, Cade had been known to have a hair-trigger temper.

"They didn't hurt you, did they?"

It was Jefferson Tucker's turn to study her. "You do know them."

"Please don't ask me how."

Again his gaze swept her face. "All right, but I need to know whether they mean you harm."

She contemplated the proper response. To allow to a stranger that they were two of her five overly protective brothers would needlessly complicate matters.

"Harm? No, the opposite, actually."

Well, now. It all began to make sense. One of those two was sweet on the lady Pinkerton. Apparently that feeling was not returned, or perhaps they had had a tiff of some sort.

Didn't matter. While he wasn't keen on getting in the middle of some sort of romantic entanglement, Jefferson did owe a debt of gratitude to Miss Callum.

He let out a long breath. "All right, Miss Callum. Do you want me to see that they leave town or just leave the situation alone?" He looked down at her. "Because I don't intend to stand in the alley with you and miss the first decent supper I've had since last May, nor do I intend to tolerate any further interruptions to my evening."

"I don't wish you to hurt them, but if you could convince them to leave, I would be happy to buy that supper for you."

"And you can assure me that these fellows aren't lawbreakers?"

She drew herself up to her full height as a lovely shade of pink climbed into her cheeks. "I am a Pinkerton agent charged with keeping the laws of this country, sir. And as such I would never allow any persons of that ilk to escape. So no, they are most assuredly *not* lawbreakers."

My, but she is beautiful when riled. He nodded and then fixed her with a look. "I don't like getting in the middle of a lover's quarrel, either."

"I assure you there is no such relationship with either of them," she snapped.

"No, I guess there isn't. Couldn't be that a Pinkerton agent charged with keeping the laws of this country would find time for romance."

Her eyes narrowed. "What do you mean by that?"

"Just that you seem to be the type who wouldn't allow love to get in the way of the disposition of her duties."

He could tell the pretty lady was trying to decide if she ought to take offense or thank him. While she thought about that, he said, "Do not move until I come back for you. Understand?"

When she nodded, he set off around the corner of the mercantile to where he had a better view of the street. The men in question had moved down the block and now stood in front of the ticket window at the rail station.

"Evening, boys," he said when he caught up with them.

"We don't want any trouble," Sore Jaw said. "Look, we're heading out soon as the train leaves for New Orleans."

"And when is that?" he asked as he glanced over at the pair of tickets the clerk was handing the other man.

"The train will be pulling out any minute," the clerk told them. "You ought not to dally, fellows. What about you, mister?" he said to Jefferson.

"I'm just here to tell these two goodbye." Jefferson made sure he had both of the travelers' attention before continuing. "If I see you around, I won't hesitate to consider you two the criminals you are."

"We're not criminals," Sore Jaw protested.

"Then why don't we take a stroll down the road to speak to the law and see what he thinks? The way I remember it, I was taking a bath when the two of you barged in my room and—"

The train's whistle interrupted him before he could finish. By the time the sound had ceased, the interlopers were climbing aboard.

Jefferson made sure the train left with them on it and then went back for Miss Callum. "Sent them packing on the train to New Orleans," he told her as he escorted her across the street toward the entrance of the hotel. "Now, about that supper?"

"You mean they left? Just like that?"

He wouldn't tell her the boys were already heading out of town when he gave them good reason not to change their plans. Instead, he nodded. "Just like that. Just like you kissed me."

"That was not a kiss."

"Miss Callum, that was definitely a kiss, and a memorable one too." He paused just long enough to let her think about that. "You know, I'm of a mind to have a nice steak. Will you join me?"

"Yes," she said as she stepped inside. "I'll be glad to pay up."

"I wouldn't think of it. I've come into some money recently, and I would be much obliged if you would let me pay back some of your kindness by buying you dinner."

She looked as if she might argue, and then instead she merely nodded. Once they were seated at a table near the back of the room and had ordered their meals, Jefferson broached the topic on his mind. "The truth. Are you in danger, Miss Callum?"

Eight

Since when did a simple question about whether a person was in danger meet with such surprise? Miss Callum laughed, sobering only when Jefferson did not join her in an expression of humor.

"You're serious," she said, the remains of her smile still in place at the corners of her lovely lips.

"I am."

She removed the napkin from the table and placed it in her lap. A gesture likely meant to delay a response, and yet he was determined to be patient.

In the lamplight, her fair hair took on a golden glow, and the color in her cheeks rose. She was a beautiful woman, this Pinkerton agent, a fact that made him wonder why she'd chosen this line of work instead of busying herself as a rich man's wife.

"There is always an element of danger, Mr. Tucker," she said without the slightest fear in her voice. "It is a hazard of my occupation, and one I can neither repair nor concern myself with."

"Because to do so would be crippling to your work?"

Her expression softened. "Indeed."

"So those men—"

"Fall under the category of things, or rather persons, I cannot concern myself with at the present time."

"I'll grant you that, then. But I still say that was quite a kiss."

"Suit yourself, but it was merely a diversionary tactic meant to—"

"Detract attention due to the fact the behavior was something those two would never assume you would do," he supplied. "Acting against character can be effective."

"And apparently it was."

"Oh, it affected me," he admitted.

Sadie shook her head and resolutely changed the subject to the weather and resulting flooding that had taken place the last few weeks in the surrounding countryside. Though he might have commented to say that weather of any sort had not permeated the depths of his prison cell, Jefferson decided against it. The diversion of speaking about anything not related to a case was surprisingly refreshing, as was the relaxed expression on Miss Callum's lovely face.

Soon enough, the food arrived. Though the meal would never be compared to fine dining in any way, the fact that it was hot, palatable, and not infested with anything that moved when he stabbed it with a fork made this the best dining experience he had in a very long time, the picnic lunch notwithstanding.

Jefferson caught Miss Callum watching and realized his plate was emptying much faster than hers. "Delicious," he said as he speared the last piece of meat and downed it with as much restraint as he could manage. "Thank you for tolerating me tonight. I find I'm out of the habit of recalling how to dine with proper ladies. I cannot recall when the company was more pleasant."

She prettied up her expression with a smile. "What are your plans once you return to Mobile?"

So she intended to deflect with a change of topic. Of course she would pick that one.

He exhaled as if the moment might pass and Miss Callum would cast her interests elsewhere. Failing this, he elected to answer with the most truthful thing he could say.

"I have no idea."

Though her brows lifted, she offered no advice as she sipped gingerly at her steaming mug of tea. His esteem of her rose, for a woman who did not tell a man what to do was a rare creature. At least in his experience.

Her silence prodded him to pick up the thread of conversation in a safer place. "Once you're rid of me, where will you go?"

Her beautiful green eyes met his gaze. "I think that's a subject only discussed between Pinkerton agents, don't you?"

"Oh, of course." He suppressed a smile. "None of that spy-to-spy courtesy here. I do understand."

She sat back amused. Or perhaps perturbed. The expression she offered could have been either.

"Spy to spy?" She glanced around the empty dining room. "Really, Mr. Tucker? Is that what you think we are?"

Jefferson let out a long breath as he reached for the sugar bowl in an attempt to make the rather vile coffee palatable. After adding two spoonfuls of sugar, he took a sip and then reached once more for the spoon.

"What I think is that you and I are not so different, at least in our careers." He paused to move the sugar bowl back to the center of the table between them. "And in this case, I think a decent argument can be made for the fact that our careers have intersected quite nicely."

"You act as if we are working together, Mr. Tucker, which we decidedly are not."

"I beg to differ, Miss Callum. You are looking for my brother and so am I." He shrugged, an affectation designed to allow the woman to consider him harmless and not the least bit interested in the topic. Neither, of course, was true.

"Actually, once my replacement arrives, I will

hand over your custody as well as the job of finding your brother."

"And you will move on to another case."

She almost smiled. Almost but not quite. "That is my hope."

"Ah, so your interest in finding the larcenous Will Tucker, as he's known in the newspapers, pales in comparison to something more interesting?"

"After a brief respite, yes."

"A visit with home and family, perhaps? I'm sure your husband will be happy to see you return."

She shook her head. "Are you making polite conversation, or was that an attempt to uncover personal details about me?"

"Yes. Is it working?"

"It is not." She crossed her arms over her waist, all pretense of dining set aside. "You're a curious man."

"And you are changing the subject, Agent Callum."

"Yes. And it *is* working." At his chuckle, she continued. "You count your freedom in hours with no idea of what you will do and—"

"I never said I had no idea as to what I would do." He leaned slightly in her direction. "What I said was that I had no idea of my plans once I returned to Mobile. The two are separate issues."

"I don't follow."

"I was pursuing a suspect when I was wrongly incarcerated. I intend to continue that pursuit. That is what I will do."

"I see." She paused as if deciding what to say next. "Then I wish you much luck in the pursuit of your suspect and the execution of whatever plans you undertake."

"That is kind of you."

"No, it's not. Anyone thinking of taking up detective work for a living should be considering another line of work." She looked away. "I'm sorry. I shouldn't have said that out loud. It has been a rather long day. If you will excuse me, I will say good night."

She rose, and Jefferson followed suit. "I wonder if I might change your mind."

"About what?"

"Retiring early." He paused to collect his thoughts, not an easy task with a beautiful woman watching. "And maybe about detective work."

"I doubt it."

Yet as she said the words, Sadie found herself wanting to be talked out of them. What was it about this handsome man that had her so befuddled?

She was a Pinkerton agent. A professional just doing her job. And yet she couldn't recall having more fun sparring with a dinner guest in quite some time.

And despite the fact he'd been a grizzled and grimy stranger only hours ago, she had found somewhat of a kindred spirit in Jefferson Tucker. Perhaps it was their shared professions.

He caught her attention and held it. "I realize this may be more than a man should ask a woman he does not know, but I wonder if you would keep me company just a little longer."

Before she could respond, he continued. "I was locked up alone in a cell for almost a year, Miss Callum. I find I'm rather enjoying the conversation and not looking forward to going back to that empty room."

"Oh."

There were a half dozen answers she could have made to flat out tell him no. Another half dozen that would let him down easily and still allow her to escape his company.

"I don't suppose it would hurt to continue our conversation," she found herself saying. "As long as we do not discuss cases or whether I have a husband waiting for me at home."

"You don't."

She ignored his statement. Of course a man trained as a detective would have to press his point. That did not mean she had to acknowledge it.

"So," she said brightly, "it's still early and the rain appears to have stopped. Where would you like to go on your first night as a free man? I'm sure we could find a theater performance or something of the sort. Would you like me to ask the desk clerk what he would recommend?"

"Actually . . ." He said the word slowly, almost sheepishly. "What I would really like is to see the stars. It has been a very long time."

Sadie gave him a sideways look. "I take it you had no window in your . . ." She looked around the dining room to be certain they were still alone before returning her attention to Mr. Tucker. ". . . your previous accommodations?"

His laughter held no humor. "I did not."

"Then it is time you renewed your acquaintance with the night sky."

He offered her his arm and she took it. "Lead on."

Though she was quite familiar with the Louisiana capital, her experience was more suited to political events attended with her father or, more often, social events attended with her brothers or mother. A walk beneath the stars would be a new experience for her as well.

They stepped out onto the sidewalk, where she spied her driver lounging comfortably against the carriage. "What are you doing out here, Sam?" she asked.

The look that passed between him and the former prisoner was one she could not miss. "Just enjoying the night air, ma'am," he said when he once again met her gaze.

Sadie studied him a moment and then nodded. "All right. Do continue."

"A little longer and then I believe I'm done for the night. I'm beginning to lose interest and it's been a long day."

"It has," Mr. Tucker said. "You may want to get your rest."

"I believe I will," Sam said before tipping his hat to Sadie. "Good night, ma'am. Sir."

As Mr. Tucker led Sadie down the sidewalk toward the river, she slid him a sideways look. "What was that about?"

"Hmm?" His brows rose as his face became a picture of innocence. Guilty innocence, she decided.

"That conversation was not about a man enjoying the night air. So what was it about?"

"Sure it was," he said and then nodded toward the end of the street. "What is that up ahead? If I didn't know for certain I was in Louisiana, I would swear we were coming upon a proper British manor house."

"Manor house?" She chuckled. "More like a castle. However, it is the state capitol building."

They turned the corner, and the edifice came into full view. The magnificent structure, with its twin turrets, crenelated battlements, and white façade, did indeed resemble some sort of medieval castle. With the wash of moonlight and the lamps lit, the building looked especially noble.

"My mother's ancestral home looks very much like this." His tone was wistful. "I miss it."

"The home?"

He shrugged. "England. Home. All of it." He adjusted his cuffs, all the while keeping his attention fixed on the capitol building. "Have you ever been to England, Agent Callum?"

"Yes, several times. I liked it very much."

He looked down at her. "What did you like about it?"

"The museums, the history. London was magnificent. We went to the theater . . . the Alhambra in Leicester Square, I believe. Is that the one with the statue of Shakespeare out front?" At his nod, she continued. "Oh, and there was one memorable occasion. The Inventions Exposition where Sir Francis Bolton put on the most amazing—"

"Electric light show," he said along with her. "Yes, I know. I was there."

"Were you?" She tried to imagine the staid detective enjoying himself at such an event and failed. "Then you know it was just lovely."

"Indeed. And yet as nice as London is, there's something about the English countryside. Where a man can look up at the stars and actually see them at night."

Sadie followed his gaze. "They do not appear to be as visible here," she said as they continued on. "Perhaps down closer to the river?"

He steered her that way, walking in silence as a

city trolley pulled by a team of horses plodded past. She looked over at the conveyance, its windows filled with blank-faced passengers mostly hidden in the evening shadows, and took note of every detail. Even now she could not let her guard down and just enjoy an evening stroll.

Apparently neither could Mr. Tucker, for she caught him looking in the same direction until the trolley had disappeared around the corner.

"Sorry," he said as he went back to looking straight ahead. "A habit of mine."

She smiled. "Mine as well."

His nod was the only response he made until they reached the end corner. "Shall we take a look at the river? I heard the men in the barbershop talking about the flood. Apparently the water levels are going down, but the river is still well over its banks."

"What they probably neglected to tell you is that the Mississippi has a mind of its own and tends to try to change course regularly."

"Is that so?"

A horse cantered past as they walked on, its color so dark that only its hooves were visible until it emerged from the shadow of the buildings across the street. The rider was a man in uniform, probably a police officer. With a nod in their direction, he continued on his way.

A few minutes later the road ended in a confusion of warehouses and ramshackle buildings.

Beyond them were wharves where steamboats rocked at anchor beside vessels of all sorts of sizes and levels of seaworthiness. Snippets of conversation, punctuated here and there by sounds of laughter, drifted toward them on the not-so-pleasantly-scented breeze.

Though most of the day's work was done, there were still a few stevedores working, their crates and cartons moving silently down the docks to disappear into the vast buildings that housed the commerce brought in by the river's vessels. On board the steamboats, lights flickered and people moved about on the decks.

They moved off the sidewalk to a path worn through the undergrowth along the river. The view was better here, much more open sky and with far less activity to distract the eye.

Jefferson Tucker stood tall beside her, his posture that of a man with an extensive military background. His hands were behind him now—parade rest was what the children of workers who staged mock-wars behind the smokehouse called the stance. And while his body did not move, his eyes seemed to be sweeping the scene unfolding before them.

Sadie took the opportunity to study him. Like his brother, this Tucker bore the sandy hair and handsome face that could easily capture a woman's attention.

When he caught her looking, she pretended

interest in the steamboat rocking at anchor just down the wharf. "I believe that's the *Anna Belle*," she said. "It's a lovely vessel. One of the finest in all of Louisiana."

"Lovely," he echoed. "Yes, indeed."

But when she returned her attention to him, he was not looking at the steamboat. Oh, but those eyes did gaze at her with interest.

Warmth began to climb her neck and flood her cheeks. Ridiculous. And yet there it was.

"So," she said, her voice an octave higher than she expected. She cleared her throat and tried again. "What do you think of our river? She is quite impressive."

"Impressive," he said, this time so softly that Sadie was not certain she heard.

She felt herself drawn to him. Felt an interest in spending more time in his presence. It was an odd feeling, this attraction. No, she quickly amended. There could be no attraction. She was a grown woman. A trained Pinkerton agent whose family life was more complicated every day. A daughter whose father must be placated before the next case could be tackled. And a sister who could expect one or more of her brothers to pop out of the darkness at any moment, as Brent and Cade had done this afternoon.

And yet, at that moment, her only wish was to stand there beside the water and let the lull of the quiet strength of the man beside her tug her closer.

As if he had guessed at her thoughts, Mr. Tucker moved to place a protective hand on hers. Again he looked down at her.

With his expression cast in moonlight and shadows, there was no indication of the direction of his thoughts. Owing to his profession as a detective, would his thoughts even show should she manage to see his face?

Perhaps. Or perhaps not.

A recollection of their kiss rose unbidden. Kisses, she amended as she allowed the slightest shiver.

"Are you cold?" His arm slid around her and gathered her close.

Hardly. Heat enflamed her face.

"Look."

Sadie followed the direction he pointed and spied a falling star. "Oh, my. Wasn't that something?"

"Something." Mr. Tucker continued to gaze up at the sky. "My grandmother used to tell me that seeing a falling star meant my wish would come true."

"Did you believe her?"

"Of course. When I was a child, anyway."

"And now?"

He shrugged. "I am older and wiser. Not by choice."

His grip on her waist tightened slightly. He was watching her again. Smiling.

Out of the corner of her eye, she saw something move. A second look told her it was a snake. One of those nasty cottonmouths that populated the riverbank.

She reached for the gun in her pocket and dispatched the intruder with a single bullet.

"What in the . . ." Mr. Tucker pulled a match from his pocket and struck it. "Good shooting. That snake was well over five feet long and headed for us."

Shrugging, she returned her revolver to its hiding place. And then, quick as that, the moment was over and he stepped away to thrust his hands in his pockets.

"Well," he said, his voice sounding oddly strained, "I have seen the stars and the local wildlife. Thank you."

"My pleasure." She nodded toward the direction in which they had come. "After you, Mr. Tucker."

He led the way, and Sadie fell into step beside him. At the corner they paused long enough to allow a pair of wagons to pass before crossing the street.

In each alley and doorway, Sadie watched for Brent or Cade or one of the three others. When the train station came into view, she searched the platform and looked into every window.

"Ever the Pinkerton agent, Miss Callum?"

She met his gaze with a smile. "Yes, I suppose so."

"And yet you are not enthralled with the occupation."

"What gave you that idea?"

A whistle blew at the station and a plume of steam rose over the roof of the station. A moment later, the evening train pulled away and silence once again reigned.

"You gave me that idea. Something about anyone thinking of taking up detective work for a living ought to consider a different line of work."

"On occasion I speak when I should remain silent."

"And I tend to remain silent when I should speak." He stopped and grasped her wrist, halting her progress up the street. "So I will remedy that right now."

"Oh?"

"Thank you, Miss Callum. I know these clothes came from money you gave the driver. I saw you hand it to him."

She shrugged. "I'll note it on my expense report."

"I doubt that," he said, and she did not argue.

"So," he continued as the entrance to their hotel drew near, "why is it that you remain in a profession you cannot recommend?"

"I said I could not recommend it. That hardly means . . ." She stopped short. "Do you have a family, Mr. Tucker? Other than your brother, I mean? A wife, fiancée, or lady friend?"

He grinned. "Family, yes. A woman who fits any of those titles you mentioned? Not at the moment."

She tried again. "Before your unfortunate incarceration, perhaps?"

He shook his head. "There were ladies of whom I was fond. They might have become . . ." He seemed to be searching for the words. "What I mean is, I had the opportunity several times over, but the job . . ."

A look of realization came over him. Apparently the London detective had finally gotten her point.

"But the job," she echoed. "Exactly. Which is why I cannot recommend this profession. Now, if you will excuse me, I believe it is time to say good night."

It probably was time to say good night, but Jefferson still wasn't ready to part ways with her. He couldn't just say so. Not when he'd already gone well past the point where he felt comfortable in admitting he needed more time with her.

So he nodded politely and then kept up with her brisk pace as she crossed the final distance down the sidewalk toward the hotel. Had he not known that Sadie Callum was a Pinkerton agent, and an exceptional one at that, he might have mistaken her for a well-bred young lady from an aristocratic family.

Lady Sadie. He grinned at the thought. And

yet she could easily pass for nobility. Even his mother, the arbiter of all that was fashionable, would have been fooled.

That thought stopped him in his tracks. A Pinkerton agent who looked like a society girl. With the bearing of a princess and the deadly aim of a sharpshooter.

The possibilities for a woman with those talents were endless. And while he could easily convince himself to take her on as a partner in the case he would be returning to, it might be a bit more difficult to convince her.

Jefferson smiled. Somehow he would manage.

He must.

Nine

The next morning, Jefferson gathered up his revolver and knife, the sum total of his belongings now that the suit of clothes he'd left prison in had been thrown into the trash bin, and headed downstairs.

Miss Callum met him at the same table where they had dined last night. She was reading the *New Orleans Picayune* when he walked in.

"Care to join me?" she asked, and then she lowered the newspaper to slide an envelope in his direction. "The judge was prompt in his response. This arrived last night. I think you'll be pleased."

The telegram had been sent to her but the subject was him. Or, rather, the funds that were owed him for the weapons that had been taken. A deposit was being held for him at a bank in Mobile. All that remained was for Jefferson to retrieve it.

Which meant he could also write to the pawnshop and retrieve his watch once he arrived there.

"There's something else." She reached into the side of her skirt and retrieved a small pearl-handled Remington pistol, likely the same one that had dispatched the snake last night, and then slid it across the table toward him.

"What is that for?"

"You'll be in the company of a Pinkerton agent, but it's always good to have some sort of weapon." Her gaze fell to the telegram now sitting next to the gun. "Whatever you do once you're back in Mobile, I assume you'll need a little something to reclaim your life with."

A muscle worked in his jaw as Jefferson sorted out the mix of emotions. That the woman was trying to take care of him irked him. He'd never been put in that sort of position before.

And yet he knew he must look at the thought behind the gift instead of the reason she expected he needed it.

"I appreciate that, Miss Callum," he said gently, "but I have weapons enough to see me to

Mobile." He punctuated the statement with a press of the weapon back in her direction.

Then her attention went to his midsection. "Doesn't a man with a fine pocket watch usually wear the chain on the outside of his vest, Mr. Tucker? I wonder where you might have found the money to purchase weapons."

He schooled his expression to not give any hint that she was correct in her assumption. Instead, he searched for a diversion and found it in the date on the newspaper in front of her.

"Doesn't a person generally read a newspaper that is less than four months old?"

Before she could respond, Jefferson snatched it up. The headline caught his attention immediately: *LOCAL HEIST HAS INTERNATIONAL CONNECTION.*

There, in the first line of the report, was the name of the man he had been sent by the London Metropolitan Police to the States to find nearly a year ago. This man's abilities as a forger were well known in certain circles in Europe, and informants had claimed he was intent on moving into a more lucrative market with his goods.

Only this time the criminal was declaring himself the victim.

"I'll have that back now, please," Sadie said calmly as she silently berated herself for being so careless as to read case documents in public. Mr.

Tucker complied, although with far too much humor in his expression.

What she had not mentioned was that Henry had sent good news for her. Though she would still be allowed a few days respite once Mr. Tucker was handed off, which she would use for her trip back to Callum Plantation to placate Daddy, she would be immediately placed on the Astor case.

Though the message was written in code that made discerning details difficult, Henry had been clear on one point. Owing to new information, the Astor case looked to be much bigger than one woman's trouble with a questionable Rembrandt.

What those details might be piqued Sadie's interest even further. Until she could arrange a meeting with Henry or, failing that, could receive more information through safer channels, she was left to wonder.

After placing an order for enough breakfast to feed several men, Mr. Tucker returned his attention to her. "Your next assignment?"

Drat!

Sadie folded the newspaper and slid it inside the valise beside her. "Did you sleep well, Mr. Tucker?"

She punctuated the question with a polite smile. As their gazes met, she could see that his humor had given way to open interest.

"My sleep is beyond the topic at hand, Miss Callum." He paused while the waiter delivered strong chicory coffee, a sugar bowl, and a pot of honey. "However," he said as he dipped his spoon in the honey and then drizzled it into his cup, "since you've been so kind as to inquire, yes, I will admit to the best rest I've had in a long time. Now, about the Valletta case."

How could he have known?

"I'm sorry?" she said carefully.

"Your case. Sergio Valletta? He would be your victim in the article you've been reading."

"Oh, yes. Interesting story. A suspected art thief is robbed. Or at least that's what's been claimed here." She slowly lifted her gaze to meet his. "Are you familiar with this case?"

"Four months ago I was in prison, Miss Callum. How could I be familiar with the case?"

And yet he had referred to the Italian by his correct name, a name that was misspelled in the newspaper article now safely tucked away in her valise. Further questions were prevented when Sam appeared in the doorway.

Sadie beckoned him to approach with a wave of her hand. "Mr. Tucker's breakfast has not yet arrived. Are we running late?"

"Not exactly," he said as he held out yet another telegram. "And this is not exactly good news, either."

The man's habit of reading her telegrams was irritating. She fixed him with a look that let him know this and then accepted the paper he held.

"Your man's not coming," he told Mr. Tucker. "At least not today. There's been an accident up the line. Derailment, they say. Probably due to tracks being underwater. Looks like our fellow's one of the lucky ones who wasn't seriously hurt."

Sadie read the words. *Derailment north of Shreveport. Unharmed but no means to travel today due to floods. Have alerted Henry.*

She folded the page and tucked it into her valise just as the waiter brought a platter of breakfast for her companion. The truth of the matter was that until someone arrived to relieve her of her duty, she was still the agent in charge of Jefferson Tucker. The agent required to see that the former prisoner arrived in Mobile without incident.

"There's just one thing to be done." Sadie looked up at the waiting driver. "Please see that my trunk is loaded onto the train with Mr. Tucker's things."

"But, Miss Callum, is that proper, the two of you traveling alone?"

She knew he meant well. Meanwhile, Mr. Tucker dug into his meal with the zeal of a starved man, all the while watching her.

"I am a Pinkerton agent, Sam, and as such I am bound by the need to protect my charge. In the absence of another agent, I am required to see to the safe arrival of Mr. Tucker in Mobile."

"But you're a lady—"

"Whether I am male or female does not matter. Whether I carry out my duties as a Pinkerton agent matters very much." She paused only long enough to allow him to consider this. "Am I explaining this in a way that makes sense to you now?"

He swallowed hard and managed a nod. "Yes, ma'am. I'll just see to your trunk."

"Thank you." She waited until Sam had left before facing Mr. Tucker again. When she looked over at him, she saw that he was watching her carefully.

"I am fully capable of seeing myself home," he said as he loaded a bite of scrambled eggs onto his fork.

"I'm sure you are." Sadie collected her valise and held it in her lap. "However, as my duties are not yet discharged, accompanying you is my responsibility."

How she would explain that to Uncle Penn and Daddy was another issue entirely. And yet, she truly had no choice. A Pinkerton agent did not merely walk away from an assignment because it had become inconvenient or conflicted with family schedules.

Nor did her brothers, now that she thought of it. Sadie glanced around to be certain none of them was in sight. Brent and Cade had left awfully fast to suit her investigator's instinct. Unless Mr. Tucker's response was sufficient to make them believe she was not around, they would soon return.

He nodded toward the bag in her lap. "What about your next case? Isn't that your responsibility too?"

He'd asked Miss Callum a question she obviously did not wish to answer. No matter, for Jefferson knew the correct response. The London Metropolitan Police had required the same commitment to duty from him.

He had ended up paying the price for veering off course from his purpose for being in the States. Though he was tempted to dwell on the choice to honor his mother's request to visit John, nothing would change the fact he had made his choice and suffered the cost.

Never again would he be lured away from his duties. If he still had duties, that is, for as yet he had received nothing in response to letters sent to his superiors.

Or, if responses had been sent, they had not been delivered to his cell.

Two more bites taken as his companion sat in stony silence were all he could manage. "All right, Agent Callum," he said as he cast his napkin aside and took a quick sip of coffee. "Shall we?"

She rose without comment, leaving a trace of the lavender-and-lemon scent of her perfume in her wake. She paused only long enough to stop at the front desk to check for any further messages.

Finding there were none, she straightened her back and marched outside, leaving him to catch up.

Once at the train station, Miss Callum made short work of arranging the changes to her ticket and then escorting him to the train. "After you, Mr. Tucker," she said in that businesslike tone of hers.

"You know, Miss Callum, I see a potential problem that you and I should discuss before we get on this train." He nodded to a more private area of the station. "Might I trouble you to come with me for a minute?"

She pursed her pretty pink lips and then nodded. "If you'll be brief."

"After you," he said as he led her away from the train and the prying eyes of the conductor. After he found a quiet corner, he said, "I wonder if you considered the undercover aspect of our mission."

"I don't know what you mean."

"If we are to pass our time on this trip unnoticed, then perhaps you should consider that a woman looking for all the world as though she is protecting a man is going to draw unwanted attention." He paused just long enough to let that statement soak in. "It may even cause people to wonder."

Her eyes narrowed. "I assure you, Mr. Tucker, I am not concerned."

"But I am. I propose the best course of action is

to decide what our cover story is and see that we keep to acting out those roles until we arrive in Mobile. At least, that's what we would do at the London Metropolitan Police. Perhaps you've not gone undercover before."

"Actually, that is my forte."

Of course it was. He smiled. Indeed, he would find a way to convince this woman to join him in his investigation. Eventually.

She let out a long breath. "All right, then. We are the Jeffersons traveling home to Mobile."

"The Jeffersons. Easy to remember and simple enough not to draw attention. All right." He nodded toward the train. "After you, Mrs. Jefferson. And remember, when all else fails, you can kiss me."

She met his gaze, barely blinking. "No, you misunderstand," she said sweetly. "I am Miss Jefferson, your sister. And do not expect that kiss."

Leaving that declaration in her wake, Sadie marched toward the train. Even when he expected she would glance back, she did not.

Brother and sister? He took in her elegant figure and pretty eyes and couldn't imagine her as any sort of relation to himself. And yet she did have the coloring and fair hair to fool all but the most discerning.

"I didn't expect the last one," he called to her retreating back.

She ignored him.

The train whistle sounded, propelling him into motion. Jefferson caught up to Miss Callum just as the conductor called, "All aboard!"

"After you, sis," he said with an exaggerated bow.

She shook her head, but not before he thought he spied a fleeting grin. Any sign of humor was gone by the time they reached the passenger car.

Once they were seated, their tickets punched by the conductor, Jefferson stretched out his legs as best he could, given the confined space, and settled in. A few minutes later the whistle sounded, and the train pulled away from the station in a cloud of steam and smoke.

Miss Callum appeared to have no interest in the passing scenery, busy as she was making notes in a journal she had pulled from her bag. Watching her was tempting, and yet her looks in his direction prevented Jefferson from studying her as he wished. Thus, he feigned exhaustion and closed his eyes. He'd almost fallen asleep to the rocking rhythm of the rails when his companion called his name.

He opened one eye just enough to find her digging in that battered valise of hers. "Here they are," she said as she retrieved a stack of folded papers tied with a ribbon and then thrust them in his direction.

"What's this?"

He sat up and took note of the contents of the stack. Letters.

"There was an issue in getting your mail delivered." She pursed her lips. "Another situation the judge was keen to handle with some expediency. I'm terribly sorry I forgot to give them to you until now."

Loosening the ribbon, he let it fall into his lap. The first letter was dated several months ago and postmarked London. Several others bore the same postmark but with earlier dates.

All were opened, their contents obviously read by someone. And though the address on the letterhead was the same, apparently the London Metropolitan Police were now being called by another name.

"Scotland Yard," he said softly.

"I beg your pardon?"

"Nothing. Just noting a name change."

Jefferson returned his attention to the packet of correspondence. Fresh anger simmered as he shuffled the letters to put them in order of their posted dates, the oldest one first.

If he had not received the letters that came in, could he then assume that those to whom he had written had not received any correspondence from him, either?

There was only one way to find out. Only one way to discover not only what he had missed, but whether he still held a position with the newly named Scotland Yard.

He gave Miss Callum a sideways look. "Would you have any writing paper in that valise of yours?"

Ten

Sadie found paper and pencil for Mr. Tucker and then returned her focus to the trees and farmlands passing by outside the window. While the tracks followed the river, thick underbrush and trees obscured the muddy water in many places. Here and there she saw fishing boats and even the occasional steamboat.

Mostly, she allowed the scene to blur as her thoughts concentrated on the days ahead. Uncle Penn would be waiting in New Orleans to fetch her home. Or perhaps Daddy would come himself or send one of the boys. In any case, she might have been sleeping in her own bed tonight had duty not required otherwise.

Mr. Tucker was scratching out another letter beside her, his masculine scrawl unreadable at this distance. His expression told her these were not correspondences that pleased him to write. Or perhaps such was his concentration that his handsome face was pinched into a most decidedly angry countenance.

He caught her looking at him and ceased his writing. To look away would mean she had been gazing with some intention to read his missives, which she absolutely had not. She had been studying him, measuring him against her recollections of his criminal brother.

She offered a smile but nothing further. Nor did she move her attention from his face.

"I suppose you're wondering what has me riled up," he said as he set the pencil aside and shook his right hand as if it pained him. "Beyond your kiss."

"Not particularly," was her truthful answer. She forced her thoughts away from the kiss he appeared insistent on teasing her about. "I fear I'm caught up in my own thoughts. I apologize for not being an attentive companion."

If her response surprised him, he didn't show it. Instead, he gave her a curt nod and went back to his work. By the time the announcement was made that their arrival at the next station was expected shortly, he had several letters folded and addressed for mailing.

"Thank you," he told her as he returned the pencil and few sheets of paper that remained.

"I take it you were glad to receive these letters," she said as she stuffed the blank pages back into her valise. "Or perhaps not so glad. Your expression as you were writing seemed as if you were irritated."

"Irritated," Mr. Tucker echoed. "Yes, I'd agree with that. I thought some matters were being ignored. Now I see that was not the case."

Outside, the landscape slid past at a much slower rate now, the lush green of the springtime countryside giving way to the city and its buildings.

"After reading your letters, have you made any decisions about what comes next for you?"

He looked down at the correspondence in his hand and then up at her. "Not yet."

A cryptic answer, and yet she was not inclined to pry. Not when this Tucker was not the intended subject of the ongoing investigation.

"I suppose you'll figure something out," she said when she realized he was still watching her.

They rode in silence for a few minutes. "I wonder if I might ask you a question, Miss Callum." At her nod, he continued. "What makes a woman like you choose a career with the Pinkertons?"

Several responses occurred, but none she wished to share. One did not casually mention the fact that joining an organization that, at its heart, allowed a person to pretend to be someone else was a benefit. Nor did it seem appropriate to mention the reason she wished to hide.

"I think my best answer is that the career chose me," she offered. "What about you?"

"That is not an answer at all," he said as he

settled back against the worn leather seat and looked past her, presumably to the scenery passing outside the window.

"Nor do you seem to be forthcoming, Mr. Tucker. Perhaps those of us who are in a line of work that requires secrets to be kept have a few of our own as well."

"Perhaps so." He gave her a direct look. "If this career hadn't chosen you, what would you be doing?"

"That depends. What would I wish to do or what would I actually be doing?"

"Don't make me choose. Answer both questions."

"Only if you will."

"Agreed."

Sadie considered her answer a moment and then smiled. "All right. If I had not become a Pinkerton agent, I would probably be auditioning husbands or, more likely, decorating some grand home and planning a nursery. Apparently, that is what my parents believe I was put on earth for."

"And if you were able to do what you wished?"

"Probably the same, although on my own timetable and not married to a man chosen for me."

"Chosen for you because your parents care for your future?"

"They do," Sadie said with another smile. "Alas, I am cursed with a mother and father who love me."

He met her gaze. "What would you do first, if given your own timetable?"

"Paint." The word slipped from her mouth unbidden. She'd never told that secret to anyone. Even at the Institute, she had settled for a course of study in art history instead of the more hands-on arts. "I'm awful at it," she hurried to say. "My skills run more toward the history of art rather than the creation of it."

"Perhaps with more practice?"

She laughed. "I would only be poor at it rather than awful. No, I'll keep to the study of ancient Egyptian and Iraqi artifacts and oils by the Old Masters."

"Egyptian and Iraqi artifacts?" He gave her a sideways look. "Seriously?"

Shrugging, she brushed off his question. "Any course of study in art history begins with the Egyptians and their cuneiform tablets, hiero-glyphic papyri, and such. And one can hardly make a complete study of the era without including the Iraqis."

"Yes, of course," he said thoughtfully.

"And you?" she asked, happy to direct the questions back to him and away from herself. "What would you do if not for the career you left back in England?"

He thought only a moment, or so it seemed. "I would probably become a gentleman farmer. Hopelessly boring, I know, but it gives a man a feeling of accomplishment to know he is tilling soil handed down to him through the generations and in the process leaving something for future offspring."

"That is noble indeed and not the least bit boring. My father is much like you've described, only his legacy consists of sugarcane fields and the processing mill he and my brothers keep innovating."

Further questions would have to wait as the brakes squealed and the conductor passed through the car.

By habit, Sadie searched the faces of those gathered on the platform outside. Though she half expected to see her brothers waiting, she did not expect to find Kyle Russell there.

Before she could gather her things and exit the train, Kyle had climbed aboard. When he noticed Sadie's companion, he stopped short, eyes narrowed.

"Agent Russell," Sadie said as she urged him forward. "I would like to introduce you to William Jefferson Tucker." She turned to Mr. Tucker. "Jefferson Tucker, please meet Kyle Russell, formerly of the Pinkerton Agency."

"And your escort to Mobile," Kyle said as he moved close enough to shake the man's hand.

"Oh? I thought you retired."

"I did, but Henry can be persuasive." He looked past her again to the Tucker twin.

"I'm pleased to meet you, Agent Russell," he said to Kyle. "Unless I am mistaken, your name appears on my brother's arrest warrant as a witness against him."

Kyle barely blinked. "You are correct."

Jefferson held his gaze for a moment and then offered a curt nod. "I hope you understand that while John and I might resemble one another, that resemblance stops at our appearance. We are quite the opposite when it comes to behavior."

It was Kyle's turn to nod. "So I understand. You have an impressive record at London Metropolitan. Or do I call it Scotland Yard now?"

"Scotland Yard, according to their letterhead."

"About that." Kyle paused to allow a particularly rowdy pair of boys and their parents to slip past in the aisle. "You do look exactly like the man I arrested. My understanding is there was some consideration given to the fact that the state of Louisiana did not release the wrong man."

"Consideration that was withdrawn when Mr. Tucker and I testified on his behalf," Sadie offered.

With another appraising look, Kyle's expression softened. "A pity that hearing took so long."

"Indeed." Jefferson Tucker nodded toward the exit. "Before we board the train for Mobile, I need to see that these letters are mailed."

"Yes, right." Kyle reached for Sadie's valise, only to have her step away.

"Thank you, but I can manage this," she said. "The trunk that will need to be transferred is another matter entirely."

Kyle shared a laugh with her and then quickly sobered. "You won't have to transfer, Sadie. This train's going to New Orleans, and I promised Henry you would be on it."

"Did you?" It did not escape Sadie's notice that Mr. Tucker watched their exchange with great interest. "Did you promise Henry anything else?"

"Two things, actually."

"Oh? And what would those two things be?"

"That I would deliver an envelope for you to read once you're alone." He reached into his jacket pocket and retrieved said envelope. The handwriting was unmistakably Henry Smith's, as was the seal on the back.

"And the other?" she asked as she tucked it into her valise.

"That I would steer clear of your father until the situation with the *Picayune* is remedied to his satisfaction."

"Really, Kyle? There was no situation with the *Picayune*. Surely Uncle Penn has been able to talk sense into Daddy by now."

"He hadn't two days ago when your father paid me a visit to demand I do right by you and make a public statement denouncing the claims made in the paper." He paused as if to allow her to take that in. "It was all very civil, really. Apparently, he and my father have a passing acquaintance that goes back several decades."

Sadie shook her head. Much as she appreciated the depth of her father's love and protection, the fact that he tended to do such things wore on her. "I'm terribly sorry. He didn't harm you, did he?"

"No. He neither harmed me nor made any promise of injury I wouldn't have suggested had a daughter of mine been caught in a similar situation."

She lowered her voice and leaned toward Kyle. "But there was no *situation*—"

"Those that's leaving need to go," the conductor called from the doorway. "Gonna get underway here soon."

"Sir," Kyle called to the railroad man. "The lady's ticket will be changing. Can you see that her trunk remains on the train as far as New Orleans?"

"Sure can, sir. Miss Callum, is it?"

"Yes, that's right. Should I settle up with you for the additional charge or go down to the station and purchase a new ticket?"

"That's been taken care of." Kyle nodded to her valise. "The new ticket is in the envelope."

Satisfied, the conductor went off in search of Sadie's trunk, leaving the three of them in the nearly empty railcar. Sadie took advantage of the moment to turn to Mr. Tucker.

"I suppose this is where we part ways." She

offered her hand to shake his. "I wish you the best in whatever it is that you will be doing."

"Thank you, Miss Callum." He lifted her hand to his lips and then released his grip. "And thank you again for all you've done to secure my release and get my valuables back."

"About that." She held up her index finger. "If you'll wait just one more minute, I have something else for you. I had hoped to give it to you upon my departure from Mobile, but since Agent Russell will be escorting you for the remainder of your journey . . ."

Sadie reached into her valise, pulled out a gold pocket watch, and then handed it to him.

"But how? It's impossible that this is the same one and yet . . ." He shook his head as he weighed the watch in his palm. "It is my watch."

"The watch that you sold so that you might have weapons should I have need of being protected. Am I wrong?"

He did not deny her claim. Instead, he said, "How did you manage this?"

She pasted on the smile she used when the need to charm a gentleman arose. "Simple, Mr. Tucker," she said sweetly. "I am a Pinkerton agent. I've been taught to do the impossible. Sometimes the impossible requires that I send Sam Fenton out on an after-hours errand to a Baton Rouge gun shop where an item was taken in trade."

"I cannot allow this. You will be repaid."

Sadie shook her head. "Never mind that. I am pleased I could manage it. Now, I believe you two have a train to catch."

"And you have a father to appease." Kyle offered a commiserating look. "I wish you the best. I should warn you that he is now aware that I am a Pinkerton agent. Or rather, that I recently retired as such—this errand notwithstanding."

"What did you tell him about me?"

"That you would explain everything when you returned home." He shrugged. "I thought it best that I not elaborate, as I felt he did not have any idea that his dear defenseless daughter—his words, I might add—was a Pinkerton agent as well."

Wonderful.

"If it helps, my wife stepped in at that point to tell your father that she holds you in high regard."

"So Millie was there too? Funny, but I did not get that impression from her the one time we met."

Rather, the former Mildred Cope had made it quite apparent that she did not appreciate the fact Kyle was seen in public with Sadie. Of course, at the time he and Sadie were conducting Pinkerton business and carrying on the ruse that the two were romantically linked.

"She has since seen the error of her ways and, in fact, would love to get to know you better should your travels take you to New Orleans for longer than just the time it takes for your father to fetch you home."

"Yes, I would like that very much," she said and found it was the truth. In her line of work, she met so few women who understood what it was to be a Pinkerton.

Turning his attention to Mr. Tucker, Kyle once again studied the recently released prisoner. "And you're certain you're not the man who ought to be behind bars in Angola? You bear a striking resemblance."

"And yet our mother could always tell us apart. As can Miss Callum."

Kyle returned his focus to Sadie. "How so?"

"The eyes, for one. This man's are gray and yet they can look blue. As I recall, your Mr. Tucker's eyes were gray but under certain circumstances looked green."

"Green, yes," Kyle said as he leaned forward to study the former prisoner's eyes. "And blue they are." He returned his attention to her. "For now, if you say this is not our suspect, I will bow to your expertise, Sadie. I will, however, have questions of him."

"I welcome them, Agent Russell," Mr. Tucker said. "And as such, I will have questions of my own regarding my brother."

Kyle seemed to consider the statement. "I will tell you what I can." He turned to Sadie. "We part ways here, Agent Callum."

"It's good to see you back at work, Kyle, even if it's only for a short while," she told him as she shook his hand.

"I confess I have grown comfortable enjoying my wife and my work in the scientific arts."

"About that, I am always interested in hearing about your latest breakthroughs in crime fighting technology. Is there anything new to report?"

"There is always something new, although I am not always willing to report it."

His expression offered a genial smile but his posture told Sadie he wouldn't be saying anything more with Jefferson Tucker in their midst.

"Fair enough. Please give my best to your wife." She looked beyond Kyle to Mr. Tucker. "I wish you both a safe journey."

Mr. Tucker nodded. He seemed poised to speak and then appeared to have thought better of it. His smile became the goodbye that did not find voice.

With the men's departure, Sadie found herself well and truly alone. Only as the conductor came back through, several passengers following in his wake, did the car return to a lively hum of voices.

She spied Kyle and Mr. Tucker conversing on the platform. The two looked cordial enough. And yet Sadie knew Kyle's suspicions would persist until he no longer had his doubts about the man's identity.

Moving her attention from Kyle to Mr. Tucker,

she studied his features. Had she been told this was the man whose stench filled the carriage on the ride to Baton Rouge, she would have argued that it was impossible. Beneath a year's dirt and unkempt clothing was an extremely handsome man.

A man who had sold his prized watch to see to her protection. And who was awfully pleasant to kiss, now that she thought on it.

He looked up and caught her watching. Rather than offer an innocuous smile or look away, she held his gaze until the whistle blew and steam obscured the platform.

Even as the train lurched forward and Sadie settled in for the last leg of her journey home, she thought of Jefferson Tucker. A pity she had to meet him now. Here. Because of the criminal Will Tucker. For had she seen him across a New Orleans ballroom or caught sight of him in a drawing room in Manhattan or Paris, she might have given him a second glance. Might even have allowed his attentions.

But any man who knew her as a Pinkerton agent could never find an interest in her as a woman. The two were impossible to mix, and any thoughts to the contrary were a waste of time.

Oh, but they would always have that kiss.

Actually, as she leaned back against the seat and allowed herself to recall, there had been two kisses. Two memorable kisses.

Eleven

Jefferson climbed into the railcar a step ahead of his Pinkerton nursemaid. Though both Agents Callum and Russell claimed their escort was for his safety, Jefferson figured the real reason was to stick close in case John showed up.

It was John they wanted, but Jefferson wanted him more. As much as he wished to exact revenge for losing almost a year of his life, his brother had even more than that to answer for.

"After you, Tucker," Agent Russell said as he gestured toward their seats.

He obliged, following the conductor until he stopped at a bench near the front. "You in first," Russell said as he watched Jefferson take the seat by the window before moving beside him on the aisle.

"You realize I was released from prison a free man."

"And you realize I'm tired of putting Will Tucker back in prison."

"Point made. However, the William Tucker you're looking for is not me, nor do I have any idea how to find him."

All his statement got was an appraising look from the man seated beside him. Jefferson turned

126

his attention to the passengers milling about on the train platform below.

The agent waited until the train lurched forward and left the station before beginning his interrogation. And there was no mistaking Kyle Russell's pointed questions about home, family, and his early history for polite conversation. Not when the conversation quickly turned to his brother's penchant for lying.

"He even told my wife he was interrupted on occasion by telephone calls from London," Russell said. "Nothing of the sort is possible, and yet he said it with just enough authority that she believed him."

So that was his issue with John. Somehow his twin had ingratiated himself with the woman to whom Russell was married. The extent of that relationship was likely something best not asked about, and yet Jefferson could not help himself.

"Indeed, my brother has always been persuasive. Our father said he could sell igloos in the Arctic Circle." He paused to slide a sideways glance at his companion. "Considering his association with your wife, I must ask whether your concern for his case is more than professional."

Color instantly flamed Russell's face, and a muscle worked in his jaw. Only an idiot would miss the fact that he was truly angry.

The conductor returned to take their tickets,

buying Jefferson a few minutes' time. He could have apologized. Probably should have. But years of training had taught him that an angry man often spoke closer to the truth than one who was calm enough to hide his intentions.

And so he watched. And he waited.

As soon as the conductor moved on, Russell let out a long breath. Jefferson continued to watch him closely, both with an interest in finding out who he was and in self-defense should he have to deflect any well-deserved punches.

The Pinkerton agent's fingers curled into fists that ground into his knees. "Because I am seated next to you in the discharge of my duties, I am obliged to ignore the fact you have just made an erroneous assumption about the relationship between my wife and your brother."

"Is that so?" he asked in the most neutral tone he could manage. Still, he watched those fists and expected he might be greeted with one between the eyes any moment.

"However," Russell said slowly, "as husband to a woman whose reputation is uncompromised and above reproach, I am currently uncertain as to my ability to carry out my duties as a Pinkerton agent."

Jefferson quickly amended his statement. "Forgive me," he said, and meant it. "I can see that I was incorrect in assuming that you held some sort of grudge against John."

"Is that what you call him? John?" The agent looked away, his hands now crossed over his waist. "No, you were not wrong in making that assumption. My grudge with him goes way back beyond the time when I first met the woman who was to become my wife."

Again he responded with, "Is that so?"

Russell's gaze swung abruptly back to Jefferson. "He not only duped my best friend's wife before Lucas met her, but he was also responsible for the death of Lucas's sister Mary McMinn."

"I know."

The agent's brows rose. "You do?"

"I've read the dossier on him. You forget I wasn't always considered an accused criminal." Again he allowed the statement to sink in. "Or rather a wrongly imprisoned man."

"What else do you know?"

"I know the substance of the testimonies against him as well as all the documentation used to swear out warrants in Mississippi, Louisiana, and Tennessee. I also read the arrest reports for both times he was caught and the list of suspected victims for the times when he was not."

What Jefferson did not say was that he had committed every page to a memory that never forgot anything he read. Nor did John, for that matter, although he left that tidbit also unsaid.

"Do you dispute any of it?"

Jefferson thought only a moment. "I do not."

"And the theory that twins are more closely connected than other siblings?"

"That I will dispute."

"Even as children?"

"I assure you no twins have been born to rival our differences. Our mother likes to say that the only similarity between us is in our appearance."

"So you were not close?"

"For a time, I suppose we were close enough. But boys become men, and men make choices that . . ." He shook his head. "Suffice it to say that when I walked into that prison last May, it had been quite some time since I had seen my brother."

"Yet you were there to pay him a visit."

"At my mother's request." He would stop with that.

"When do you expect to see your brother again?"

"I assure you it will go better for me if I do not see him alone. And I would certainly tell you where he is right now if I had any idea myself."

"You don't expect he'll be waiting for you in Mobile?"

"I expect that you will have an agent there watching my grandparents' home with instructions to prevent any such visit." He met the agent's gaze. "And do not misunderstand me when I tell you I welcome that interruption. You have my word as a fellow law investigator and a gentleman that I will not stand between you and the return of my brother to his rightful place behind bars."

Russell once again studied him, likely looking for the same signs Jefferson would have watched for had their roles been reversed. Then he let out a long breath. "I believe you, Tucker. Much as I don't want to, I do."

"Thank you," was the best he could think of to say before returning his attention to the scenery passing by outside.

"Tell me about your work at Scotland Yard."

Jefferson swiveled to put his back to the window. Finally, a topic safe to discuss.

"When last I spoke to my superior officer, I was employed as a detective." He shrugged. "Until I can return to London or receive a letter answering that question, I am not sure as to my status."

Of greater concern was whether he was employed at all, although the correspondence seemed to indicate a position would be held for him. How long that spot would remain open was a matter he had been putting to prayer well before he read the seven-month-old dispatch this morning.

The statement seemed to placate Russell, for they passed the remainder of the trip in polite but firm silence. Their truce lasted until Jefferson arrived on the steps of his grandfather's home on Springhill Avenue.

"Nice pile of rocks," Russell said as he admired the white-columned city home the judge built for his wife and children.

"My grandmother was pleased with it," Jefferson said as he pushed open the front door before the uniformed butler could manage it. "Grandfather much preferred the cotton plantation in Lowndes County to this place, but Grandmother Tucker needed a place to enjoy the social season."

Stepping into the wide hallway, time tumbled backward until Jefferson recalled the thrill of hiding in the nooks and crannies of the grand home awaiting John or one of the local boys to come find him. An adventure, it was, those pilgrimages his father made to call on his relatives and show off his growing sons.

"Welcome back, Mr. Tucker," the butler said as he took Jefferson's hat and coat. "You were not expected this week, so I fear dinner will be somewhat delayed."

"Yes, of course," Jefferson said as he nodded toward the stairs. "Is my grandmother no longer in residence, then?"

"She is indeed, sir. Not much for leaving her chambers for fear the Yankees might return, but for nearly ninety, she's still going strong. Just as she has since your last visit."

Nearly ninety. Was that possible?

"Take a look at this, Tucker."

Jefferson jerked his attention back toward the open front door, where he'd forgotten all about the Pinkerton agent's presence. He found his shadow going through the stack of mail that had been languishing on the sideboard.

"You there," the agent said to the retreating butler. "Has Mr. Tucker been staying here?"

The older gentleman's expression showed confusion. "Yes, sir, for several months now, although you might ask him yourself as he's standing right there."

Jefferson realized the butler thought he was John at just about the same moment the agent did. And then Russell held out an envelope.

"It appears you've missed the Knights of Revelry event. Back on the seventh of April it was. Eight o'clock at the Princess Theater. A pity."

Again he turned his focus on the butler as he set the letters back down on the silver platter meant to hold them. "Is there a reason the mail has not been opened since the beginning of the month?"

"Go ahead and tell him," Jefferson offered, willing to play at being John one more time if it helped the agent in his quest to find the runaway Tucker.

"All right, Mr. Tucker, but it does seem odd that I'm to answer and not you."

Jefferson forced a grin. "My friend here is something of an odd fellow, so let's just humor him, shall we?"

A glance at Russell told him the agent had not taken offense. Rather, he appeared to find the ruse somewhat amusing.

"We don't answer mail, nor do we talk about whether the gentleman of the house is at home or away. That's the rule Mr. Tucker told us, isn't it, sir?"

"That was the rule," he amended. "I think we can now go back to the way things were before that rule, don't you suppose?"

"Whatever you say, sir," the butler said, as if used to the foibles of the wealthy. "If there's nothing else, I will see if the kitchen can scrape together a cold supper."

"Actually, why don't you send someone down to Klosky's Delmonico on Common Street for oysters. It is still there, isn't it?"

"Yes, sir."

Jefferson glanced over at his guest. "Unless you don't like oysters, Mr. Russell?"

"Why don't you call me Kyle? And the way I look at it, if a man hails from this part of the country—I am from New Orleans, just so you know—and doesn't like oysters, then he hasn't had them prepared correctly."

Jefferson grinned. "Indeed. I believe you and I are going to get along fine, Kyle." He paused to address the butler once more. "I have another question that may seem odd to you. One year ago a box was delivered here with my name on it."

He offered a brief description that included the sender's address and the size and color of the package. "Do you know where that box went?"

"Of course, Mr. Tucker. It's in the storage vault awaiting your further instruction on its disposition. Shall I deliver it to your bedchamber?"

"No, the judge's library, please."

"As you wish, sir."

The butler then ushered Kyle up to his room, leaving Jefferson to pay a visit to the matriarch of the Tucker family. However, as he opened the door to the bedchamber where his grandmother held court, he found a candlestick flying in his direction before he could say a word.

"I told you to stay out of here, you no good scamp!" she declared as Jefferson quickly stepped back into the hallway.

"Cease fire, Granny. It's Jefferson. I just want to talk to you."

Silence greeted him until he braved another peek into the room. This time a vase of cut crystal in a deep blue went flying. Jefferson neatly caught it and then set it aside to close the door.

"Throw all the things you can reach, Granny," he said to the woman whose hand had stilled on the handle of the silver biscuit dish where she usually kept a stash of sweets. "But if you manage to hit me, it won't be John Tucker you wound. It will be his twin."

"Jeffy?" She sat back up against the pile of

pillows, each a riot of color that attested to her hobby of needlepointing flower bouquets on every possible surface.

"Yes, Granny. May I approach, or do I need to find the helmet I left here the last time I visited?"

"You left no such thing," the silver-haired former beauty said. "Get yourself over here and hug your grandmother, William Jefferson Tucker. Then we shall discuss the reason why you've neglected me so long and what we will do about your brother."

Twelve

Sadie stepped off the train and into the arms of Seamus Callum. His grip was firm, his smile broad.

"Sarah Louise, my ray of sunshine."

"Daddy," she whispered against his lapel as she held him tight.

He smelled of fresh air and soap with just the slightest hint of the earthy Louisiana soil that grew his sugarcane. His red beard, incongruous in comparison to his blond hair, scratched against her face. Even now, with so much to hide and so little time to spend at home, there was no better feeling than to be held by her daddy.

Then he held her at arm's length, his eyes searching her face as if memorizing it all over again. Concerned, unconditional love, that's what his face told her. What his eyes said. All the more reason to never allow disappointment to show in those eyes.

"I wondered what kind of reception I might get," she said carefully. "Considering the letter you wrote."

His expression softened, though his grip on her arms did not. "And I stand by what I said. You cannot be showing yourself on the pages of the newspaper for all the world to see. It's just not . . ."

Daddy paused and seemed to be at a rare loss for words. Though she was glad for the temporary silence, Sadie felt no compunction to allow it to continue.

"I know you must be disappointed, but I promise nothing untoward was happening when that picture was taken. It isn't at all what it appears."

"I don't suppose you want to tell me what it is, then?"

If only she could. "I was doing a favor for Kyle Russell," she said as she chose her words carefully. "He was on an assignment. His wife . . ." What to say? She let out a long breath and then continued. "His wife was fully aware that I would be attending with her husband. What none of us expected was to be photographed."

"Obviously," he said as he looked away.

"Daddy, I'm sorry I've caused you and Mama trouble. I never meant to."

Slowly her father returned his attention to his daughter. "You never do." Again he paused. "Just one question and then we'll leave this topic alone. If you answer truthfully, then maybe I'll see that Mama doesn't bring it up either."

"All right. I will answer if I can."

"Fair enough. This person you did the favor for? Might that be Allan Pinkerton?"

She felt a flush climb into her cheeks. "No," she said slowly.

"He was the one who hired you as a secretary up there in Chicago. I figured he was the one to blame for putting you in front of those cameras with Agent Russell. And I ought to warn you that I know Russell's daddy and have been aware that Russell has been with the Pinkertons for some time now."

The truth demanded more than a one-word response. "Daddy," she said slowly, "I am no longer a secretary to Mr. Pinkerton."

"So you quit that job." He shook his head. "I cannot say I'm sorry to hear that."

"No, I did not quit my job." She paused again as she determined just exactly what to say. "But I no longer work for Mr. Pinkerton himself. Instead, I have been shifted to another department. It was in the discharge of those duties that I happened to be called on to help Agent Russell."

Daddy seemed to be considering her statement. Meanwhile, Sadie allowed a small amount of relief over the fact that while she had told the truth of her current situation, she had not been forced to admit the full extent of her duties in working for the Pinkertons. Merely allowing her to continue as a secretary, when she was not traveling with Uncle Penn, had taken quite some time and energy. She would not add any further grief to what had already been expounded upon unless she absolutely must.

"All right then. I suppose the subject's closed for now. I'll see what I can do about keeping your mama from bringing it up."

"Thank you, Daddy. Now can we go home?"

"Is the one trunk all you have?" he asked as he shepherded her through the crowd and outside to the family carriage. "You packed light this time," he said with a chuckle. "And didn't do much shopping."

"That's all," she said as she allowed Daddy to help her in. "And all the shopping I did fit easily inside."

For all that his good humor raised her suspicions, Sadie allowed herself to feel a small measure of relief. Given the warnings sent through Uncle Penn, she had fully expected her father to give her what-for right there on the platform before they ever left the train station.

As she settled back on the padded seat, Daddy

excused himself to step outside and speak to the porter about her trunk. A folded newspaper, likely her father's entertainment while he awaited the train, had been left on the seat across from her. Sadie picked it up to reveal the front page of *L'Abeille de la Nouvelle-Orléans*, the French language newspaper also known as the *New Orleans Bee*.

Among the advertisements for Pharmacie Americaine on Canal Street and Mmes. Godin et Martinet Robes et Confections on Bourbon Street was a notice for the grand opening of yet another library sponsored by the Millie's Treasure Foundation.

Sadie smiled as she thought of Kyle Russell and his bride, Millie, the couple behind the foundation that had done so much in the past year since its inception. That smile dimmed as she wondered whether she might someday find love as her fellow Pinkerton agent had.

For to love would mean to share secrets that Sadie was unsure she might ever be able to share. She folded the paper along with her dreams of a life beyond her beloved Pinkerton work and pressed them away.

A moment later, with the trunk safely loaded, Daddy was back and they were off. Seamus Callum still bore the fair-haired good looks he had passed on to two of her brothers, but Sadie couldn't help noticing that the eyes that sparkled upon her arrival bore smudges beneath them.

"Are you tired, Daddy?"

"I suppose I am. Had some trouble with an evaporator that broke down. With Brent and Cade off who knows where, I'm shorthanded."

"Did you send them after me again?"

The question, bold as it was, hung in the air between them. Until this moment neither had ever spoken of the way Callum men shadowed her. Rather, by tacit agreement, Daddy pretended he didn't send them and Sadie pretended she didn't mind when one or two of her brothers arrived unannounced.

He studied her, or at least he appeared to. Barely blinking, he rested his square jaw against one scarred fist until Sadie was sure he didn't intend to answer at all.

"Never once have I sent anyone after you, and that's a promise. But now that we're talking about it, where is it you go, Sarah Louise?"

Swinging her gaze toward him, she found all evidence of his former good humor gone. Instead, his big hands rested on his knees, fingers drumming against his trouser legs as if the energy required to hold them still was too great.

"Different places," she answered carefully.

"That's no answer for a man's only daughter to give her father. I know you're grown, but when the good Lord gave you to me, I promised Him I would look after you best I could."

"And you have, Daddy." She reached across the space between them to rest her palm over his knuckles. His movement ceased. "Thank you for that."

He turned his hands over to capture her wrist. "Where is it you go?" he repeated. "Tell me the truth."

"I did. Different places is an honest answer. Wherever Uncle Penn goes, I tag along," she added.

"Then I'll know the answer why."

That she couldn't tell him. Not without giving away the exact nature of her employment at the Pinkerton Agency.

"Now, Daddy, you know I have acted as traveling companion to Uncle Penn ever since Auntie decided she was too old to leave Mobile and I finished my course of studies at the Institute. Maybe you should be asking him why he goes to the places he's gone."

The statement was a risk. Sadie was banking on the knowledge that Daddy and Uncle Penn said as little as possible to one another.

"I have."

Oh.

"He's a spy, sunshine. So I need to know if you're one too."

"A spy?" She laughed. "Daddy, that's the most ridiculous thing I've ever heard. The war ended more than two decades ago. What could Uncle

Penn possibly be spying on?" His expression stopped her. "You're serious."

"I am."

She gave him a sideways look. "Did he tell you that?"

"Not in so many words."

Sadie thought carefully before speaking. "Well, then, I will allow that he might have done some sleuthing during the war as you've claimed over the years, but a spy? If he is, then he's a good one because I've seen no evidence of it."

The truth. What she did not add was that her ability to do her own spying would have called attention to any similar proclivities in her uncle years ago.

Her father's eyes narrowed and he moved his hand away as he shifted positions. "If he was good at it, then you wouldn't see any evidence of it, would you?"

He had her there. And yet Penn Monroe was a harmless but interesting older gentleman with a wife who had turned into a homebody in her old age.

A man who called Henry Smith a trusted friend. Yet he had showed no interest in the cases she had handled, preferring instead to be used as her reasons for travel and nothing more.

"I can see you're thinking about it now, aren't you?" Daddy shrugged. "I'm no genius, but if Penn didn't tell you, then maybe that just makes all those travels you two have done together all the more suspicious."

Sadie recovered in time to say, "Honestly, Daddy, I have never seen Uncle Penn do anything the least bit suspicious. He goes to zoos and museums and draws lovely sketches in his notebooks just like I do. Art is our shared interest, as is travel. If that is suspicious, then you and I have a different definition of the word."

Daddy looked her square in the eye. A muscle worked in his jaw. "As I said, that just means he's good at what he does. I knew I shouldn't have gone along with your mama when she said you could go up to Chicago to study art."

"Art history, Daddy. There's a difference."

"It took you away from River Pointe, so it's all the same to me." He paused. "And I still say Penn Monroe's up to no good."

Sadie sighed. Better for Daddy to suspect Uncle Penn than her. Better still if the subject could be changed to anything else.

Outside the carriage, the ancient buildings and narrow streets of the familiar French Quarter were behind them. Ahead was the river, and beyond that the land showed itself lush and green.

"And while I'm on the subject of my sister's husband," Daddy continued, "don't you wonder what he told me about why he came back to Louisiana without you?"

She schooled her expression but couldn't

manage to look her father in the eyes. "Actually, it hadn't occurred to me to ask, but now that you mention it, I am curious. What did he say?"

Daddy made a snorting sound. "Not much at first. Then I insisted he tell me where my girl was or I was going after you."

Sadie could easily imagine that conversation taking place. What she could not figure was how Penn might respond.

"He told me that a matter of importance caused him to hurry back here. 'A matter of importance,'" he repeated with some measure of emphasis. "I ask you, what is more important than seeing you home safely?"

"Well, Daddy, you did say he was a spy. Perhaps it was a matter of great importance."

"I don't care what his excuse was. I was ready to get on the next train north, and then I found out you were heading home. Good thing too. Of course, I know the flooding slowed you down."

"Yes," she said truthfully. "There were certain difficulties in the railroad schedules."

"A derailment north of Shreveport too. I thank the Lord you weren't on that train. Anyway, you're here now, no thanks to the man my sister was fool enough to marry."

The carriage slowed to turn onto the River Road. Inwardly relieved that Penn's excuse was at least accepted if not approved of, Sadie inhaled deeply of the fresh air, a welcome change from the cinder-filled train and the smells of the city.

She exhaled slowly. Indeed, it was a beautiful spring evening in Louisiana.

"You sound content to be back here," her father said.

"I suppose I am." And she was, if even for just a few quiet moments. "What have I missed while I was away?"

Daddy shrugged. "Got two new foals from the bay mares, and the Southern Pacific Company's decided to build a railroad siding over on the eastern side of our land."

"That will be convenient."

"And the Trahan boy, he's come home from Tulane. Your mama would know more about the topic, but I believe he's planning on setting up his medical practice soon."

When she did not comment, he continued. "You remember him, don't you? Fine boy. A hard worker at the sugar mill before he took himself off to college."

Of course she remembered Gabriel Trahan. He had stolen her first kiss at the parish fair. Not that it had meant anything. They were practically babies at the time.

Unfortunately, Mama and Mrs. Trahan had never managed to forget. In the years that followed, the conniving pair had taken every opportunity to encourage another kiss.

Or, rather, an engagement.

"Not you too, Daddy," she protested.

"I don't know what you're complaining about. Gabe is a fine man. A good man."

"And no doubt he will make some woman a good husband someday."

"That's what we're counting on," he said under his breath. "You know you missed Jeanette's wedding."

"I sent my regrets."

"I understand George will be taking on a job at his father's law firm. He's a Harvard man, but I believe he studied the law at Columbia. Several fine fellows he introduced me to at the wedding inquired about you."

Sadie sighed. More likely it was the other way around with Mama or Daddy—or both—talking her up to whichever unmarried fellow would listen. The fact she'd missed the nuptials of the decade, as Mama had referred to the Lapeyre–Waugh wedding, was a blessing.

Rather than allow discussions of weddings and available bachelors to continue, Sadie decided a change of topic was in order. "Tell me about the new foals. Are any more expected? And what sort of new gadget is Ethan trying to get you to use in the sugar mill?"

And thus the topic was happily changed. For as much as Daddy wanted to care for her—and apparently that meant renewing his resolve to find her a husband—he was a horseman at heart. And a planter.

With very little effort on her part, Sadie was able to keep that topic going until the massive iron gates of Callum Plantation came into view, but as soon as she saw those gates, she sighed again. She was home. For all the good and the bad that the word meant, she was home.

The drive to the house took another five minutes as the road wound through sugarcane fields and past the sugar mill, where Daddy's machines ground more sugarcane into sugar than what human labor had once accomplished. Those who came and went through the doors of Callum Sugar and Refining were employees who were loyal and well paid.

For Daddy had long ago discovered that one went with the other. The cluster of white frame cottages off in the distance also testified to his belief that those who were given more than a job tended to stay longer and work harder.

As a child, Sadie recalled playing with the children who resided in those cottages. Recalling the cozy spaces where boys and girls bunked two or three on a mattress at night made her vast canopy bed with its carved headboard and blue silk curtains seem terribly lonely when the shadows fell.

So she had turned to books. And later, to art. Neither were good substitutes.

After a few more curves in the road, the vast white marble home that formed the center of Callum Plantation came into view. She knew the path ahead by heart, and yet each time she returned and saw the lush canopy of two-hundred-year-old live oaks marching like sentinels down the avenue, her heart soared.

Home. Again the word pierced her heart and settled her mind all at the same time.

The carriage turned down the last quarter-mile toward the front entrance of Mama's grand palace on the river. Twenty-eight live oaks. Twenty-eight equidistant columns spanning all four sides of the massive mansion.

Peering out from between the columns were four windows on the top floor and four more on the ground floor below. Each window was flanked by shutters of deep green latched closed only in times of severe weather or the odd cold spell that touched this part of Louisiana.

In the center, upstairs and down, were double doors that opened onto wide porches. Delicate iron lace framed the balcony above and kept those who wandered too close from landing on the lush green lawn below.

Home.

Sadie sighed. How many secrets had she hidden there? Too many. And yet here she was returning with even more.

As she stepped out of the carriage, she glanced

up at the balcony to see curtains fall back into place. Likely her mother had been sitting by the window awaiting the carriage's return for some time. She was vigilant, her Louisiana-born mama, and she was a prayer warrior who would have been petitioning the Lord on Sadie's behalf ever since her only daughter stepped on the train to Chicago.

The double doors opened downstairs, and three of her brothers poured out onto the wide porch, followed close behind by most of the household staff and two of Daddy's hunting dogs. The entire assemblage hurried down the steps toward her, the boys calling her name, the dogs barking, and the rest of the group offering broad smiles.

Oh, but it was good to be home.

Daddy came up beside her and placed one arm around her waist. "Welcome back, Sarah Louise. I hope you're not considering an escape anytime soon."

Her father's use of the word "escape" made her cringe even as she quickly turned her expression into a smile for her family. For that was exactly what leaving Callum Plantation felt like every time she passed through the gates with her traveling bags beside her in the carriage. An escape.

From what, she didn't bother to consider. Not when there were necks to hug and laughter with a generous dose of the cook's fried chicken and shrimp gumbo still to be had inside the only place she could truly call home.

No, the need to escape would sneak up on her slowly, gradually. Would seize her like a thief in the night, grasping at her throat until she felt as if she could not breathe unless the carriage was heading away down the River Road with her inside.

Thirteen

Jefferson pushed away from the table, the pile of oyster shells and empty plates indicating an evening well spent. As firelight flickered across the polished wooden floor, he rose and gestured for the Pinkerton agent to follow him across the wide center hall to his grandfather's library, where his box of evidence and case notes was waiting unopened on Grandfather Tucker's desk.

He let out a long breath of relief. At least John hadn't tampered with it.

A fire had been lit there as well, rendering the room much more comfortable than it might otherwise have been on this chilly night. Kyle gravitated toward the mantel and the array of items placed there by Grandfather Tucker that no one yet had dared remove.

Edging a pair of miniature bronze Civil War

cannons and a judge's gavel out of the way, he picked up a silver-framed miniature of a woman wearing the formal gown of a Mardi Gras queen and held it up to the light. "A beautiful woman. Your mother?"

"My grandmother." Jefferson smiled as he took a seat behind Grandfather's massive desk and then reached for the humidor. As expected, the staff still kept the box filled with the late judge's favorite cigars.

While Jefferson had never taken to the vice, tradition dictated that he offer one to his guest. "Thank you, but no," Kyle said as he returned the miniature to its place on the mantel.

Jefferson closed the humidor's lid and set it aside. Moonlight filtered through the open shutters of the floor-to-ceiling windows, mingling with the golden glow of the fire to turn the multi-colored carpet a rich silvery shade.

Of all the rooms in Grandfather's home, this was Jefferson's favorite. The lone place where he felt well and truly at peace.

"You're certain your grandmother has seen John recently?" Kyle said when he had settled across from him in a leather chair beside the fire.

"She may be near to ninety and confined to her bed, but her mind is as sharp as yours or mine. According to Granny, my brother was last here some eight or ten days ago. She based this on the fact that while she appeared to be napping, she saw John rifling through her jewelry cabinet."

Kyle met his gaze. "That would fit the profile. I don't suppose she called the police."

"You suppose incorrectly. Granny was insistent that a report be made, even though it doesn't appear that John escaped with anything of value."

"And he has not returned?"

"According to Granny and the butler, no."

Jefferson lowered his gaze to study the amber paperweight that bore a chip from the time he threw it at John and missed. One of the rare times he had not hit his target.

"I doubt John will give up on having a nice roof over his head so easily." He returned his attention to Kyle. "Especially since the police officer who arrived to take the report has elected not to file charges unless John were to cause any further trouble."

"Despite the fact that the man has plenty of charges already filed against him?"

"A fact that the officer was apparently unaware of."

"Then he needs to become aware of this. I'll pay the chief of police a visit tomorrow." Kyle stared at Jefferson for a moment and then shook his head. "You will have to forgive me, but your resemblance to the thief Will Tucker is uncanny."

"Under the circumstances I'd say that wasn't all so remarkable."

"No, I suppose not." Kyle shifted positions

and seemed to be studying his hands. "I know we have not discussed how long I will be staying in Mobile. However, given the fact that your brother may well return at any time . . ."

"You would like to remain here, at least until you are certain you've exhausted all possibilities of capturing him?" At Kyle's nod, Jefferson continued. "By all means. Consider yourself a guest in my home. Or, rather, my grandmother's home, for I'll never consider it fully mine as long as she holds court upstairs."

"Then I would like very much to meet your grandmother and thank her myself for her hospitality."

"Perhaps, although if you don't mind I would prefer that she not know the reason for your stay. I have faith she will not give away your identity to John should he slip past the both of us, but I would prefer that no one but I know what your real purpose is. When I was with the Met, I found that the policy of keeping a tight circle of informed persons worked quite well."

"Agreed." He paused. "I wonder how long you will remain here in Mobile. Considering you have a life and employment in England, that is."

Jefferson's inelegant snort of derision caused the Pinkerton agent's eyebrows to rise.

"I'm awaiting responses to correspondence that went missing while I was in prison. As I said earlier, I am unsure of my present status with

Scotland Yard and at loose ends until those questions are settled."

"I hope they will be settled to your satisfaction," Kyle said. "Though my greater hope is that we capture your brother and return him to prison before that happens. Purely selfish here, of course."

Jefferson understood. As a man whose livelihood had centered on the pursuit of justice and the solution of cases presented to him, he would have no qualms feeling the same way were their roles reversed.

"So," he said as another thought crossed his mind, "tell me about Agent Callum."

"Sadie?" Kyle chuckled. "She's something, isn't she?"

"That she is," he said as he considered the fair-haired beauty he'd kissed twice. The woman who apparently knew a cuneiform from a hieroglyphic papyrus and could make even the plainest dress look like something worthy of wearing to Buckingham Palace.

Jefferson centered his thoughts and continued. "How does a woman of her quality end up a Pinkerton agent?"

"That is the million dollar question, isn't it?" Kyle shrugged. "I suppose you'd have to ask her. Although, I warn you I doubt she'll give you a straight answer."

"And why is that?"

"Sadie has her secrets. But then, don't we all?"

"Oh, I don't know." Jefferson leaned back against the old leather of Judge Tucker's favorite chair and exhaled slowly. "I suppose we do, although if we're worth our pay as investigators, we are as good if not better at finding them out than keeping them."

"I suppose so, but don't even think of trying to find out whatever it is Sadie is hiding. It'll be a waste of your time, I promise, and it might even get you smacked around by one of her brothers." He paused. "She has four, you know? Or is it five? Anyway, they are all older than she is and fiercely protective. So is her father."

"Might those brothers think to disturb her while in the discharge of her Pinkerton duties?" he asked carefully.

Kyle chuckled. "At least once that I witnessed myself. Denver, last year." His chuckle dissolved into a grin. "The eldest stepped right into a surveillance operation Sadie and I were carrying out. He told her he was in town thinking of buying into a copper mine or some such nonsense. She was hopping mad."

Brothers? That explained the two fellows who were so anxious to find Miss Callum that they were willing to break the law and disturb his privacy to accomplish the feat.

"But no husband?" he inquired and then wished he hadn't. Sadie had answered that question. Why did he care to have her response confirmed? And yet he found that he did. Very much.

"No husband." If Kyle suspected any motive other than curiosity, he did not let on.

"So four or five brothers and a father who wish to protect her, and yet she manages to perform her duties as a Pinkerton agent in spite of all that?"

"And very well," he said as he stifled a yawn. "Forgive me, but the early morning has taken its toll. Could we continue this conversation over coffee in the morning?"

"Of course," Jefferson said as he rose to usher Kyle out into the hallway and up the stairs. After leaving him at the door to his chambers, Jefferson stopped briefly to peek in on his sleeping grandmother before heading back downstairs to the library.

Bypassing the desk, he went to the window and opened the shutter to peer out into the darkened night. Jefferson's image taunted him from the glass, the face that so closely resembled his brother's.

And then that face moved when Jefferson had not.

John.

Jefferson bolted from the room and out into the night, only to find himself alone in the vast front garden. A lantern might have shed light on whether tracks were there to follow, but he hadn't thought to bring one. He came to a stop in front of the window, his back to the house as he stared out into the darkness.

Calling out to his brother was foolish for several reasons, not the least of which because the Pinkerton agent upstairs might be the one to answer. He had promised to inform Kyle of anything relating to his brother. He had not promised at what point he would offer that information.

Speaking to John first was Jefferson's intention, and he couldn't do that with the agent looking on. So he stood his ground and willed his brother to show himself. Practically dared the coward to move into the puddle of light left by the open window behind him.

And a coward he was, for no other sort of man would leave his own brother to rot in the Louisiana penitentiary. Jefferson crossed his arms over his chest, his eyes still roaming the depths of the thicket.

Then suddenly there he was. John Tucker. Or was it?

Jefferson moved closer to the spot where he thought he spied a man standing. Only then did John step out of the shadows.

"Jeff," he said, his tone just as congenial as if the two were greeting one another across the dinner table. "I need your help."

"My help?"

"I realize the request may come as a surprise,

but you were always the one who did the right thing."

The truth, and yet it took all Jefferson had not to argue the point or laugh. Instead, he stood mute, his mind on deciding how to best capture John before he slipped away again.

Slowly he reached down to press his palm against the revolver at his side. As he maneuvered to retrieve the weapon, he was careful to lean into the shadows.

"So you won't answer? Or is your lack of answer a response on its own?"

"I have no answer because I don't know what you're asking of me, John." He paused. There, the gun was now firmly in his grasp. "Or why you would think I would assist you at all, considering the fact you left me in that prison to do the time you were given."

"You're made of tougher stuff than I am. I couldn't do that time. Not there."

"You're always hiding behind some excuse. And yet I have to wonder if any of them are true."

John stared back at him, his expression blank. Likely he would run. The only question that remained was whether Jefferson could capture him without harming him.

"Turn yourself in so I don't have to," Jefferson finally said.

"Turn myself in?" He laughed. "That's funny."

"I won't help you."

His brother sobered. "Oh, you'll help me all right. There are people who think you have betrayed them. Important people."

John's taunting smile made Jefferson want to take aim and relieve himself of the burden of caring for his brother at all. Still he waited, his training taking over where his anger threatened to win out.

Revenge is Thine, not mine.

"Does the name Valletta mean anything to you?" John asked.

He knew it would. Jefferson could see that much on his brother's face. He kept silent.

"Thought so. He knows you as well." He chuckled. "Or he thinks he does."

"What does that mean?"

"He's a dangerous man, Jeff. Watch out for him."

The moon momentarily went behind a canopy of clouds, rendering the gardens a deep, velvety black. Though he never saw his brother move, when the moon once again peered out, John was gone.

Jefferson followed as best he could, trailing his footsteps until he lost them in the thicket. And still he kept moving forward.

Finally, the edge of the Tucker property gave way to a narrow logging road, where pine forests were being cut away for export. By the light of the moon he could see that there were no footprints in the mud. John had not come this far. But where was he?

Jefferson backtracked to the house and did a circle around the perimeter of the big white clapboard home. Unless he had removed his shoes, footprints would have been easily detectable on the porch boards surrounding all sides of the house. With the night too cool for windows to be open, John's ability to slip inside easily was questionable at best.

Still, he continued his search, finding no evidence of his brother's presence in any of the outbuildings that dotted the property. It was as if John Tucker had vanished.

Which, when Jefferson thought of it, was exactly what his brother's best talent was. No, he amended. His best talent was in finding trouble. Running from that trouble to disappear came in a close second.

Fourteen

"Make way, all of you," Daddy shouted above the din of Sadie's homecoming. "I'd like to get this girl inside before suppertime if you don't mind."

The noisy crowd of older brothers parted, allowing Daddy to get as far as the front porch steps before Mama appeared in the doorway.

"Sadie," she said as she closed the gap between them and enveloped her only daughter in a tight embrace.

For a tiny woman, Mary Callum was strong. Strength of bone and muscle ran as deep as strength of character and mind in the New Orleans family from which Sadie's mother came. Qualities her daughter prayed had been passed on should the time arise and a need for it come.

"Mama," Sadie said against her mother's soft neck. "You look beautiful."

And she did. The ebony hair several of her brothers had inherited showed strands of silver only upon the closest of inspections, a testament to her Acadian heritage. And those big dark eyes, fringed with thick lashes, seemed to miss nothing as she inspected Sadie from hat to traveling slippers and back up to her face again.

"And you look as though you've been on a train since daybreak," she said as she turned Sadie toward the door. "We've been waiting lunch. You know I adore it when all my little chickens are under the same roof at mealtime."

Her other little chickens, overgrown and apparently hungry males the lot of them, cheered at the mention of food on the table. Mama's chastising went unnoticed as they rushed around the side of the house to the well out back to do their obligatory washing up before they were allowed to join the civilized folk in the dining room.

There was a time when Sadie would have joined them. Would have counted herself as a member of that rarified league of Callum males who could hunt, shoot, and fish with the ease that seemed to come with their genetic makeup.

It seemed acutely unfair that, although her older brothers were well into their twenties, with Aaron solidly past thirty and Brent and Cade near to it, on occasion they still behaved as wild as the heathens they had been as children. It was also quite humorous to Sadie when these same hooligans dressed up in their city finery to impress the ladies.

Apparently, it was fine for a Callum man to carry on as a fool on Callum land and then call himself a gentleman elsewhere. Not only was it fine, it was encouraged.

Daddy stomped his boots on the porch boards and then must have noticed Mama's frown. "I'll just go around back and slip these off," he said.

The servants went back to their duties, while Daddy's hounds trotted happily behind him to disappear around the side of the house, leaving Sadie and Mama alone in the quiet.

There was another appraising look, this time with a less guarded expression. "You've not been eating properly," Mama said as she retrieved her embroidered handkerchief and dabbed at a smudge of cinders on Sadie's traveling coat. "That dress needs taking up. What am I going to do with you?"

Sadie linked arms with her mother and put on her best smile. "You are going to fatten me up, insist on accompanying me into town for a proper wardrobe for the coming season, and then fret over me in prayer like always."

She lifted her gaze to meet Sadie's eyes. "You know me so well, my daughter. Why is it I feel I no longer know you?"

"Don't be silly," Sadie said, though she quickly looked away. "I'm still your baby girl."

She wasn't, of course. She hadn't been for quite some time. But saying the words made her feel less as though she had left something important behind at Callum Plantation that could not be retrieved upon her return.

Before Mama could inquire further, all five Callum brothers trooped in with their hands clean and their manners now in place. Sadie allowed herself to be swept into the dining room on a wave of enthusiastic conversation. By the time Daddy joined them at the head of the long table, Mama's good humor had returned.

And so had Uncle Penn.

"Well, look who's arrived," he said as he stepped inside the dining room with a grin and wearing what appeared to be his Sunday suit.

"Goodness, Penn," Mama said as she gestured to the nearest empty seat at a table that would have held twice their number. "You look as though you've been out paying calls."

"I've been out," he said firmly but cheerfully, "and I'll just leave it at that if you don't mind."

Daddy captured Sadie's gaze with an I-told-you-so look. She ignored him to nudge Ethan, who sat to her left. The nearest to her in age, Ethan had inherited Mama's ability to peer right into Sadie's soul.

He leaned near as if to give her a swift kiss on the cheek. "So, is it a man you're pining for, or are you just here long enough to get away with leaving again?" he asked so softly that Sadie wasn't sure she'd heard correctly.

She gave him a soft jab with her elbow. "Hush."

His impish grin gave him away. Until he snagged her napkin and teased her with it.

"Because if you've already found a man, you ought to be mentioning it quick." He glanced around and then, apparently satisfied no one was paying attention to them, continued. "I happen to know there's a manhunt on, and the first of the prey will be arriving for supper in a day or two."

"Sarah Louise, did you hear what your mama said?" Daddy asked.

Sadie jolted her attention to her father and then to her mother. "No, I'm sorry, Mama. What did I miss?"

Mama's sweet smile gave Sadie the impression of an aging angel. "Just that I've taken the liberty

165

of arranging a little supper for Thursday night. I do hope you hadn't planned on running off again before then, because if you have, you'll need to cancel."

Ignoring Ethan's jab to her ribs, Sadie nodded. "I'll be here."

"Good." The look that passed between Mama and Daddy was hard to miss. "Seamus, would you bless the meal? I can hear Brent's stomach growling all the way over here."

Daddy spoke the blessing over the food and the hands that made it and then added a plea for rain, good crops, and a few other things. Oh, but Daddy did love to offer the blessing, and he did it in a baritone voice with only the slightest Irish inflection left over from his immigrant parents.

When he said a hearty "Amen," the rest of them joined in to echo a like response.

"Pass the food," Brent said next, earning him a look from Mama.

"And speaking of you, Brent," Daddy said, "I'm wondering where you two got off to the past couple of days and why you and Cade have come back sporting bruises."

Cade turned toward Daddy, revealing a nasty blue mark on his clean-shaven jaw. He was the family peacemaker, whose speed at deflecting arguments generally kept him above the fray. Seeing a bruise on him was quite the rare occasion.

Sadie took note of Mama's almost imperceptible change of expression, which she quickly hid behind her napkin. So this time Mama had done the sending and Daddy hadn't known. Interesting.

The question was where they got those bruises. Nothing in Mr. Tucker's demeanor indicated he'd had any trouble with either of them. Rather, he'd spoken firmly and sent them on their way.

She would never know, of course. There was no good way to ask.

"It was a little case of mistaken identity," Brent interjected. "But we handled ourselves just fine."

Donovan, the fourth son, leaned to his right to inspect his older brother. "Is that some of Mama's powder on your eye, Brent?"

Rather than respond, Brent shoved Donovan back into place. This earned him a reproving look from Mama and a royal dressing down from Daddy.

"Well," Uncle Penn said as he adjusted the napkin in his lap. "As you can see, Sadie, things are exactly the same around here. Nothing much changes at Callum Plantation except the weather."

"And the weather is looking to be nasty later tonight," Aaron said. Eldest son and the one most likely to take over the family sugarcane business someday, his penchant for preferring talk of crops and weather over just about anything else made him the least favorite conversationalist at the table most of the time.

Thankfully, Daddy and Aaron's weather discussion took on a life of its own that caused all talk of bruises and mysterious trips to pale in comparison. Uncle Penn tucked into his soup as soon as the bowl was set before him, giving Sadie no cause to believe he had anything new to converse with her about.

The sun had set hours ago, leaving the night sounds of the river and its creatures to fill the mild yet sultry air. None of the nasty weather Aaron predicted had yet arrived, but the ring of white clouds around the moon seemed to indicate storms would soon occur.

Sadie wandered downstairs, refreshed after a long nap and a cold supper brought up on a tray. Solitude suited her most of the time, but tonight she wandered down to the wide porch that fronted the house, eager to join two of her brothers in conversation.

Over the symphony of lapping water and crickets, she sighed. Indeed, this was something she could get used to, if only for a brief time.

Ethan swiveled to face her, his expression half hidden in the shadows. Still, Sadie could see that her brother was concerned.

"Look out, sis. They're worried about you, and when Mama worries, Daddy takes action."

"Or vice versa," Donovan said.

Of all the Callum sons, Donovan was the tallest

and leanest. With long legs and arms that could reach well up into the branches of the pecan trees Sadie used to love to climb, he had been the brother most likely to come to her rescue should she find it impossible to reach the ground.

In a way, Donovan was still the brother to whom she turned when she needed a rescue. But only because of the five, he asked the fewest questions.

He handed Sadie a packet wrapped in brown paper and then moved past her to lean against one of the columns that spanned the length of the porch. "A messenger brought this today. I figured you would rather see it before you had to answer questions from Mama or Daddy."

"Oh," she said as she weighed the packet in her palm. Definitely from Henry, though the packet bore no markings to indicate that beyond the Chicago postmark. "Thank you."

"What's that?" Ethan made a swipe for it just as Sadie moved it out of his reach. "Something from a secret admirer?"

"Don't be silly." She looked past Ethan to Donovan. "It's a book, that's all. I do appreciate seeing that no one opened it."

"Believe me, it wasn't easy." Donovan's attention turned to Ethan. "Certain people think everything that happens at Callum Plantation is their business."

"It will be someday," Ethan said, now serious.

"We're all going to need to know what's going on here. Daddy won't live forever, and we can't leave everything up to Aaron."

"Somehow I don't think we're still talking about the package." She allowed her gaze to land on first Donovan and then Ethan. "Is something wrong with Daddy? Is he sick?"

"Our father is healthy as a horse," Donovan said. "Your brother there is just nosy and likes to tag along with the adults."

"You'll thank me when tagging along turns into helping make a difference in the way we process sugarcane." He paused, his hands now grasping his knees. "We are all for one and one for all around here, Don, and we each have something to contribute to the family. Never forget that."

Sadie smiled. It was easy to forget that Ethan was a Louisiana State graduate. Newly returned from the university with a passion for engineering, he was determined to mechanize the process even further than the modern techniques Daddy was already using. Unfortunately, his youth and lack of experience caused Aaron to ignore much of what he suggested.

Sadie ruffled her brother's ebony curls and then offered him a smile. "Have patience. They'll see things your way soon enough. And in the interim, I appreciate the fact you're trying to innovate. Now, if you'll excuse me, I think I will go up to bed now. It's been a long day."

"And you have a new book to read," Ethan said in that teasing tone he took when he didn't believe a word she was saying.

"Yes," she said, offering the youngest Callum male a look that told him he'd best not pry. "I have a new book to read. Good night to both of you."

"Get your beauty sleep," Ethan said. "Mama's going to want you to look your best for her special supper Thursday night."

Sadie stepped inside and closed the front door on the sound of her brother's laughter. An early night's sleep was not in store for her tonight. Not with the package she'd been expecting from Henry in her hands.

Anticipation propelled her forward, the parcel tucked discreetly under her arm and, she hoped, out of view. Only the fear of capturing Mama's attention by making a spectacle of herself racing upstairs kept her to a sedate pace.

She had her hand on the doorknob of her childhood bedroom when Uncle Penn surprised her by calling her name. Sadie froze and then glanced first to her right and then to her left. With only Uncle Penn in view, she went toward him and fell into a hug.

"I'm glad you arrived safely, my dear. But safely and swiftly would have been much better."

"Agreed. But there was an issue with . . ." Again she looked around. "With the man who was to meet us. I was afraid I was going to have to travel all the way to Mobile, but thankfully—"

"Why in the world would you be traveling to Mobile?" Mama said as she rounded the corner. "And if you don't tell me, I know my brother-in-law will."

"You've come in on the middle of the conversation," Sadie's uncle responded smoothly. "No one had plans to go to Mobile today, for goodness' sake. Not when this resident of the city was right here under your roof."

That was indeed true. Until her replacement failed to arrive, Sadie had no plans to go anywhere but home. Only her duty as a Pinkerton agent had put that plan in jeopardy, something she could never tell Mama.

Or could she?

Her uncle glanced down at Sadie, mischief showing in his eyes. "Perhaps I should take that package you've been kind enough to deliver for me and say good night to the both of you. It is well past the hour when men of my age should be abed with a good book."

Sadie handed the parcel to Uncle Penn with a smile she hoped her mother would believe was real and then watched him kiss Mama on the cheek. Next he leaned in toward Sadie. With a hug and a discreet wink, he stepped into his chamber.

Sadie turned to find that her mother's expression indicated she was still reluctant to let this line of questioning die. Of course.

Anyone who might wonder where Sadie gained her interrogation skills would do well to pay a visit to Callum Plantation and spend an afternoon shadowing Mama. Actually, an hour would do the trick, as it rarely took much time for her mother to accomplish whatever goal she set out to achieve.

"You worry me, Sarah Louise."

"Truly, Mama, there is no reason for it. I'm fine."

"Are you?" Dark eyes searched her face. "Then why continue going around as your uncle's traveling companion when it is far past time to settle down and be mistress of your own home and mother to my grandchildren?"

Sadie laughed in spite of the situation. "Well, there it is. You are wishing for grandchildren."

"There is nothing wrong with such a wish."

"Of course not. However, I suggest you speak to any of your five sons if you wish grandchildren to come sooner rather than later. Goodness, Mama, Aaron is well past the age when he ought to be finding a good woman and starting the next generation of Callums."

"And yet he cares more for crop science than finding a lifetime love, that son of mine. Ethan too, although your father doesn't believe that book learning has the same value as Aaron's years following in his daddy's footsteps."

"A pity. I'd say both have value." Sadie reached to tug on Mama's sleeve. "And both of those men could use some help in finding the right woman. But then, so could the twins and Donovan."

"Don't be silly. Those men are busy sowing their oats. I've never seen a woman who can capture any of their attentions and keep it for any length of time. I fear my sons are either easily bored or difficult to please."

"Neither are problems you cannot repair. Why don't you expend the matchmaking skills you were planning to use on me at your supper to find them someone?"

Mama's attention went to Sadie's eyes. "So you're on to me?"

"Tipped off by one of my brothers, but yes, I'm on to you." She let her arm fall by her side. "Please don't, though."

"Don't?"

"Don't get ahead of what the Lord wants for me."

Her mother's expression went slack. Then color rose in her cheeks. "Get ahead of the Lord? Sarah Louise Callum, how dare you accuse me of such a thing?"

"I am not accusing," she hurried to say. "I am only suggesting that it may not yet be time for me to settle down. I feel as though there are so many more things left for me to do."

"Such as travel to Mobile? I know what I

174

heard, Sadie. You said you were afraid you would have to travel all the way there."

"To deliver the package."

"Don't be ridiculous. Your uncle was right here and you knew it. You're making no sense."

Sadie consoled herself with the knowledge that was a germ of truth in the statement about a "package." After all, Uncle Penn had used that word in his telegram, although in reference to herself and not to Mr. Tucker.

She hadn't fooled Mama a bit, that much was clear from the way her mother watched her carefully and said nothing. Mama's silence was far more calculating than anything she might say.

Finally, she sighed and said, "I can see you do not want to clarify your statement."

Sadie thought to protest and then decided against it. In truth, she did not want to clarify anything. Could not.

"I'll allow this diversionary tactic of yours, Sadie, but do not mistake me when I tell you that I am suspicious of the conversation you've just had with your uncle. And for that matter, I've been suspicious of your travels with him for quite some time now."

"Mama, truly, I—"

"Do not bother arguing this point," she said with a sweep of her hand. "Your daddy was right when he said you needed to come home after boarding school. But no. I thought you would enjoy that art institute in Chicago. Now I have to wonder if I made the wrong choice."

"Mama, really, I—"

"The hallway is not the place to carry on a discussion like this." She looked first to her left and then to her right down the long passageway. "Like your uncle, I find the hour is later than I prefer to be about."

Once again, Sadie grasped Mama's sleeve. "I assure you there is nothing untoward going on, either with my travels or in any other aspect of my life." She paused to be certain her point was made. "I am thankful Uncle Penn has made these travels possible, and I do thank you and Daddy for allowing it. And for allowing me the time to study art history."

"I miss you terribly when you're away," her mother admitted, "but I do understand the wish to see the world. I suffered from that yearning myself when I was young."

"You are still young, Mama, and there's nothing keeping you from traveling. Don't be like Aunt Pearl."

"My sister-in-law is older than me by many years, daughter," she said in an icy tone. "Her health has always been delicate. Perhaps that is why she stays home and allows Penn his travels."

"Whatever the reason, I still say you do not need to be a hermit like her. London and Paris are closer than ever in this modern world. Why not leave the plantation in your sons' care and take Daddy on a tour of the Continent?"

"I do well to get Daddy in to New Orleans or Baton Rouge for the occasional dinner and socializing, but you have given me something to consider. And perhaps if Daddy won't go, you will."

A statement, not a question, and thus no need to respond. Instead, Sadie gave her mother a hug while she sent up a quick prayer that the Lord might not cause that to ever happen.

As she bid Mama good night and went to her bedchamber, Sadie allowed the briefest thought of a vacation abroad. Just her and her mother and all the time in the world to visit the shops and dressmakers of London and Paris.

It would be, in short, a nightmare.

Fifteen

Sadie waited for the knock that would indicate Uncle Penn was returning her package until she could no longer sit still. Peering out her door, she found the corridor dark and empty, though it appeared a light was still burning in her uncle's room.

Making her way quietly down the hall, she lifted her hand to knock but found the door already cracked slightly open. Sadie pushed against it and called her uncle's name as softly as she could. It only took a moment for her to see that the room was empty.

A brief thought about a note being in order was discarded when Sadie couldn't find pen or paper handy. Surely when he returned, her uncle would realize she had retrieved the item in question.

Snagging the package from on the desk, she hurried back to her room and closed the door. Turning the key in the lock, she leaned back against the cool wood and closed her eyes. Sneaking around in her own home felt wrong, and yet she could not allow anyone to know what Henry had sent.

A noise outside startled her. She placed the package beneath her pillow, doused the light, and then moved toward the open window.

In the moonlight she noticed a movement in the trees. Her window faced the front of the house and the vast alley of oaks that lined the drive up to the grand entrance downstairs.

Though the moon's soft glow cast the alley in shades of silver and black, two male figures—one of them possibly Uncle Penn but definitely not Daddy—walked side by side despite the late hour. Snatches of conversation floated up on the spring breeze as the pair turned to disappear into the shadows.

Sadie closed the curtains and then lit the lamp at her bedside before tearing into the package. As expected, she unwrapped a copy of *Gulliver's*

Travels, one of Henry's favorite means of sending important information. Inside the book she easily found the date and time of the meeting place encoded on the pages.

Tomorrow afternoon? She checked again to be certain. Henry rarely wished to meet on such short notice, although it had been well over a week since they had last spoken. Perhaps something new had been discovered in an old case.

Or perhaps she was being called into duty much sooner on the Astor matter. Her hopes rose as she reached for her valise and tucked the book inside.

Tomorrow she would find a good reason to visit her favorite dressmaker in New Orleans, the one who kept a closet of disguises and asked no questions. In the meantime, she would read up on the Astor case and add to her notes, for surely that was the cause of his need to meet so soon after departing from the Tucker case.

Sadie arrived at the breakfast table the next morning ready to plead her case for use of the carriage.

"How did you sleep, dear?" her mother asked.

"Very well, thank you."

"There is something to be said for sleeping in one's own bed." She peered at her daughter over the rim of her teacup.

"Yes," Sadie said as she screwed up her courage and tamped down on her enthusiasm to meet with her supervising agent. "Mama, I would like to see the dressmaker today. I've given no thought to a spring wardrobe, but I'm certain Madame Theriot can remedy this."

Was that surprise she spied on her mother's face? Or perhaps it was annoyance.

"Actually, I need the carriage today, so I'm afraid your errand will have to wait," her mother said, her voice clearly showing annoyance.

But why?

"Of course," Sadie said cheerily as she poured a cup of strong chicory coffee. "I can put off my trip until later in the morning."

She carried her cup and plate to the table and set them across from Mama before taking her seat. Outside the window, a blue jay trilled loudly as it made a diving sweep at one of the barn cats before disappearing into the oak tree once more.

"I have calls to make in the city and no way of knowing how long they will take." Mama set the teacup down a bit too loudly. "Another day, perhaps? I'm sure you understand."

She held her mother's gaze. No, she did not understand.

"There is no need to make two trips to New Orleans when you could let me off at Madame Theriot's and then come back for me after making your calls. Or I could do the same for you. Really, either is fine."

Her mother rose with a polite smile. "Hurry with

your breakfast, then," she said as she whisked out. "I would like to get the day started, and it feels as if it's already half over."

A glance at the clock over the mantel told Sadie it was not yet nine. What in the world was wrong with Mama?

Jefferson walked past the Presbyterian church and then Barton Academy to step inside the bank and complete his first errand of the day. With money in his pocket and a bank draft securely deposited in his account, he could tackle the more important mission of sending a telegram to his superiors back in London.

His carefully worded message cost a fortune to send, but the knowledge that it would arrive at Scotland Yard well before the letters he'd posted yesterday made the price slightly less painful.

A check of his pocket watch told him it was not yet ten o'clock, although the time was late afternoon in Britain. He should alert his parents of the situation now that he had been freed. However, not knowing whether they had been informed of his false imprisonment, Jefferson decided a letter of sufficient length to explain his absence was in order.

How to explain the situation with John was a much trickier proposition. The man had been caught committing several inexcusable crimes, and if Agent Russell was correct, his brother had also been indirectly responsible for a woman's death. There was no good way to tell a mother and father awaiting news of sons on the other side of the Atlantic this kind of information.

Jefferson returned home with these thoughts trailing him. Kyle met him on the porch, his smile noticeably absent.

"Why didn't you tell me your brother was here last night?"

"Good morning, Agent Russell," he said, as much to buy time as to decide exactly how much he was willing to admit.

Kyle reached out to grab him by the arm, stopping his progress across the porch. "I asked you a question, Tucker."

"I heard the question," he said as he yanked free of Kyle's grasp. "Yes. John showed up outside the library window after you went upstairs."

"Convenient."

"Think what you want, but I was not expecting him and you had already gone upstairs to bed."

"Nor did you awaken me to inform me of his visit, which brings me back to my original question."

Jefferson shook his head and then looked the man in the eyes. "I doubt you would believe me if I told you I simply didn't think of it."

Not when he'd spent most of the night trying to figure out how John knew anything about Sergio Valletta. No one knew about his connection to the man except his superiors at Scotland Yard and his contact at the British Museum.

"You're thinking about something," Kyle said.

Jefferson leaned against the porch post with a frown furrowing his brow. "It was something John said before he ran. And to be clear, I was making the attempt to capture him when he fled."

When Kyle said nothing, he continued. "He mentioned the name of a man I had been investigating."

"And?"

"That's all. He asked for my help. I refused. He made a threat and then ran."

He left off the part where John specifically stated that Valletta thought Jefferson had betrayed him. That claim was the source of much of his lack of sleep. The possibilities for what John had done were endless, but he had been able to narrow things down to several options.

None of them appealed.

"And this man you've been investigating is here in Mobile?"

"No. Or at least I can't imagine why he would be."

Kyle removed a small notebook and pen from his pocket. "I will need that information."

"Sorry, but I can't tell you that. Until I hear otherwise, the investigation is still ongoing, and I'm enjoined not to give any details unless specifically ordered to do so by my superiors. I'm sure you've been under similar orders on the cases you've worked."

Kyle looked as if he might argue. And then, slowly, he put away the pen and notebook.

"I will remind you, Tucker, that the case I am currently working—at least until my replacement arrives—is the one where I put your brother back into prison."

Jefferson straightened and offered Kyle his hand. "And I give you my word I will help you in any way I can. Once you are replaced by another agent, I will extend the same courtesy to him." He paused and then added, "Or her."

Kyle took his hand, albeit grudgingly. "Then we have no further quarrel, unless I hear that you have once again gone without telling me about a meeting between you and your brother. And I will have to inform the chief of police when I meet him shortly."

"Of course."

"Perhaps you should accompany me and tell the chief yourself."

"All right, though I won't be telling him about John's mention of the subject of my investigation."

"Fair enough. For now anyway."

A welcome breeze blew past, ruffling the leaves in the trees and sending a cat skittering after a limb that fell onto the lawn beyond the house. Jefferson watched the orange tabby paw at the leaves and then lose interest before he returned his attention to his guest.

"I'm curious. How did you find out John was here?"

"A deduction, really. I was out indulging my passion for astronomy last night by watching a bit of the Lyrids meteor shower and happened to see you looking around as if you'd lost something. I went to investigate, but you were already in your bedchamber."

"It was dark. How could you possibly see me?"

Kyle grinned. "Apparently you have no idea of my penchant for inventions."

"Inventions that allow someone to see in the dark? I would think that could come in handy for a man working on a criminal investigation."

"Absolutely."

Jefferson shared his grin. "Tell me more."

"Actually, it is easier to show you. Perhaps this evening after the sun goes down I can offer a demonstration. Unless you're expecting your brother to return."

"I'm not expecting anything of John. However, wouldn't it be easier to track him with a device like you're describing should he decide to run again?"

"It would." Kyle leveled him a serious look. "I want to be perfectly clear on this. Should I have the occasion to arrest your brother, you will not stand in my way?"

"Should you have occasion to arrest my brother, not only will I help, but I'll be the first in line to testify against him. In fact, I cannot promise to be responsible for my behavior in the event he is captured, so it's probably best that you find him instead of me."

Again Kyle gave him an appraising look. "Yes, I suppose you have as much reason to be angry with him as I do. More, perhaps, considering he stole a year of your life from you."

"Eleven months and a few weeks," Jefferson supplied. "And possibly my career as well." That he would know with more certainty once he received a response from London.

"When my replacement arrives, there will be at least one vacancy at the Pinkerton Agency. If you were considering relocating to the States, that is."

"You're leaving the Pinks?"

"Between my wife, her charity work, and the inventions, I have plenty to occupy my time."

"I envy you that." The words slipped out before Jefferson could reel them back.

"I wasn't always an advocate for marriage, but now I find it suits me well. Or, rather, Mrs. Russell suits me well. We are hoping to expand our family soon, and that also suits me."

"Good for you," Jefferson said genially.

"Spoken like a confirmed bachelor."

"Indeed." Jefferson had no need of any further argument. For while he envied the happiness

Kyle had found in hearth and home, he knew all too well that this sort of arrangement would never work for him.

"A word to the wise, then," Kyle said. "Those men who are certain they will never find the right woman are just the ones the Lord likes to use to prove otherwise. I speak from experience."

Sixteen

Using the back door, Sadie left Madame Theriot's Dressmakers and then doubled down Royal Street to slip around the corner to find the meeting place Henry Smith had indicated. She was early, but only by a quarter hour, and she was famished. And though no genteel lady ate beignets in a public establishment without benefit of the proper table setting and well-placed companion, she ordered two.

After all, in the disguise she had donned at her favorite—and very discreet—dressmakers shop, no one would mistake her for Sarah Louise Callum of the River Pointe Callums.

Unfortunately, the rather plain garment she chose was black, befitting her disguise as a widow in mourning, and it only took a slight wind off the river to create a mess with the powdered sugar before she'd had more than one bite of her tasty treat.

When a gentleman handed her his handkerchief, she glanced up through the black net of her veil expecting to see Henry standing there. Instead, she looked up into the smiling face of the very man Daddy had mentioned yesterday.

Gabriel Trahan?

"Hello, there. Ethan didn't mention you had returned to Callum Plantation."

So he knew who she was. She tried to put a neutral face on what was an unfortunate situation. "It's so good to see you again, Monsieur Trahan."

He joined her at the table. "That would be Dr. Trahan, Miss Callum. You may not recall, but I'm a Tulane man. Newly graduated." He paused as if assessing her. "And I know we are grown now, but shall we dispense with the Mr. and Miss and use the names we've always used, Sadie?"

"Yes, of course. Gabriel it is." She dabbed at the sugary mess she'd made on her bodice, smearing the sugar more than removing any of it.

He lifted his hand, and a waiter hurried to them. "Water or seltzer, and do hurry." He returned his attention to Sadie, his dark eyes studying her with humor.

She recalled her brothers' friend, the hopeless tagalong with a shock of dark hair and a slight stutter who spent countless hours trying to best anyone who would take him up on his outrageous adventures. Gone was the gangly boy and in his place was a surprisingly handsome man.

"You have grown up," she said as her hand stilled. "You're so tall. And well spoken."

He shrugged. "God answers some prayers quickly. Others He is a bit slower in response. And on the topic of slow . . ." Gabriel glanced around and fixed the waiter moving their direction with a frown.

"I understand you're considering opening a medical practice in River Pointe."

"I am, although New Orleans suits me, and I've had a nice offer to join a practice here in the city. I am as yet undecided—Finally," he said to the waiter before accepting a glass of water and turning to Sadie, his smile restored. "Dip the handkerchief in there, and you'll have much better luck in removing the evidence of your beignet."

She did and the problem was solved. When she attempted to return the handkerchief to him, Gabriel shook his head. "Keep it for now. You still have beignets to eat, and besides, I will see you on Thursday."

She clutched the damp handkerchief. "Oh, yes. Now that you mention it, I believe Mama said something about inviting you out to visit."

Not only visit. Unless Ethan was wrong in his assumptions, every effort would be expended to make a match between her and Gabriel.

She debated warning him and then despaired of it. Better that she pray Mama would not take that step after all rather than give the handsome doctor the wrong impression about Sadie's participation in the scheme. For she would most decidedly *not* be helping Mama make any matches. That was the last thing she wanted.

The very last thing.

"I am looking forward to an enjoyable evening." His eyes swept the length of her and then returned to meet her gaze. "However, I must ask if condolences are in order."

"Condolences?" She glanced down. "Oh, no . . ."

What to say? Sadie leaned forward, and her childhood friend did the same.

"May I ask a favor of you?"

He seemed to consider the question before lifting one dark brow. "That would depend on the favor. I've taken the Hippocratic oath, and one of its basic tenants is that I do no harm. So . . ."

"You're teasing me."

He shrugged. "Well, you do see how this could become complicated should you ask something of me that would conflict with this oath."

Sadie laughed. Indeed, he was the same Gabriel she recalled. "I assure you that your oath will not be broken."

"Then ask away. If you're sure."

Sadie toyed with the edge of the handkerchief as she formulated just the right words for her request. Finally, she looked up to see he was still watching her.

"All right. I don't know how you managed to

find me. I've donned somewhat of a disguise."

"I assumed as much when you said you did not have a husband languishing in the grave."

"Yes, well, I would first request that you not ask for the details as to why I wish to pass an hour or so undetected. And then I would also ask that you not tell anyone you've seen me."

"Ah." He sat back and stroked the well-trimmed beard on his chin as if considering her words. "So you wish to make two requests. That does change things a bit."

"It does?" She gave him a sideways look. "How so?"

"If you were only asking the one favor, then I could justify complete agreement." Again he paused to stroke his beard in mock thoughtfulness. "However, in light of things I must ask for a promise in return should I agree to your terms."

"A promise in return?" Only the twinkle in his eye gave him away. She grinned. "And what is that?"

"I will request a promise that you take a walk with me after supper on Thursday." He shook his head. "No, I will require it. And perhaps you may even tell me what causes a woman to want privacy enough to hide in order to get it."

Gabriel's mock-serious expression had her laughing again. "We are agreed. I will take a walk with you after dinner, and you will not tell any-one we have spoken today."

"Don't be silly. The only person I had occasion to speak to was a lovely woman in widow's garb who had need of my assistance with a handkerchief and a glass of water." He paused to rise. "Now, if you'll excuse me, I have an appointment to keep. I will see you the day after tomorrow."

She watched him go as the reality of her situation sank in. Gabriel Trahan had caught her impersonating a widow. The truth of that statement began to sink in.

Caught her.

The childhood friend who had trained in medicine at Tulane University spied her from beneath the disguise of her widow's veil and *caught her*.

Sadie looked down at the handkerchief in her hand, at the doctor's initials stitched in bold letters on a corner of the linen square. A Pinkerton agent bested by an amateur. Her fingers shook.

"Is this seat taken?"

Her gaze lifted to find Henry standing there. Relief shot through her.

"Please do sit," she said as she folded the handkerchief and put it away. "I'm very glad to see you, sir."

"Because you've been discovered by someone who recognized you?" Henry asked as he lowered himself onto the chair Gabriel had only just vacated.

"How did you know?"

"An agent of mine does not smile sweetly at an

intruder, Miss Callum. And considering I have been waiting for more than five minutes to find you alone, your unexpected visitor would be classified as an intruder. Unless the man was expected."

"No," she hurried to say. "He was not, although you are correct in assuming he is no stranger."

"No?" Henry waved away the waiter. "Who is he?"

"A childhood friend." She pushed the plate of beignets in Henry's direction, but he waved them away as well. "His name is Gabriel Trahan. He is newly conferred with the degree of medical doctor from Tulane and was anxious to tell me about it."

"I see." His gaze swept her person. "And did he indicate surprise that his old friend was a widow?"

"I believe I explained the situation to his satisfaction." At Henry's raised brows, she continued. "No, sir, I did not tell him I was meeting someone. I merely said I wished some privacy, and donning a costume seemed to be the best way to achieve that."

"And you're certain he believed you?"

"I think so. However, my mother has invited him for dinner on Thursday, and I promised a walk after the meal in exchange for his discretion in not mentioning he had seen me today."

"So seeing him here was just a coincidence. How convenient."

A Pinkerton did not believe in coincidence. How many times had Henry told her this? Either he was showing a rare instance of sarcasm, or he had changed his philosophy on human nature. Neither seemed likely.

Sadie was about to comment on this when he lifted his index finger to tap his chin, the signal for silence. She glanced around carefully, not seeing any reason for concern, but kept quiet.

Finally Henry looked her way once more. "Miss Callum, why exactly are you so interested in regaining the Astor case?"

Not the question she expected, and yet one easily answered. "It's a fascinating case, sir. Between the accusations Mrs. Astor is making regarding her Rembrandt and the possibility that, if those accusations are proven true, other works of art could be involved causes the mind to reel. This is a case that could involve the British Museum and perhaps several other entities. And, as you may know, I am a student of the arts thanks to the stodgy finishing school Mama insisted on and my time at the institute in Chicago."

"All this I know. Tell me what I don't know."

She thought a moment. "Imitation is not merely the sincerest form of flattery but also a profitable business among thieves of antiquities. Aren't you the least bit curious whether this Rembrandt is the tip of an iceberg that could rock the art world?"

"Could it?"

She leaned in, impassioned by the topic and yet acutely aware she must not draw attention to their conversation. "The British Museum believes someone is selling antiquities that have come directly from their archaeological site in Iraq. The items that have been found were a mix of the genuine article and the forged. Could that same someone also be selling other items? One dealer's name continues to appear. He sold Mrs. Astor her Rembrandt. I think the matter is worthy of investigation."

"That's a nice speech, Miss Callum."

He removed his spectacles, cleaned them with his handkerchief, and then returned them to his nose. His attention, however, remained on the square of cloth in his hand.

"Sir, my response was not intended to be nice but rather to indicate the passion I feel for the subject. I want this case, and sooner rather than later. If too much time passes—"

"Yes, I am aware of what can happen if we allow further time to lapse." He folded the handkerchief and returned it to his pocket. "And that is why I have agreed to allow Mrs. Astor her Pinkerton agent. However, there is a complication."

"Something not already mentioned in the case documents?"

He nodded. "I've had a report that one of our more pressing cases may have overlapping facts."

"Oh? Which one?"

Again he glanced around, but this time he did not give the signal for quiet. Instead, he met her gaze with a look that told Sadie he was most unhappy.

"The Tucker case."

"What?"

His nod was almost imperceptible. "It seems that duplication exists in both the Astor and the Tucker cases, and that in neither have the victims been certain as to whether they were duped."

Sadie sat back and regarded her employer with curiosity. "You're speaking in riddles, sir."

"These cases are riddles," he said as he leaned forward to rest his elbows on the table. "Or rather they have similar riddles at their core. You had occasion to spend an amount of time with Mr. Tucker recently. What did you make of him?"

Unfortunately, her first thought was of their kisses. She firmly pushed the recollection aside. Then came the starry evening, the polite manners.

"I found him to be a gentleman in every way."

His appraising look stalled at her eyes. "I am not asking whether he is able and qualified to fill your dance card, Miss Callum. I am asking your thoughts on his behavior." He paused. "And whether he may have pulled off a trick under all our noses."

"My answer would be the same, sir. His behavior was never untoward. In fact, he was kind and protective of me."

She elected not to mention the efficient way he handled the swift exit of her brothers or the fact that he pawned a family heirloom in order to purchase weapons with which to offer that protection. Instead she said, "I must ask what trick you believe he may have pulled."

"You are certain the man whose company you kept for those two days was indeed William *Jefferson* Tucker and not William *John* Tucker?"

"Sir, I'm not sure where you are going with this line of questioning. I am the one who testified as to the fact that the state of Louisiana had imprisoned the wrong man. So, yes, I am certain of his identity."

"Bear with me, then, as I present an alternative scenario." He beckoned the waiter to order a café au lait for both of them and then waited until the fellow had hurried away. "What you testified to was that the facts indicated the man who was behind bars was not the man who originally should have been put there."

"Yes. The facts indicated that the Tucker who received the original sentence was indeed the Tucker who should have remained in jail. That someone took it upon themselves to listen to a man claiming his position had been switched by his twin is ludicrous."

"Is it?"

The question stalled her. "Yes, of course," she finally said. "The evidence is clear."

"Tell me what is clear about it."

"In essence, John Tucker's eyes are gray but tend to green, and Jefferson Tucker's gray eyes tend to blue. Every woman duped by Tucker, except for Miss McMinn, testified that the man had green or gray eyes. None claimed his eyes were blue."

"His eye color was the basis for your testimony?"

"That is something women notice, sir, and it is certainly something that cannot be changed." She shrugged. "Of course, there were other things, such as the fact that Jefferson was a man whose abilities as an officer with Scotland Yard were above question. If he was guilty of impersonation and was indeed John, not Jefferson, why would he pay a visit to his brother if he suspected his brother would cry foul and have him arrested?"

Henry's expression never changed. "I would have you answer your own question. Why would a guilty man return to the scene of the crime, as it were?"

"Are you speaking in generalities? Or are you asking me to comment specifically on the Tucker twins?"

"Start with generalities."

She gave the matter some thought as the waiter returned with their steaming coffees and then departed again. Though her study of the criminal mind was most incomplete, she had learned a thing or two about human nature during the four years she had worked as a Pinkerton agent.

She called on that experience now as she formulated a response. "In general, that sort of behavior would come from someone who has something to prove. One twin who has been bested by the other and then returns to gloat."

"Is that all?" he said as he lifted his cup to take a careful sip of coffee.

"No, sir. In the case of a policeman and a criminal, I would say that either the policeman visits the criminal to feel a measure of superiority or perhaps does so in a gesture of pity." She allowed the thought to take hold. "Or maybe he is a good son and merely visiting at the prompting of his mother, as Jefferson Tucker stated at the hearing."

"The coffee's quite good, Miss Callum. You should try it." Henry returned the cup to its saucer. "Since we are now speaking in specifics, shall we consider another possibility?"

At Sadie's nod, Henry continued. "Is it possible that these two men are in collusion? They are, after all, twins. That relationship suggests a level of kinship that goes beyond the usual, don't you think?"

"No. I cannot see it. They are far too different. Or at least my impression of the criminal Tucker from everything I have read about him leads me to believe that he would be very different from the Tucker I spent time with."

"Remind me of your impression of Jefferson Tucker again, please."

"He was charming, carefully protective of me, and a perfect gentleman."

"And yet, Miss Callum, that very same record of evidence against John Tucker would indicate he is charming, carefully protective of whoever has his attention, and a perfect gentleman."

He sat back to allow her time to consider the truth of that statement. "I wonder if you've considered that these two men may be playing on their individual strengths to achieve a common goal."

"No, sir. That never crossed my mind."

"Well, consider it, because Scotland Yard fired William J. Tucker just last month."

"For his absence?" She looked down at her untouched coffee and then up at Henry. "He was falsely imprisoned. I hardly think that's fair—"

"No, Miss Callum. He was summarily dismissed without explanation. That's the official response. However, my sources tell a different tale. Apparently, someone within the department where the man was employed suspected Tucker of collusion with a known suspect in a case he was working for the British Museum. Out of professional courtesy, the facts were not made public."

"And the case?"

"Trafficking in antiquities of questionable provenance."

The pieces of the puzzle fell into place as Sadie regarded Henry with surprise. "Such as the Rembrandt Mrs. Astor purchased?"

"The very same."

She paused only long enough to collect her thoughts. "And so our overlapping situations."

"Exactly. The question I need you to answer is whether wc have one Tucker or two to catch. And once that is determined, which Tucker will we be catching?"

Seventeen

Jefferson stared at the telegram and then read it again. He had been dismissed? Summarily and with cause?

Surely there was a mistake.

He would write again. Would send another telegram asking for clarification.

And yet the words on the paper in his hand werc as clearly written and unmistakable as any person could manage. It was as if his superiors thought he knew exactly to what they referred.

There was nothing for it. Returning to London to have a face-to-face discussion with whoever was in charge now was the only remedy he could figure.

He ordered his bags packed and then went to visit with Granny. He found her propped up on her pillows, a lady's maid reading to her from a Robert Louis Stevenson novel.

"Aching for adventure, I see," Jefferson said as he stepped inside the room.

"Aching, yes, though I doubt I'm to see any further adventure. Seen enough in my years. Come now and give your Granny a hug." To the maid she said, "I'll call for you when I'm ready to resume our reading."

The girl set the novel on the bedside table and went out, not sparing a glance at Jefferson as she walked by him. He moved closer to the bed, reaching down to embrace his grandmother.

"Sit," she told him as she indicated the chair the maid had just vacated. "And tell me what I'm missing outside this room."

They chatted about the events of the day for a good half hour. For a woman who claimed no touch with the outside world, his grandmother managed to keep an eye on current news items, and she could discuss politics with the expertise of one who was closely involved.

"And while all of that is interesting, what I really want to know is what has you all tied up in a twist, Jeffy?"

"Me?" He shrugged. "Just some travel plans. I'm not keen on going back to London, but I must."

She studied him a moment. "Does this have anything to do with your brother?"

"Not directly. I fear this situation is of my own making."

"Or is it because your mama decided you needed to pay John a visit?"

"That was the beginning of what became an unexpected detour, yes." He gave the idea more thought. "I need to meet with my superior officer to clear up any concerns he has about keeping me on the payroll."

"So there are concerns?" She shrugged. "I see the man's problem if that is what we're discussing here. A fellow who hires a detective to track down the criminal element does not expect to find his employee behind bars."

"Nor did this employee expect it, obviously."

"No, you never did see any of John's dirty tricks coming until they hit you square between the eyes."

His grandmother's common sense and plain way of speaking did his heart good. The truth of her words, however, had the opposite effect.

"I'll answer for you," she continued. "No, you did not. And like as not you thought your little detour to pay a call on John was a kindness that just might change the man."

"I confess the thought did occur."

She lifted up off the pillows and then reached over to swat his arm.

"What was that for?" he asked.

"It's the same fool thing John has done all his

life. He's conned you. When are you going to stop trusting him?"

"I don't trust him."

"I'll rephrase the question. When are you going to stop believing John will change? You know the analogy of the leopard not changing his spots, don't you?"

"Yes, Granny."

"Well, John's spots haven't changed since he was a child. He has as much spunk in him as his daddy but with none of the good sense." She fixed him with a look. "You, however, are as kind-hearted as your mother. Thank goodness you inherited your father's ability to see truth, at least when you want to."

"What does that mean?"

"That means if anybody else did the things your brother did, you would have them lined up and shot."

"You're exaggerating."

"Of course I am, but I'm also trying to get your attention." She paused to settle herself back down on the pillows. "And here's what I want you to promise."

"What's that?"

"That you pray the Lord gives you an understanding of just how to handle your brother the next time the two of you meet up."

He reached out to grasp her hand. "I promise, Granny."

She placed her other hand atop his. "I know you will. And the next time I see that fool brother of yours, I am going to dare that leopard to change his spots. Maybe that'll do the trick. That, and I'll be praying. The Lord, He does love to help those who ask."

"He does at that."

"I am glad you agree." Granny gestured to the table. "Now, pick up that book and start reading to me, would you, please? That girl's sweet and smart as a whip when it comes to reading, but this is a book that ought to be read in a man's voice."

Jefferson complied, opening the book to the midway point where a bookmark held its place. "I fear I won't be able to read all of this before I leave."

"That soon, then?"

He ducked his head slightly. "Tomorrow, if I can arrange it."

"Well, I suppose I'll have to have that handsome Pinkerton man finish it for you."

"Granny," he scolded playfully. "Do you think Agent Russell will be willing to prolong his stay just to finish reading this book to you?"

"He will if I hire him to."

Shaking his head, he placed his finger on the first line of the page and began to read. He wouldn't put it past his grandmother to make good on that threat. As a favor to the Pinkerton who might be called on to finish the job, Jefferson determined to read as many pages as he could manage tonight.

After a while his grandmother stopped him. "I'm tired now, Jeffy. Give me a hug and promise you won't stay gone so long this time."

"You know I can't promise that, but I promise I'll try. How's that?"

"I'll take it. Now go on out of here and warn that handsome man he's about to get a job offer he ought to consider."

"I won't do it. Maybe I'll stay here and read to you tomorrow." In truth, the idea held more appeal than jumping back into a fight that would include not only his brother but possibly his superiors at Scotland Yard. And for what? So he could regain his job? Could prove himself competent? Even then he might not be welcomed back to his former position. Nothing in that plan was certain. Perhaps he should abandon it altogether and wait until he had a better grasp on the situation.

"Nothing is certain, Jeffy. Live a little."

"I'm sorry, Granny. What was that?"

"I said, nothing is certain. Live a little." She reached to grasp his hand in hers. "You don't know what I mean, do you?" When he shook his head, she continued. "You have something powerful bothersome on your mind. What it is, I don't need to know. But what you need to do about it? Well, that's what I'm telling you. Live a little, Jeffy. Take a chance. Nothing is certain."

She was right, of course.

Leaving her room with a chuckle, Jefferson went down to the library, where he found Kyle apparently waiting for him. At least that was his impression of the pacing the Pinkerton agent was doing.

"You're leaving?" he demanded when Jefferson stepped into the room. "Exactly when were you planning on informing me of this?"

"Good evening, Kyle." Jefferson forced a cordial expression on his face as he walked over to sit in Grandfather Tucker's chair.

"We had an agreement."

"Yes, we did." Jefferson settled himself comfortably and then watched as the Pinkerton agent sat in a chair across from him. "However, the situa-tion has changed, and I was only informed of this a few hours ago."

"You mean you were informed that you were dismissed with cause."

"How did you know that?"

Kyle lifted one brow. "The real question is why you think leaving town will fix this problem."

"I will ask again. How did you know about my dismissal? Were you reading my telegrams?"

An impossibility, of course. The folded piece of paper was still in his pocket, where he'd put it at the telegraph office.

The Pinkerton agent leaned forward and rested his elbows on his knees. "Suffice it to say our organization has a good working relationship with your former employer."

"I see."

He did. Information was exchanged all the time between such entities with a common goal. The real question was why.

And yet Jefferson knew even if he asked, there was no guarantee that the answer Kyle gave would be a truthful response.

"And as to how I knew you were leaving, your butler was kind enough to ask whether I wished to travel with you or stay longer in the city. So, now that you're off the case you were working on, are you still inclined to not discuss it?"

"Just as you would be disinclined to give me any information on any of *your* cases. We've had this discussion, Kyle. Why belabor the point?"

"Even now that you are no longer in their employ."

"Especially now."

"Fair enough." Kyle sat back and regarded Jefferson for a moment. "When do you leave?"

"Tomorrow," was all he would say. "You're welcome to stay until you can make other arrangements although I would ask that you respect the fact my grandmother is under this roof."

"And if I were to offer an alternative to the time and expense it will take to stand before your superiors and hear the reason for your dismissal?"

Jefferson shook his head. "I see no alternative."

"And yet there is one." Kyle paused as if considering his words. "You were dismissed due to inconsistencies in your reports and dereliction of duty."

"Impossible!" Taking a deep breath, Jefferson let it out slowly. "And how was I to have committed these acts while wrongfully imprisoned?"

Kyle merely stared, allowing Jefferson to work out the answer himself. "Your brother. He had almost a year to do whatever he wished."

Jefferson paused to think of the possibilities of that statement. Of the warning John had offered upon their last meeting. "Including impersonating me."

"Or, is it you impersonating him?"

"That's outrageous—"

"Is it?" Kyle regarded Jefferson impassively. "As twins would you not have similarities and differences? What if one twin has skills the other does not possess? Would that not be reason enough to exchange places?"

Blood pounded at Jefferson's temples as he stood. "I assure you, Agent Russell, there is nothing on this earth that would be worth going to that prison for, be it treasure or pride. Nothing."

"If you say so."

"I do," Jefferson snapped. "And so do you. A man who was uncertain as to whether I was friend or foe would not have showed me the array of crime-fighting inventions you have at your disposal."

Kyle gave Jefferson an appraising look. "I had to hear what your answer would be. I guarantee you will be asked this question more than once in the future."

Jefferson let out a long breath as his temper subsided. Still, he remained standing. "I suppose you're right."

"I am, and I think you've done well by your response. There's another possibility I've been considering. This case you were working on, is that what brought you to the States?"

"Yes."

"And not the need to pay your brother a visit?"

He tried not to consider how different things might have been had he not made that stop in Louisiana. "My mother requested I see to his health and safety. It was not something I would have done otherwise."

Kyle's expression sobered as he seemed to be considering his next words carefully. "Then is it possible that your brother did not arrange to switch places with you on his own?"

"I don't follow."

"Would it be out of the realm of possibility to assume that your investigation might be making certain people nervous?"

Jefferson thought of the last letters he received

from his informant at the British Museum's archaeological site in Iraq. With relics disappearing only to reappear on the London market, someone was profiting while the museum was taking great losses. Any disruption of that arrangement would very likely make certain people nervous.

"No. It wouldn't."

He returned to his seat, his mind reeling. Anything was possible when it came to John, although he rarely got along with others for any length of time, especially not when the other person was male instead of female.

"I can see you are considering this," Kyle said.

He reached across the desk to toy with the paperweight. "I am."

"And?"

Setting aside the glorified rock, Jefferson returned his attention to the Pinkerton agent. "There is merit to the argument."

Merit also to taking action and finding a solution himself without depending on the expertise of others. Jefferson once again rose, his mind made up as he moved toward the door. Kyle followed after him.

"Still planning on leaving for England?"

"Leaving? Yes, but not for England."

"Where, then?"

Jefferson stopped short, one hand on the newel post. "Suffice it to say I've realized I have two options. I can either plead my case before my superiors in London, or I can solve the case and then arrive to witness their apologies firsthand. I like the latter situation better."

Eighteen

"Was that you I saw walking in the moonlight the other night, Uncle Penn?"

Sadie had caught her uncle in a rare moment of solitude, for his activities were such that he rarely made an appearance at the Callum table. Or, for that matter, anywhere on the property.

He appeared to welcome her presence, even moving over so she could sit beside him on the bench that boasted the best view of the Mississippi River on all of the plantation. She settled her skirts and let the warm sunshine penetrate fabric and skin to seep deep in her bones.

"It was me indeed," her uncle said just when she'd decided he would not be responding at all.

"But not Daddy you were walking with."

He swung his attention from the slow-moving river to her face. "No, it was not."

She allowed the brief answer. If Uncle had his secrets, who was she to pry? And yet Daddy's accusation rode high in her thoughts. Too high to ignore any longer.

"Uncle Penn," she said gently as she swiveled

to face him. "Daddy thinks you're a spy. Is he correct?"

If Penn felt surprise, his expression showed none of it. Instead, he allowed a deep rumbling chuckle. "Seamus would think so, of course. He never did approve of Pearl marrying me."

"But is he right?"

Again it appeared as if her uncle would not answer. Then, slowly, he nodded. "I expect in the narrow definition he meant it, yes."

"Are or were?"

"Ah, now there is an important distinction." He shrugged. "I came down to this lovely part of the world with a less than honorable purpose, at least as far as your father sees it."

"To spy for the Union?"

"To gather information." He nodded in her direction. "Something you ought to know a little about."

"And then you stayed," she supplied as a way to steer the direction of the conversation to more neutral ground.

"For love. Something you ought to allow yourself, Sadie."

She laughed. "Now you sound like Mama and Daddy."

"They have your best interests at heart."

Her quick study of his features told her he was serious. "Yes, I know they do."

"I understand the matchmaking begins this

evening." He returned his gaze to the river. "What are your plans for avoiding the matrimonial trap?"

"Running is impossible given the wardrobe requirements, so I thought perhaps I would make myself intolerable. That certainly works for Aaron."

"My dear, I doubt young Dr. Trahan could ever find you intolerable."

"About him . . ."

Again his attention went to her. "Yes?"

"I had an encounter with Gabriel in New Orleans a few days ago."

"Unpleasant?"

She shook her head. "Quite pleasant, except for the fact that I was wearing a disguise and awaiting a meeting with Henry Smith."

He let out a long breath. "I see. That would be inconvenient."

Henry's statement regarding coincidences came to mind. "Disconcerting, actually. I've never been found out like that. I . . ." She paused to center her thoughts. "I've since thought that perhaps I'm losing my ability to perform my duties."

"Nonsense."

Sadie offered him a smile. "You're saying that because you're my uncle."

"I'm saying that because I was there."

"What?"

He shifted positions. "Or rather I should say that I saw you going into the dressmakers and then waited in hopes you wouldn't be long. I thought I might treat my favorite niece to café au lait and perhaps some beignets."

"I see."

"When you came out in widow's garb, I assumed you were on assignment, although you did not appear to have any backup—at least, none I recognized. So I thought I'd best trail you at least as far as wherever you were headed."

"I didn't see you."

"Yes, well, I kept out of sight, as it were. I made certain you got your beignets and then when the gentleman arrived at your table . . ."

"You assumed he and I were to meet. Secretly."

"I assumed you had good reason to be where you were, so I did not make myself known. My dear, have I ever interfered in your work?"

"No." She did wonder how many times he had watched unnoticed, though. A question she chose not to ask. "But how did you know it was I who walked out of the dressmakers? Perhaps my disguise was not a good one after all."

"I know my niece. And I knew you had gone in alone. When a woman of your height and size left, I suspected it was you and assumed you had good reason for hiding your face."

Sadie decided not to ask any further questions. She also decided not to use the costume of a widow again anytime soon.

"You'll see the fellow again tonight, yes?" At

her nod, Uncle Penn continued. "Does he know?"

"About my work as a Pinkerton? No, and I do not intend to tell him."

"You will have to tell him something."

She met her uncle's gaze. "I told him I donned the disguise in order to find a measure of privacy."

"Did he believe you?"

"I think so. Although I suspect I will find out for certain tonight when we take that walk I agreed to."

"I suspect you are correct." Uncle Penn nodded toward the house. "I also suspect you will have your mother and perhaps your father to deal with once the young doctor states his intentions. Aren't you the least bit interested in him?"

"He's a childhood friend, Uncle. Seeing him all grown up is a bit disconcerting."

"The same word you used to describe your meeting with him." He reached over to touch her sleeve. "Not exactly the word a young lady uses when describing a man for whom she has an interest."

Sadie looked down at her uncle's hand and then placed her own atop it. "It isn't, is it?" When he shook his head, she continued. "I should let Gabriel know that anything more than a friendship is not to be."

"Suit yourself, my dear, but if you do, be

prepared for another fellow to be invited to supper. And should he not suit, another."

She groaned and withdrew her hand. "You're right, of course."

"I am, and yet I wonder when your Mr. Smith will have you out solving another case."

"I believe it will be soon," was all she felt comfortable saying. If Uncle Penn saw Gabriel, wasn't it possible he had also seen Henry? And yet nothing in the conversation thus far led her to believe he had.

Her uncle let out a long breath. Though his attention was focused straight ahead, Sadie had the oddest notion he was studying her.

"Perhaps you and I should head back inside and spend what little time we have left here with those who love us."

He stood and she followed his lead. "Does that mean you're going back to Mobile, or are you coming along with me again as my reason for traveling?"

"It means I miss my wife dearly, and if I cannot convince Pearl to come to me here at Callum Plantation, then I shall be forced to return to Mobile and her. So no, I shall not be traveling with you any time soon."

"I see." She paused. "Then I do wish she would pay us a visit. I haven't seen Aunt Pearl in far too long."

Uncle Penn offered Sadie his arm and she

217

took it. "Perhaps you should add your letter of invitation to mine. With two of us pleading our cases, how can she deny us?"

Jefferson stepped off the train in New Orleans, the Pinkerton agent still in tow. "I can manage from here," he said to his persistent shadow.

"I'm sure you can." Kyle hefted his bag onto his shoulder and stood waiting for him to do the same. "However, I thought maybe you could use some help."

"Help?" He shook his head. "In what way?"

"Oh, I don't know. Solving your case, maybe?"

A train's whistle blew and steam rose as a conductor called out a warning to board. The crowd was thick on the platform, a great milling mass of humanity that stood between Jefferson and the city where his quest for justice would begin.

He started to walk ahead without responding. There was no need.

Kyle stepped in front of him, blocking his way into the station. "Hire me. Together we can remedy the situation."

"Hire you? I think not. Nor do I need your assistance. I'm sure you have other ways to find my brother without pretending to help me."

"Pretending?" Kyle appeared ready to argue and then seemed to think better of it. "All right," he managed through a clenched jaw. "But if you're going it alone, keep in mind that there won't be anyone there to back you up if you need it."

"I won't need it." He let the remainder of his argument go in favor of reaching out to shake the other man's hand. "Thank you, Kyle. Without your agency's assistance, I would still be behind bars waiting for someone to believe they had the wrong Tucker locked up."

"You can thank Sadie Callum for that."

Jefferson nodded and then parted ways with Agent Russell. "Maybe I will," he said under his breath as he stepped out into the afternoon sunshine.

Kyle caught up to him. "I'd like to make a deal with you, then."

"A deal?" Jefferson kept walking, sparing his companion only the briefest of glances.

"A few of my inventions in exchange for your promise that you will report back to me should you have any information on your brother."

He stopped short and Kyle followed suit. "Why would you trust me?"

"I don't." Kyle waited until a pair of matrons passed them to continue. "But I know you're the only link we have to the man I want to put back in jail. I'm going to keep looking for him until my replacement returns to duty. Then John Tucker will be someone else's problem."

"Fair enough. But your inventions?" He shook his head. "Why would you offer that?"

"Same reason." He shrugged. "I've already told you I have a vested interest in catching the man. If I can help you, then I'm thinking you'll help me."

"You'll want them back." A statement, not a question. And yet Kyle seemed ready to respond.

"You won't get any of the good stuff," he said with a grin. "Only a few things I have extras of. You can keep them if they suit you or return them if they don't. I only ask that, as a man of honor, you help me or my replacement to put a guilty man back behind bars."

"I see." Jefferson thought only a moment before nodding. "I don't suppose I can turn that offer down."

"I didn't think you would." He lifted his hand to wave at a vehicle parked just down the block. The driver pulled the closed carriage up to them a moment later. Kyle tossed his bag in and then climbed inside, motioning for Jefferson to join him.

"I don't live far from here," Kyle said. "You're welcome to stay with us as long as you'd like."

"Thank you, but I won't trouble you any longer than necessary."

Kyle gave him an appraising look and then slowly nodded. "I warn you that my wife will insist you stay to supper. And lest you think you'll be able to tell Millie no, I should also warn you that when I met her I didn't have any thought of spending more than a few minutes in conversation with her before I went on about the business of testing my personal flying device."

"That's a first meeting that sounds different than most."

"It was indeed. But then my Millie, she is definitely different than most."

Jefferson's smile was swift and genuine. "Then I will not waste my time in trying to leave until after supper."

As it turned out, he not only stayed to supper but also returned the following day for lunch. As promised, Millie Russell was an engaging and personable hostess. She was also a brilliant scientist, something he discovered when Kyle showed him the laboratory the two shared in their home near the center of the city.

"My father would love this place," he told Kyle later as they sat together in the ground floor library. "He always was a man of science."

"Was?" Kyle asked. "Is he no longer alive, then?"

"Oh, he is quite well. I received a telegram from him this morning, actually. I suppose that is why I had him on my mind just now."

Kyle remained silent a moment. "And your brother? Any further news?"

"If I had news, I would have shared it." He bit back on his temper. "I'm sorry."

His companion shrugged. "I don't suppose I

would take well to the topic either if I was in your shoes. Perhaps we should return to discussing your father. Is he still sailing?"

Jefferson looked up sharply to meet the Pinkerton agent's blank stare. So he had done his homework, not only on the Tucker brothers but also on their father.

"He is. When he can manage it, that is. The life of a ship's captain appeals to him much more than the daily business of running a shipping company."

"I thought perhaps a man at his level of success would leave the sailing to others."

"I always suspected he took the helm of his vessels and sailed away in an attempt to keep John and me landlocked and perhaps to coax us into running Tucker Shipping. Now I think it's just the life he loves and nothing more."

"So you weren't always a detective?"

"I was. John was learning the ins and outs of running the company until he got bored and disappeared."

"Disappeared?"

"He was like that, my brother. The best at anything he attempted but always prone to bad endings."

"That much has not changed."

"Sadly, no." He shifted in his seat and then said, "I wonder if I might ask you something about Sadie Callum before I go."

Kyle lifted a brow. The beginnings of a smile quickly followed. "You can ask . . ."

"But you will not guarantee an answer," Jefferson supplied.

"Exactly."

"Fair enough." He let out a long breath. "I need her to do something, and she may not agree. Any suggestions on how I can remedy that?"

Kyle chuckled. "Absolutely. The remedy is to not even make the attempt. Once Sadie has her mind set on something– or against it—nothing is going to change it."

Not what he had hoped to hear. "I see."

"There is one thing to consider. I'm just guessing here, but I noticed she sets great store by the opinions of her parents. Last I heard, they didn't know she is a Pinkerton agent. So if you can figure a way to convince her parents, then maybe you have your remedy."

"Both parents, or is there one who would be preferable to speak with?"

"Divide and conquer? Yes, I see your point. In that case, based on a recent meeting I had with the man, I suggest you speak with Sadie's father. Name is Seamus Callum."

"Seamus Callum. Got it." He rose to shake Kyle's hand. "I do thank you."

"Don't thank me," Kyle said as he also stood. "You'll see why when you meet him."

Jefferson got as far as the door before he

stopped. "One more thing. You've told me who Sadie listens to. Any idea who Seamus listens to?"

Kyle shrugged. "Himself? And perhaps his wife, although I doubt that. The Lord, maybe?"

Jefferson nodded. "Then I will start praying."

Two days later, Jefferson stepped out of New Orleans' Hotel Monteleone onto Iberville Street. He glanced around to be certain he hadn't been followed and then climbed inside the waiting carriage. The conveyance jerked forward, its wheels turning slowly on the rain-slick street.

"I trust your trip went well."

Jefferson reached out to shake his host's hand. "It did, thank you. And yours?"

"A day at sea is always a good day."

How many times had he heard the expression? Not enough to tire of it, especially coming from this man.

He affected a casual expression that belied the fact he carried a substantial amount of cash and several weapons on his person, as well as a few choice inventions loaned to him by the Pinkerton agent.

The folding knife tucked into the sleeve of his shirt felt cool against his skin. It was a welcome diversion as the carriage rolled on and their conversation fell into pleasantries about the weather and the condition of the shipping industry. Not once was John's name mentioned.

"Are you ready to tell me what this is all about?" the man asked.

"I need transportation by sea. Discreet and on short notice."

At his companion's nod of agreement, Jefferson relaxed. Indeed, he could manage this.

Nineteen

Thursday evening came before Sadie was ready for it. Despite her prayers to the contrary, Gabriel arrived right on time and seemed ready to give her more than her fair share of his attention.

Mama kept her dinner conversation light and decidedly away from any hint of matchmaking. Sadie gave thanks for that, although her nerves were still stretched taut after the conversation with her uncle earlier that afternoon.

As the time came to join Gabriel on the walk she had promised, Sadie was more than ready to bolt from the confines of the dining room in favor of the more expansive outdoors. Her mother, however, appeared ready to linger.

"Since Gabe was raised on the property, you should show him all the new things Daddy has been working on in his absence," Ethan said. "Or I can, if you'd prefer, Gabe."

"No," Mama and Gabriel said in unison.

"You have things to do, Ethan," Mama said, her

smile never slipping as she set her napkin aside and stood.

"I don't, actually." Ethan trailed Sadie and Gabriel out of the dining room and into the foyer. "And I do not mind."

"Then come along," Sadie said casually as she moved to open the front door. She would owe Ethan a debt of gratitude for this, something she had no doubt he would eventually come to collect.

"Ethan," Daddy called, "I believe you were going to show me your new idea for the evaporator. Now's as good a time as any, don't you think?"

Her brother shrugged. "I suppose I ought to take advantage of the opportunity. You'll have to manage this stroll without me."

Sadie smiled, although her disappointment rose. With Ethan as entertainment, she might not have been called on to make polite conversation with Gabriel. And tonight she had too much on her mind to consider polite conversation with anyone, least of all the man who had spied her in disguise two days ago.

Sauntering out into the late afternoon sunshine with what she hoped would be a casual expression, Sadie inhaled deeply of fresh Louisiana air and then exhaled slowly. She never tired of the view from the porch, of the stately avenue of trees that swayed in the gentle breeze off the river.

A bell clanged, announcing a steamboat passing

by, and Sadie looked over in that direction. The vegetation had grown too thick to allow for an unobstructed view of the river from her vantage point, but she could see the pair of smokestacks and the string of words indicating the name of the vessel above the tree line.

For a moment she thought of the last time she had stood and watched the river go by. With Jefferson Tucker.

Gabriel stepped between her and the river's view and offered his arm. "Shall we?"

"Yes, of course," she said as she stepped away to walk down to the lawn.

The evening was warm for early May, and the breeze was just light enough to allow for no need of a shawl. She chose their path, taking the lead as they strolled down the avenue beneath the oaks.

"I always wondered how these trees got so big so quickly," Gabriel said when Sadie paused to look back at the house perfectly framed in the distance.

"Surely you have heard the story."

He shook his head. "No. Or if I did I've forgotten."

Sadie shrugged. "The trees were planted some thirty years prior to constructing the house," she said. "Apparently, the property's previous owner envisioned a home there someday, but unfortunately he did not live to see it built."

Sadie said the words by rote, the story behind

the Callum home committed to memory after years of hearing it repeated on far too many occasions. Interesting as it was that Seamus managed to build a monument to Mama on the very spot where another man had hoped to do exactly the same thing for the woman he loved, the story had lost its luster in the retelling.

The steamboat bell rang again, sending her attention to the river and the conversation held upstream of these same waters that afternoon in New Orleans. For all the reasons stacked against the plan she and Henry had formulated, it was so far out of the realm of possibility that it just might work.

"All these years of playing all over this property with your brothers, and I feel as though I am only just seeing it." He reached to take her hand. "Very much the same way I feel about you, Sadie."

She tore her attention from the avenue to the man standing beside her. "I'm sorry. What did you say?"

Frustration etched his handsome features and then quickly disappeared to reveal a smile. "You weren't paying a bit of attention to me, were you?"

"I was. Mostly."

"Mostly?"

"Forgive me," she said, and she meant it. "I'm just distracted this evening."

"Unlike our last conversation." His statement,

casually made, belied the serious look he slanted down at her through the dappled shade.

"That conversation never happened." She paused to look up into eyes so different than she recalled. "Remember?"

Whatever she'd seen was now gone as Gabriel ducked his head and then looked up with a grin. "Do you still read those stuffy books on the arts, Sadie?"

"I'll ignore that."

"I will take that as a yes."

She caught sight of two figures walking in the distance. Daddy and Ethan, heading for the sugar mill. The way Ethan's hands were gesturing and Daddy's head was nodding, it appeared the conversation between the two was going well.

It did her heart good to see that her father was actually taking an interest in the changes her brother was suggesting. Or at least he was finally willing to listen.

"Sadie, where are you?"

Gabriel stepped into her line of sight, obscuring her view. "You look every bit as deep in thought as you did the other afternoon in New Orleans."

Her eyes narrowed. Would Gabe ever let the matter rest?

"And you seem insistent on bringing up an event we had agreed we would not discuss."

Sadie took measure of him, judging his expression and the way he stood. Confidence and something else. Not amusement, despite the hint of a smile on his face. But what?

Was he offering torment in the form of good-natured jesting? No matter. She would put an end to the conversation or leave him to stroll the gardens alone.

And though the former was the better choice, the latter had great appeal.

"Gabriel Trahan," she said with the full force of her Pinkerton training. "I welcome any questions from you on what you saw. Ask away, but when you've been answered, I will require that you never bring up the topic again."

Her assertiveness must have caught him off guard, for his smile slipped. A moment later it was back in place.

"No questions at all. You wished for privacy," he said with the nonchalance of a man suddenly captivated by something off in the distance.

"And you aren't curious as to why I resorted to a disguise?"

"No, of course not. A woman of your beauty and social standing must find it difficult . . ."

Gabriel's words slowed to a halt as whatever captivated him took precedence. She looked behind her to see what had interested him and found nothing more than the sight of a carriage coming up the road.

"Expecting visitors?" he asked, his attention on the approaching conveyance.

"No, but that doesn't mean someone else isn't." She turned her back on the carriage and resumed her walk. If Gabriel wanted to greet the guest, he could do it without her.

Veering off toward the river and the bench where she and Uncle Penn had sat earlier in the day, Sadie contemplated her uncle's advice. She did find Gabriel disconcerting, not a quality that would endear him to her beyond maintaining their tenuous link to shared childhoods.

He followed, finally, and arrived at the bench with the news that the carriage had apparently come to retrieve Penn. She found it odd that Gabe would care about the comings and goings of her uncle.

No, disconcerting. She turned her attention to the river, where a few logs were slipping by, buoyed by the downstream current. With the motion of the tide came thoughts of the case notes she would be studying again as soon as she could get upstairs alone.

Her mind reeled with the possibilities of what the merging of the Tucker and Astor cases might bring. While she was glad she didn't have to seek out the missing Tucker to apprehend him, managing some sort of arrangement with—

"All right, I admit it. What happened in New Orleans is still on my mind," Gabriel said abruptly. "I am curious."

It took Sadie a moment to return her rambling

thoughts to some semblance of order. "I have secrets," she said crossly. "Is that what you're thinking?"

"That is how things appeared, yes."

"And yet a few minutes ago you weren't concerned at all."

Before he could respond, she held up her hand and then stood, her attention still focused on the river. "Forgive me," she said in what she hoped would be a gentle tone. "It's just that I'm a bit confused about your interest in my activities and why you can't seem to let what happened go. You were offered a chance to ask questions, and you declined. You promised to never mention it, and you can't seem to manage that."

She turned to face him, her arms crossed over her midsection. Gabriel first appeared to be stunned, but then, by degrees, the corners of his lips turned up to reveal he was apparently amused. This only fueled her irritation.

"Go ahead and smile," she snapped. "But you will do it without an audience."

"Wait, Sadie," he hurried to say. "I'm sorry, though I fail to understand what is so confusing. I've had an interest in your activities since we were children. Are you only just noticing this?"

Apparently he wanted an answer. She had none. Nor did she have any recollection of him treating her differently from anyone else when they were young.

His expression sobered as he rose. "I meant no harm. I just thought we might renew our acquaintance now that we've both returned to River Pointe, and your parents seemed to believe . . ."

He looked away, his voice trailing off as she saw he was sincere. Sadie's anger evaporated.

"My parents mean well," she said gently. "However, they have conveniently ignored the fact that I am a grown woman, and as such am fully capable of making certain decisions for myself."

She paused only a moment. "Among those decisions would be the choice of whom to wed." She allowed another pause as he lifted his gaze to meet hers. "And when."

"Perhaps I should go." He turned toward the house and began walking in that direction.

Hurting him had not been her intention. She hurried to catch up to him.

"Yes, you should," she said as she slanted him a sideways glance. "But only because I'm awful company this evening."

His steps faltered as he looked down at her. She could almost read his thoughts as he tried to make sense of her comment.

Sadie quirked her brow to lighten the mood, even as she pretended serious concern. For although Gabriel likely did not realize he had interfered in a Pinkerton meeting of grave importance, he had spotted her in a situation she did not wish for him to repeat. There was nothing to gain and everything to lose by allowing him to leave in his current state.

"I am blaming myself," she said. "Now it appears we are at an impasse."

"I don't follow."

"It's simple. Will you forgive me my lapse into impolite behavior or not? If not, I fear my matchmaking parents will require an explanation. They despair of me even as they not so subtly hunt for a suitable match for me, hence the need to go out in disguise on occasion."

"Ah, well. Things are beginning to make sense, although I cannot imagine how anyone would despair of you."

"I am difficult at times." That was the truth and she knew it.

He chuckled, an indication she had soothed over his rumpled feelings. "You forget I've known you long enough to recall that Sadie as well as the one who is very sweet."

"I miss Sweet Sadie. She was lovely." Again, the truth, although there would be no return to the naive girl she had been all those years ago.

Gabriel offered his arm and she took it. Together they set off for the house, likely much to the delight of her mother who was unsuccessfully attempting to hide while watching them from an upstairs window.

"I suppose you know we're being observed," she said.

He nodded. "You may not have noticed that Brent is pretending to exercise his mare in the pasture over there, and yet he has been sitting still astride the horse for some ten minutes."

She cut her eyes in the direction of the pasture. Indeed, Brent was in the saddle, reins in hand and not budging. When she waved, he pretended not to see as he dug in and sent the mare racing away from the fence.

In the process, she spied Cade standing beside the smokehouse a few yards beyond the house. Nudging Gabriel, she watched as he did the same and waved. Cade responded with a nod and then ducked inside the outbuilding.

"You have three other brothers and a father. I wonder where they are. Or do they take turns?"

"I apologize. On those occasions when I fail to remind myself how much my family loves me, I get a bit perturbed at being unable to move about without observation."

"Unless donning a disguise?" he supplied. At her nod, he continued. "Then perhaps the next time we meet, I should wear my own disguise. Perhaps an organ grinder or some fellow who paints portraits in front of the cathedral?"

"Honestly, painting portraits might be fun, though I had no idea you held any interest in the arts."

Gabriel seemed taken aback for a moment.

"No. I don't suppose that would be something you would know."

"What an odd statement." Sadie's Pinkerton training kicked in, albeit with some measure of skepticism. "What are you hiding, Dr. Trahan?"

"Hiding?" He held out his hands, palms up. "I have nothing to hide, Miss Callum. I am but the boy who left here now all grown up."

She laughed, and he joined her. "All right then, grown-up. Tell me something I don't know. Tell me what's happened with you in the years since we last saw one another."

His smile faded as he nodded. "All right. Where do I start?"

Talk of Gabriel's days at Tulane and his experience learning the practice of medicine took them all the way to the front porch, where they paused beside one of the columns.

He paused as if surprised they had reached the house so quickly. "It's getting late, and I should go." He reached to take her hands in his. "I'm very glad you're home again at Callum Plantation. I do hope you'll stay a while so we can become reacquainted."

"I thought that's what we were just doing, Gabriel," she said firmly.

"Indeed." He released her hands to offer a somewhat formal bow. "I'll be watching for you under a widow's veil or behind an easel, then."

As he walked away toward the carriage awaiting

him, Mama slipped into Sadie's view. "What did he mean by that?" she asked, her attention fully on the retreating doctor.

Sadie studied her mother's profile and then turned to reach for the door handle. "I have no idea, Mama, but please don't invite him to supper again without telling me first."

"And why is that?" Mama's words followed her through the open door. "Does he not suit you? There are others who might."

Sadie paused on the stairs to turn around just as the carriage rolled away down the avenue of oaks behind Mama's silhouette. "He is nice enough," Sadie said gently, "but I do not think he and I would make a companionable match."

"Because he is of a mind to find a wife?" Mama rested her hands on her hips. "That is generally the first thing you dislike about any fellow who comes calling, and I am not going to hear it any further."

"Was he coming to call, Mama?"

Her mother seemed completely nonplussed with the question. "I had hoped that tonight's supper might cause Gabriel to believe he was welcome to call on you, yes. And I understand that you might be reluctant to allow a young man to call on you, but you needn't have worried. Should he have made any untoward moves, you were completely safe."

"Is that why you sent my brothers to spy on me?"

Mama's posture went rigid. "That is ridiculous," she said in a voice so high and tight that Sadie knew it wasn't the truth.

She rested one hand on the stair rail to steady herself as a thought bore hard on her. "Mama," she said on a sharp intake of breath, "you have been sending them after me for quite some time, haven't you?"

When her mother turned to walk away, Sadie hurried after her. "I am a grown woman, and you cannot keep sending my brothers to see to my safety."

Her mother whirled around so quickly that Sadie almost slammed into her. "No? Well, we both know there have been times when you were not here and should have been. Are you ready to explain your reluctance to remain at home?"

The breath went out of Sadie.

She readied herself for the confrontation she expected would now happen. Instead, her mother swept past her and moved gracefully up the stairs.

At the top of the staircase, Mama paused to look down at her. "I've ordered a bag packed for you. Tomorrow you and I will be paying calls in New Orleans and then staying over for the opera and perhaps a soiree or two. I've asked the new girl to act as your maid for the trip since you've not taken the time to choose someone."

"Yes, that's fine."

Though seemingly willing to comply, inwardly she sighed. This would never do. With Henry giving her permission to move forward on the Astor case, Sadie had hoped she might find a way to leave. An unexpected trip to New Orleans would derail her plans.

Twenty

Mama's determination to see her daughter wed knew no bounds. Sadie came to this conclusion after the two nights at the French Opera House and a half-dozen visits to old friends had resulted in a dance card that had only one empty slot left for tonight's soiree.

Sadie resisted the temptation to complain as the maid squeezed her into the gown of pale blue satin that had arrived just this afternoon. The girl was newly moved upstairs from the laundry and of sufficient talent, according to Mama.

Talent or not, the girl gave the stays another tug, and the last of Sadie's patience fled. "Truly, that is fine," she implored. "I will have no ability to breathe should you continue."

A girl she guessed to be no more than sixteen or seventeen, the maid had seemed smitten with the idea of attending a grand ball and dancing the night away ever since she swept into the room with the ball gown.

"I'm sorry, but the missus wishes you to look your best tonight," the red-haired girl said. "She left specific instructions that should she pull out her tape measure, your waist would be less than twenty inches. I gave her my word I'd at least try."

"Then I shall be certain to hide her tape measure." Sadie paused to attempt a deep breath and failed. "And you have certainly tried. I can attest to that."

She rose and moved toward the bench, where she would accept a second round of torture in the form of having her hair styled in the latest fashion. In the mirror, she caught a glimpse of the girl as she pirouetted in a circle, the basket of pins and brushes tucked under her arm.

"Do you like to dance?" Sadie asked, catching the girl off guard.

Stuttering to a halt, the maid ducked her head and hurried to her side. "I'm sorry, miss," she said as she awaited Sadie's positioning herself onto the bench. "My mum says I get carried away and forget myself sometimes."

"No need to apologize, at least not to me. I recall the days when I did not think these social occasions were such a chore." The truth, though barely and never with such enthusiasm.

"Thank you, miss. I appreciate your understanding."

"That's a lovely accent you have," Sadie remarked as she found a comfortable place on the bench and rested her hands in her lap. "Are you Irish?"

"By way of Cornwall. I was born in Armaugh, but only because a winter storm kept my mum with her people when she'd planned to rejoin my pa."

She met the girl's gaze in the mirror's reflection. "And your name?"

"Julia, it is. Julia Katherine Oakman's the name my mum and pa gave me, but I . . ." She shook her head and reached into the basket for the brush. "Sorry, miss. I do go on."

"No, it's fine, Julia. You're doing a wonderful job of making me forget about the evening ahead. Tell me about your home and how you came to leave Cornwall."

By the time Sadie's hair had been dressed and the last jeweled hairpin set into place, she knew Julia's tale of traveling from her beloved Cornwall to follow a young sailor, only to find he had a girl in more than one port.

"What an awful thing for a man to do."

"No, miss," Julia said as she went about the business of putting away the instruments of torture. "There's much worse a man can do, and I praise the Lord that I wasn't fool enough to allow it. My mum and pa raised me right, they did. I do miss them."

"Are they still alive?"

"Goodness, yes." She crossed herself and then moved quickly away to set the basket back in its place. "I'll see the both of them soon as I'm able. That's my plan."

"To return to Cornwall?"

"Well, yes, though don't you worry now. What with the cost of such a trip, I'll be working for your family for a good long time, I will. Are you happy with the way your hair is styled, or would you prefer I do something different?"

"No, it's lovely. Thank you. You have quite a talent." Sadie swiveled on the bench to face the girl.

An idea took root, and she considered it. "How old are you?"

"Twenty years last Christmas Day, though I'm told I don't look it."

"No, you do not. And you would like to go home and see your parents?"

Ginger-colored brows gathered. "Forgive me, miss, for being so familiar." She shook her head. "I'll just go and fetch your dancing slippers. The missus will be wondering where you are."

Just as the girl's hand touched the doorknob, Sadie said, "Julia, are you well paid?"

She bit her lip and then worried with the trim on her sleeve before nodding. "I am."

Though she said the words with confidence, Sadie doubted her. "Then you would not be interested in any sort of travel."

"Wait now," she said quickly. "What's this?"

Sadie shrugged. "Just that I may be looking for someone to . . ." She paused to judge the girl's expression. Indeed, she did appear interested. "Well, never mind," she said with a wave of her hand. "You're likely not interested in leaving Callum Plantation."

"I'm not. Truly." She wrung her hands and then studied them before looking back up at Sadie. "But if I were, then . . ." She seemed to be considering her words carefully. "Then where would this travel be, exactly?"

Sadie rose and moved to the window, where the reflection on the panes of glass worked just as well as the mirror had. "Oh, here and there. A traveling maid must be prepared for all sorts of places."

Sadie paused just long enough to appear as if she might not continue. "Both here and abroad," she finally said.

"Abroad? Is that so?" Julia said, almost too softly to be heard.

"It is." Sadie turned to lean against the window-sill. "But there's a terrible burden such a maid must bear."

Her brows rose again. "Oh?"

"Yes. Complete discretion is required, and any maid who would take on such a duty would be forced to keep secrets she couldn't share with anyone else. Not a soul."

Now the girl looked less enthusiastic. "Miss, I don't know what you're referring to, but a woman who would let her tongue flap to anyone other than her employer . . . well, she doesn't deserve such a post."

"Agreed. Now, I believe you were going to fetch my dancing slippers, weren't you?"

Sadie watched the maid scurry away as a plan began to formulate. Travel with Uncle Penn had become more complicated, especially given the fact that Aunt Pearl could very well be headed for River Pointe right now.

But travel with a maid, now that just might be the way to accomplish her purposes. Sadie had been watching Julia for a few days, ever since she overheard the girl fussing at one of the parlor maids for a slip of the tongue regarding one of her brothers.

The more she had watched the young maid, the more convinced she became that the girl could be trusted. She would still have to convince Mama and Daddy to allow Julia to leave. And her brothers must realize they could not continue to follow her.

Those were issues for another day, however. For today, it appeared the first piece of the puzzle as to how she would depart New Orleans for the Astor home in Manhattan had been put into place.

"It's time, miss," Julia said when she returned with Sadie's slippers and then helped her down the stairs and out into the carriage.

"How is the new girl working out?" Mama asked absently as her finger traced the edges of her filigree bracelet.

"Very well," she said as she watched the girl in question walk back inside and close the door.

As the carriage pulled away to head down Saint Charles Avenue, Sadie glanced back at the double gallery house where she had spent snatches of her childhood. The city house, as Mama called it, was a lovely two-story home with columns and arched doorways that would later find echoes in the big house out at Callum Plantation.

The home had once belonged to Mama's parents, but now it sat empty unless used by the Callum family on one of the rare occasions when they did not return home at the end of a day in New Orleans. Sadie's favorite childhood memory involved dancing beneath the splashing water of the fountain situated in the center of the back courtyard.

Mama had not been amused, but Daddy waited until she went back inside to hoist Sadie back into the warm water and allow her to play to her heart's content. To her recollection, that had been the last time her father stood up to her mother and allowed Sadie to have her way.

"You're woolgathering," Mama said. "Or was that expression meant to be pouting?"

Sadie swung her attention back to her mother. "I am far too old to pout. I was just thinking about the courtyard and the fountain."

"A noisy thing, that awful fountain. I never did understand why my grandmother insisted on it.

She would say it disguised the sound of carriages going up and down St. Charles Street, but I am here to tell you it did no such thing, although I promise it drew mosquitos."

Mama muttered on about the inconveniences of city life, all the time looking as if she might bolt from the carriage the moment it arrived at their destination. As for Sadie, when the time came to alight from their conveyance, she did so carefully and with great trepidation. This evening was something merely to endure rather than enjoy. One more evening placating Mama and then she could make good her escape.

The lights of the second-floor ballroom beckoned, and Mama quickly allowed the crowd to swallow her whole. Sadie kept a slower pace, first offering her evening wrap to the butler and then scanning the crowd with purpose and, at the same time, a practiced air of indifference.

In these situations her Pinkerton training automatically kicked in. From one side of the expansive room to the other, she made a mental note of whom she saw, with whom they were speaking, and what sort of expressions they wore.

Next she found all of the windows, doors, and other means of escape. Finally, she reached to slide her hand over the Remington pistol hidden in her skirt, and then she was ready to make her arrival known.

Several of the gentlemen who had happened to

be home when she and Mama paid their calls glanced her way. Sadie was certain their interest was due to conversations between Mama and their mothers.

What she did not know was how many of the others whose names she did not know failed to make the cut. Or perhaps they were new to the city and had not yet been noticed by Mama's network of matrimonial spies.

"Miss Callum, what a pleasure to see you."

She turned to see Gabriel execute a perfect bow. When he lifted his head once more, merriment was in his eyes.

"Are you here to dance or shop?" he asked as he offered her his arm.

She took it knowing full well he might get the wrong impression. And yet it behooved her to arrive on the arm of a fellow rather than alone.

"Apparently, it is to be both," she said as she leaned toward him in order to be heard above the orchestra. "I am required to dance while my mother shops among my dancing partners for just the right man to marry me."

His lips turned up in a smile, and yet Sadie thought she caught the slightest sense of disappointment about him. "A pity she did not judge me adequate for the task."

"Oh, she did. In fact, I would wager a guess that you were her first choice."

"But not yours?"

"I thought we were clear about that, Gabriel," she said gently. "You are a friend of many, many years. The boy with whom I caught polliwogs and climbed trees, for goodness' sake. How can I forget that and look at you differently now that we are both grown?"

"And yet I had hoped . . ."

She was just about to try to rescue the conversation when he began to snicker. He was teasing her. The cad.

Jabbing him with her elbow, Sadie once again leaned close. "All right. Now that you understand and realize no offense is intended, I need you to tell me who some of these men are. Mama had them rotating through the parlor so quickly that I've lost track of names and relationships to her friends."

Gabriel happily complied until the orchestra struck up the first dance of the evening. "And this is where I lose you," he said as he nodded toward a man heading her way. "Alphonse has boasted he has your first dance, and so it appears he does. However, I have carefully positioned my own name on your card to be used as rest or for dancing. The choice is up to you."

She gave Gabriel a grateful smile and then allowed the planter's son to escort her onto the dance floor. Just when she thought she could not stand another stomping upon her toes, the music ended and he handed her off to the next swain whose name was listed on her card.

And so the hour went until finally the band rested and so did Sadie. Refreshments were served in the parlor, but she took the opportunity to escape the confines of the crowded ballroom for the more sedate atmosphere on the wide porch that surrounded the genteel home.

Ferns drooped over iron rails to cascade down to a courtyard not so different from the one at their home on St. Charles Avenue. The fountain, painted deepest black and completely invisible except when the moon peeked out from thick clouds, gurgled and splashed. Somewhere out in the garden soft voices murmured.

Owing to the pale color of her gown, Sadie knew she was easily visible standing at the black iron rail. And yet she made no move to hide, nor did the couple that strolled down the path and out into the dark abyss of the thick foliage of the formal back garden.

"There you are." Mama glided up beside her and handed Sadie a cool drink. "You certainly looked as if you were enjoying yourself."

"I was. Mostly."

In truth, she was bored out of her mind with the small talk and smiles that passing for socially adept required. Bored even more with the idea of spending the rest of her life in such numbing pursuits.

Then there were her aching feet. Perhaps she should suggest that Kyle Russell's next invention be a pair of dancing slippers that prevented men from trouncing on toes.

She took a sip of the sweet punch and then looked up at the dusting of stars teasing the edges of the dark spring sky beyond a bank of heavy clouds. The moon peeking out was just past full, with only a small sliver missing from its perfectly round shape. The scent of rain filled the air, and tree branches hung low as if already bending beneath the weight of the raindrops that would eventually fall.

"This thick night air is ruining my hair," Mama said. "Do listen for the sound of the orchestra returning. If I recall correctly, you've arranged for several very nice young men to dance with you in this set, and I do not wish for you to miss any of these opportunities."

Her use of the word "opportunities" was quite telling. Indeed, to her mother, the sons of friends and business associates were very much opportunities for her daughter to secure her station in life. To be set, as Mama liked to say.

And perhaps she was correct. With any of the males who filled Sadie's dance card, there would be no need to concern herself with anything other than keeping a fashionable house and considering what to name the children.

That was her mother's life, however, and not one that Sadie planned for herself. Not now. Or at least not yet.

"You arranged them, Mama," she corrected, albeit gently. "And I will not disappoint."

"No," she said with what appeared to be her first genuine smile of the evening. "You never have disappointed." And then she was gone, slipping back into the ballroom as if she hadn't just given a very nice and yet exceedingly rare compliment.

Buoyed by that, Sadie took another sip of punch and then looked around for a place to leave the cup.

"I'll take that for you."

Turning quickly to see the source of the statement, Sadie lost all ability to respond. The man stepping out of the shadows was Jefferson Tucker.

Or was it John?

Twenty-one

The moonlight painted all it touched a pale silver, including the handsome man standing before her. Sadie handed him her glass, and he set it aside.

He was tall, taller than she recalled, and he wore his expertly tailored formal attire with the same casual air as his prison garb. The difference, she noted with a smile, was in the scent of him, which was an exquisite blend of soap and warm spices.

251

A recollection of the diversionary tactics that had resulted in a pair of memorable kisses threatened. She pushed them away with determination not to allow them to return and instead gave thanks that the man whom she would have been forced to find had found her.

"I didn't expect to see you here," she said as she continued to search his features for the clue that would tell her which Tucker he was.

"No, I didn't suppose you would." His smile was dazzling. "I had business in the city and thought tonight's soiree might prove interesting."

"Business? Would that be the sort of business you were working on when last we met?"

He dipped his head slightly. "It would be, yes. But enough of that. What brings you to the city?"

"My mother, although I must warn you that she's on the prowl for a husband for me, so you're in danger of falling into her trap if you even pretend you know me."

"Is that so? Then I will have to choose carefully whether to make her acquaintance or not." He glanced over in the direction she had gone only moments before his arrival. "She's a lovely woman, by the way."

"Don't even think of it. My mother needs no encouragement, and I highly doubt she would understand that you are merely toying with her."

He reached for the dance card tied to her wrist.

"What is this? Oh, my. You are the popular one, aren't you, Miss Callum?"

"It's merely an indication that the opening salvo on the war to wed Sadie off has been fired tonight in the form of a laundry list of eligible suitors."

"Have you found any who might be husband material?"

"Do not be ridiculous. It is my mother who is shopping, not me."

"And yet you may find you have an interest in purchasing."

"You do not know me very well, Mr. Tucker. I am committed to other interests at the moment."

"I see. So you're one of those ladies who wishes to forego marriage and family in favor of a more exciting life of adventure? And I thought yours was a life you could not recommend."

"I prefer to think I am wishing only to delay rather than forego." She shook her head, ignoring the remainder of his comment. "Anyway, enough of that. I am more interested in hearing how you fared in Mobile."

"I fared quite well. Now, unless I miss my guess, the orchestra has taken their seats and will begin the next set. Who is the lucky fellow?"

She glanced down at her card. Gabriel Trahan. Perfect.

"The lucky fellow is an old friend who won't mind if I sit out our dance." She nodded toward a bench situated midway down the wide expanse of the balcony. "Care to join me?"

Behind her, the orchestra struck up a waltz. Gabriel had not yet sought her out. Perhaps he had chosen another dancing partner who might return his affection.

"No."

She looked up at the man whose eyes she willed to be blue. The dim light refused to confirm that fact. "No?"

He shook his head and repeated the word. Out in the garden, murmured voices faded as only the splash of the fountain and the rare sound of a night bird echoed up toward them.

Her heart stuttered as she searched for something brilliant in response. It was those stupid kisses that rendered her unable to think, given in the line of duty with no emotion attached.

Until after.

"I see," was what she finally settled on.

"Don't pout. I was teasing you." He turned her around and pointed her toward the door. "Come on. If your friend won't waltz with you, I will."

Sadie stalled momentarily, but then her companion's palm at her back moved her along until they were standing at the edge of the dance floor.

"What I said was—"

"Sadie, forgive me for interrupting, but we are missing the dance." He leaned in to speak softly. "And I have found that dancing gives a man and woman the ability to speak without being over-heard."

"Oh."

"You sound disappointed." He shrugged. "Would it help if I were able to promise that what I have to say is worth being seen with me in public?"

Out of the corner of her eye, she saw Gabriel watching, his expression unreadable. She would owe him an apology later. Or perhaps he did not mind at all. In either case, she would speak with him because the options he had offered did not include replacing his name on her dance card with another.

"Something wrong?" her companion asked.

"What?" She looked up to see him smiling, although his attention seemed to be focused in the same direction as hers had been. "No."

"Then shall we?"

Following his lead, she stepped into place. Sadie looked up into his eyes and spied the distinct blue the moon had hidden. Immediately she smiled.

"What's that for?"

She answered with a shake of her head. It would not do to let him know she had questioned his identity.

As Jefferson Tucker swept her into his arms, Sadie found the cloak of boredom falling away.

Though the crowd swirled around them, her dance partner expertly guided her across the dance floor. Just when she had forgotten the reason for their dance, he leaned in.

"Nod if you can hear me." When she complied, he continued. "I came here specifically to see you."

She angled a look up at him. "Why?"

Leaning close once more, he said, "Because you and I have a common goal."

"Which is?"

"Which is something we need to discuss in a less public setting."

"Then I will make arrangements to meet with you next week once I've settled my mother back at home." *And contacted Henry to see just what he would have me do about this unexpected conversation.* "How do you wish I contact you?"

"No, Miss Callum, I will be contacting you. Just leave your window unlocked."

"What you're suggesting is scandalous, Mr. Tucker."

"What I am suggesting is business, Miss Callum. Just a conversation between two persons with extensive training in solving cases and the potential to help one another in that endeavor. I have no idea what you're suggesting."

The cad.

And yet she had no one to blame but herself. Hadn't she stressed on more than one occasion during their brief time together that she was to be viewed as a Pinkerton agent and nothing more, their walk under the stars notwithstanding? So a meeting between two agents, albeit of different agencies, was nothing to raise an eyebrow over. Or was it?

When the music ended, he stepped out of her arms to lead her toward the edge of the dance floor. Though he stood by attentively until the next fellow whose name decorated her dance card arrived, Sadie found he had already disappeared into the crowd when she turned to bid him good-bye.

After his abrupt departure, Sadie found she had little interest in the others on her dance card. Still, she smiled and danced and thanked each man as he stepped away and another took his place.

When the last song of the night was played, she smiled at the thought of having no one to fill that lone empty spot on her dance card. To that end, she made her way toward the table where Mama had been holding court all evening.

Sadie was within sight of her mother when someone called her name. She turned to see Gabriel standing at her elbow, arm outstretched.

"May I trouble you for this dance?"

Dancing with him was much simpler than making an apology, so she put her smile back on and offered it to him. "Yes, of course."

They danced in silence. When they reached the far end of the dance floor, however, her companion led her away from the others to an alcove behind the stage.

There the genial friend from her youth lost his smile. "Who was that man you danced with in my place? And how do you know him?"

The sharpness of his tone took her aback. Rather than respond, she slipped out of his grasp and walked away. This time she reached her mother without incident, though she knew without looking behind her that she had been followed.

"Don't you two look lovely even after such a long evening," Mama said as she looked up from her conversation with one of the matrons they had visited just yesterday. "Come and sit with us, Sarah."

Sarah. Not Sadie. She sighed. What a silly game society small talk could be.

She settled beside her mother and then watched Gabriel take the seat next to her. Once Mama went back to her conversation, Sadie swiveled to face her childhood friend.

Though her expression bore no hint of her exasperation, Gabriel must have realized his behavior had been beyond the pale, for he quickly reached to grasp her hands in his.

"I mean you no harm, Sadie," he hurried to say. "It's just that the man is not one of us, and you and he seemed quite chummy."

She listened without response, for there was no need to answer. Nor would she have given one even if he had demanded it.

"And you seemed to be in serious conversation with him," Gabriel continued. "So as a friend, I find I am concerned that some in this room might misinterpret his behavior as being overly familiar."

"Stop now!" she snapped and then thought better of it. "I appreciate your concern, Gabriel," she said a bit more gently, "but I assure you that none of the men I danced with tonight were in the least inappropriate or conducted themselves in a manner that might be misinterpreted."

He released his grip and sat back as if to study her. Several emotions crossed his face before his expression softened.

"Yes, of course. Gentlemen the lot of them and all looking to win the fair lady's hand. But do any of them know you as I do?"

Had he intended such a cryptic meaning? She decided he did not.

"Don't be silly. I have known you longer than any man in this room. Now do be a dear and stop acting this way. If I hadn't the good sense to know better, I would think you were jealous of . . ."

As soon as the words left her mouth, Sadie wished she could reel them back in. Of course. He was jealous. All that playing at being just her friend, despite his initial bid for her hand, was just so much smoke and mirrors.

"Oh, Gabriel," she said softly. "Do forgive me for taking your statement of concern the wrong way. I certainly did not intend offense."

"None taken." He nodded toward the dance floor. "Shall we finish what we began?"

Gabriel's dancing abilities were every bit as smooth as she expected, and Sadie soon relaxed. One last dance, just a few more turns around the dance floor, and then she could escape.

Finally the orchestra sounded its last note, and Sadie smiled. "Thank you," she said as Gabriel led her off the dance floor toward her mother's table.

While Gabriel stopped to speak to Mama, Sadie scanned the room and noted nothing unusual beyond the customary exit of guests.

When her attention returned to the table, she found Mama and Gabriel both looking in her direction. "She does this to me as well, Gabriel."

"Does what?" Sadie asked as she moved closer.

"Never mind, dear." Mama nodded toward the Tulane doctor. "Remember your manners and tell Gabriel goodbye while I collect our wraps."

Sadie watched her mother rise with her friend's help and then walk away without a backward glance. Slowly she returned her focus to Gabriel. "What was that about?"

"Apparently your mother is disappointed in her matchmaking efforts," he said as he offered her his arm. "I fear I did not help when I told her you needed no assistance in that area."

Laughing, she allowed him to escort her toward the door, where they waited for Mama and then stepped outside. The carriage was nearby, so this time Gabriel offered his assistance to her mother instead of Sadie. Once he handed Mama inside the carriage, he turned to her.

"Here is where we part ways, then."

She glanced around and then looked back at him. "May we offer you a ride?"

"Thank you, but no. I'll walk."

"All right, then," she said as she reached to shake his hand.

To her surprise, Gabriel bypassed her handshake to envelop her in an embrace. "Watch out for Tucker," he said against her ear. "He's a dangerous man."

Releasing her abruptly, Gabriel turned and walked away. Sadie wasted no time catching up to him.

"You're not leaving me with that statement unexplained!"

He stopped short and regarded her with what appeared to be amusement. "That statement stands without explanation," he said as he took up his stride once more.

Sadie fell in beside him, ignoring the looks from well-dressed society folks who took umbrage to her brisk stride. "Gabriel, tell me how you know Mr. Tucker."

Still he kept walking. She picked up her skirts to hurry her pace as he hailed a cab.

"I'll have an answer."

Ignoring her, he stepped out into the street to

climb inside the hack. She reached the conveyance before the driver could pull away.

"Stay right there," she said to the driver, who
grinned in response. Then she looked at the man
inside. "Gabriel Trahan, you will *not* walk away
without telling me what you mean by your cryptic
warning. Do you understand?"

Her irritation had no effect on his calm expression. "I understand you're a woman, Sadie
Callum, and as such you do not always need
answers to your questions."

He called to the driver, and then, as the hack
pulled away from the curb, looked back at her.
"Let it go and take my advice. That is the only
answer you will get from me."

Twenty-two

The next morning, Sadie endured Mama's questions all the way back home to Callum Plantation
while barely managing to keep her eyes open.
She had waited for Jefferson Tucker to appear,
only to decide he likely had no idea where to find
her, either in New Orleans or River Pointe.

Sometime around dawn, she realized that while
the Tucker and Astor cases might be connected,
she would get nowhere trying to sort through the
details of both. Sadie decided that two days
hence she would offer up some plausible excuse

and slip away from Callum Plantation to follow the leads on the Astor case.

Surely Agent Russell could keep tabs on Mr. Tucker in her absence. And perhaps he could decipher the riddle Henry had presented regarding the Tucker brothers and their possible participation in the scheme.

Having no good plan for her exit in place had been the reason for choosing to wait two days. However, if Mama continued to pester her, the time line just might shorten.

By feigning sleep, Sadie had almost managed to derail her mother's inquisition, just as she had done last night. Almost, but not quite, for the moment she opened her eyes again, the questions would continue.

She envied Julia and Mama's maid, who were given the responsibility of riding back with the wagonload of furniture, crates of dresses, and other purchases Mama had made during her time away in the city. Though their pace might be slower, there would be no need to dodge unwanted questions.

Finally, Sadie had enough. "All right, Mama. You want to know why I chased Gabriel Trahan down the sidewalk in full view of anyone coming out of the ball and then dared to keep his carriage waiting when he tried to leave?"

"Yes, dear," she said sweetly. "I do wish to hear your explanation so that I might answer those who will surely be contacting me with their concerns."

Concerns? Gossip was the proper term, and yet Sadie knew she had thrown caution to the wind when she chose to behave as she had.

"I am a Pinkerton agent, and Gabriel has information I need for a case."

There. She said it.

"You know," Mama said slowly, "if you were going to make a statement like that, you could have done it last night."

Sadie's pulse throbbed against her temples, mimicking the plodding of the horses' hooves. "Well, I've done it now. Although I can see that I should not have made the attempt."

"There are several things you should not have done, Sarah Louise," Mama said with the icy tone she reserved for special occasions. "Telling me some tall tale about working for the Pinkerton Agency as something other than a secretary is far from the top of the list."

"Please spare me the list," she said wearily. "I am keenly aware that I took momentary leave of my senses."

"At least that is an explanation that makes sense. Perhaps I will mention as an excuse your recent travels and the difficulty in returning home due to all that terrible flooding."

"Whatever makes you happy, Mama."

"Not having to say anything in your defense

would make me happy," she said, her voice now almost as weary as Sadie's.

"Then don't."

"And let people speak ill of my daughter?" She shook her head. "Perish the thought. I love you far too much to allow it."

"And I love you too."

Sadie watched Mama closely. Her mother returned the favor. Together they sat in silence as the carriage rolled down the River Road, the windows open to allow in the crisp breeze.

"Pinkerton agent?" Mama shook her head, her attention shifting to focus somewhere outside the carriage. "Truly, Sadie. I know that little event made you fearful of men but . . ." She shrugged as if the ability to say anything further on the subject was beyond her ability.

"Little event?" Sadie thought back to the moment when she had most unwisely ignored parental wisdom to investigate a commotion in the woods outside Callum property lines. "Mama, a man was strung up and about to be killed. That is no little event. Someone had to speak up."

Even as she said the words, Sadie understood now what she did not perceive as a girl of just past eleven. Adults who spoke out risked harm beyond themselves, while children were not held to such liabilities.

"And you've been crusading for the underdog ever since. Why do you think your daddy let me talk him into sending you off to that nice boarding school and then later to study art in Chicago?"

When she realized Mama was waiting for an answer, Sadie let out a long breath. "You always said it was to wash the Louisiana mud off of me."

Mama chuckled, though there was no humor in it. "Daddy didn't want anything to happen to you. Me? I know bayou people are smart. None of those men were going to raise a hand to a Callum child."

Nor would any of them ever see a day in jail for their crimes. The injustice had plagued Sadie long after the image of what she saw had faded.

Mama looked across the confines of the carriage to meet her daughter's gaze. Her expression held the promise of a smile.

"Unfortunately, I set you off running and you haven't stopped yet."

"And I will be leaving again soon."

Her mother waved away the statement with a sweep of her hand. "Sadie, enough of that."

"Someday, when you look back on this conversation, you will realize that what I tried to tell you was true. Until now, I never thought about a connection between what I saw as a child and the path my life has taken."

Mama looked poised to speak and then must have thought better of it. Instead, she merely shook her head.

Sadie looked away, satisfied she had finally

found the courage to speak the truth to her mother. The fact that Mama didn't believe a word of it was something she had never considered. Exhaustion tugged at her until she finally succumbed to a deep sleep that lasted all the way until the carriage slowed to turn onto Callum Plantation.

"It looks as though we have company," Mama commented as they traveled slowly beneath the avenue of oaks leading to home. "I wonder whose carriage that is. It's certainly a fine one."

Giving the vehicle only a brief glance, Sadie climbed down the moment the wheels ceased to turn and then hurried up to her bedchamber, where she fell into bed. Some time later, she awoke to the growls of an empty stomach echoing in a darkened room.

Lighting a lamp, she ran a comb through a hairstyle that had been ruined by her nap and then set off down the back stairs to see what was left from the evening's meal. The kitchen was dark, but Sadie easily found a match and lit the tallow candle the cook left for emergencies.

The glow was sufficient to illuminate the room without drawing any unwanted attention. A few minutes later, Sadie wrapped a roast beef sandwich in brown paper and blew out the candle with the intention of slipping back upstairs to enjoy a quiet meal alone.

Laughter of a decidedly male variety derailed her plan and sent Sadie diving beneath the big wooden table with her sandwich tucked under her arm. Thank goodness Mama insisted the kitchen floors be clean enough to eat off of, for that was practically what she had resigned to do as Daddy spoke to whomever he was entertaining on the other side of the only door that offered any means of exit.

Eventually retreating footsteps echoed. Sadie waited until she was certain the hall was clear before going back up the stairs to her room.

Though she was certain she had left the lamp burning, the room was now dark. Instinct instantly had her reaching for her gun, and then she recalled where she was. Julia had most likely turned the bed down, readied the room for slumber, and then turned off the light when she departed.

Sadie's fingers reached across the expanse of space searching out the lamp. From across the room, a light blazed.

"Hello, Sadie," a familiar voice said from the center of the blinding illumination.

She blinked to adjust her eyes and still could not see the source. The voice she recognized immediately. "Mr. Tucker."

The light lowered just enough to make out a vague image of the man, who had situated himself in a chair by the window. Apparently Kyle had loaned the Tucker fellow one of his gadgets.

"Considering the fact I am sitting in your bed-chamber, I think we can dispense with the formalities. Call me Jefferson."

Sadie deposited the paper-wrapped sandwich on the table beside the door and then crossed her arms over her waist. "What are you doing in my bedchamber, *Jefferson?*"

"I told you I would find you." He nodded toward the table. "What's in the package? It smells like the same thing I had for dinner."

Shaking her head, she grabbed the sandwich and moved toward the window seat. Just to be certain, she searched his face to see that his eyes indeed were a shade of blue.

She opened the folded brown paper and revealed her sandwich. "I doubt your meal was better than this. Our cook makes the most delicious roast."

"She does," he said as he leaned back and smiled. "I especially like how she cooks the onions and carrots just enough to make them tender but not so much that they lose their crispness."

"How would you know that?"

"I asked. After I thanked your father for inviting me, of course." Jefferson nodded to her sandwich. "You haven't taken a bite yet. I highly recommend you do before I'm tempted."

Snatching up the sandwich, she tore it in two and offered him the larger piece. He waved it away.

"Are you certain?" she said as she lifted her portion to her mouth and took a bite.

"I am. Enjoy your snack."

"Supper. I slept through the meal and awoke hungry."

"That would explain why you did not come down." He studied her a moment. "Out late last night? I wondered about that Trahan fellow. He seemed to have an interest in you that went beyond a shared childhood friendship."

"About him." She paused to recall what Gabriel had said. "How do you know him?"

"Me? I don't know him."

"And yet you called him by name."

"I read his name on the dance card you showed me. If you recall, I stole his dance." He reached for the other half of the sandwich and took a bite. "Good earlier," he managed when he finished chewing. "Even better now."

His story made sense. But how, then, did Gabriel know Jefferson's name? She decided to ask.

"I have no idea. He specifically called me Jefferson Tucker?"

"Yes, I think so. Or did he?" She tried to recall. "No. He said Tucker."

Jefferson took another bite and appeared to be thinking. "Then it is likely he knows John. And you say this is someone from your childhood?"

She nodded.

"Interesting. Have you established a connection between him and my family?"

"None that I can determine. He grew up in River Pointe and went off to Tulane to study medicine."

He sat up a little straighter. "I would like to meet him."

"I'm sure my mother can arrange it."

He took another bite and chewed it before shaking his head. "No, I prefer to make those arrangements myself."

"All right." She paused. "How exactly did you come to know my parents well enough to wrangle an invitation to supper?"

"That's a great story, actually." He enjoyed another taste of the sandwich. "Your mother and I had plenty of time to chat at the soiree last night while you were dancing with half the eligible men in New Orleans."

She thought of what Mama must have said during the course of the evening. "I hope you don't believe anything she told you. She wants me married well and soon."

His smile told her it was very likely that Mama had said something to that effect. "I assure you she was most complimentary when discussing you."

"The better to see me wed, I believe I told you."

He laughed. "Yes, but what you haven't told me is how an extremely capable Pinkerton agent has a family who feels they must take care of her. It makes no sense."

"It makes perfect sense."

He paused to tap the side of his forehead with his index finger. "I cannot think of one good reason to keep this information from your family."

She set aside the remains of her sandwich. "About that. Just who was at dinner last night?"

"Your parents and your brother Ethan."

A thought occurred. "Only Ethan?"

"Yes. Why?" A look of understanding dawned. "Sadie, would those two fellows who paid me a visit in my hotel room back in Baton Rouge happen to be your brothers?"

"I'm afraid so." She fixed him with a look as she recalled the supper table conversation regarding the bruises Brent and Cade were sporting the same day she arrived home. "You didn't tell me you fought them, Jefferson."

"Because there was no fight. Just a little self-defense on my part." He shrugged. "Trust me, Sadie. They didn't get much chance to defend themselves."

"Oh?"

"Perhaps you recall how I reacted when you surprised me in the carriage."

"Yes . . . I see your point."

"As to your brothers, men who have some-thing to hide are usually more eager to listen to a proposition that keeps them out of trouble."

She gave the matter a moment's thought. Neither of her brothers cared much for getting in trouble with Daddy, although they might care that Mama's part in the escapade was revealed. "Do what you must, then."

"I plan to. And your father?" He tilted his head

as if recalling a particularly pleasant memory. "Apparently your mother had already spoken highly of me, so he was well prepared to like me."

Sadie shook her head. "So you've won over both my parents. And how did you manage that?"

"By telling them I am in need of a wife."

Laughter bubbled up. "No, the truth. What did you tell them? As a student of human nature, I'm always looking for the best ways to guide subjects toward a specific outcome."

His expression sobered. "That is what I told them, Sadie. Actually, I did tell them a little more than that, but I was careful to let the conversation naturally flow in that direction."

"What direction?"

"As a student of human nature, I'm sure you understand that information freely given is suspect, but information that the subject—or in this case, subjects—feel as if they are prying out of by way of confession is the information most believed."

She leaned forward, her heartbeat throbbing at her temples. "*What* else did you tell them?"

"That my first acquaintance with you was both memorable and impossible to forget."

"Those two things mean the same, Jefferson."

He chuckled. "In the strictest sense, I suppose so. However, neither your mother nor your father pointed that out."

"What other information did they pry out of you?"

Twenty-three

Sadie was obviously riled up and ready for battle. Jefferson decided he would avoid telling her the details of his lengthy conversation with Seamus Callum and his wife.

Just how he would avoid this remained to be seen. And yet she would likely not take well to the fact that not only had he gained the favor of both Callums and their youngest son, but he had also secured permission to court Sadie.

It was all a means to an end, and yet Jefferson allowed himself to feel just the slightest bit of enthusiasm at pretending to be the pretty blonde's beau. He would do it all up right, if he could recall just how to make a fuss over a woman. It had been far too long since he'd spent time paying a call on a lady.

But then he'd realized that the first time he laid eyes on Sadie. Their fall in the carriage had reinforced the knowledge.

And then came the kiss.

Kisses, he corrected, for the second one had been all his to initiate.

And their evening under the stars.

"Jefferson."

He swung his gaze to collide with hers. "Yes, dear?"

"Truly you are insufferable. What possessed you to ingratiate yourself to my family?"

Time to come clean with at least part of the plan. "The better to steal you away when the right moment comes."

"I don't follow."

He paused to consider how to best gain her trust. "You and I have cases that may very well be connected."

"You have no idea what case I am working on."

He had not expected that comment, although he had to give her credit for the casual way she offered her response. The only thing to do was bluff.

"Your case involves a dealer in arts and antiquities named Valletta."

There. The way she blinked. Tried to hide her surprise. This girl was good, but he was better.

"You haven't said anything in response, Sadie."

She continued to stare.

"No matter. I want Valletta and so do the Pinkertons. We can work together to achieve this or I can do it alone. However, if I do it alone, you may not get your chance at him."

"Is that a threat?"

"No. It's a promise."

"I am not yet confirming or denying your supposition." Sadie shifted positions. "However, theoretically, what do you propose?"

"I propose that we help one another to determine just what Valletta is up to, and in exchange both cases are brought to a satisfactory resolution."

"For argument's sake, I will ask how you think this will be accomplished."

Jefferson suppressed a smile. He understood her reservations. He also knew she would accept his terms. She had to.

"We work together, as I said, sharing sources and forming a team to bring Valletta and his associates down." He sensed her next question. "And no, I do not know why you want him or what he has done to make the Pinkertons find cause to investigate. What I do know is that he's been a source of irritation for me and the British Museum for a very long time."

At the mention of the British Museum, her eyes widened. Only for a moment, he noted, and yet impossible for him to miss.

Her recovery was swift, as was her rebuttal. "You assume I am investigating this man because you saw me reading an article about him."

So she recalled that. He allowed a smile. "In a newspaper that was four months old."

Sadie rose, her sandwich obviously forgotten. As she moved toward the other side of the room, Jefferson wondered if she might be heading for the door. When she turned to retrace her steps across the carpet, he feigned indifference.

The lovely blonde stopped in front of him and

crossed her arms over her tiny waist. If the effort and the expression she affected were intended to make her look stern, she failed miserably.

"I suppose you believe that gaining my parents' trust will convince them to allow me to leave with you."

"Much as I am enjoying my visit—and your cook has promised a tasty ham for supper tomorrow night, by the way—I cannot solve my case from the comfort of Callum Plantation."

She was looking out the window now, but he resisted the urge to follow the direction of her gaze. "If you're thinking my father will let me climb into a carriage and leave with you, I assure you that will not happen."

He leaned back to watch her as she settled once more on the window seat and returned her attention to him. "It will."

Color rose in those pretty cheeks. Oh, but she was lovely when she was angry.

"Explain yourself, then."

"They want you wed." He shrugged. "So I will marry you. A honeymoon is a wonderful time to travel. I thought we would start with a trip to Newport."

Again he noted her brief look of surprise. So Newport was the location where she would be doing her investigating. It had been a guess based on the season and the fact that New York's elite— most of whom outdid one another regularly with purchases of art and artifacts—gathered there this time of year.

Her laughter once again filled the room. "That is the most ridiculous thing I've heard in a very long time. And believe me, I've heard some ridiculous things lately."

Jefferson held his ground. "It can work, and it will."

"It cannot work if I refuse to go through with it." A door closed somewhere down the hall, and she jumped. "And I will not lie to my parents," she said in a much softer but no less insistent voice.

"I am not asking you to lie, Sadie," he said gently. "In fact, I am not even asking you to play along beyond the obvious request that you not mention my plan to anyone."

Someone knocked, and once again she jumped. She exchanged a worried glance with him and then rose to walk toward the door. He sat very still. If he were to be caught in Sadie's bedchamber, it would not bode well for her. It would, however, hasten the next part of his plan.

"Yes?" she said, one hand on the knob as she softly turned the skeleton key to lock them inside.

"It's Julia, miss. I'm wondering if you'll be needing anything further tonight."

Jefferson relaxed and thought about what he had learned recently regarding an Irish lass with lovely red hair and a fresh heartbreak, courtesy of a rogue whose reputation with the ladies had him fleeing New Orleans some time ago. It was amazing how much the hired help were willing to tell a man the boss trusted. Even more amazing was the depth of the hired help's knowledge.

But then he'd long ago learned to go to the source, to those who were in a position to see and be trusted. They were the ones who generally had the most information. And that information was much more likely to be true than anything he would get from other sources.

Jefferson grinned and then reached for the sandwich he'd set aside. Indeed, the Callum cook did make a fine roast.

Had there not been a pressing case to solve and his reputation to regain, Jefferson might have considered prolonging his time at Callum Plantation at least until he tired of the food and the company. And that could have made for a lengthy visit.

"No, Julia. Thank you, but I'm fine," Sadie said through the closed door.

"And your breakfast tomorrow?" the girl continued from the other side of the door. "Will you want a tray brought up?"

Jefferson nodded, hoping she would think he wished her to avoid the dining room at breakfast time tomorrow.

"That won't be necessary. I believe I'll dine downstairs. Good night now."

She turned back toward him with a triumphant expression.

He smiled, happy he was the one who got what he wanted. He might be rusty after almost a year behind bars, but he still had the skills. Soon he would be convincing his superiors at Scotland Yard of this fact as well. But first he must complete this part of the plan.

"Well, then," he said as he rose. "I suppose I'll leave you for now. Please wear something pretty to breakfast. I do like you in blue."

"Of all the nerve." When she saw he intended to walk out her door, she hurried to stand between him and the exit.

"Can't bear to see me leave?" he asked as he extinguished Kyle's personal lantern, plunging the room into darkness.

"Hardly, but I cannot bear the thought of being caught having a man leave my bedchamber. So wait here." Sadie opened the door, peered out, and then closed it once more. "All right. The hall is empty. Hurry and go."

When Jefferson had successfully slipped into a room at the far end of the hall, Sadie closed her door and sagged against it. What in the world was she going to do?

Her attempt at telling Mama about her employment as a Pinkerton agent might have failed miserably, but she had no doubt that Daddy would have believed her. He already believed Uncle Penn was a spy. Why wouldn't he think the same of her since she regularly kept company with her uncle?

She let out a long breath, reached over to light the lamp, and then moved toward the wardrobe, where Julia had hung a nightgown on a peg for her. Telling Daddy was something she should have done four years ago when she came home the first time after agreeing to a job in Pinkerton's Chicago office.

Though she arrived on the doorstep of the downtown office building with the intention of applying for a secretarial position that would justify her desire to remain in Chicago instead of returning to Louisiana, Mr. Pinkerton had other ideas.

Indeed, her skills with a revolver and her ability to blend in with society types had made her just the candidate the agency had been seeking for a troublesome case. On Sadie's part, she decided to accept the position, but only as a lark and just until the one case was solved.

What began as a lark became something much bigger. Much more. She found she was good—very good—at performing the duties of a Pinkerton agent. While she had been adept in her studies of the history of art and slightly less talented at the actual execution of art pieces, her abilities as an operative for the agency were stellar.

Upon the successful conclusion of the case, Mr.

Pinkerton offered her a raise and a promotion to field agent. While a few of the men groused, none who worked with her ever complained.

In fact, the only persons who thought her ill prepared for the duties she was required to perform were the ones who loved her the most: her family. And that was her own fault, Sadie mused as she hung her skirt and shirtwaist on the peg and slipped the nightgown over her head.

As she had told Jefferson, it was much simpler for her parents and brothers to remain ignorant of the fact rather than suffer their worries and concerns. Or at least it had been simpler until the boys began arriving unannounced and in hopes of shadowing her to keep her safe.

Snatching up her valise from its hiding place under the window seat, Sadie climbed into bed and spread the facts of the Astor case out in front of her. Every document that mentioned Sergio Valletta went into a separate stack that she gathered up and began to read.

Though she had gone over every line of these pages, she had not looked at the facts in light of the new evidence Jefferson had provided. Somewhere in all of this were the clues that would explain why art and antiquities dealer Sergio Valletta had cried wolf when a wooden mummy case had gone missing from his Royal Street shop four months ago.

The robbery had indeed made the papers, both

in New Orleans and across the country, but police had found nothing to substantiate the crime. But then a crime is difficult to commit when the victim refuses to allow the police to study the scene for clues.

Sadie leaned back against the pillows and smiled. New Orleans police might not have been allowed in, but she would be. The only question was which of several plans to choose.

Twenty-four

Jefferson arrived at the breakfast table to find five curious Callum males awaiting his arrival along with the pretty Pinkerton agent. Two paled immediately as he found his place between Sadie and Ethan. He offered his soon-to-be-wife a smile she promptly ignored.

"There's the man of the hour," Ethan said as he clapped a hand on Jefferson's shoulder. "I trust you slept well and are ready to walk the property with me as promised."

"Walk the property?" Aaron echoed. "Whose idea was this?"

"Mine," Ethan responded. "And if you recall, my vote has just as much value as yours around here."

Aaron offered an inelegant snort at the statement and said nothing further. Meanwhile, the two

Jefferson had learned were Brent and Cade sat in stony silence. Though they were likely plotting a conversation with him later, apparently the pair was in no hurry to admit they had made his acquaintance on a prior occasion.

Only the other brother, a lanky fellow named Donovan, seemed oblivious to the tension swirling over platters of pancakes, bacon, and butter-milk biscuits that served as a dividing line on the table. And yet he kept what Jefferson decided was the closest watch of all on him.

Though the Callum males varied in coloring between the swarthy tones and inky hair of Mrs. Callum and the fair complexion and fair hair of Seamus, they all had one characteristic in common. They were protective of their baby sister. He would have to be careful how he navigated the treacherous waters of his pretend courtship with Sadie. One false move, and any or all of the men at this table would make short work of pounding him to a pulp.

"How exactly do you know this man, Sadie?" Aaron asked.

"He and Sadie met on a train traveling to New Orleans," Ethan offered. "Jefferson was heading to Mobile to visit his grandmother, and Sadie was on her way back here. It was love at first sight."

Sadie appeared ready to protest and then must have thought better of it. Instead, she shook her head and gave all of her attention to the spoon that swirled sugar into her tea.

"And yet our Sadie hasn't mentioned a thing about him," Aaron said. "Nor has she answered my question."

"There is no need to repeat what Ethan has just told you," she said, her voice as cool and calm as if she were discussing the weather or the latest hat she'd purchased.

Aaron, however, appeared ready to jump from his seat and demand Jefferson leave immediately. "Then perhaps you can tell us why a woman in love thought it just fine to take a stroll after supper with Gabriel Trahan?"

"The supper that our mother arranged?" Ethan turned to Donovan. "Remember how I warned her that Mama was up to matchmaking?"

Donovan's nod was barely perceptible. Still, he continued to stare at Jefferson, his expression bland but with a look in his eyes that Jefferson recognized as quietly lethal.

Sadie stood, her palms on the table as she addressed the now-quiet Callums. "Since every last one of you was watching us, did any of you see anything that appeared to suggest a romance between Gabriel and me?"

None of them responded, although Jefferson detected the slightest bit of humor on Ethan's face.

"That's right," she said. "There was none. Nor do I claim any such feelings for this man."

"Sadie darling," Jefferson hurried to say. "Truly it is fine that you stop pretending. The truth is out now."

"The truth?" Her laugh held no humor. "Isn't that just perfect? I could stand here and tell you the truth all day, but no one will believe me."

"I believe you," Ethan said.

"You don't," Sadie protested, "else you wouldn't be repeating what Mr. Tucker has told you. Now, if anyone else wishes to discuss my personal life, I would ask that you wait until I have left the room. I am tired of hearing what Sadie needs to do and who Sadie ought to be seen with. Do any of you realize I am a grown woman who has long ago earned the right to—"

Applause from the doorway interrupted her rant. She turned toward the noise, as did Jefferson. Seamus's broad grin sent Sadie quietly back into her chair.

"That was a nice speech, Sarah Louise," Seamus said as he took his place at the head of the table. "What think you, Mr. Tucker, of our girl's opinionated ways?"

"I applaud her ability to tame her brothers, and I expect she will be performing the same feat on me once we are . . ."

Something sharp jabbed him mid-thigh. Jefferson looked down to see Sadie's fork poised to poke him again.

"Something wrong there, Tucker?" Seamus

asked as he tied an embroidered napkin around his neck and gestured to the platter of biscuits just out of reach. "Please pass those my way, Cade. Now, Ethan, you may continue your plea for the mechanized equipment you think we need to purchase."

"We need no such thing," Aaron said. "There's nothing wrong with the way we have been processing sugarcane for the past fifteen years."

"And yet there is always a need to consider new and better ways, son, if they exist. The floor is yours, Ethan. Make your case while I enjoy my breakfast, and then, Aaron, I will hear your thoughts once I've considered Ethan's proposal."

Tensions diffused, Jefferson returned his attention to the plate in front of him, though his gaze covertly studied Sadie's father. He leaned toward Sadie, who had yet to remove her fork from close proximity to his thigh.

"While they are speaking of proposals, should I add my own?"

"No!"

Ethan stopped talking to look past Jefferson at Sadie. "Do you have an opinion on mechanization too?"

Her smile was weak, wavering, but the tines of the fork pressed hard against his leg. "Actually, I was speaking to Jefferson . . . that is, Mr. Tucker. Do go back to your speech, Ethan. As Daddy would say, it is nice."

She winked and Ethan did the same before returning to his discussion. Jefferson smiled at Sadie and then once again moved close enough for her to hear his whisper.

"Poke me again with that fork, and I'll drop down on one knee right here and propose marriage to you in front of your father and brothers."

Sadie's gaze collided with his. "You wouldn't dare."

He barely blinked. "Try me."

A moment passed and then she returned the fork to the table. Dabbing the napkin against her mouth, Sadie dropped it beside her plate and stood. "If you'll excuse me, it's time I went on with my day."

Ethan and her father barely noticed her, although the other four brothers looked up sharply. Jefferson took note of their expressions and found they all appeared concerned.

"Something wrong, Sadie?" Donovan asked. "You never miss a chance to have biscuits and honey. I brought in that honeycomb just yesterday, so it's fresh and tasty."

"I'm sure it is, but I'm not hungry. Perhaps later."

And then she hurried from the room, leaving Jefferson with a decision to make. "I'll just go and see to her," he said before following after her.

He caught up with her on the stairs and reached out to grasp her wrist. "Want me to go and get a biscuit and wrap it in paper? I can bring it up to your room. Or I'll get two and we can split it like we split that roast beef sandwich last night."

He meant it as a joke. As something to lighten the mood. However, her expression of horror told him the teasing had backfired.

Slowly he glanced over his shoulder to see that Brent and Cade Callum were watching their exchange with great interest. "Hello, boys," Jefferson said. "May I have a word with you?"

"That's funny," Cade said. "I was about to ask you the same thing."

Jefferson glanced back at Sadie. Did she hope her brothers would give him what for? Her expression told him yes.

He turned to take the stairs two at a time and then pressed past the Callum brothers. "This way, gentlemen," he said as he stepped out the front doors into the morning sunshine and then waited for them to follow.

Pasting on a look meant to indicate he found the situation irritating at best, Jefferson turned to face the second and third sons of Seamus Callum. Though his fists were ready, he prayed his words would strike the first blow.

Cade came at him first, his posture threatening action. Brent stepped between them and regarded Jefferson calmly. "Start talking, Tucker."

Fear was what they sought, but the idea he might be worried about these two doing him harm was laughable. Instead, he stood his ground, his shoulders square and his backbone firmly in place.

"I heard you were cozy with Mama and Daddy at supper last night," Cade said. "But do they know about Baton Rouge?"

"Baton Rouge?" He lifted a brow and tried not to laugh. "The way I recall things, you two were in danger of ending up in jail until I decided to show you some leniency and let you leave town quietly." His gaze landed squarely on Brent. "Does your father know about that?"

"He has a point," Brent said to Cade.

"But he was there in the place Mama said . . ." He closed his mouth and shook his head. "He was where Sadie was supposed to be."

Interesting. So Sadie's mother was somehow apprised of her location. The quiet and doting Mrs. Callum certainly had another side to her, one he hoped he would not run afoul of.

Brent seemed to consider his brother's statement a moment. "Why were you in Baton Rouge, Tucker?"

"Same reason you were. To catch a train."

"Where you met my sister?" Brent offered.

"Actually, yes."

"I knew it." Cade nudged past Brent. "If you've compromised her, I'll see that you pay."

The door opened again and Seamus stepped outside with Ethan and Aaron on his heels. "If Mr. Tucker here has compromised your sister, I will be the one to see that he pays."

The Callum boys moved aside to allow their father to step closer to Jefferson. "You understand my meaning, son?"

Seamus Callum was a big man, although no bigger than he. Yet this was a man defending his daughter, which made him dangerous beyond his years.

"I have nothing but the best intentions toward Sadie. In fact, I'd like to talk to you about those intentions, sir."

"No time like the present." Seamus nodded to Aaron. "Go with your brother and listen to what he has to say. I'll be out there directly."

"But I—"

"Aaron, a man who can't hear another opinion is one who might need to find another line of work."

"Yes, sir. Come on, kid. Educate me on the improvements you think we need to make."

Aaron glanced over at Seamus with a see-I-can-cooperate look and then fell into step beside Ethan. Meanwhile, Brent and Cade continued to watch Jefferson closely.

"You got somewhere else to be, or maybe you want to stay here and explain to me what you were doing in Baton Rouge?" Seamus asked them.

The pair hurried off in two different directions, although Jefferson figured the conversation about Baton Rouge was not yet finished.

"Having trouble with those two?" Seamus asked.

"No trouble at all, sir. Now, about Sadie—"

"Walk with me, son, else my wife and daughter and likely half the household staff will be listening to what you say."

Jefferson glanced around and thought he saw a swirl of skirts disappear from one of the front windows. Likewise, a door closed somewhere inside.

Seamus chuckled as he stepped off the porch and headed off down the avenue of oak trees that led away from the house. Hurrying to follow suit, Jefferson matched the older man's pace.

"Nice place you have here, Mr. Callum."

"I reckon it'll do," Seamus said, with more than a little pride in his voice. "Mary thinks it's time we parcel out pieces to give to the boys so they'll settle down. I think they're going to do what they're going to do, and no piece of land is going to cause them to do it any faster."

Jefferson listened to the man as he spoke of home and family. Of what he wished for his children, how he intended to help them, and what he wouldn't do.

And as the Callum patriarch spoke, Jefferson began to realize just what family meant to this father of six. Suddenly his plan to steal away

Seamus's daughter under false pretenses did not seem so brilliant after all.

In fact, it felt like the lie it was.

Seamus stopped short and crossed his arms over the broad expanse of his chest. "All right. Talk to me, son."

There it was. His chance. And the words refused to come. The lie stuck in his throat, lodged there by his own sense of what was right and what was very, very wrong.

"Cat got your tongue?" Seamus chuckled. "How about I help you? You like my Sadie, don't you?"

He did, so Jefferson felt fine in nodding.

"And she's someone you would like to spend more time with?"

Again he nodded, as the statement was true. Beyond her abilities as a Pinkerton agent, he found he enjoyed spending time with her.

"I think I know what you're trying to say then."

"You do?" he managed.

" 'Course I do. I was young once." He turned to face back in the direction of the house, both hands on his hips as he seemed to survey the monument to his success as a sugarcane planter and refiner.

"Her brothers don't seem to care for you much, excepting Ethan. But they mostly don't like any-one who comes too close to their sister." He paused to glance in Jefferson's direction. "You hurt one of us, you hurt us all. You understand that, son?"

"I do, sir."

"I'll admit I was skeptical when my wife invited you to supper. If Kyle Russell hadn't vouched for you, I guarantee you wouldn't have stepped foot on Callum property if you were looking to cozy up to my daughter."

Kyle had spoken to him? Interesting.

"I do understand, sir, and I appreciate your care of your family."

Seamus shrugged. "I have a sister in Mobile. A brother-in-law too, but I don't trust him farther than I can throw him. Don't suppose you've met Penn Monroe yet. He's made himself scarce lately, although usually not at mealtimes. He's probably up to his usual tricks."

Jefferson listened while the elder Callum expounded on the topic of family relations. He, too, had a family member he did not trust, but unlike Seamus, he wouldn't be making mention of John today.

Sadie stepped out onto the upstairs porch and seemed to be watching them. She hadn't worn a blue dress, but he'd figured she wouldn't do as he asked. Still, he had to test her to see how best to manage her.

"You haven't asked, so I'm not offering," Seamus said as he nodded toward the house and, presumably, Sadie. "The question is, do you plan to ask?"

"Sir," Jefferson said slowly, "I came here planning to ask."

The planter turned back toward him and shaded his eyes with his hand. "And?"

He hesitated only a second before looking back in Sadie's direction. "And I still think it's a good plan."

Twenty-five

With her brothers scattered to the four corners of the property and Daddy busy with Jefferson Tucker, Sadie decided now was the best time to manage a visit to the city. Slipping down the back staircase, she hurried to the carriage house. She followed the sound of snoring until she found one of the drivers sound asleep in the tack room.

Clearing her throat produced no result, so she stepped back outside and knocked loudly. Snoring quickly became snorting, and then the driver stumbled out.

His eyes widened when he saw her waiting. "I do apologize, Miss Callum. I didn't hear you come in."

"No, I suppose you wouldn't, what with the fact you were sleeping." She paused to allow that statement to sink in before adding, "And loudly."

His face flushed bright red. "Yes. Well, about that. You see, I worked hard to get the carriage in good order, and then when I finished, well, I . . ."

"You took a brief rest?"

"Yes," he said sheepishly. "That would be about the size of it."

Sadie glanced around and saw that the two of them were alone. "I don't suppose there's any harm in a brief rest. Jack, isn't it?"

"Jack Barnes. And thank you for understanding, Miss Callum."

"It's quite all right." She paused and leaned slightly forward. "Rest assured I will not tell Daddy. Oh, but there is just one little thing."

"Yes, miss?"

"I am in need of the carriage," she said with as much confidence as she could manage. "And you, of course. There is an errand I must see to in the city."

"An errand, Miss Callum? Will any of the family be joining you?"

Sadie thought a moment. As much as the driver might be chastised for not remaining awake during working hours, they both knew he would catch much more trouble from Daddy should he even consider taking Sadie into the city alone. It simply wasn't done. Ever.

"Actually, if you could send one of the stable boys for my maid, Julia, I would be much obliged."

"Julia." He nodded. "Yes, Miss Callum. Right away."

"Oh, and would you be a dear and not mention my errand to anyone in the house?"

Jack turned to offer her a confused look. "Not mention your errand?" He shook his head. "I don't follow, Miss Callum. Are you asking me to hide your errand from your father?"

Goodness, but he was being stuffy. "No, of course not," she hurried to say. "What I meant is I am in a bit of a rush and, well, Daddy did say he would be busy with Ethan and Aaron this morning, so I do not wish to interrupt them."

"Yes, miss And your mother?"

"She is a very busy woman, although I'm sure if you were to mention our plans to go into the city, she would think nothing of having you take her on her visiting rounds again. You do enjoy taking Mama visiting, don't you, Jack?"

"I'll just send the stable boy after Julia, miss."

When his footsteps echoed on the steps outside, Sadie let out a long breath. Why was it that she could face any number of fearsome threats without blinking an eye, only to return home to River Pointe and then find herself cowering in a carriage house in hopes of finding a way into the city? And being afraid she might fail?

He returned a few minutes later. "The girl is on her way. Where is it you would like to be taken?"

She gave him the address.

"So this is a shopping trip." His expression showed relief. "Why didn't you say so? I confess I was concerned, but now . . ." He shook his head. "Surely there will be no repercussions for taking you and your maid shopping."

Ignoring that statement, Sadie squared her shoulders and marched toward the carriage. Perhaps it would be better to have a second person along for her mission and not just her reputation. She could make good use of the maid, now that she thought of it.

Julia climbed in a few minutes later and then the carriage jolted forward. When they successfully reached the River Road, Sadie sat back and let out a long breath.

To the maid's credit, she sat quietly without asking any questions. Nor did she seem the least bit worried about what her duties might entail. Rather, she maintained a discreet demeanor and an alert presence.

"I'm doing a bit of shopping today," Sadie said. "I have an interest in antiquities, and there's a place in town I very much want to visit."

Sadie paused to allow her gaze to sweep the length of her companion. Though Julia's garments were serviceable, no one would believe her to be anything more than a maid. That must be remedied.

Thus their first stop was to Madame Theriot's dress shop for something more suitable. "Oh, miss, I don't know," Julia said when Sadie ushered her inside and insisted she choose an appropriate gown for the day's adventure.

"I believe any of these would look just right on your friend," Madame Theriot said as she held out several day dresses for Sadie's inspection.

"Try those on," she told Julia.

"Yes, miss," the maid said, although there was precious little enthusiasm in her voice.

Julia stepped out of the dressing room in a lovely emerald green ensemble that elevated her from maid to mademoiselle. "Perfect," Sadie told Madame Theriot.

"Wonderful," the dressmaker said. "Shall I wrap your purchase?"

Sadie opened her reticule to retrieve payment for the garment and then shook her head. "No, she will be wearing the dress." She glanced around before returning her attention to Madame Theriot. "I wonder if you would have something to put her dress in. The one she wore into your shop, that is?"

A moment later, they left with Julia's maid's garments neatly folded in a modest and incongruous carpetbag. Sadie placed the bag on the floor of the carriage and then allowed Jack to help her inside.

"I feel like Cinderella," Julia said as she joined Sadie, patting her new hat with gloved hands. "I do believe I am going to like working for you, Miss Callum."

"That's another thing, Julia. While we are going about our shopping today, I will need you to call me Sarah."

"Sarah?" She shook her head. "Forgive me, Miss Callum, but I couldn't possibly. It would be too familiar and most disrespectful."

Sadie fixed the girl with an even look. "Any disrespect will come from your refusal of a direct order. I thought we had an agreement, Julia, that you would do as you are told at all times without questioning the reason or the propriety of the command. I would have you practice that now, please."

She was stern, but necessarily so. If Julia were to be used as an assistant in investigations, she must first learn how to follow orders. There was no other option.

"Yes, Miss . . ." Again she shook her head as she diverted her eyes to study the carriage floor between them. "Yes, Sarah."

"All right, now look at me." When Julia complied, she continued. "Your assignment will be quite straightforward. When we reach the antiquities shop, I will require you to accompany me inside and act the part of a companion rather than a maid. You will pretend interest in some of the items but be very careful not to speak unless I ask a question or give you an order. Do you understand?"

"Yes."

The carriage turned onto Royal Street and then rolled to a stop midway down the block. Sadie took note of the green awning and the window beneath. Elegant gold letters proclaimed the establishment to be Monsieur Valletta's Antiquities and Curiosities.

Once Jack had assisted both of them to the wooden sidewalk that spanned the distance between the street and the building's edge, Sadie paused to give her maid one more assessing look.

"No questions?"

"Just one. What if someone speaks to me first?"

"Then respond briefly and with as little inflection in your voice as possible."

"So don't let on that I'm not a native of New Orleans?"

"Exactly. I wish our visit here to be as forgettable as possible to Monsieur Valletta. If there's nothing else, then follow me."

"Nothing at all," Julia said with a weak smile.

The door opened with a melodic tinkle of bells. The sound brought a short man of stout stature hurrying into the salon.

"Welcome, ladies," he said, presumably taking note of the carriage and uniformed driver waiting outside. "Please enjoy the treasures and delights I have to offer in my humble establishment."

The "humble establishment" was stuffed with antiquities of all sorts, none of which appeared to have any resemblance to objects that could be called humble. Rather, a rich assortment of items from all parts of the world had somehow been gathered to form a tableau that was at once pleasing to the eye and yet chaotic at best.

The little man inched closer, and Sadie took note of his height, weight, and eye color. She would pencil these details into her notebook later, but for now she committed them to memory along with the curious jacket of purple velvet that he wore and the odd Turkish trousers and slippers that completed his ensemble.

"Are you ladies looking for something in particular?" His attention rested on Julia, who, to her credit, did not respond.

A half-opened packing crate situated behind a table caught Sadie's attention, and she moved toward it. Cedar shavings had spilled from the crate and were scattered about on the polished wooden floor, the only sign of poor housekeeping in the room.

Just as she was about to reach for the curious carved object, an artist's sculpture of an elongated cat that looked for all the world like a mummy case, the proprietor stepped in to slide the box out of her reach with one slippered foot.

"That item is not for sale. However, I do have some lovely pieces depicting felines over here. Perhaps you would like to see them?"

"Actually, I am curious. Your piece there looks

exactly like something I have been searching for."

Color rose on his ample cheeks. Despite the cool temperature in the room, he reached for a handkerchief to dab at his forehead.

"It is Egyptian, isn't it?" Sadie put on her best smile and offered it to the shopkeeper. "Perhaps you would allow me to see it?"

"Oh, I couldn't possibly."

She reached to touch his sleeve, running her finger across the purple velvet as she looked into his eyes. "I am somewhat of a collector. Just allowing me to see the piece would mean so much." Again her finger traced the edge of his sleeve. "So very much."

He cut his eyes toward Julia, who appeared to be interested in a particularly gaudy Second Empire lamp, and then back in Sadie's direction.

"She's with you? And she can be trusted?" At Sadie's nod, he continued. "Perhaps I could allow just a little peek, but only if you promise not to tell Monsieur Valletta that I allowed it."

So this was not the proprietor. *Interesting.*

"Of course. My friend and I are quite circumspect and trustworthy."

Julia nodded on cue and then went back to her inspection of the lamp. Sadie returned her attention to the oddly dressed man. "You may call me Sarah," she said with the tone of a woman seeking a confidence. "And you are?"

"I am a man who knows what's good for him,

and so I must ask for your promise that my employer, Monsieur Valletta, will never hear of this."

Any man not forthcoming of his name had more than just an appellation to hide. Sadie proceeded with caution.

"You have my word," she said. "But I must inquire as to whether he is here in the building. For if I need to speak to him regarding any purchases I wish to make, I will."

"He is not. He is a busy man, what with his travels far and wide to gain the world's treasures for his shop."

"I see. And yet if I were to offer a sufficient amount, an amount that might cause the monsieur to consider selling . . ."

Interest etched his features. Sadie had to suppress a smile. Once she had the financial aspect of an arrangement decided, all else generally fell into place.

"I never know when he will return. And I assure you that any purchases you might wish to make will be negotiated with me at a much lower price than he would give you."

She nodded toward the box. "Then perhaps we should hurry."

"Yes, of course, although as you recall, I have said that Monsieur Valletta has indicated this item is not for sale."

So he was greedy as well. All the better to

manipulate him into showing her exactly what she wanted to see.

"And I also recall that you have said I might negotiate with you. Or perhaps Julia and I should go elsewhere?"

The man's grin rose quickly. "No need for that, my dear. Indeed, I did say negotiation is possible."

He shuffled over to retrieve the crate and then beckoned them to follow as he disappeared behind crimson curtains bedecked in all manner of fringe and crystal ornamentation.

Sadie moved in close as the mummy case was lifted from the crate. Approximately thirty inches in length and half that in width, the item was either an excellent representation of a mummy case or a decent forgery.

"May I?"

After giving the question a moment's consideration, he handed the rare item to Sadie. It was heavy but not overly so, and the wooden carvings on the top and sides confirmed her theory. With a slight shake of the box, she knew it had to hold the bones of the cat in whose honor the burial box had been created.

Authenticity was obvious in the markings and style of the piece. She gave the item another cursory glance and then handed it back to the odd fellow.

"This is a very good specimen. I'm quite interested. So I wonder . . ." She looked around, taking note of the back office, the exit to the courtyard, and the staircase that led up to what appeared to be a second-floor room. "What else does the monsieur have that might be of interest to me?"

"Mademoiselle, I have no idea what you mean." He looked to Julia. "Perhaps you might enlighten me."

Julia merely smiled and then shook her head.

"Ah. Well, then, I shall ask you for a clarification, Sarah." He carefully replaced the feline antiquity in the crate and then returned the lid to its place atop the box. "What exactly is your budget for these as yet unnamed items?"

So they had moved to speaking of price. Always a good sign.

"Budget? Whatever is that? I certainly am not familiar with the idea of worrying about cost. Are you, sir?"

"Only when it involves explaining to Monsieur Valletta why I took a customer up to his private apartment."

The private apartment where the theft had been reported. Where police had been unable to gain access.

Again Sadie reached out to touch the man's sleeve, the same gesture of familiarity that had worked to gain his confidence before. This time, it brought a smile along with a conspiratorial wink.

"You like cats?" He shrugged. "Perhaps I have another such item to show you."

Cats? *Oh, please.* And yet she allowed nothing but enthusiasm to show on her face.

"Please lead the way, sir," she said as she followed him across the narrow length of the office area toward the staircase. "Although I would admit that it is less the feline nature of the antiquity that draws my interest and more the rarity of the item itself."

He stopped short, and Sadie had to catch herself else she would have run into him. "So you are more interested in items that are rare than in any specific type of collection?"

"Exactly." She paused and then decided on a bold move. "My friend Mrs. Astor has told me such wonderful things about the Rembrandt she recently purchased, and so I wonder if ="

"Mrs. Astor?" His dark brows rose. "Why did you not say you were acquainted with such fine folks? Did she purchase this item from us?"

"As I said," Sadie offered demurely, "Julia and I are circumspect and trustworthy. I certainly would not mention names such as dear Mrs. Astor's were I not so inclined. And I do not know yet where her piece was purchased, although I expect I can find that out when I see her again very soon."

The man nodded like a fool. An eager fool.

"Yes, yes, of course. Follow me, then. I think I

have a few things you will be most interested in."

He gestured toward the stairs. "Remember, lest you draw my employer's wrath, you are not to mention what you are about to see."

Sadie stalled. "I do not understand. Why would your employer be upset if he were to profit from my visit?"

His eyes narrowed. "I have made no mention of him profiting, have I?"

"So you've nothing here for sale?"

"Monsieur Valletta is a very private man." He nodded up the stairs toward the apartment. "But that is not to say a deal cannot be made. A circumspect arrangement with a person who is trustworthy."

"I see."

She did. Given the current offer being made, it was well and truly possible that Monsieur Valletta could indeed have been the victim of theft.

Sadie glanced over at Julia. The maid was watching intently and playing her part as companion quite well. Sadie offered a nod of appreciation and then returned her attention to the man who beckoned her up the stairs.

Motioning for Julia to follow, Sadie stepped carefully up the narrow staircase and into the doorway of a room that was dark and smelled of mold and camphor.

"Just give me a moment and I will light a lamp. The monsieur, he does keep things—"

A crash and a thud and then silence. Sadie called out to him, but no response came. She stepped back to speak to Julia.

"Keep watch to be sure we aren't surprised," she whispered. "Do not leave the spot where you are standing now unless I tell you to. Nod if you understand."

At Julia's affirmative gesture, Sadie turned back around to assess the situation. Complete silence filled the room, giving her reason to believe there was no one else around. Perhaps the man just tripped. Stumbled over some object in the dark.

She felt along the wall to see if perhaps the building had been wired for electricity. Unfortunately, no switch to operate lights appeared within reach. What she wouldn't give right now for one of Kyle's illuminating inventions.

Taking a tentative step forward, Sadie kept a firm grasp on the doorframe. Now that her eyes had adjusted somewhat, she saw that the room wasn't completely dark. Weak light from the back room below spilled into the space in front of her, offering a path across the patterned Aubusson rug.

She once again called out to the shopkeeper. And then she spied the body.

Twenty-six

"Find a lamp, Julia," Sadie called over her shoulder. "Or a candle. Anything that will help me see."

"Yes, miss," she said before hurrying away.

A moment later she returned with a beeswax candle and matches. Sadie struck a match to light the candle and then handed the matches back to Julia.

She turned slowly, mindful of not losing the flame that offered a flickering light into the dark chamber. Noting the shopkeeper's huddled form, she set the candle on a nearby table and made her way toward him.

It appeared as though the man had tripped over a wrinkle in the rug and landed facedown. Resting her palm against his back, she could feel his even breathing.

When he groaned, she patted his back. "Sir, have you suffered harm?"

It was a stupid question, and yet the first thing that came to mind. Of course he had suffered harm. He'd fallen in a darkened room and knocked himself senseless.

"Open the curtains," she said to Julia. "We need daylight in here."

A moment later the room was flooded with

sunshine. Amid unopened crates and stacks of paper-wrapped parcels, the shopkeeper attempted to climb to his feet.

"Slowly now," Sadie said. "Perhaps it would be best not to try to stand just yet."

He maneuvered into a sitting position and then gingerly shook his head. "What happened?"

"I think you took a tumble." She reached past him to press down the wrinkle in the carpet but it wouldn't budge. "That is odd. I thought perhaps there was a problem with the rug, but now I think there's something beneath it."

Sadie picked up the edge and retrieved a parcel wrapped in brown paper. It matched others she saw strewn around the room. With nothing to indicate the contents or to whom the package might belong, she set it aside and returned her attention to the shopkeeper slumped before her.

While the poor fellow held his head in his hand, Sadie rocked back on her heels and looked around the room. A once-grand apartment, the chamber filled the entire back of the building and looked out over a small courtyard with a fountain that had seen better days.

A glance overhead revealed a ceiling that had been decorated with cherubs and clouds, a rather impressive fresco for the upper floor of an antiquities shop. So this was the place where the theft had occurred.

She stood and moved toward an armoire that

rose to an impressive height well above her head. Even if she spread her arms out, she could not have possibly reached the edges of the massive piece.

Louis XV, she decided. The curlicues and carvings certainly marked it as a piece of substantial value. Indeed it looked very much like the armoire Mama brought with her to Callum Plantation upon the occasion of her marriage to Daddy.

Sadie moved closer and turned the ornamental key. Both doors opened, revealing the wardrobe's contents.

The interior had been filled with shelves, and each was stacked to overflowing with framed pieces of art. Of pastoral scenes, sea battles, and portraits of long-dead persons of obviously noble birth.

She picked up a small watercolor approximately ten inches in length and nine inches in width and gasped. Albrecht Durer's *A Young Hare*. Indeed, there was his unique signature along with the year. "Hmm . . . 1502," she whispered as she ran her index finger over the ancient frame.

This should be in Vienna. It certainly had been several years ago when she last visited the city's museums.

And yet it was here. On a dusty shelf in a New Orleans antiquities shop.

Sadie let out a long breath. Either the painting

had changed hands recently or it was a clever forgery. She would stake money on the latter.

When she noticed the shopkeeper watching her from a now-standing position, she put away the painting of the fat brown rabbit.

"That is a lovely fresco," she commented with a casualness she did not feel. A glance around the room told her Julia was no longer in sight. Sadie made a point of gesturing toward the ceiling. "And quite rare to see something of such beauty hidden away, is it not?"

He shrugged as he brushed the dust off the front of his purple velvet coat. "A century ago this building was not in use as a shop. It was a ballroom where kept ladies danced for gentlemen. At least, that's what Monsieur Valletta claims."

"It is what Monsieur Valletta knows to be true."

The man froze, the color draining from his face. "Monsieur Valletta!"

Sadie turned to find a wiry fellow of indeterminable age standing just inside the door, his arms crossed over his chest and a gold watch fob with what appeared to be diamonds encrusted on it glittering in the light. And though he smiled, there was no humor in the dark eyes that watched her closely.

As she was well and truly caught, the only response was to bluff her way out of the situation. She made her way toward the man, her hand out-stretched.

"You must be Monsieur Valletta." Sadie upped her smile as his slipped. "I am so very glad to meet you. I had hoped I would make your acquaintance, and yet your assistant said you were not here. I was very disappointed, of course."

"Of course." He leaned over to blow out the candle, its light now unneeded. "And exactly what are you doing up here in my private apartment, Miss . . . ? I'm sorry. I do not believe we have yet made complete our exchange of names."

"Callum," she said with the authority of a woman well trained to handle these situations. "Sarah Callum. And this is Julia."

"Sarah Callum," he echoed. "I do not believe I have made your acquaintance. And yet, I never forget a face. From where do I know you?"

She thought of the photograph in the *Picayune* and prayed that Monsieur Valletta had not seen it. "Perhaps we have attended some of the same auctions? I adore finding the loveliest pieces of art. Most of my buying is done in Paris or London, although recently I came upon an exquisite Rembrandt. My dear friend purchased it before I could."

"Her friend is Mrs. Astor," the man in the purple coat interjected.

Monsieur Valletta's dark brows rose. "Which Mrs. Astor? There are two, you know."

"Of course," she said lightly. "And while Caroline is a dear, Mary Astor is the woman to whom I refer. Although her friends call her Mamie."

"And you are one of that number?"

"I am."

Julia suddenly appeared in the doorway behind Valletta, her expression stricken. There would be time later to extract an explanation from the maid as to where she had gone. Sadie forced her attention back to the antiquities dealer.

"Well, be that as it may, I regret you've been brought up to my private apartment, Madame Callum—"

"That would be Mademoiselle Callum," Sadie corrected.

"Yes, well. In any case, I would like it very much if you and Mademoiselle Oakman would take your leave now."

Sadie took a stuttering step backward and collided with the armoire. The contents shifted but thankfully nothing slipped or fell. "But I had hoped to purchase a—"

"There is nothing here for sale. Albert should have told you this. And yet I must wonder how you got in here unless he showed you the way."

She turned to allow her gaze to capture the details of the room, committing the particulars of its contents to memory as best she could.

"Please do not blame Albert," she said when

her attention returned to the older man. "The fault is all mine. I can be quite persuasive when I set my mind to it, and I did so want to have a purchase I could compare to the Rembrandt when I see Mamie again. She's ever so proud of that painting."

The bells on the front door downstairs rang out, and Monsieur Valletta turned sharply. "See who it is, Albert," he said brusquely before returning his attention to Sadie. "And you, Mademoiselle Callum, shall remain where you are."

"I beg your pardon?" She reached down to touch her skirt, calculating how much time she needed to retrieve the revolver from its pocket. "I find I do not like your tone, sir. Julia, I believe it is time we made our exit. May I trouble you to alert the driver?"

"Stay where you are, Miss Oakman," he snapped.

Sadie fixed her with a stare that told her she meant business and then nodded toward the stairs. Julia's nod was barely discernable as she picked up her skirts and scurried away.

"Monsieur Valletta," Sadie said without inflection, "I fear I have upset you. That is unfortunate. However, should you persist in this manner of behavior, I will be forced to take my business elsewhere." As she spoke, she moved toward him, her attention never wavering from his eyes.

The pretense worked, for as she reached the door, he stepped aside and allowed her to pass. She made a point of moving elegantly down the steps, as if she might be arriving at a ball rather than fleeing a crime scene. Knowledge that the art dealer could at any moment cause her great harm or prevent her exit did not keep her from holding her head high, though her heart was pounding.

As Henry said, sometimes the one with the bigger weapon is the one who has no weapon at all other than the power of the bluff.

When her feet reached the ground floor, Sadie allowed a quick glance up at the top of the stairs where Monsieur Valletta remained. An idea occurred, and she decided to chance one more ruse.

She turned to face him, her hands on her hips in a show of exasperation. "I will offer one last chance for you to redeem yourself. The Egyptian feline is a fine specimen. Should you wish to earn my good favor once more, I would hear a combined price for it and the lovely Durer in the armoire."

At the mention of the Durer painting—or perhaps it was a moment before when she spoke of the Egyptian piece—Valletta's posture went rigid. Then he turned his back on her and disappeared inside his apartment. The sound of the door slamming shut brought Julia running.

"The mister, he's here!"

Sadie shook her head. "Albert?"

"No, it is I," came a familiar and decidedly male voice from the other side of the curtains. "And if Albert is the little man who nearly knocked me down exiting the building, then my guess is he is halfway to the river by now."

She groaned. "Jefferson? What are you doing here?"

He moved into the room quietly, his attention focused up the stairs behind her. "I heard a door slam. Was that—"

"Valletta? It was. He's closed himself inside the apartment. The place is filled with art. For a man who reported a robbery, he certainly has plenty of pieces left for sale. Although he said repeatedly that the items were not to be purchased."

"I'll bet he did." He pressed past her to hurry up the stairs to the door. As she predicted, he found it locked. While he toyed with the latch, she acted on a hunch and slipped outside into the court-yard. There she spied Monsieur Valletta halfway down an emergency staircase, a burlap bag slung over his shoulder.

Retrieving her weapon, she aimed it at the art dealer. "I am a Pinkerton agent, Monsieur Valletta. Stop right there."

He stopped moving and turned toward her, holding the sack at arm's length.

"I'll have the bag first, and then you can climb down."

The man lifted the burlap bundle in his fist and threw it at her. Though Sadie made a passable attempt at dodging it, the heavy bag caught her on the shoulder and struck her down. Her head hit the ground hard.

The impact knocked the breath out of her as the revolver skittered across the uneven stepping-stones to disappear beneath the fountain. She blinked rapidly, trying to clear the ringing from her head as she raised herself up on one elbow and saw Valletta coming swiftly toward her.

Her hand searched for the revolver under the dense ferns that covered the base of the fountain but connected with nothing but dirt. Rolling out of the way, she avoided his hand as he grabbed for her arm.

Or was it the bag he wanted?

She grasped at the burlap, snagged the corner, and then hauled it across the cobblestones toward her. Valletta stomped his foot on the other end and held fast, creating a tug of war.

Sadie might have won had the art dealer not pulled a knife from his pocket with his free hand. "Release the bag, Agent Callum."

Rotating on her hip, she mustered her strength to kick at the side of his knee, sending him hurtling toward the fountain. As he fell, he released his grip and a gilded mummy mask of Syros rolled toward her.

She hauled the precious artifact close and

prayed the damage to the nose and right lappet had been done before the tussle with Monsieur Valletta began.

Noticing a carnelian amulet in the form of a seated figure of Harpocrates, she held the mask against her chest and reached to cover the talisman with her palm. A second later, Valletta ground the heel of his boot into her hand, causing her to cry out as she dropped the mask.

The treasure rolled out of her reach. With her free hand, Sadie reached up to slam her fist against the back of her attacker's knee. He went sprawling forward, the burlap bag still clenched in his hand.

Baubles tumbled out. A pottery funerary cone rolled into the ferns and a limestone canopic jar followed quickly behind. Valletta snatched up the jar as well as a small painting in a gilt frame, possibly the Durer.

He dumped them unceremoniously back into the burlap bag. Looking around, he stepped off Sadie's hand to grab the funerary cone.

A shot rang out. The art dealer dove for cover.

Sadie rolled toward the ferns to once again search for her gun. When her palm connected with the cold metal, she wrapped her fingers around it and stumbled to her knees as she took aim.

Monsieur Valletta was gone and so were the mask and amulet.

Holding the gun at her side, Sadie rose and wobbled toward the gate to emerge into the alley. Jefferson's face rose before her, and then everything went black.

Twenty-seven

Sadie slowly opened her eyes. Pain zigzagged behind her ear and across the back of her head. She groaned as her vision cleared and the horizon tilted.

"Tell him to bring the carriage into the alley."

A man, she knew. But who?

"She's fine," he said. "But her head will ache for a while. Where is that carriage?"

Jefferson.

"How did you find me?" She whispered. She couldn't seem to manage more than that.

His chuckle rumbled against the ear that pressed against his chest. "I have a talent for finding beautiful women, Miss Callum. Let's discuss this later when you're home."

Looking up in the direction of his voice sent another shard of pain that caused the blackness to close in again. By the time she once more opened her eyes, she was in the carriage with a different face swimming before her.

"Julia?" she managed when she caught sight of the fiery red hair.

"Yes, miss. Just sit back and try not to move. The mister said you'll be fine if you just stay still."

Blinking to restore her focus, Sadie shook her head. The effort cost her with pain at her temples, but she stifled a groan.

"What mister? Do you mean Mr. Tucker?" At Julia's nod, she continued. "Why did he not join us? And how did he know we were at Valletta's? Did you tell anyone?"

"How could I?" Julia asked. "I did not know myself until we were well underway."

"Yes, of course." Sadie tried to focus but felt her eyes slide closed. When she could open them again, she focused on the wide-eyed maid. "Where is Mr. Tucker?"

"He told me he would be along soon. I didn't think to ask him anything else."

"Did he catch up to Valletta?"

"The man from the store? If he did, I was not aware of this. Nor did I see what happened to the man in the strange clothing once he stepped out the front door. Who was he again?"

"I have no idea, although Valletta called him Albert." Thankfully his clothing choice just might set him apart should she have to identify him again.

"They certainly had some odd things for sale there. Why in the world would a person wish to buy a coffin for a cat?"

The art historian in her rankled at the question, and yet Sadie could understand the girl's uninformed opinion. "Actually, that was an Egyptian artifact, and it was extremely valuable."

"Well, whatever it was, the thing rattled. I thought maybe it was broken and they covered up the damage somehow, although the paint they used didn't do a very good job. It looked awfully shabby."

The carriage hit a rut and Sadie groaned in pain. "That's because it's very, very old. And it rattled because the bones of a cat were inside."

The maid's horrified expression almost made Sadie laugh. "You mean someone would buy it with a dead cat inside?"

"That enhances the value to collectors." She took note of the green ensemble and then slowly straightened. "You must change out of that dress and back into the clothes you were wearing when we left home."

"Oh," Julia said as she looked down and then back up at Sadie. "I do suppose returning in such a pretty dress when I didn't leave in it might raise an eyebrow."

"To say the least." Sadie paused to consider how best to handle the situation. "Can you manage it without stopping the carriage?"

Julia gave her a sheepish look. "With help, I might."

"Draw the curtains, then, and I'll do what I can."

Sadie discovered that helping a lady dress was a skill a lady's maid acquired over time. Managing the feat in a moving carriage with absolutely no skills and a head that pounded added up to not accomplishing much.

However, Julia was out of the green gown and into her plain servant's clothing before they had traveled the length of the River Road. Sadie watched the maid carefully fold her new dress and return it to the carpetbag on the floor between them while thoughts of the day's escapade tumbled forth.

As the events fell together in sequence, a question rose. "Julia, where did you go?"

The maid looked up from fussing with her shoelaces. "Go, miss? I don't understand."

Sadie thought over the recollection and then reformed the question. "When Monsieur Valletta caught me in the apartment with his assistant, you were nowhere to be found." She paused to allow the statement to fully sink in. "Despite the fact I told you to stay with me unless I explicitly told you otherwise."

"I was there, miss," she protested as she reached to open the carriage curtains once more. "Just not where you could see me."

The maid sat back and continued to fidget with her laces, although they were already firmly tied, a clear indication to Sadie that the girl had something to hide. Perhaps now was the time to ask the question Sadie had thought she might save for later.

"Julia."

At the sound of her name, the maid looked up. "Yes, miss?"

"Where were you? And why couldn't I see you?"

She let out a long breath. "All right. I admit I had a bit of a panic. I saw that man, the one you're saying is Monsieur Valletta."

"Go on."

"He was skulking around in the back garden. Pacing, really, as if he was aggrieved at something. Or maybe someone."

"How did you see this?"

Julia sat up straight, her back barely touching the cushions. Her attention went to the window and stayed there. "You told me to open the curtains, remember?"

"And you saw him then? Why didn't you say something?"

"And alert that other man? I didn't think it was wise, miss. If you'll pardon me, I did not believe he was the least bit trustworthy."

Neither had she, but to hear such incisive thoughts from a maid gave her confidence that the girl was a good judge of people. "That does not explain why I could not see you."

"No, it does not. I know you asked me to stay put, and I would have, but the fellow, well, he looked like he might be trouble, and so I went down the stairs to where I could see better into the garden without letting the man in those strange clothes know I was spying. You see, there's a window there that looks out, and . . ."

She looked away.

"And?"

"And that's when I saw the mister."

"Mr. Tucker?" Sadie sat up a little straighter, ignoring the jab at her temples. "The man who helped me to the carriage?"

"Yes, miss. He came through the curtain, and I might have gasped. And that might have caused him to find me on the stairs."

"Might have?"

"It was the reason he found me, yes."

Outside the familiar landmarks of the River Road rolled past. They had little time left now.

"Please continue," Sadie said. "What happened next?"

"The man who was pacing the back garden came hurrying in the back door like he owned the place. The mister, he pulled me into the closet that's right next to the big room where you were doing your art shopping. Said it was so he could have the element of surprise over the fellow."

Sadie smiled at the girl's description of her purpose for being there. Art shopping was indeed the last thing she had been doing, but it pleased her to think that might be what Julia would believe.

At least she hadn't completely lost her ability to do her job as a Pinkerton agent. After Gabriel spied her in the French Quarter, she had begun to have her doubts.

"I was quiet like he said I should be. Once we heard you speaking to Monsieur Valletta, then Mr. Tucker asked that I go and see what was going on."

The carriage slowed to turn off the River Road and onto Callum property. Sadie thought carefully before speaking. "Why did you listen to Mr. Tucker and not to me?"

"But I thought . . ." Her voice fell silent as color crept into her cheeks. "I don't suppose I have a good answer for that other than what he said made sense at the time. I thought it would be what you might have said if you could have."

And perhaps it might have been. Still, the fact that Julia decided that on her own troubled her.

Sadie remained silent the remainder of the trip. Though it was customary to stop at the front of the house to let off family, the driver continued around back to return the carriage to the place where it had been parked before the day's adventure began.

When the carriage rolled to a halt just out of sight of the house, Sadie moved to place her hand over the door's handle. She fixed the maid with a serious look.

"You will tell no one of what has transpired

today. Do you understand? Not my mother or father or any of the household staff. If questioned, you will say that you accompanied me on a shopping trip. And I specifically forbid you to discuss this in any way with Mr. Tucker. Do you understand?"

"Yes, miss." She lifted downcast eyes. "I am sorry I didn't do as you asked. I thought . . ." Her words trailed off as tears welled in her eyes. "I thought I was helping."

Sadie softened her expression, though only slightly. Civilians who helped were sometimes more dangerous than the criminals the Pinkerton agents pursued.

"You are forgiven. Now dry your eyes lest someone ask you why you're crying."

The young woman nodded and retrieved a handkerchief from her pocket to dab at her cheeks. When she moved to retrieve the carpetbag, Sadie stopped her.

"I will keep that with me."

"Yes, miss."

The door opened, and Sadie allowed the driver to help her out. Though her knees felt wobbly and her head pounded, she managed to make her way inside.

Uncle Penn met her in the foyer with a worried expression. "Where have you been?"

Glancing around, Sadie shook her head as she returned her attention to her uncle. "I cannot tell you right at this moment. However, suffice it to say I've had an interesting morning."

"As have I." Uncle Penn linked arms with her and hurried her into Mama's formal parlor.

The room was tiny in comparison to the grander rooms on the ground floor. It was filled with a dizzying array of floral patterns on the wall, on the cushions of the petite sofas, and in the art Mama had chosen for the walls. Even the chandelier bore a profusion of flowers captured in crystal by Lalique in Paris and specially hung to appear as if blooming from the ceiling.

The sight of her uncle standing tall among the decidedly female furnishings would have been humorous had his expression not been so grave. "Where were you?"

She clutched the carpetbag and her reticule to her side. "I went shopping in the city."

He didn't believe her. His face told her that much. And the crease of his brow told her there was more than just his concern for her.

"Has something happened?" she asked, trying not to sway as she stood.

His hand rested on the back of a slipper chair as if he were the one who needed steadying. "We've had a visitor."

"Oh?"

Uncle Penn pulled a paper-wrapped package from his coat pocket. "He left this."

"Henry?" she asked as she accepted the package. Though it appeared slightly off size for a book, there still might be a volume inside.

"No, Sadie." He went to the door and shut it firmly. "How well do you know the Tucker fellow?"

She shrugged. "I don't suppose I can't claim I know him well. Why?"

"Because that package was delivered for him."

She turned the box over to see that indeed the name of William Jefferson Tucker had been written in a neat script with black ink. There was no return address or postmark. Nothing gave away the sender's identity.

She thrust it back at Uncle Penn. "Then give it to him. I shouldn't be opening it."

He refused the package. "Aren't you curious as to what's in it?"

"No," she said, although that wasn't completely true. "Who delivered it?"

"That's the interesting part. No one knows."

Sadie shook her head. "How can that be?"

"I don't know." He shrugged. "I only know that I nearly broke my neck stumbling over it when I went out the front door. I thought it prudent to show the curious item to you before it was delivered to Mr. Tucker because he's apparently here at your request, or in pursuit of you, depending on who is telling the tale."

"It is neither, I assure you."

"So you've not made his previous acquaintance?"

"He is the man I saw released from prison. That was our only acquaintance before he arrived here."

"I see." Uncle Penn looked away.

The headache that had abated was returning. Worse, a glance in the mirror over the fireplace revealed that her tumble in Monsieur Valletta's courtyard had soiled her dress and ripped the skirt in two places.

If Mama saw her, there would be no end to the questions she would ask. Sadie determined to decide what to do with the package later.

She tucked the wrapped item into the crook of her arm and resolved to put on a neutral expression despite the pain. "Thank you, Uncle Penn. I will see that Mr. Tucker gets this."

"I thought you might."

Moving past him to the door, she stopped when he called her name. Sadie turned to see her uncle looking more worried now than when they first stepped into the parlor.

"Your dress," he said. "What happened?"

Sadie mustered a smile. "Just a little accident."

"You do not have accidents, Sarah Callum." When she did not respond, he shook his head. "I can see you're not keen to tell me anything, so I will offer my best advice."

"And that is?"

"Hurry upstairs before your father sees you. He's already concerned he has one spy in the house. What will he do if he decides he has two?"

She gave her uncle a hug and hurried away. What indeed? And imagine if Daddy were to realize he just might have three spies under his roof?

Not that she believed Uncle Penn was anything other than a man with a curious streak and a yen to travel.

"Oh," he called from the bottom of the stairs. "I almost forgot."

Glancing over her shoulder, she watched her uncle catch up to her. The exertion caused him to pause, his breathing slightly labored. Indeed, age was catching up to Uncle Penn, something Sadie disliked greatly.

"Pearl will be joining us soon." He grinned. "Apparently one of us won her over with our letters."

Resting her hand on her uncle's arm, she looked up into his kind and familiar face. "She misses you."

"Perhaps. Will you miss me when it comes time to travel again?"

"Terribly, although I am not yet certain you won't be traveling with me."

"Oh, I am." He glanced around the empty stairwell and then leaned closer. "My traveling days are coming to an end, dear girl. I fear you may have to go it alone."

She patted his arm. "Not until I must."

"Well, should Pearl decide to stay a while, then you must. I fear my lovely bride would not be pleased if she arrived here in time to say good-bye to me. And truly, I do miss the woman. So perhaps if our Henry calls you back to duty, he will also provide a companion with whom you can travel."

"And an excuse that my father will accept?" She shared his smile. "That is a tall order, even for Henry Smith."

"As long as I have known the man, I've never found him unable to find a solution to any pressing problem."

The front door opened and voices drifted up toward them. Uncle Penn nodded toward the hallway leading to the bedchambers.

Daddy. And Mama was with him.

"Looks like rain tonight," her father was saying. "But then it has looked like rain for several nights now. I suppose that is just May in Louisiana."

Mama's response was too quiet to hear from this distance. The sound of their footsteps told Sadie they were heading this way across the marble floor.

"He can't find me like this," she whispered as she calculated the distance to the end of the very long hallway. "I'll never get inside my bed-chamber quick enough."

"Off with you, girl. I'll stall them until you can get yourself inside and do something with that dress you've ruined."

"Thank you." She turned to go and then Uncle Penn reached out to grasp her elbow.

"One more thing." He seemed to be studying her face intently. "Are you certain you don't want to tell me where you have been and what you were doing to return in such a state?"

"I'm certain," she said. "I wish I could, but—"

"Just tell me one thing. Did a man cause this?"

She almost laughed, but with Daddy's footsteps coming nearer, Sadie did not dare. "Actually, yes, but not in the way I think you mean. This was work, Uncle Penn, and yes, Henry knows of the persons involved. I plan to give him a full report as soon as I can manage it."

"All right, then. I cannot argue with that." He gestured to her head. "Summon your maid as soon as you close the door."

"I plan to," she said as she offered a kiss on the cheek and then slipped from his grasp.

"Be sure you have that maid of yours brush out your hair. Unless I'm mistaken, there's a fern stuck in your curls."

Twenty-eight

Though Julia managed to repair the damage she did to her coiffure, there was no remedy for the pounding in her head that refused to abate, even after a dose of headache powders and a cup of willow bark tea. Nor did there appear to be a fix for the dress she'd ruined in Monsieur Valletta's courtyard.

"Perhaps I can restyle it to something that doesn't require as much fabric." Julia held the dress up and studied the material. "I see potential for a nice riding outfit. What do you think?"

"I think that would be fine."

The maid draped the garment over a slipper chair near the window and then returned her attention to Sadie. "Will you be wearing the sapphires with the blue gown, miss?"

"Yes, I suppose. But just the necklace. I don't care to bother with the earrings or bracelet. It's only supper."

"Supper with the man who's aiming to marry you." She met Sadie's astonished look. "At least, that's what the staff is saying."

"Are they?"

Julia shrugged. "Not that I am adding my opinion, for I promise I am saying nothing. However, I felt you ought to know."

"Yes, thank you. I appreciate the warning."

"And next week, when you're to wear the navy ball gown?" Julia continued. "This set will also look nice with it, don't you think? Unless you do not wish to be seen in the same jewels so soon."

Sadie nodded and then winced. The party to which Julia referred was a full week away. And though she wouldn't tell the maid just yet, if at all, she would likely be gone well before then.

"I doubt anyone but Mama will notice, and she will keep our secret."

"Yes, miss." Julia went to the armoire to retrieve the necklace and then secured it at Sadie's neck. "You do look pretty. The mister will be pleased."

Ignoring the comment, Sadie rose from the mirror and went to the window. The sun had just set, leaving the oaks trailing shadows across the remains of the gold-orange light. At the edges of the horizon, purple fingers of twilight climbed up into a sky that threatened rain.

"If there's nothing else, miss, I will take this dress and begin working on it."

"Yes, of course." Sadie glanced back at Julia. "Thank you."

The maid looked as if she might blush. "Mending and repurposing the wardrobe is what a lady's maid does."

"No, I mean thank you for being willing to accompany me today." Sadie settled onto the window seat and looked up at Julia. "I think we both agree that our adventure does not fit into the category of things a lady's maid does."

"I rather enjoyed it. And I shall keep the secret of what happened no matter who should ask."

"Has anyone asked?"

Her fingers clutched the fabric. "No, miss. I just meant . . . well, never mind. I shall keep the secret, and should you need someone for another adventure, I'm your girl. And if you have any questions as to whether I'm fit for that service, I hope you will believe I learned my lesson and will await only your instructions from now on."

Julia crossed her fingers over her heart and then grinned. Sadie wanted to believe her. Unfortunately, only time would tell as to whether the girl's claim was true.

Time and perhaps yet another test.

Sadie mustered a smile. "Then perhaps we shall discover whether that's the case someday soon."

"Yes, miss. I do thank you. And I shall see that you have more of those powders and willow bark tea for when you come back upstairs after supper. You do look as if you are still not feeling completely free of your headache."

At Sadie's nod, Julia hurried away, leaving silence in her wake. Sadie glanced over at the package she had placed beneath her valise atop the armoire.

She should see that Jefferson got his parcel.

When and how was yet to be determined. Also yet to be determined was whether she would peek inside it before she made good on that delivery. After all, Henry had instructed her to keep close tabs on the man should she have the ability to do so.

Didn't that include investigating strange parcels without postmarks?

By the time she reached the dining room, the meal was about to get underway. She settled into the only seat remaining, the one directly across from Jefferson.

"I'm glad you could join us, Sarah," Daddy said. "Unless you object, I'll be offering the blessing now."

Goodness, he was cranky. She bowed her head and joined hands with Mama on her left and Aaron on her right. As her father petitioned the Lord for wisdom and then gave thanks, she risked a quick peek at Jefferson across the table.

And caught him watching her.

He seemed amused. Or perhaps his expression was one of confusion. In either case, he had best not mention a word of what happened this afternoon. Surely he understood that this was Pinkerton business and not fodder for a family discussion.

Aaron nudged her and she glanced his way. The rest of the family had said their amens and were passing the plates.

Sadie lifted her head quickly. Too quickly. Blinking from the jab of pain, she accepted the tray of rolls and then handed them to Mama.

The remainder of the meal passed in the usual way. Daddy and the boys talked farming, argued politics, and then debated whether to have one piece of pie or two. Jefferson joined in on most of the discussions, although when it came to pie, he helped himself to one slice and did not go back for seconds.

Because he seemed in no way eager to guide the conversation anywhere but the aforementioned topics, Sadie allowed herself to relax. Depending on whether Julia could be trusted, she may very well have gotten away with the escapade.

By the time coffee was served in Mama's enormous silver coffee server, Sadie was feeling the effects of the headache powder she had taken. The pain that plagued her had all but abated, but in its absence her ability to remain awake had fled as well.

A swift kick under the table caused Sadie to come awake swiftly. "Mama?"

"Yes, dear?" Her mother looked as innocent as could be, never mind the fact she had just executed a direct jab with her foot to Sadie's left leg.

Sadie's eyes narrowed. "Did you want something?"

Mama's lips turned up in a pretty smile.

"Actually, it was Mr. Tucker who was speaking. I merely assisted by getting your attention."

She turned to look over at Jefferson. "Yes?"

"Well, now." He placed his napkin on the table. "That is exactly what I hoped you would say."

"Did you hear that, Seamus?" Mama called across the length of the table. "She said yes."

A cheer went up as Sadie sat back and watched Ethan clap his hand onto Jefferson's back. "You were right, Jeff. I didn't think you were, but you sure were right."

Aaron leaned over in her direction. "Congratulations, brat."

She elbowed him and he pretended it hurt. "What is all the fuss? I merely responded to Mr. Tucker. You would think it was the Fourth of July or something."

Jefferson's laugh caught her attention. "This is better than the Fourth of July, Christmas, and New Year's Eve all rolled together."

She crossed her arms over her waist and shook her head. "If you are all having a joke at my expense, it is not funny."

"Who's joking?" Daddy said. "The man asked and you said yes. Your mama heard it. We all did."

"And that is worthy of celebration?"

"We're celebrating because someone's going to take you off our hands," Cade called from his spot next to Daddy.

"I told you so." Brent jabbed Cade with his

elbow. "And you said she was so particular that it would never happen."

Slowly the realization of just what they were celebrating dawned on Sadie. "No," she said first to Mama and then to Jefferson. "No. That is not what I meant."

Mama reached over to touch Sadie's sleeve. "Don't you go changing your mind now. You've answered our Mr. Tucker and that's that."

Donovan met her gaze, his expression stoic. Finally, he reached for his butter knife and tapped his water glass until the room fell silent.

"Maybe we ought to listen to Sadie before we celebrate?"

"Thank you, Donovan." She looked over at Jefferson, who seemed more interested than entertained, and then turned her attention to Daddy. "I wish to inform each and every one of you that I am not amused by your teasing. In fact, I believe I will beg off the after-dinner conversation altogether and claim a headache. If you will excuse me."

She pushed back from the table and tossed her napkin atop her dessert plate. When she rose, Jefferson followed suit, as did her brothers. Daddy remained seated, his expression grim.

"Don't worry, Sadie," Ethan said. "You have a good one. I just wish you had told us about him instead of letting us all find out by surprise."

"Trust me," she said as she fixed Jefferson

341

with a glare. "It was a surprise to me as well."

The man in question winked, and all good sense fled. She picked up the napkin from its resting place atop her uneaten pie and tossed it at him.

As the napkin sailed past, it toppled her water glass and turned the sugar in Mama's Waterford sugar bowl to soup. Jefferson reached out and caught the linen square, but not before a blob of piecrust landed on his black silk vest.

All her brothers except for Donovan began speaking at once. Cade and Brent shouted advice for Jefferson while Ethan taunted her to throw the entire slice of pie next time. Aaron leaned over to voice disapproval and then sat down as he shook his head.

Mama merely stared, her lips pursed in disapproval and a deep V forming between her eyes. Likely the speech from her mother would come later when she'd had time to form it properly. After all, ladies did not air their grievances before company. It was poor manners, and above all, Mama insisted on manners.

Daddy climbed to his feet and then leaned over to pound the table. "That is quite enough, all of you. Sit down and hush."

This time quiet fell hard and fast. A moment later, Sadie was the only person in the room who remained standing.

"Tucker, what's your take on this?" Daddy asked.

Jefferson snapped to attention. "My take, sir?"

He leaned back in his chair and steepled his fingers. "Yes. Did you just offer marriage to my Sarah Louise?"

"I did, sir." Jefferson shifted his attention to Sadie. "I didn't expect this would take your daughter by surprise. We have spoken of it."

"And I told him he was out of his mind." She headed for the door and didn't look back even when Daddy called her name.

"If you will excuse me, Mr. Callum," she heard Jefferson say. "I will see what has her so upset."

When her false fiancé stepped out into the foyer, she whirled around and fixed him with a look that should have stopped him in his tracks. "See what has me *upset?*"

"You are upset."

Sadie opened her mouth to speak and then thought better of it. A glance at the open door behind him told her that everyone still seated in the dining room was straining to listen.

"I have other things to do rather than take part in any further pointless conversation with you, Jefferson Tucker. Do not follow and do not go back into that dining room and congratulate yourself on becoming my fiancé." She lowered her voice and leaned toward him. "I know what you're doing, but there must be another way to do it. I will not pretend to marry you, and that's that. I will not deceive the people I love. You cannot change my mind."

Jefferson seemed to consider her statement a moment. "I see your point, Sadie. However, if you will allow me to handle the situation in the proper manner, I believe we can solve any issues that have arisen in regard to your reluctance to wed." He moved closer, his voice barely a whisper. "And as to deceiving your family, would you not put refusing to tell them that you are a Pinkerton agent in that category?"

She pointed her index finger at him. "Do not move."

His chuckle followed her as she walked back into the dining room. Sadie allowed her gaze to skip down the table, touching each of her brothers and her uncle and father before landing on Mama.

"While I thank you for your efforts in welcoming me back home, I did not expect you all to take the next step and find a husband for me so I will stay." Her look challenged Mama. "That is what you're up to, isn't it, Mama?"

"Now see here, Sarah Louise," Daddy said. "Do not be blaming this on your mama. Maybe it's me who was bent on having my girl back under my roof. Did you think of that?"

She forced her expression to soften. "I appreciate the sentiment, but I must tell you that your efforts will not work. I will find a husband, I promise. But I want it to be when the time is right for me and not when you think it should happen."

"The Lord works in mysterious ways," Mama said. "I think it would do you good to remember that."

"Don't you think if the Lord wanted me married, He would let me in on the news?"

Her father shook his head. "I sure wish you hadn't put it that way."

"It is the only way I can put it, Daddy. He's just going to have to make it plain who His man is, and then I'll have no choice but to say yes."

"I can't argue with that," Aaron said. "Although I do like your Mr. Tucker. Seems like a fine man."

A general murmur of agreement went up. Sadie glanced behind her to see if the man in question had heard. He gave her an I-told-you-so look that caused her to make a face in return.

"I love you all," she said gently as she returned her attention to her family. "But please let things happen naturally and without any assistance from you. I promise someday I will say yes. No more matchmaking, Mama."

"Tell that to your Mr. Tucker," she said. "I've never seen a man put up a more compelling argument for helping a romance along. And I don't think any of us assisted him in making his proposal today. He did that of his own mind and free will. Am I right?"

"You are correct," he said. "Although, considering we're going to be family, I do wish all of you would call me Jefferson."

"I like the sound of that, Jefferson," Daddy said as her brothers joined in with similar statements.

Shaking her head, Sadie bid her family good night. This time, she brushed past Jefferson without a word.

"If you all will excuse me," she heard him say, presumably to her family. And then his footsteps echoed behind her.

Had she not been lashed in to the hated corset and hobbled by the ache in her temples, Sadie might have picked up her skirts and run. Her family already thought her the worst sort of heathen anyway given her behavior toward the man they all apparently adored.

Jefferson caught up to her and then trailed a step behind as she walked quickly down the hallway. He stepped in front of her in the foyer. "The plan *will* work if you cooperate, Sadie. However, it will also work if you do not."

She faced him down, or rather looked up, and then let out a long breath. "How can you worry about that right now?"

"What better time to worry about it? Maybe you don't feel any sense of urgency, but I have a strong interest in finding a solution as soon as possible."

He was right, of course. And yet the way he had gone about executing his plan without listening to reason irked her. Like it or not, he had involved her family in his scheme and then left her to deal with the result.

It was all too much. Perhaps tomorrow she would have a reasonable alternative to his ridiculous plan. Or, failing that, she would find the words to explain the situation to her family so that she might leave Callum Plantation unimpeded by concerns that her brothers would follow.

But that was for tomorrow. Tonight, especially in this man's presence, she could not think straight. She might blame it on the headache powders she had taken or the effects of the willow bark tea, but there was something to be said for a man as ridiculously handsome as Jefferson Tucker standing in close proximity and claiming to want to solve all her problems that made her more than a little lightheaded.

So she would think about it all tomorrow. Sadie stepped around him without comment and went up the stairs.

She didn't care whether he followed or not. When she successfully closed her bedchamber door behind her without him stopping her, she smiled. And then she spied the parcel atop the armoire.

Had Mama not raised her better, she might have said a few choice words. Instead, she clamped her mouth shut and retrieved the valise, ignoring the paper-wrapped package beneath it. She would see he got the item tomorrow, perhaps. Maybe it would be delivered unopened. Or maybe not.

But tonight she could not consider worrying

with it when she had much bigger issues to consider. After today's fiasco with Sergio Valletta, the time for lingering at Callum Plantation had come to an end.

If Jack could be convinced to take her to New Orleans on a shopping trip, he certainly could be convinced to drive her there one more time. What he would not know until after the journey was well underway was that he would be taking her to the railroad station.

After she dropped a letter for Henry at the post office, of course.

She rang for Julia, still unsure as to whether she would include the maid in her plans. She considered the idea as the girl helped her through her bedtime routine and into her wrapper even though the sun had not yet gone down.

Because Sadie was lost in her thoughts, she noticed Julia's silence only as she was making her exit. "Is something wrong?"

The girl paused, one hand on the doorknob. Slowly, she turned around, her expression troubled. "Just a little fuss with the cook. Nothing of concern."

"All right." Sadie picked up the newspaper she hadn't managed to read that morning and then noticed that Julia hadn't moved from her place by the door. "Is there something else?"

The maid lifted downcast eyes. "Are you truly going to marry the mister?"

"I am not."

Her face brightened. "Cook says she heard Dr. Trahan talking to your daddy and brothers, trying to convince them the mister isn't who he claims."

Sadie moderated her expression. "And just who is Mr. Tucker claiming to be?"

"I don't exactly know." She moved away from the door to settle onto the chair nearest Sadie. "But when Dr. Trahan told your daddy that the man who wanted to marry his daughter was a spy for a foreign government, well, you would have thought he had just told the funniest joke ever."

"What did my daddy think?"

"Mr. Callum, he started laughing and Mr. Ethan and Mr. Aaron, they both joined in. According to Cook, there wasn't a thing that came out of Dr. Trahan's mouth that made sense."

A spy for a foreign government. The statement was chilling in its accuracy and in the fact that somehow Gabriel knew this and tried to warn her family.

"Did Dr. Trahan say anything else?" she asked when she noticed Julia watching her closely.

"Just that if nobody would listen to reason he would have to show them. At least, that's what the cook told us."

"I see. And what do you think?"

She let out a long breath. "I think that a man who goes to that much trouble to keep a lady safe isn't such a bad fellow."

"Are we talking about Mr. Tucker or Dr. Trahan, Julia?"

The maid rose. "I suppose the same could be said for both, miss. Dr. Trahan, he does fancy you. But Mr. Tucker, well, he carried you all the way to the carriage and made sure I had proper instructions on how to care for you until I could get you home. I think if given the chance, either of them would make a fine husband."

"Not you too! I wish you could have heard the speech I just gave to my family tonight about matchmaking."

"Oh, miss, we all heard it." A flush of bright red climbed into her cheeks. "What I mean is, it would have been hard not to hear, considering the pantry's just on the other side of the dining room door. Now, if you'll excuse me, miss, I thought I would go back to my sewing."

"Yes, of course."

Long after the door closed behind the maid, Sadie was still thinking about the girl's words. Why was Gabriel warning her family about a man whose last employer was Scotland Yard?

And how did he know so much about Jefferson Tucker?

Twenty-nine

Jefferson sat back in a comfortable leather chair, all eyes now on him. "How does this man know so much about me?"

None of the Callum males seemed willing to offer a response. For once, Jefferson was sorry that the tradition of after-dinner conversation didn't extend to the females in the family.

While Sadie had obviously been delighted to leave him standing alone in the foyer, Mrs. Callum might have taken the same amount of pleasure in following the group into Seamus's library to share what she knew of the man.

And he had no doubt she knew plenty.

"Come now," Donovan said. "Aren't the rest of you keen to tell this man just what Gabriel's trouble is?" When no one responded, he continued. "That fool's been in love with Sadie since they were kids. She's oblivious to it, of course. Or at least she was. I believe Trahan made her an offer of marriage and she turned him down."

"That's how it looked to me." Aaron shrugged when his father glanced over at him. "You know how Mama wants us to watch out for her. That's all I was doing."

Jefferson caught Brent and Cade watching him

and decided now was the time to act. "These two know something."

They exchanged glances and then Brent shook his head. "Don't know a thing," he said, though his sullen expression told Jefferson there would probably be a different sort of conversation later.

Penn rose from his place in the corner to move to the center of the group. While he reached for a cigar in the humidor on the corner of the desk, he made no move to trim or light it.

"You got something to say, Penn?"

Jefferson couldn't help but notice the gruff tone with which Seamus addressed his brother-in-law. There appeared to be no love lost between the men.

If he had more time, he might have looked into the cause, if for no other reason than the fact that it always interested him when brothers—or in this case, brothers-in-law—found themselves at odds.

Penn Monroe lived in Mobile. That made finding out about him much easier, especially if he was acquainted with Grandfather Tucker, and possibly with his father.

However, time was short. Very short.

Penn tapped the end of the cigar against his palm and then directed his attention toward Seamus. "For reasons I'll not go into, I do not trust Gabriel Trahan."

Seamus snorted. "That's it? You're just going to make a statement like that and then say you won't explain it?"

"That's right."

Apparently Seamus did not expect such a direct answer. He recoiled almost as if he had been hit. When he recovered, he shook his head.

"I've known that boy since his mama birthed him, Penn." He gestured toward the north. "He was born in one of my employee houses just up beyond the mill. His daddy was one of the hardest workers I had. The boy just came back from Tulane. Gonna make a doctor of himself. And you're going to say that you don't trust him? Do you even know him?"

"That is a nice speech, Seamus." Penn's iron-gray brows gathered. "Do you? Know him, I mean."

"I just said I did," he sputtered.

"I would submit that you do not. You know who he was. Do you know who he is now? He has been away. Is it possible he has changed?"

This could go on for quite some time. And unless Jefferson missed his guess, it might spiral out of hand quickly. He thought carefully about what he wished to say and just how he might best say it. Finally he cleared his throat. "May I interject something?"

All eyes turned toward him.

"I believe the question was in regard to how

Dr. Trahan came to know so much about me. Can anyone in the room enlighten me on why he would tell you that I am a spy for a foreign nation?"

Seamus's eyes narrowed. "How did you know he said that?"

"I told him." Ethan pointed at Jefferson. "He needed to know what has been said about him so he could answer for it." The youngest Callum male looked to his father. "It's what you've taught us to do. Go to the horse's mouth and let it talk to you."

Seamus nodded. "Indeed I have."

"And yet you do not believe Trahan," Jefferson said to Seamus.

He crossed his arms over his chest. "How do you know this?"

"Because if you did, you would not approve of your daughter marrying me." Jefferson held the planter's gaze. "And if you did not approve, you had ample opportunity to say so at supper tonight. In fact, I would go further and say that if you did not approve of me, I would not have been sitting at that table at all."

Seamus grinned but said nothing.

"He approves because I've vouched for you, boy," Penn said with a broad smile of his own. "I told him all about your granddaddy the judge and what a fine family you come from. Doesn't hurt that your daddy and I had somewhat of an association before he headed out on that last mission of his."

Jefferson's attention whipped toward Penn. "How did you know—"

"Don't waste your time trying to figure it out, son," Penn said with a chuckle. "Suffice it to say that Mobile was a much smaller town during wartime."

"What he's trying to say is that he's a spy," said Seamus. "Or was. I can't decide if he still is or not, and the old goat will not tell me."

Penn chuckled. Apparently this line of conversation had a lengthy history.

Seamus returned his attention to Jefferson. "I also can't decide if it is his fault that my Sarah went to work for Henry Smith up at Allan Pinkerton's operation in Chicago or if that was her idea alone."

The Callum boys began speaking at once, all but Donovan voicing an opinion on why their father couldn't possibly be correct. Jefferson noticed the middle brother's silence and met his gaze.

"You're not disagreeing."

Donovan paused only a moment before grinning. "Actually, I am hoping it's true."

"Oh, it's true," Seamus continued. "Why do you think I tolerated those trips she made with Penn here? And that picture in the *Picayune* with Agent Russell? I wasn't pleased, I'll tell you, but my concern was for her safety and not her reputation."

"Then why put up with it at all, Daddy?" Ethan said. "If it's dangerous, that is."

"Son, do you think I would let my baby girl go off with a Union spy if I hadn't already made my peace with the fact she was doing something important?"

Again, the brothers called out protests. "Uncle Penn," Donovan said above the din. "What do you say about this?"

Penn surveyed the group and then smiled. "I say very little. That's why I am good at what I do. And if I have any response, it's this: It takes one old goat to know one." When the laughter stopped, Seamus's included, Penn continued. "However, I believe Mr. Tucker may have more to say on this topic."

Jefferson acknowledged Penn's statement with a nod and then returned his focus to Sadie's father. "I do, but if you don't mind, I need to speak to Mr. Callum alone."

Seamus looked around the room and then stood. "Come on with me, then. I don't figure we'll get privacy any other way."

A few minutes later, Jefferson found himself astride a black bay gelding riding along a path that wound along the Mississippi River. With Seamus in the lead, he was left to take in the beauty of the evening and the vast expanse of the plantation where Sadie was raised.

Glancing back at the house, now small and

barely visible in the distance, he thought of the lady Pinkerton and what she might have been like as a little girl. He found it hard to believe she'd run free through this property as a barefoot child, but then he could barely imagine the elegant woman as anything but who she was now.

Thick stalks of sugarcane rattled in the evening breeze, their green leaves swaying as far as Jefferson could see. An open expanse of land came into view ahead, and Seamus slowed his pace to motion that Jefferson come alongside him.

At one end of the clearing, a dirt path trailed off and circled around, presumably to end at the cottages whose rooftops were visible in the distance. Thin plumes of smoke indicated the homes were occupied, as did the shrill laughter of children at play.

"Most of my employees live back there," Seamus said as if anticipating the question. "A few more live in town. Not as many as we used to have before we mechanized, though. Until we start cutting, I don't need more than a few dozen men."

Seamus looked off in the direction of the cottages. "You're wondering if I kept slaves out there?"

"My grandfather raised cotton in Alabama before the war. I figured you must have."

Seamus turned back to Jefferson and then lifted his hand to shield his eyes from the sun. "Yes, I

357

did, though I found it an unpleasant business altogether and something I couldn't reconcile with what I learned from the Good Book. My wife threatened to go home to her mama and daddy the day I freed them all and then offered the best of the lot a salary. Said she might as well because we'd be losing the house and land soon anyway."

"But she was wrong."

"In more ways than one." Seamus grinned. "Best of it was that she admitted it to me about a year later when we brought in the biggest crop we'd ever had."

The older man leaned back in the saddle, his attention now focused toward the river. "I bought this parcel of land for half of what it was worth thirty-two years ago next month from a fellow who ran the whole operation poorly and using slave labor to do what men paid a living wage could have done just as well. I figured the best way to succeed was to do the opposite of what didn't work. I've done quite fine using that logic."

"Yes, sir. It appears you have."

He shrugged. "Fewer hands to do the work meant I had to improvise. And machines don't have to be fed, clothed, or tolerated beyond the point where they don't make sense."

Jefferson nodded as he surveyed the collection of structures that might have been barns, tool-sheds, or any sort of farm building. Each bore the evidence of mechanized machinery inside through the series of pipes leading between them and the bricked fireplaces that marked the end of several of them. Behind the largest of the group a half-dozen wagons that had been fitted with curious lifting devices were huddled together.

"The hardest part of the season is where all I can do is watch," Seamus said. "Come September we'll be using all of those wagons plus as many more as I can find in town to rent to get the cane harvested. But right now all I can do is wait."

Silence fell, and Jefferson got the idea that something in the man's speech was a lesson meant for more than merely growing sugarcane.

"Gabriel Trahan wants his part of my land."

The statement took Jefferson by surprise. "I don't follow."

"The boy grew up here, but he never did like that his daddy worked in my mill. He was like his mama. Too good for the cane fields and determined to get out." He paused. "She did, you know. Get out, that is. Ran off and married someone else the day after they laid Gabriel's daddy in the grave. The boy never forgave me."

"How can that be your fault?"

Seamus seemed to be giving the question serious consideration. "What I didn't stop I got blamed for. That's what I'll say on that and no more."

"Again, I'm sorry, sir, but I don't follow how that has Gabriel upset with you."

He nodded. "The man making accusations against you has more to his claims than good intentions. My wife thinks he's the man for Sadie. I know for a fact that he's not."

"Because she's a Pinkerton agent?"

"No, he's wrong for her because she is my daughter, and I'll leave it at that."

Then, as if shaking away a memory he found distasteful, Seamus rolled his shoulders and dug his heels in to set his horse moving once more. Jefferson was left to follow.

By the time they turned their mounts down the narrow path that ran next to the river, the sun was slanting long shadows across the muddy brown water and night birds were dipping across the bank. Here and there magnolias hung thick with Spanish moss and bent their branches down toward the river.

What Jefferson thought was a branch hanging as long as a man's leg began to move and then fell into the water below. A cottonmouth. He urged the gelding carefully past the tree. He never had liked snakes.

The moon rising behind the cottages bore a ring of clouds around it that foretold another stormy night ahead. From the direction the river rolled, Jefferson could tell they were now heading south and would be in sight of the Callum home in another quarter mile or so.

"You had something to say, boy." Seamus slid

him a sideways glance. "Now would be the time to say it. I reckon I'll help you decide, just in case you don't know where to start. Why exactly are you making a fuss of wanting to marry my daughter when she clearly doesn't intend to be wed?"

"Because it is the only way the plan will work."

Seamus pulled up the reins and stopped. "You'd better keep talking," he said, his voice ominous. "And start by telling me who you are exactly, and I don't mean who your mama and daddy are because I already know that."

"Yes, sir. Until a year ago I was an investigator for the London Metropolitan Police at Scotland Yard. If you know of my parents, then you know that is where I was born."

"Your brother too."

"Then perhaps you know that while in Louisiana pursuing a lead on a case, I paid a visit to John."

"At Angola. Yes, I read the papers. I also know the jail set you loose recently. Did my daughter have anything to do with that?"

"She testified as to my identity and proved I was not the Tucker who should be behind bars."

"Because you and she were previously acquainted?"

"No, sir." The horse stamped and snorted, but Jefferson held tight to the reins as he calmed the gelding. "Your daughter testified based on her knowledge of my brother's case. Until I stood in the courtroom that day, I had never laid eyes on her."

"Go on."

"I recently discovered that I lost my job during my incarceration. I intend to get it back by solving the case I was paid to sort out."

Mr. Callum gave him a look that told Jefferson he was being studied closely. "Even though you have no obligation to do so?"

"But I do. I made a commitment. That has not changed despite the fact I am no longer on the payroll. In fact, I am more determined now than ever."

Seamus continued to observe him. Then, slowly, he nodded. "Finish your story."

"There is an overlap in the case I was working on and the case recently given to your daughter. I need her to partner with me on this."

"And she isn't willing?"

"She is, or rather she was. I think she may not like the idea of how I plan to go about securing her release from your custody."

Seamus laughed. "I suppose it would feel as though she's under house arrest here, what with Sadie's ability to do what she wishes as long as she doesn't try to do it under my roof."

"Apparently she values your opinion of her. And your wife's too. She cannot stay at Callum Plantation and solve this case."

"Is that why she went to New Orleans today?"

Jefferson paused. "I cannot say."

"Cannot or will not?" He waved away a response. "Never mind. So let me see if I understand. You wish to facilitate my daughter's escape from River Pointe by making it appear that you are heading off on a honeymoon so I won't make a fuss and my wife won't send a couple of my boys after her?"

"Exactly. Although, now that you've said it, I admit I don't like the idea that we're deceiving the family. I only thought it a better way to handle the issue of allowing Sadie to leave."

Seamus gave him a sideways look. "Can't you do your job without her?"

"Easily, but she's good at her job, sir, and I would prefer to have her expertise. With Sadie along, I can use her ability to secure invitations into society I might otherwise be unable to get. Her presence will help me do my job better and much faster."

"Deception is never the better way, son." He gave Jefferson a moment to consider that statement. "However, I see your point. Maybe we can figure out something."

"We, sir?"

Seamus fixed him with a look. "She's my daughter, Tucker. I think I know better than you how she thinks and why she does what she does."

Why did she kiss me? The thought emerged seemingly from nowhere.

"Tucker?"

He shook off the recollection but allowed that he might revisit it. When her father wasn't watching, that is.

"Yes, Mr. Callum."

Sadie's father reached across the distance between them to shake Jefferson's hand. "You might want to call me Seamus, seeing as we're about to become family."

Jefferson waited for the smile that never came. "You're serious."

The older man shrugged. "Sarah Louise will think so, and more importantly, so will her mother. Now, here's what we're going to do."

Thirty

Sadie looked up from the notes on the Astor case to answer Julia's knock. The maid hurried in with a folded piece of paper that she presented with a look of urgency.

She tucked her hands in her apron pockets. "The mister says I'm to wait for a response."

"All right."

Sadie opened the note and read Jefferson's demand for an immediate meeting on a matter of great importance. Unfortunately, he did not offer any insight as to what that matter might be.

Her lack of proper dress, coupled with the fact

that she was making progress in analyzing a rather complicated index of purchases made by Mrs. Astor for the Newport home she called Beaulieu made Sadie's first response a definite no.

And yet at this late hour, what could he want except to discuss something related to the case? For surely she had said her last word on the subject of his ridiculous plan to marry her.

A glance up at the paper-wrapped parcel on the armoire sealed her decision. She carefully folded the index and returned it to her valise along with her notebook and pencil and then allowed Julia to help her dress once more.

Retrieving the carpetbag from its hiding place in the back of her armoire, she removed Julia's green dress and stuffed it into the recesses of the wardrobe. Reaching for Mr. Tucker's parcel, she gave it one last looking over and then placed it inside the carpetbag.

She reached for her shawl and then slipped downstairs and out into the night. By the time she found the groom and had a horse saddled, the entire adventure was bordering on the ridiculous. Why couldn't the man just request a conversation in the parlor with her like a normal fellow?

Because there was nothing normal about Jefferson Tucker. And he had come to her rescue earlier today.

As Sadie guided the mare along the path that led toward the clearing, a lantern latched onto a stick fastened to the saddle illuminated what the moon-light did not. And that same moon bore signs that the heavy night air would eventually give way to rain.

For now, however, only the earthy scent of the cane fields, the chirp of crickets at the river's edge, and the soft breeze that swished their green tops disturbed the quiet. Ahead she spied the outline of a man on horseback.

Jefferson.

She urged the mare forward, keeping the lantern steady and the carpetbag firmly hung on the saddle horn until she reached her destination. Tucker's mount whinnied a greeting, but the man remained silent as he took the lantern and set it aside to help her down from the saddle.

"Thank you for coming," he said as he took her horse's reins and tied them to the post near where he had already secured the gelding. "Let's go in here where we can be assured our privacy."

If he wondered about the carpetbag, he said nothing to that effect. Rather, his arm guided her until she had crossed the uneven ground in the clearing and reached an all-too-familiar building.

She followed him inside the old schoolhouse and then waited while he lit the personal lantern he pulled from his pocket. Sadie hadn't stepped inside the one-room building since Mama decided to send her away to be further educated.

The smell of old lumber assaulted her senses

and sent her mind tumbling backward. For a moment she was that little girl who sat midway down the second row, her blond hair captured in braids that the boys whose parents worked in the mill loved to tug.

Resolutely turning from the neat rows of desks, she watched as Jefferson pulled a chair near the fire and then set a blaze going in the fireplace. The golden glow bested the harsh light from Kyle's invention.

Jefferson must have felt the same, for he extinguished the device and then brought a second chair to place before the fire. "Sit with me."

She did, and then impatience got the better of her as she placed the carpetbag on the floor beside her. "Couldn't this have waited until morning?"

He looked up from stoking the flames, and Sadie's breath caught. Firelight slanted across his features made him even more handsome.

"There is no time to waste, Sadie." Jefferson returned the poker to its place on the hearth and then sat back to fold his arms over his waist. "Tell me what happened today."

"You know what happened."

He shook his head. "Humor me and start from the beginning."

She thought to protest and then decided against it. "All right. I paid a visit to Monsieur Valletta's shop. He was not there when my maid and I arrived, or at least his assistant claimed his absence. I was able to gain access to Valletta's private apartment at the invitation of that assistant upon the guise of purchasing an item of particular interest."

"And what item was that?"

"An Egyptian feline burial crypt. Apparently with the bones still inside."

His brows rose, indicating surprise, and then lowered again. Definitely interest in that expression. "And then?"

"And then you know exactly what happened after that. You were there, after all."

"No, Sadie. I was not."

Her breath stuttered to a halt as she searched his expression for signs he might be teasing her. Finding none, she shook her head.

"You were," she insisted. "You saved me in the courtyard. Or rather you assisted me to the carriage. Julia saw you, as did our driver. In fact, Julia had a conversation with you beforehand as well while I was in Valletta's apartment."

Jefferson rose to take a few steps away, his boots echoing against the wide cypress boards. "I was here all day. With Ethan."

"That's not possible. You were . . ."

"I was fishing with Donovan. And then later Ethan took me on a most impressive tour of the building where your father's sugarcane processing takes place."

She searched his face. "Oh, that is a funny joke."

"It is no joke. Think Sadie. What did we have for supper?"

"Fish, but—"

"Fish that Donovan and I caught. Lest you think I'm not telling the truth, I can now tell you that the evaporator is located just north of the boiling house, bagasse is used as fuel for the boiler, and, thanks to his time at Louisiana State University, your brother has some interesting ideas for mechanizing several aspects of the refining process. Care to hear more?"

She shook her head and the reality of what happened this afternoon—of who exactly was standing in the courtyard with her—sunk in. "That means . . ."

"The man at Valletta's shop was my brother."

Sadie leaned forward and grasped her knees as a sudden wave of dizziness hit her. "I swore to arrest him, and instead . . ."

"You allowed him to help you to the carriage." He stopped his pacing to stand before her. "Tell me everything that led up to the moment John spoke to you in the courtyard."

"Monsieur Valletta . . ." She paused to recollect the details. "He was climbing down the back stairs with a burlap sack. When I called to him, he threw the bag at me. I fell and . . ."

"What happened to the bag?"

She let out a long breath. "Valletta took it. I

tried to save an amulet, but he ground his shoe into my hand."

Sadie showed him where a red blotch on the top of her right hand marked the spot. Jefferson took her hand in his and seemed to be examining the remains of the injury.

"Go on."

Sadie shrugged. "I don't recall much beyond that moment, at least not clearly."

"But my brother assisted you to the carriage?" At her nod, he continued. "Did he say anything?"

"Nothing that I remember beyond reassuring me that he would see to my safety."

"And before that? Did he speak to you or perhaps have a conversation with Valletta in your presence?"

"No." She thought a moment. "Do you think he was following me?"

"My guess is that he was meeting Valletta and did not expect to see anyone but him." Jefferson released his hold on Sadie's hand and then rose to resume his pacing. "I have seen John once since my release from Angola."

"What?" She stood and caught up to him. "And you did not think it prudent to mention that fact to me? Did you tell Kyle?"

"It happened when I first returned to Mobile. And yes, Kyle knows."

"Go on."

Her echo of his phrase made Jefferson smile.

"There's nothing further to tell beyond a cryptic remark John made about Valletta. Something about how Valletta thinks he knows me well but he does not."

"John has been passing as you."

Jefferson offered a weak smile. "As you can attest, it would not be the first time."

"Indeed." She went to the window. Outside the cane swayed and a cloud drifted lazily over the moon. "Does he mean you harm?"

"An interesting question," Jefferson said as he moved to stand beside her. "What do you think?"

"I think he wishes he were you." She slid him a sideways glance. "And when someone wishes to be someone else, that can make for a dangerous situation."

"I'm not afraid of him. Nor is he my first priority right now." He paused only a moment. "I have secured passage to Newport for us."

She stepped away from the window to respond carefully. "I have plans to take a train to New York City at the end of the week."

Jefferson shook his head. "The Rembrandt is in Newport. At Beaulieu. And I can have you standing in front of it well before you can manage it on your own."

At her astonished expression, he chuckled. "Was that a test, Sadie? If so, you failed it miserably. Or perhaps you do not wish to have me along as you solve your case."

"I work best alone."

He dipped his head and then met her gaze. "As do I."

"Then we are agreed."

He stepped in front of her. "Hardly. I need you. And you need me."

"Hardly."

She moved around him, her eyes on the door. Once again, he blocked her path and then turned her around to walk with her back to their place near the fire. She allowed it as much for the warmth as the fact that though she wanted a hasty exit, the rain that threatened was not exactly beckoning her outside.

"You cannot gain access to Mrs. Astor and her friends without me," she said. "That is why you're keen on coming along."

"And without me, you cannot leave Callum Plantation unless you wish to invoke the wrath of your mother and father and likely end up with one or more of your brothers in tow. I have it on good authority your uncle's traveling days are over."

His smile irked her, as did his stance. Worse, he was right. She moved to go past him again and he countered.

"I know why Brent and Cade were in Baton Rouge. Your mother wishes you to have protectors. I understand Aaron was sent to Denver, and I believe Donovan was called upon to attend a particularly interesting meeting between you,

Kyle Russell, and an agent by the name of Lucas McMinn in Natchez. Or was it New Orleans?"

She knew the answer but would not reply. What she hadn't known was that Donovan had followed.

"I can see that you do not doubt me. I wonder if you're willing to listen just yet. Or perhaps I need to offer more examples?"

"No, you've made your point." A jagged flash of lightning heralded the bad weather that the moon had predicted. "However, I believe any further conversation on the topic can wait. If you'll excuse me."

"Not yet."

Thirty-one

Jefferson looked down into Sadie's eyes and tried to decide if he could go through with the plan he and Seamus had decided upon. It would work. But should it?

Something about this woman had rendered her unforgettable, even beyond the way she had taken on a judge to see him released from prison. Though she was stunning, one of the most beautiful women he had ever laid eyes on, the depth of what lay behind those eyes, that smile . . . that was what captured his attention and held it.

"You're looking at me in the oddest way, Jefferson."

The object of his thoughts swept past as regal as a queen escaping her throne room. When she paused at the door, he took the moment to consider her in silhouette.

Though Callum Plantation with its grandeur and beauty suited her quite well, Sarah Louise Callum was made for greater things. And thus his mind was made up.

"We need each other, Sadie. Let me get you out of River Pointe and back to work as a Pinkerton agent."

She turned toward him, her face still hidden in shadows. He heard her soft sigh.

"You know I'm right," he added gently.

Her chin tilted up and her shoulders dropped. He knew that pose: Resignation. Again she allowed him to lead her back into the circle of firelight.

"Hear me out," he said gently. "That's all I ask."

"I won't pretend to marry you, Jefferson. That's ridiculous."

"And it would cause you to be required to arrest your pretend brother-in-law, which might prove uncomfortable at family gatherings."

"You're teasing me."

"Only slightly."

She crossed her hands over her waist. "I will not lie to my family."

"I am not asking you to."

"No?" Her voice held a measure of interest that gave him hope she might actually cooperate.

"I have spoken to your father. He approves of my plan."

Only after he made the statement did Jefferson consider the fact he probably should have termed the scheme *their* plan. Seamus had certainly provided his input.

"You *what?*" Indignation rose on her pretty face, accompanied by the loveliest color of pink in her cheeks. "How dare you go to my father and tell him—"

"I told him nothing, Sadie. Nothing beyond the fact that I had business that required travel and needed your assistance."

"I doubt he believed you."

"Then you would be wrong." Jefferson leaned in, inhaled the lavender and lemon scent of the Lavande perfume that was uniquely Sadie. "Trust me."

"I shouldn't." And yet her expression told him she would. "I will speak to Daddy before deciding."

"You have one hour. Pack what you can, including at least three of your ball gowns as I expect we will be called upon to socialize. Then you can speak to your father, although I warn you he will tell you that what I've said is true."

"One hour?" She laughed. "Stop teasing me."

"I assure you I am quite serious." He paused to nod behind him toward the river. "Our means of escape docked this afternoon."

"Here? At Callum Plantation?"

He decided his nod was answer enough for her. "Unless we leave in one hour, your mother will be home from her benevolence society meeting and, unless your father and I are wrong, will very likely prevent you from leaving quietly."

"Yes, I would imagine she might put up a fuss."

"Agreed. So you will tell no one. Not even your maid."

Sadie shook her head. "But I had hoped to take Julia with me. For propriety, if nothing else."

"You can't, Sadie. Not this time. And I assure you propriety will not be an issue."

Behind Sadie, Jefferson spied Seamus standing in the doorway. Right on time. He tipped his head in greeting, and Jefferson did the same.

Sadie reached out to place her hand on Jefferson's sleeve, drawing his attention. "But, if I leave in an hour without saying a word to anyone, Mama will—"

"Your mother will believe what I tell her," Seamus said.

"Daddy?" Sadie bounded across the room and into her father's arms, now heedless of anything so mundane as propriety. "Is it true? Have you and Jefferson spoken?"

Seamus chuckled as he held his daughter at arm's length. "We have. Listen to what he says and do it."

"But . . ."

"You wonder why I give my blessing to this?" At her nod, he continued. "The Pinkerton Agency needs you to do what you do best."

At his use of the word "Pinkerton," Sadie gasped and then turned back toward Jefferson. "You told him!"

"No, Sadie," her father said. "Your Mr. Tucker said nothing of the kind. I've known for quite a while."

"But how? Uncle Penn?"

Again Seamus chuckled. "That old goat wouldn't tell me the time of day if he thought I really wanted to know. No, sunshine, I figured it out on my own."

"How?"

His tender expression made Jefferson smile.

Her father smiled too. "Don't you think I know you at all, Sarah Louise? You're suited to this, and I applaud Allan Pinkerton for recognizing he had an agent in you instead of a secretary."

"You knew about that too?"

Her father shrugged. "I will admit I paid the man a visit when I suspected. He wouldn't say a word either way, but when I left Chicago, I knew in my heart what was the truth. And, Sadie?"

"Yes?" she said as Seamus gathered her into his arms.

"A daddy couldn't be prouder of you than I am. Worried sometimes, yes, but proud."

"But why send the boys? And why demand I come home?"

"I miss you. I won't apologize for that. As for sending the boys, that would not be my doing."

"I see." She glanced over her shoulder at Jefferson, who upped his grin. "So you approve of this plan for me to leave with Mr. Tucker here?" Sadie returned her attention to her father. "He says I have one hour to get ready."

Seamus met his gaze. "Then you should listen to him."

"And Mama?"

"Your mother has no idea about your employment as a Pinkerton or your plans to travel tonight." He reached to sweep a strand of blond hair away from her face. "If she's not worrying about you, then she might start using some of that energy to worry about me. I prefer to keep things as they are."

"Yes, Daddy. All right."

"Then perhaps you ought to go and do as I say," Jefferson said. "Time is short."

"Yes, of course." Her smile was radiant as she stepped out of her father's embrace.

"Oh!" Sadie scooted around Jefferson and hurried over to the fireplace. She returned to hand him a package wrapped in brown paper. "This is yours."

He tucked the parcel under his arm. "I will open it once our journey is underway. Now go. And hurry."

"Why don't I see our girl back to the house before the rain drenches us all?" Seamus said.

"One hour," Jefferson called as he watched the Callums slip out into the night arm in arm.

Only as he was banking the fire and preparing to leave himself did Jefferson take note of Seamus Callum's parting words.

Our girl.

Yes. In other circumstances, careers and detective work notwithstanding, he could easily see Sadie Callum as his girl. A sobering thought.

And an intriguing one.

Sadie stuffed Julia's green dress back into the carpetbag and returned the bag to its hiding place in the armoire. With one last look around the room, she gathered up her valise and turned toward the door.

The knock surprised her, and she gasped.

"Do have some patience. It has not yet been an hour," she said as she opened the door to find her maid standing there.

Julia looked down at the valise in Sadie's hand and then past her, likely seeing the trunk that had been hastily packed. "Are you leaving, miss?"

What to say?

Her hesitance must have been answer enough for Julia, for the maid's expression quickly fell. "You're going without me."

After glancing both directions down the hallway, she gestured for Julia to come inside her room. Shutting the door behind them, Sadie set the valise aside and then took a deep breath and let it out slowly.

"If this is because of the way I didn't completely listen to all your instructions this afternoon, I am ever so sorry. I didn't intend to ignore what you said. I just didn't expect that the mister would come in and surprise me, and then that Valletta fellow . . . well, he did give me a start."

"I assure you this has nothing to do with what happened there." Sadie paused to consider a question that had been niggling at her thoughts. "I do wonder something," she said slowly, her gaze never leaving Julia's face. "How did Monsieur Valletta know your name?"

The maid's eyes widened and then her expression quickly shuttered. "Likely he heard you call me Julia."

"No," she said evenly. "Your *last* name, Julia. How did he know it was Oakman?"

The girl opened her mouth as if to comment and then resolutely shut it again. Wherever the truth was, it appeared the maid was not eager to offer it.

"Julia?"

Another knock, this one much louder, much more insistent. "It's time."

Jefferson.

She moved past Julia toward the door, opening it slightly to reveal her soon-to-be traveling companion. Behind him were two stable boys, likely the means by which her trunk would be delivered to the river.

"A moment, please."

"There's no time to spare," he insisted as he reached beyond her to open the door. "We must be off before your mother returns from her meeting . . ." He paused, his gaze fixed on Julia. "Oh."

"I was just speaking with my maid about a private matter. Why don't you have my trunk taken down and then I'll follow in a moment?"

"All right."

Sadie leaned in. "You're certain she cannot accompany me?" she whispered.

"No, she cannot."

Nodding, she turned to face her maid while the stable boys hefted the trunk onto their shoulders and carried it out behind Jefferson. Being careful to close the door behind them, Sadie returned her focus to Julia.

"Is there something you wish to tell me?" she asked the maid.

The girl lifted her chin, her expression now kind rather than blank. "Nothing, miss. I swear it."

"And Monsieur Valletta's use of your last name?"

"I do not recall it," she said emphatically. "Are you certain of it? Perhaps in the excitement and hitting your head and all, you don't recollect things as they actually were?"

Grudgingly admitting this might be possible, Sadie still elected not to give voice to the thought. Rather, she nodded toward the armoire.

"The carpetbag containing your green dress is in there. You may have it."

"Truly?" Her lips turned up in the beginnings of a smile. "You're certain? How will I explain it to the cook and the others?"

"Tell them it is a gift from me. A gift bestowed from a trust in your discretion." This time her expression held none of her previous patience. "And the belief that your allegiance lies with me. Do not prove me wrong, Julia."

"No, miss. And thank you, truly." She offered Sadie a hug and then stepped back, stricken. "I do apologize. My emotions did get the better of me."

"See that indiscretion does not." Sadie once again reached for her valise. "You will tell no one of this conversation. Do you understand?"

"I do, miss. But when will you return?"

"I cannot say." She met the girl's gaze. "However, I will return. You have my word."

"And then may I count on traveling along with you?"

"I had hoped that would be the case." Sadie reached for the doorknob. "However, whether you travel with me or not will depend on your actions in my absence. I cannot travel with someone I cannot trust."

Julia nodded vigorously, the carpetbag clutched

to her chest. "You can count on me. I give you my word. Not a peep of our conversation to anyone, and that is a promise."

Sadie stepped out into the hallway, leaving Julia to follow in her footsteps as she made her way downstairs to find Daddy waiting for her at the front door.

Without a word, he welcomed her into his arms and then ushered her out into the night. When they arrived at the Callum Plantation docks, Jefferson was waiting.

Sadie tarried only long enough to offer Daddy a quick hug. "Thank you," she said as she kissed his grizzled cheek.

He shook his head. "Don't thank me. You're doing what you're supposed to be doing. I'm just making it more likely you'll leave without your mama following."

She gave him one more hug and then stepped back from his embrace. "About Mama . . ."

"Leave her to me."

"But what are you going to tell her?"

He looked past her to where Jefferson was waiting. "Just let me handle it. Go solve this case. I'll be waiting for you when you get back."

Stealing one last hug from Daddy, Sadie did as she was told, allowing Jefferson to assist her up the gangplank and onto the deck of the three-masted schooner emblazoned with the name *Lizzie*. As she moved out of their way, crewmen hurried to loosen the ropes and ready the vessel for departure.

Daddy stood still and tall on the dock until the vessel pulled away. Only then did he raise a hand to wave.

Behind him, a carriage appeared heading down the River Road toward Callum Plantation. *Mama.*

Though tempted to hide, Sadie doubted her mother could see her. For that matter, she probably would give little heed to yet another set of sails unfurling to move the vessel downriver toward the open seas.

Still, Sadie kept watch until Daddy and the docks disappeared around a bend in the river. Only then did Jefferson tap her on the shoulder. She turned to find him standing next to a handsome older man dressed in what appeared to be a naval uniform of impressive rank.

"Hello," she said to the gentleman before focusing on Jefferson.

"Sadie Callum," he said, "may I present the captain of our vessel and the man who promises our arrival in Newport will be made in record time. He also happens to be my father."

"Harrison William Tucker, at your service," he said.

Wonderful. Another Will Tucker.

Thirty-two

Captain Tucker was every bit as charming as his son, and also every bit as good a navigator as he claimed to be. The vessel arrived in the Gulf of Mexico ahead of schedule and skirted the coastline past Mobile without stopping.

"No visit to your mother this time around?" Jefferson asked his father as they sat together in the large captain's suite that had become their living area during the voyage.

"You know she wouldn't allow a quick visit. I figure I'll appease her by spending a few weeks there once I've deposited you and the girl in Newport."

The conversation continued, father and son chatting easily as the day fell toward dusk outside. Though Sadie pretended interest in the novel in her hands, her attention refused to be caught by the words on the page. Finally, she gave up and set the book aside, allowing her gaze to travel the length of the salon.

While her accommodations were luxurious by maritime standards, the expansive room that was Captain Tucker's private domain made hers look like the maid's quarters. From the paneled walls to furniture that would have looked just fine in Mama's fanciest reception room, the space was much more than merely a place for the Tuckers to keep out of the glaring May sunshine.

Jefferson had appropriated the captain's desk, and it was now covered in handwritten pages and pieces of evidence he had collected prior to his imprisonment. As yet, Sadie had not decided whether to offer her own notes to compare with his. Still, she eyed the pages with interest anytime she managed to come near them.

"You still do not trust me?" Jefferson said when he noticed her peering over in the direction of the desk.

"Let the girl be," Captain Tucker said as he headed out of the cabin. "I'd say she has good instincts. A woman cannot fully trust a man she does not know. Rather, ask yourself 'How well does she know me?' "

She gave the older Tucker a grateful smile as he disappeared into the corridor, leaving them alone. Jefferson crossed the salon to settle in a Louis IV chair nearby.

The sea breeze had tousled his hair, while the sun had bronzed his skin. Were she not absolutely certain that Jefferson Tucker was a British detective to his core, she might suspect he took well to life at sea.

"Is he right?"

"About not trusting you?" Sadie shrugged. "Not completely."

"If you do not completely trust me, then you

don't trust me at all." He rose to move to the desk. "Come take a look at this."

She thought only a moment before joining him. Jefferson arranged the pages before her and then nodded.

"Go ahead. See what you think."

Settling into the captain's chair, she picked up the first page she saw and began to read. The document was an account of a merchant vessel captain who had taken possession of several crates from a shipper in Baghdad and delivered them to London.

Among the items on the manifest, most of which were Iraqi in origin, was an Egyptian feline casket that appeared similar in description to the one Sadie had examined in Monsieur Valletta's shop. Jefferson nodded to another page.

"The amulet," he said. "Would it be similar to any of those mentioned in this list?"

"Yes, this one." She pointed to a note in the ledger that referred to a carnelian amulet in the form of a seated figure of Harpocrates.

"You're certain it is the same one?"

"Of course I'm not certain, Jefferson," she said as she pushed the manifest away and looked up at him. "But it could be."

He slid the pages back in her direction. "Take another look and see if anything else seems familiar."

Her gaze landed on a pottery funerary cone

and a limestone canopic jar. She pointed both out.

"What else did you see in Valletta's apartment? Think, Sadie."

"I *am* thinking," she snapped before letting out a long breath. "All right. There were boxes and crates very much like the one I . . ." Sadie looked up at him. "The parcel that was delivered for you. Did you open it?"

"I forgot all about it. I'll get it."

He headed off down the passageway, leaving Sadie alone. She rose to wander to the porthole, where the last rays of sunlight flooded the cabin. Ahead, a lighthouse stood high above a thick cluster of buildings, the beam from its lamp teasing waves with a dance of brilliant light.

"Good news, son. We're dining with Joe Porter tomorrow. You remember him, don't you? Oh . . ."

Sadie turned to see Jefferson's father standing in the doorway. "He's just gone to his cabin to retrieve something. I'm sure he'll be back in a minute."

Captain Tucker smiled. "That's just as well. I've wanted a moment alone with you."

The floor rumbled beneath her feet, causing Sadie to steady herself against the wall. "Oh?"

"You'll get your sea legs soon enough, Miss Callum." He nodded toward the chair she had only just vacated. "You may want to sit while we're passing by the reef, though. It's a bit choppy out here."

She complied and then watched as Captain Tucker joined her. "Enjoying yourself so far?"

His voice was as deep as Jefferson's, with more of the Southern tones she was accustomed to. His eyes were a deep blue, a shade darker than his son's.

"I am, actually. Most of my travel is by train anymore. I haven't taken a sea voyage since . . ." She almost said since she became a Pinkerton agent. Instead, she added, "Since the last time I traveled to Europe."

"How do you know my Jefferson?"

The change of topic caught her off guard. "He hasn't told you?"

"He has, but I'm not sure I believe him."

"I suppose the simplest answer is that I first knew John, and then, when my employer called upon me to decide which of the Tuckers was being held in Angola Prison, I came to know Jefferson."

"Your employer," he echoed. "That would be who?"

"The Pinkerton Agency." She watched him nod. "Was that not what Jefferson told you?"

"Oh, he did say that, but I found it difficult to believe that a woman of your beauty and obvious intelligence would be employed at all. I rather thought he was playing a joke on me or perhaps making an attempt to steal away with a pretty lady."

"I assure you neither is the case."

"I understand. I had a moment to converse with your father whilst my boy was breaking the news to you of your travel plans. Nice fellow, Callum."

She easily offered a warm smile. "Yes, I rather like him."

"As to your being an agent?" He waved away any protest she might have made with a sweep of his hand. "Don't misunderstand me. I have nothing but the utmost respect for the Pinkerton Agency, their stance during the War Between the States notwithstanding."

"He's not telling you how women should be waiting at home while the men go off to work, is he?"

Sadie smiled as she glanced over at Jefferson, who now held the parcel in one hand. "Not exactly."

"Not at all," Captain Tucker said to his son. "My point was completely misunderstood. It's just that you are so lovely and delicate, my dear," he said, his focus now on Sadie. "I cannot imagine you would find it interesting at all to work in a man's field."

"Yes, Dad, that is so much better than just telling her she ought to be home awaiting the return of a husband." Jefferson shook his head. "Any doubts of Sadie's abilities were gone when she dispatched a snake at close range. In the dark."

"I will ignore your sarcasm, Jefferson. And I will not ask why the two of you were within range of a snake after dark." He watched as his son joined them. "Instead, I will ask what you have there."

"A package delivered to Callum Plantation with my name on it."

Jefferson turned the parcel over and studied it carefully. Then he removed his folding knife to cut away the paper, revealing what appeared to be the back of a small painting. Tossing aside the remainder of the wrappings, he turned the painting over.

"The Durer," Sadie said with a gasp. "Jefferson, that is the painting I saw at Monsieur Valletta's shop."

He met her gaze. "You're certain?"

"You're going to ask that again?"

"Sorry," he was quick to say. "I merely meant to inquire as to whether you were certain this was the exact same painting."

She thought back to the stacks of parcels all wrapped in the same paper. Her mind recalled the crates piled randomly around the apartment and situated here and there in the shop below.

"It is possible there are many copies of the same painting, but yes, I saw this exact one unwrapped and stacked on a shelf in his armoire."

"Well, then," Captain Tucker said as he rose. "It appears the two of you have a right and proper mystery to solve, so I will leave you to it. Just so you're aware, we will be making a stop in Key West. Joe Porter's invited us to dine tomorrow, and I accepted on your behalf."

"Wait, that's not possible," Jefferson said. "Sadie and I need to get to Newport as soon as possible."

"And you will. However, I have an interest in looking at a nice piece of property that's recently come available. If I wait to stop in on the way back to Mobile, I could very well run into storm season. And you know what that means."

Growing up on the coast, Sadie did. And from the expression on Jefferson's face, so did he. Storms brewed in the Gulf only to blow on shore with little notice. Taking chances in a vessel of this size when those chances could be avoided was foolish.

"We'll drop anchor sometime after midnight. Dr. Porter isn't expecting us until lunch, so don't feel that you need to get up too early. I, however, will be saying good night as I don't expect to come back and bother you before bedtime."

Jefferson watched his father leave the salon and wondered what in the world had gotten into the man. Lecturing Sadie on why she ought not remain a Pinkerton? Questioning her as to why she joined up?

"I apologize for him. My father means well, but

392

he doesn't understand the modern woman's ability to choose a life outside of the home."

"Nor does mine," she said. "Or at least I didn't think he did. Now, well, I suppose he's making an exception with me. Temporarily, is my guess."

He watched her hold the painting without actually looking at it and wondered where her thoughts had gone. And then, just as quickly, her attention returned to him and to the Durer.

Setting the painting aside, he leaned back to consider his next statement carefully. "So now that we've decided our fathers are hopelessly mired in the past, can we also agree that we are now working together on this case? Or do I still need to earn your trust?"

"It is in our nature to question things, don't you think? That's what makes for good detective work."

"I agree, but that does not answer my question."

Sadie met his gaze with a direct look. "Part of my assignment is to determine which Tucker, if either of you, has a part in the Astor case."

Jefferson shook his head. "I don't follow."

"The agency is aware that there have been mentions of Will Tucker's involvement with Valletta. Part of my job has been to determine which Will Tucker is the guilty party." She paused. "Or whether you both are involved."

The admission was a surprise. And yet he should have expected as much. If the Pinkertons had enough information on him in their files to free him from Angola Prison, then they certainly ought to also be aware of other information regarding his whereabouts and associations.

"I see. And have you decided?"

"Jefferson, my father decided for me."

"I don't follow."

"I am here because Seamus Callum made it possible. And while you have not yet completely earned my trust, Daddy has."

"So, trust by proxy then? I'll take it." He nodded toward the desk. "Shall we go and see what we can make of these clues?"

Sadie rose. "Not yet."

Irritation flared as he watched her walk out of the salon. What more could the woman want than what he had already offered as proof of his allegiance?

Thirty-three

Jefferson stalked to the desk muttering under his breath about the irrationalities of the female persuasion. Situating himself in his father's chair, he began to put the pieces of the puzzle together in what he hoped would be an orderly fashion.

Testimonies from British Museum officials at the Iraq dig site went in one pile. Those he would use to document the antiquities that had been excavated and declared under the purview and ownership of the museum.

A list of officials and employees of all agencies associated with the dig went into another stack. To that stack, he also added the roster listing the names of all persons and shops known to possess or sell items that were either directly connected to the dig or possible forgeries of those items. These would be used to compile a list of suspects.

Then came a most perplexing set of documents. These fit into neither category and seemed to defy classification beyond the fact that some of the same persons, shops, or bills of lading were involved. His gift of the Durer painting fit in that category too.

He set them aside and began to read the topmost page carefully, although he had already committed each document to memory.

"Jefferson?"

Startled, he looked up to see Sadie standing in the doorway, a battered valise tucked under one arm. The fact she'd managed to take him by surprise was most disconcerting.

As was her smile.

"What do you have there?" he asked when she set the valise on the desk between the two large stacks of papers.

"The full resources of the Pinkerton Agency. And the expertise of one of its best agents."

She laughed when she said that last part, and

yet Jefferson found no humor in it. She was good, and though he had nothing with which to compare, given her quick thinking and critical skills, a case could certainly be made for that statement.

What he did know was there couldn't possibly be another agent who combined brains with beauty the way Sadie Callum did.

He met her gaze. Allowed his attention to fall to her smile. Her lips. Indeed, he would have a most difficult time of concentrating in her presence.

"Jefferson?"

She shook her head when his eyes found hers again and then tucked a strand of straw-colored hair behind her ear. The faintest scent of lavender and lemons teased him as she settled into the chair across from him and then proceeded to unload the contents of her valise.

Several notebooks and a collection of news-papers wrapped with a yellow ribbon landed on the desk. Next she retrieved three file folders and placed them neatly atop the newspapers.

With each movement, each moment of concen-tration, her expression softened. Thick lashes teased cheekbones of creamy ivory skin warmed by the lamp's glow as she paused to open yet another notebook and glanced down at the pages.

Her gaze lifted to sweep the contents of his desk before returning to her task. When she was finished, the notebook now set atop the others and Sadie looked up at him expectantly.

"Somewhere in all of this is a connection. We just have to find it."

"Simply put," he said. "And yet you're correct."

She sat back and directed her attention to the pencil she held. "Perhaps if we each were to write the facts of the case in some order, chronological I think, then maybe we will see a clearer path to the solution."

"All right," he said as he retrieved writing paper from the desk. He offered a sheet to her, but she declined and retrieved her notebook once more.

"Beginning to end?" Jefferson asked.

"Yes, I believe so."

Sadie applied herself to the task with vigor while he struggled to recall just what he was to be writing. Yes, the genesis of the case from the moment he was called into service until his incarceration. He wrote the dates of his travels, almost three years in all, and then noted the cities where he had found pieces of the puzzle that lay on the desk before her.

It all added up to nothing more than a travelogue. Certainly no new clues emerged.

Then he decided to follow the trail of one piece to see if the facts became clearer in specific rather than in general. After drawing the piece, he thought of Baghdad, where he had occasion to watch a particularly valuable coin being painstakingly pulled from the muck after centuries of debris had covered it. To Rome, where that same coin was cleaned and prepared for shipping. Then came Paris, where the piece was spotted for sale in a shop in the Fourth Arrondissement before disappearing. And finally to London, where a coin that appeared startlingly similar was sold at auction by Sotheby's.

Only after the sale did the owner cry foul and claim forgery. That case was still pending, though the reputation of the auction house and thoroughness of their staff precluded any such nonsense as selling forged coins.

However, the word among Jefferson's informants was that while the Sotheby's coin was real, the person making the claim against the venerable auction house might very well be fake. It was an odd conundrum he hadn't quite worked out yet. Why would a person whose identity was false make a claim against an artifact that was real?

He considered Sotheby's as the connection and then quickly discarded it. They didn't deal with most of the items on the list.

Sadie looked up and then leaned forward to peer down at his notes. "That coin," she said. "I've seen it."

He shrugged. "I don't doubt it. There are many of them. Most are real."

"May I?" At his nod, she retrieved his notes and read through them.

"So your case hinges on provenance? If an item

was part of the museum dig, then it belongs to the museum?"

"Yes."

"Then that means there is a common thread in how these items got from their place of origin to the place where they were sold."

"Yes," he said again, his frustration rising. "And yet I cannot find one connection to tie the facts together."

"Surely there must be. Think, Jefferson," she said in an echo of his previous demand of her.

Unbidden came the recollection of their kisses. Of how she felt leaning against him in the moonlight on the banks of the Mississippi with the stars falling overhead.

"I'm trying not to." He pushed back from the desk. "Let's talk about the Durer. And Valletta."

"All right." She sat back primly as if waiting to be questioned. "What do you want to know?"

"Tell me your impression. What does your gut tell you about Valletta?"

"He's a forger?" She shook her head. "No. Too plebian. That man is a collector. Oh! That's it. He is a collector. But he cannot have what belongs in a museum. So . . ." She stood, her fingers gripping the back of the chair. "So he hires out forgeries of the pieces he wants and then . . ."

She began to move, stepping around the chair to walk the length of the room. Outside a watch bell clanged.

"And then?"

"And then he realizes how much money is to be made in the trafficking of these forgeries. The next step is to cultivate a network of artists and a pool of buyers." She stopped short. "Yes, that would explain all the wrapped parcels and crates in his apartment. But . . ."

She gave Jefferson a stricken look. "But what does that have to do with your case? The antiquities appearing on the London market are real but stolen. The ones Valletta had were forged but not stolen. Oh, Jefferson, it's all too confusing. Then there is the connection to John. And the Durer that mysteriously arrived at my home with your name on it."

She returned to her chair and sat with a most unladylike plop. Her eyes met his.

"Thoughts?"

Yes. I want to kiss you again.

"Yes," he said as he stood and walked around the desk to help Sadie to her feet. "We table this discussion for now and get some sleep. Sometimes what makes no sense at night becomes perfectly clear in the morning."

"I suppose you're right." She reached out to gather up her documents and return them to her valise.

Sadie awakened the next morning to a strange and eerie quiet, punctuated here and there by snatches of conversation spoken in hushed tones, the clang of a ship's bell in the distance, and the staccato of birds squawking overhead.

Key West.

Dressing quickly, she hurried past the salon and up onto the deck, where the brilliant sunshine stopped her in her tracks. Placing her hand over her eyes, she moved forward at a more decorous pace to join Jefferson as he stood in conversation with his father on the aft deck.

"Good morning," he said, and his father echoed the greeting.

Captain Tucker wore what appeared to be a dress uniform complete with gold buttons that gleamed in the morning sun. Jefferson, however, looked as if he were a planter on holiday with his summer suit and Panama hat.

"Indeed it is," she said as she surveyed the city sprawled out before her. From the red brick buildings to the collection of various structures tumbled together, Key West was indeed a treat to the eye. "We are going ashore, aren't we?"

"Yes," Jefferson said. "I will be happy to escort you."

"We can leave now," the captain called to both of them. "I've a meeting in half an hour and then I visit with the Porters. If you promise not to miss the luncheon, I will forgive you for not keeping an old man company this morning. But only if you'll see that I get where I need to be first."

Jefferson nodded toward the gangplank. "After you, Sadie," he said. "Have you been to Key West before?"

"Never."

"Let's remedy that then," he said as he helped her down the moveable bridge connecting the ship to solid ground.

Her feet were now on dry land, but her legs protested, leaving her knees feeling as if they might buckle. Putting a brave face on the silly infirmity, she pressed on and followed Jefferson across the docks and around the warehouse district to where a redbrick building, still under construction, loomed large among a dozen smaller buildings.

The morning was warm for May, and the breeze off the water scented the air with the briny smell of salt and fresh fish. Sadie allowed Jefferson to help her up into a small open carriage pulled by a sand-colored mare.

"Whitehead Street?" Jefferson said as he set the rented carriage in motion.

"Just down from Porter's place. Do you think you can remember where the doctor lives?"

"It hasn't been that long ago, Dad. I believe I can find it."

Jefferson eased the carriage into the throng of vehicles and set off away from the docks. Glad for the hat that shaded her face from the harsh sun, Sadie sat back to enjoy the ride.

The bustling city was larger than she expected, its population apparently divided among a mix of dandies in fancy dress, exotically costumed foreigners chattering in unrecognizable languages, and persons who might easily pass for a more criminal element elsewhere. A cluster of buildings, shops of many types, hugged Duval Street and provided a backdrop for the chaos that reigned on the avenue.

After making a left onto Southard Street, they were traveling where palm fronds dipped toward a dusty road clogged with carriages and wagons. Here chickens and pedestrians fought for what little space remained. Behind fences made of ironwork or wood were homes of various sizes.

As they turned down Whitehead Street the homes became larger and more uniform in size. And though the locale was tropical, Sadie only had to look beyond the hibiscus and palms to find mansions more suitable to the finer streets in New Orleans than here in such a remote location.

"Up there," the captain said.

Jefferson guided the carriage to a stop in front of a wedding cake confection of a home with porches and fretwork all around both levels. Bidding them goodbye, Captain Tucker headed toward the front door of the home as Jefferson eased the carriage back onto Whitehead Street.

"What would you like to see?" he asked.

"Just give me the grand tour," she said with a smile.

And so he did. After an hour's drive around the small island, they ended up back at the docks. Sadie noticed that a crowd had gathered.

"May we go see?" she asked Jefferson.

He took out his pocket watch and noted the time. "I don't suppose it would hurt," he said as he parked the carriage and then helped her down.

Her legs bothered Sadie less now, although if she paid close attention she could feel the phantom roll of the waves when she stood still. She stretched, happy to be on solid ground and yet feeling slightly guilty that she was enjoying a pleasurable morning as a tourist.

She linked arms with Jefferson and allowed him to escort her toward the group now gathered in a tight knot around a man who was nailing something to the broad side of a wall. A sign, she decided when he moved away.

Owing to his superior height, Jefferson could easily read what Sadie could not see for the crowd standing in her way. "What does it say?"

"It appears there will be an auction," he said as he released her arm and moved closer. "I didn't realize wrecking was still going on here. Apparently there's been a salvage."

The crowd parted as the man moved to open the doors of the warehouse. A moment later, most of those watching filed inside. Sadie joined them, leaving Jefferson to catch up.

Another set of doors opened on the opposite side of the warehouse, flooding the cavernlike space with light. Tables lined up in rows that went down the length of the room and offered a seemingly unrelated array of goods. Items too large for the tables were stacked in heaps wherever space could be found.

Sadie made her way toward a table covered in bolts of fabric, some decorated with elaborate embroidery and flecked with strands of gold and silver, stacks of waterlogged books, and a tangle of fishing nets. Beneath the nets, she saw a child's doll and a pair of ladies dancing shoes.

At each table she found a similar combination of oddly placed articles, some of value and others seemingly worthless. Jefferson came up beside her and reached for a glass epergne. The delicate crystal vase, with its tall center flute that rose up from a wide bowl on an elevated foot with a lovely enameled pattern just beneath a wide row of gold gilding, was exquisite.

"Lovely," she said as she ran her fingers on the stripe of gold. "Eighteenth century. Probably English, and definitely handblown. Look at the craftsmanship."

"Yes, very nice," he said, though his expression showed more confusion than appeal.

Jefferson's attempt at finding an interest in the

delicate piece made her giggle. "You don't know what this is, do you?"

"Yes, of course." He held the epergne up to the light and seemed to be examining it. Then he shook his head. "No, I have no idea."

Sadie laughed again. "It's a glass epergne." As his brows gathered, she tried again. "A flower vase." She pointed to the tall flute in the center. "Flowers with long stems go here. Usually roses, although other varieties would look just as lovely. And here," she said as she gestured to the bowl attached at the bottom of the flute. "That is where flowers with shorter stems would go. Often this means the stems are removed altogether and left to float in the water. It's really quite lovely."

Jefferson returned the vase to the table. "I'll take your word for it."

She glanced around at the large pieces of furniture against the walls—a pair of Louis XIV armchairs over there and a late seventeenth-century Gloucestershire carved chest over there —and then returned her attention to Jefferson.

"What is all this? I mean, how do all of these odd items end up being jumbled together for a single auction?"

"Oh, that." He nudged her past a group of townsfolk who were debating whether to bid on several pieces of Spode serving pieces. "What do you know about the wrecking trade?"

"Wrecking?" She shook her head as they continued walking toward the door. "Nothing."

They emerged into the sunshine once more, the crowd outside now dispersed. "It's a nice morning. Perhaps we could walk?"

Sadie nodded and linked arms with him. They strolled away from the warehouse and down the sidewalk that snaked alongside the pier. Fat white gulls dipped and dived as fisherman mended nets down by the water, their vessels secured to the pier by ropes that held them taut against the tide.

"The wrecking trade," Jefferson said when they had walked a little farther, "was once the most profitable industry on the island." He stopped to turn toward the horizon. "Out there is one of the most treacherous navigational channels in the region. Until the lighthouse was built, vessels that were not piloted by captains familiar with the reef often ended up on it. And if there was a storm? Then even the most seasoned mariners were left to the mercy of the waves."

She followed his gaze out to the water and the blue sky beyond. "What does that have to do with all those items up for sale?"

"Often a ship could not be saved, but its passengers and cargo could. See that lookout tower over there?" he asked as he pointed to a platform off in the distance. "When a wreck was spied, the wreckers were called to duty. The first one to reach the ailing vessel was declared in charge of the salvage."

"So they saved the passengers and as much cargo as they could. And then they sold anything of value?"

"At regular auctions supervised by a judge, yes. I'll spare you a recitation of the rules and percentages and the requirements for licenses and such, but suffice it to say that even after the underwriters were paid, a man could become quite wealthy in this business."

"I see."

She noticed sails on the horizon and watched as they drew near. "So anything could end up for sale in a single auction?"

"Yes, theoretically."

A thought occurred. "Such as antiquities? And without having to prove any sort of provenance?"

Jefferson shrugged. "If they were on board a vessel at the time it was wrecked, then yes." He slanted her a look. "Why? What are you thinking?"

Sadie shook her head. "Don't mind me. I'm always trying to connect the dots in a case when I'm in the middle of it."

Thirty-four

Thoughts of the wreckers and their curious industry still plagued Sadie even as Jefferson removed his hat and escorted her into the front parlor of Dr. Porter's lovely home on Whitehead Street. Captain Tucker and the doctor were engaged in a discussion regarding the potential eradication of yellow fever when the butler announced them.

"Look who is here." The doctor turned his attention to Sadie as Captain Tucker made the introductions.

As they were led through the center of the home to an elegant dining room, Sadie noted the paintings and furniture and their contrast with the rather simple architecture. Had the doctor benefitted from the wrecker's auctions in purchasing these things? It appeared so. Or perhaps he merely had eclectic tastes.

After luncheon, where the men continued to discuss matters of business and public health and Sadie silently contemplated the particulars of the Astor case, the trio returned to the carriage. And while Sadie was no closer to solving any of the riddles presented in the documents she and Jefferson had studied last night, Captain Tucker was in great humor.

"Stop up here, would you, son?" he said as he gestured to a two-story house situated on a piece of property just down the street from the Porter home.

When Jefferson complied, his father jumped out of the carriage and strolled up to the front door to let himself in. "What do you suppose he's doing?" Sadie asked.

Jefferson's soft chuckle surprised her. "When it comes to my father, I rarely inquire." He swiveled in his seat to better converse with her. "You were awfully quiet earlier."

She mustered a small smile. "I thought it wise to listen rather than expose my lack of knowledgeof the particulars of the transmission of yellow fever."

"So you weren't mulling over the facts of our combined cases?"

She lifted her gaze to meet his. "I might have been."

"Oh, Sadie." His gentle, almost melancholy tone was not what she expected. "You're on a beautiful island on a lovely day in May. Can't you forget about the job and just enjoy yourself for a few hours?"

"Of course I can," she protested. "But under the circumstances I don't think we—"

"Ahoy, there," the captain called as he stepped out onto the porch. "Go on back to the schooner. I'll be along directly."

Jefferson gave Sadie a doubtful look and then went to speak with his father. After a few minutes of what appeared to be serious discussion, he returned.

"Apparently, he is considering the purchase of a home. This one."

"Oh." She shook her head. "Why? I mean, it's lovely and all, but why here? And why this one?"

Grasping the reins, Jefferson set the carriage in motion again. "The Tift family is selling, and it appears that my father is interested in buying. Beyond that, I have no idea."

"Well, this *is* a seaport. And your father has interests in shipping. Perhaps he wants a place convenient for that purpose. And wouldn't you think that most of the ships leaving from Southern ports would have to pass this area, at least indirectly?"

He looked over sharply. "How did you know that?"

"It was in the dossier on your brother."

The fact she knew about his family's background was, to say the least, disconcerting. That it was caused by an interest in John's past, however, was understandable.

"Yes, of course," he finally said.

Returning his attention to the road, Jefferson drove the remainder of the way to the docks in silence. After returning the carriage to the livery, he stepped out with his grin back in place.

"What is that for? I was certain you were upset with me for mentioning your brother."

"If by 'that' you mean my smile, then you will just have to wait. You see, I have my doubts about a statement you've made, and I am ready to allow you to prove it."

"Prove what?"

He set off down the sidewalk and she hurried to catch up. When a gust of wind captured her hat and hauled it into the air, Sadie stopped to fetch it from the gutter and then lost sight of her companion when he turned a corner. Only the fact that his hat still sat securely on his head kept her from losing him completely.

"What has gotten into you, Jefferson Tucker?" she asked when she found him again.

Slowing his pace, he allowed her to fall into step beside him. "Your hat. There's mud on it."

He paused at the walkway leading to the pier and took it from her hands. Retrieving his handkerchief, Jefferson made a futile attempt at wiping the hat clean.

"Never mind. I'll buy you another," he said as he tossed the ruined hat up and then watched it plummet into the sea.

"Jefferson! Whatever possessed you to do that?"

"You won't need it. Come with me."

Grasping her hand, he led her down the pier. "Wait here," he said before going over to speak to a fisherman who was busy mending his nets.

Sadie watched as the men carried on a lively discussion. A moment later, Jefferson motioned for her to join them. The boat behind the man was wretched in condition but lively in the choice of colors it had been painted. She couldn't imagine a less seaworthy craft.

"Come on," he said as he followed the fisherman to the water's edge.

She did as he asked, picking her way across the sandy shoreline. The fisherman eyed her with a grin and then handed Jefferson a pair of oars.

"Climb in," he told Sadie as he removed his Panama hat and tossed it into the boat.

"Into that?" She shook her head. "I don't think so."

With the sun glinting off his golden hair, and those blue eyes watching her closely, Sadie almost agreed to join him. Almost, but not quite.

"Enjoy your boat ride, Mr. Tucker," she said, sidestepping the surf as it splashed inches from her feet. "I will await your return aboard a proper sailing vessel."

He shrugged. "All right, Miss Callum, but you've proved my point."

Sadie put her back to the sun, the better to see the face of the man who had obviously lost all good sense. "And what point would that be?"

"That you cannot forget about your job and enjoy yourself."

He stuck one oar in the sand and leaned on it,

allowing the other oar to trail behind him. And then he grinned.

A man should never be so handsome and so persuasive. And yet it would be complete folly to climb into a boat that would very likely sink before they were more than a few feet from shore.

Then there was the matter of her hat, or rather the lack of one. A woman bent on fitting in with the well-born ladies of Newport society need not even make the attempt with freckles on her cheeks. To even consider it was pure madness.

So she turned her back on the fool and marched three steps up the beach before a rogue wave soaked her skirt almost to the waist. Startled, she landed in a puddle of skirts on the sand.

Tossing the oars into the rowboat, Jefferson hurried to help her stand. "Are you injured, Sadie?" he asked as he surveyed the damage.

"Just my pride," she said and then looked past him to the water. "However, you might want to see to your boat, Captain. It appears to be setting sail without you."

Jefferson turned to see the little boat slipping further from shore with each wave that tossed it. With a cry that sounded suspiciously like her daddy's version of the Rebel yell, the former detective went racing across the sand and into the water.

He lunged at the boat, catching the edge on the second try. Somehow he managed to tumble into the vessel without toppling it over or sinking. A moment later, he had both oars in hand and was rowing back toward the shore.

"Well done," she called as he drew near.

"Come on aboard," was his response as he swiped at the seawater dripping from his hair with the back of his hand. "I dare you."

"You dare me?" She laughed. "Truly, Jefferson, we are not children. Did you think I would take a dare?"

"No, of course not." He was almost close enough to touch now, his arms working the oars so that the little boat remained almost stationary despite the waves pounding against it. "Someone who is far too busy thinking of work instead of play would definitely never consider taking a dare of any kind. Especially one where she might actually enjoy herself."

"You are impossible!" she exclaimed, her hands firmly planted on her hips in what she hoped he would take as a sign of disapproval.

"Not impossible. Improbable, perhaps, but never impossible. Now get in the boat. People are beginning to stare."

A glance over her shoulder confirmed his allegation. Indeed, a half dozen or so of Key West's less stellar citizens had congregated at the near end of the pier and were watching intently.

To leave Jefferson to his game would mean walking past them. Alone. In a dress that was already soaked with seawater. The alternative was to sail away in that leaky tub with a madman at the helm.

Neither choice appealed.

"Come on, Sadie. Maybe we will catch up to your hat. Or I could take you out to the shallows and show you the mangroves where crabs climb all over and a vessel can sail through without seeing the sky. And though it's all the way out there, the water is only three feet deep. You can see down to the bottom and, if you're brave, you can touch starfish. Pluck lobsters right off the ocean floor."

That did sound interesting. The mangroves, that is. Her hat could float all the way to England for all she cared. And she certainly wouldn't be plucking lobsters any time soon. Not unless they were steamed and on a plate beside drawn butter.

She inched forward. "You're certain that thing can stay afloat?"

"Nothing is certain, Sadie. Live a little."

Nothing is certain.

She slipped out of her shoes and held them loosely in one hand. Still, she didn't move as the water teased her bare toes and rippled against her ankles, swirling at her skirts.

Live a little.

Something in that statement jolted her forward and sent her racing across the sand and into the warm water of the Gulf of Mexico. Her shoes landed next to Jefferson's Panama hat as the water swirled around her.

Mama would be appalled if she had seen the way Sadie threw herself into the little rowboat, emerging dripping but laughing as she climbed into a sitting position and wrung the seawater out of her skirts.

Her sputtering laughter combined with the taste of saltwater on her lips to sear a memory in her mind of a moment when she let go of all caution and concern. When she let go.

The coiffure she had hastily pinned into place this morning now tumbled down around her shoulders, but to worry with such a detail would mean she must release her grip on the seat. And to release her grip could very well mean that she would end up back in the ocean before the vessel itself went under.

With Jefferson seated behind her, the only evidence of his continued presence was the oars that appeared and then disappeared from sight as they met the tide head-on. Warm water splashed over the bow and dotted her bodice and face.

And it was glorious. Every terrifying moment of the battle to remain upright and out of the water was absolutely glorious.

Graceful gulls dipped low as if curious as to the identity of the heathen who laughed louder than their cries. A fish shot out of the water and then plopped down just inches from the side of the boat as if escorting them along their way.

Despite all odds, the little rowboat withstood the crashing waves and remained intact as Jefferson steered it into deeper water. Here the waves became ripples, the stiff wind a calmer breeze.

Sadie let go of the wood and felt the sting of a splinter as the feeling returned to her fingers. No matter. The saltwater would cure what she could not remedy at the moment.

"Look, Sadie, over there. Those are the mangroves."

Rising up on the horizon were thick clusters of what appeared to be nondescript shrubbery. As the little rowboat drew closer, it appeared as though these shrubs were growing directly out of the ocean's floor with no dry land to be seen.

Her fingers trailed in the warm water, the splinter nearly forgotten. Overhead the sun beamed warm but not unpleasantly so. She let out a long sigh.

"Look to your right," Jefferson said, the oars now still.

She looked down in time to spy a school of tiny fish, their bright hues a stunning contrast to the sandy ocean floor. The fish dispersed in a sparkling shot of color as a small shark with a black tip on its fin brushed past.

Jerking her hand from the water, she swiveled

around to find Jefferson grinning in her direction. "That shark could have bit my fingers!"

"It was just a baby and hardly concerned with either of us."

"It was a shark, nonetheless, with teeth and likely an appetite for fingers."

He responded with a shake of his head and then gestured to the mangroves. "You'll want to look up once we get inside."

"Look up?"

"Trust me. You'll understand once you see where we are going."

"All right."

She turned back around, resettled her skirts around her ankles, and then watched as the mangrove forest drew near. While she had been correct in guessing that the shrubs grew out of the ocean's floor, she did not expect that there would be gaps between the plants large enough for the rowboat to maneuver through.

"Sit down on the floor of the boat and then lean back against the seat so you can look up," Jefferson urged as he pointed the rowboat toward the largest of the openings into the forest.

Sadie did as he asked and then gasped when leaves blocked out the sunshine. Through the twisted branches of the mangroves, only dappled light filtered down, a welcome change.

"See the crabs?" he said softly. "They're climbing up the branches."

And they were. Dozens of them, most no bigger than her fist. Speckled and gray, the creatures skittered up and down the bent fingers of branches and roots that filled the little forest.

Disconcerting as it was to lay back and watch as sea creatures scurried about, it was also fascinating. Somehow green trees and sea life flourished this far from land.

"Fascinating."

"It is," Jefferson said softly, "and so are you."

He brought in the oars and let the rowboat drift, using his hands to move the craft along through the mangroves.

And then he rested his hands in his lap, allowing the water to chart their course. When the rowboat came to rest against a tangle of mangrove roots, Jefferson maneuvered himself into place beside her and threaded his fingers behind his head.

They sat there side by side watching the crustaceans as the breeze ruffled through the mangrove leaves.

"Thank you," Sadie finally said.

Jefferson turned his head just enough to see her. "For what?"

"This." She closed her eyes as a soft sigh escaped her lips.

And then he kissed her.

Thirty-five

He kissed her.

Jefferson scrambled into a sitting position and prepared to make his apologizes to the bedraggled sea creature who had stolen his good sense and replaced it with the need to hold her in his arms.

Any moment now Sadie Callum of the Pinkerton Detective Agency would express her righteous indignation at his presumptuous behavior. And he certainly would not blame her.

So he was not prepared for the fact that she opened her eyes and merely offered him a lazy smile.

Nothing is certain. Live a little.

What was he thinking? The answer? He wasn't. In fact, he was out of his mind entirely.

Retrieving the oars, he climbed into the back of the rowboat and maneuvered the craft back into open sea. When the sunlight hit Sadie's face, she opened her eyes and then shielded them with her hand.

"Can we do that again?"

For a moment Jefferson wondered whether she meant the meandering trip through the mangroves or the kiss. And then she smiled.

"I don't suppose there's time," she said.

"There's always time," he replied, still unsure as

to whether he was being called upon to kiss or row.

She sat up then and swiveled around to face him, her elbows resting on her knees and her chin cradled in her palms. "Yes, that's true. Only not always when we want there to be."

"You're speaking in riddles."

"When I should be solving them." Sadie straightened her back and then snagged the tangles of her hair and began taming them into a thick braid. "Curious, don't you think, that my father would just let me go with you so easily. Why do you believe that is?"

Her eyes collided with his, even as her fingers continued to work their magic with her blond tresses. She knew something or suspected it. Or perhaps she only wanted to be reassured that she should feel no guilt over her hasty exit.

"I think your father realized that your need to go was greater than his need to keep you."

"Because I am a Pinkerton agent. Yes, I've thought of that." She stilled her movements and held the tip of her braid between her thumb and forefinger. "But why you? Why allow me to climb aboard a schooner with a stranger when before he raised a fuss when I left with my uncle? And why was he amenable to a match between us? That was all rather sudden, don't you think?"

He had thought the same thing, actually, although Jefferson preferred to attribute that to his persuasive talents. "All right," he said. "What do you make of it?"

"That is the riddle I've not yet solved. Well, one of them."

"What do you mean?"

"I was thinking about Valletta and—"

"Sarah Louise Callum," he said in the sternest voice he could manage. "Just when I thought you were capable of forgetting you were a Pinkerton agent for a few minutes—"

"All right. I won't say anything else about the case right now. But if I were going to comment, I would say that—"

"Sadie!"

She laughed, her fingers still clutching the end of her braid. "I was teasing," she said as she plucked his Panama hat off of the floor of the rowboat, plopped it atop her head, and tucked her braid underneath.

The sight of the prettiest Pinkerton agent he'd ever seen wearing his hat along with a day dress covered in sand and saltwater made him laugh out loud.

"What?" She affected a pose. "Am I not glamorous enough for you? I suppose I'll have to find something else to wear to Mamie Astor's ball."

"I wouldn't hear of such a thing," he said as he dug the oars into the crystal blue waters and propelled the rowboat toward the shore. "You far outshine anyone who could be in attendance. I cannot imagine that Mrs. Astor will be anything but jealous."

"You, sir, are a rogue and a terrible tease."

"I beg to differ. I am actually quite good at teasing. As are you."

Sadie made a face but did not press the point further. Instead, she leaned back again, allowing her fingers to trail along in the water but keeping a watchful eye for any sea creatures that might swim too close.

"You didn't answer my question, Sadie. About having time to do something again?"

She offered a smile. "No, I don't suppose I did."

Jefferson shook his head. "And you have no intentions of telling me now, do you?"

Soft laughter was the only answer he got.

"So," she said a few minutes later, "you've been coming to Key West for a long time, haven't you?"

"Yes. Why do you ask?"

"No particular reason. I was just thinking about how lovely it is here. How peaceful." Her focus returned to him. "I can see why your father would want a home here."

Jefferson nodded. "Key West was always a stop for us when we visited Mobile. Being from England, my mother never quite understood the attraction, but she was a good sport about it."

"Then I hope she is a good sport about the home she may be getting soon."

Jefferson laughed. How little she knew Lizzie Tucker. "Trust me. My mother is always a good sport about the homes my father collects. If she doesn't like one, she just doesn't stay long."

"A pity."

Not the answer he expected. "What do you mean?"

"Someday, when I marry, I would hope that wherever I am, my husband would always be. And vice versa, of course."

A proper response escaped him. Only a fool would wish to rid himself of the company of a woman like Sadie. So he said nothing even as he allowed his imagination free rein to consider just what it might be like to wed a woman like her.

They traveled back toward the beach in much this fashion, Jefferson rowing and Sadie contemplating whatever it was she thought of when she said nothing. As tempting as it was to prolong their seafaring adventure, he only slowed their progress slightly when he realized just how quickly they were making their way back to shore.

"Sadie," he said, and then realized she had fallen asleep.

The waves were breaking closer to them now, and the rowboat shuddered as it rose and then fell again. Rivulets of water ran down the floor of the vessel, likely from a leak somewhere out of sight.

He should be hurrying them back to dry land.

Should stop studying her face, shaded as it was by the brim of his hat, as she slumbered.

Soft breaths in. Soft breaths out. And still he rowed.

"Sadie?"

She moved but only to swipe at a lock of hair that had fallen across her face. And then she murmured something. Words so soft he could see her lips move but not hear what she said.

So he leaned down, closer to her and to the lips that spoke his name. "Sadie?" he said as moved nearer.

Lips he had kissed under the mangroves.

And he kissed her again. Softly. Gently. A brush of his lips to hers. Then he sat back and watched. Waited.

Her eyes flew open. "Jefferson?"

"Hey, sleepyhead," he managed in his most casual tone.

She sat up and stretched before adjusting his Panama hat so that it rested just so on her head. And once again, Jefferson had the strongest urge to turn the rowboat around and head for open water with his passenger.

But it was too late to turn around. The fisherman from whom he had rented the boat had seen them and begun wading out in their direction.

A few moments later, Jefferson jumped out and then reached for Sadie. "I can do it," was her response.

"I'm trying to keep you dry. Cooperate, would you?"

Teetering on the edge of the boat, the current pulling against the rope the fisherman held, Sadie made a tentative move toward him. "All right. If you're sure you will catch me."

"I'm sure."

She fell into his arms as a wave toppled them both. Jefferson emerged from the water with Sadie in his arms. "See, I told you I would catch you."

"Oh, no!"

She slid from his grip and made a dive for the Panama hat that the tide was carrying away. When she missed it by inches, Jefferson lunged for it and caught the brim.

"Ouch," she said as she leaned back and lifted her foot. "I think I cut myself."

Jefferson saw blood and frowned. "Where are your shoes?"

"I left them in the boat." Sadie glanced back. "Yes, I see them."

"I'll go get them."

"No," she said as she grasped his elbow to keep from floating away. "Let's just get out of the water. I'm sure I've ruined them beyond repair anyway."

"You're certain?" At her nod, he handed her his hat. "Here, you take care of this and I will take care of you."

"Jefferson," she said, her tone filled with warning. "What are you going to do?"

Situating the chapeau back on Sadie's head, he held her close against him and moved toward the sand, lifting her out of the water. While the formerly staid Pinkerton agent squealed with laughter, Jefferson marched past the fisherman and back to the shore.

Once on the sand, she attempted to wriggle out of his arms. "Thank you. I can walk from here. It is just a little cut."

"Be still. I told you I would take care of you, and I plan to do exactly that. Do not make me trip or we will both be limping tomorrow."

Though they must have looked a spectacle, Jefferson ignored the stares of those who watched them pass.

Sadie's gown was soaked through, rendering it a less than adequate covering for her modesty. To let her walk would only draw attention to that fact. "I'm going to put you down just long enough for you to put my jacket on," he said. "And I'll not hear a word of argument."

She glanced down at her skirts and then back up at Jefferson. When he handed her the jacket, she quietly complied.

"All right," he said as he lifted her in his arms once more. "Off we go. I suggest you either smile or cover your face with my hat. I'll leave the choice up to you."

"Cover my face? What happened to the man who said nothing was certain? Who told me to live a little?" she said as her smile remained in place.

"Thank you for that reminder." Jefferson greeted all who dared to look his way as he headed down the street to the docks and then carried Sadie all the way back to the *Lizzie*.

As he stepped off the gangplank and made his way down to the main salon, he saw that his father had company.

"Mr. Callum?" he said when he stepped inside, still holding a dripping and laughing Sadie against his chest.

"Daddy?"

Thirty-six

"Sarah Louise Callum, what in the world has gotten into you?"

Once Jefferson had released Sadie from his arms, she kept her injured foot elevated slightly to keep from getting blood on Captain Tucker's rug. She kept her eyes on her father as she braced herself against the wall and tried to decide what to say in response.

"Daddy, what are you doing here?" Then her gaze fell on the chair where she had sat with Jefferson last night. "Uncle Penn?"

Her uncle stood but remained by the chair. "Good afternoon, my dear. And to you as well, Mr. Tucker."

Her attention went to the captain, who sat behind the desk with an expression that gave away nothing of what he might be feeling. Finally, she looked over at Jefferson, who seemed to be taking it all in.

The first rule of Pinkerton training was to take charge of a situation, and it appeared as though Jefferson might say something at any moment. Sadie determined to commandeer the conversation before he could.

"Daddy, I will ask you again. What are you doing here?" She put her free hand on her hip and narrowed her eyes just enough to look perturbed. "You followed me, didn't you?"

"Well, of course I did." He shifted his attention to his brother-in-law. "That was part of the plan, wasn't it, Penn?"

Her uncle cleared his throat and then nodded. "Yes." And then he cleared his throat again. "Yes, that was the plan all along."

Sadie immediately suspected it was not.

Daddy took two steps forward and then stopped short. "Your mama made a fuss, as you and I both expected. I told her I would find you, and that she and the boys were to stay put while Penn and I headed out. It worked too. She stayed put and . . . well, I found you."

Sadie shook her head. "All right. You found me. How?"

He looked perplexed. "I knew where you were going. Following wasn't difficult, nor was finding the schooner docked here in Key West."

A plausible answer, but only if Jefferson had told Daddy they were heading for the East Coast. She allowed that was possible and changed her line of questioning.

"Now what?"

He stood a bit taller, any sign of good humor gone. "What do you mean, now what? I will let your mama know I found you."

"Is that all?"

"Again, I don't follow."

"You think Mama's going to be fine with your just finding me and not bringing me home?" She paused to moderate her tone. "I am not going back with you, Daddy, so if that is what you were thinking in coming here, you can think again. We had an agreement, and I was to be allowed to conduct the particulars of this case without any interruption from my family."

"Well, isn't that a lovely speech?" Her father took another step and stopped beside Uncle Penn. "Considering it's coming from a girl who looks like something the cat might have dragged in, I will say it is quite bold of you to be the one asking the questions at all right now. And I will start by asking why you are wearing

431

a hat and coat that belong to that man over there."

Captain Tucker caught Sadie's attention and winked before looking past her to Jefferson. "You know, son, I also was wondering how you allowed the young lady to return in such a state."

Jefferson stood a little straighter, his expression very much the same as the one on his face when he had stood up to the judge back in Louisiana. "Well, Dad, as you were otherwise occupied, I thought I might show her—"

"Never mind, Jefferson. The ones who owe an explanation are those two." Sadie gestured first to Daddy and Uncle Penn. "Uncle, you of all people should understand."

"And you should realize I was not letting the old goat chase after you without me."

The look of mutual admiration that passed between the brothers-in-law stunned her. What in the world was going on here?

Sadie returned her attention to Daddy. "Now that you've seen me, you can go home and report to Mama that I am fine. I'm sure between the two of you a reasonable story can be told to prevent her from sending the boys after me."

"But you're not fine," Uncle Penn said. "In fact, my dear, you're bleeding."

"Yes, I am." She held her chin up. "But I will survive. My best guess is I stepped on a piece of coral."

"And I will remedy this right now." Jefferson linked arms with Sadie and met her gaze with an insistent look. "Let's get you bandaged up, and then we can all sit down and talk about who was where and why."

Sadie opened her mouth to protest but he was too quick. He lifted her once again into his arms and walked out of the salon and down the hall.

"Where are you taking me?"

"Were you not paying attention?" He continued down the passageway and then made a sharp turn into her bedchamber. Gently easing her down onto the small settee under the porthole, he fixed her with a stern look. "Do not move."

Then he was gone.

Sadie glanced down at the mess she had made of her dress. At Jefferson's damp and wrinkled jacket that hung off her shoulders and hid her hands. And then she realized she still wore his Panama hat with the bedraggled braid tucked underneath.

Leaning back against the velvet cushions, she closed her eyes and allowed the rocking of the schooner to lull her. What an interesting day this had been.

"Miss?"

Her eyes flew open. The day just got more interesting. "Julia?"

The maid wore the green ensemble Sadie had bought for her, and her hair was styled in a more fashionable way. In the crook of her arm, she carried a basket.

"Yes, miss. Mr. Callum said you'd been injured, and I . . ." She shook her head as she closed the distance between them. "Oh, miss, you're bleeding. Here, I've brought bandages and something to take the sting out of your cut. And you have a sunburn. Your mama would be beside herself if she knew."

"Then it is a good thing she will never know. Julia, why are you here?"

As Julia set the basket on the floor and knelt in front of Sadie, Jefferson appeared in the door. In his hand was a roll of cotton and some scissors. He looked down at Julia and then back up at Sadie, confusion etching his features.

"What's she doing here?" he mouthed silently.

Sadie shook her head to indicate she did not know. "Julia," she said slowly as she watched the girl cut a length of cotton. "I will ask you again. Why are you here?"

She kept to her work, setting the roll of cotton back in the basket and reaching for a pot of ointment. "The missus said it wasn't proper, your traveling without a maid." She looked up and met Sadie's gaze. "She asked me if I would go if Mr. Callum agreed to it and, of course I said I would."

"And my father agreed, obviously."

Julia nodded. "He did, I suppose, because here I am."

"Here you are," Sadie echoed as she put on a smile and then lifted her focus to Jefferson, who stood quietly at the door. While she watched, he shook his head and then walked away.

Julia caught her looking and turned to see what she found so interesting. By then Jefferson was gone. "Something wrong?"

"No. Nothing," Sadie said. "So tell me. How did my mother react when she discovered I had left without telling her goodbye?"

"She was plenty mad." Julia went back to her work. "She went to fussing and . . . well, there weren't nothing for it but that your daddy took her for a ride down by the river. She came back happy as could be. Didn't anyone say what went on, but I'm guessing they came to an agreement because your daddy had me packing up and out of the house before the sun set that day."

"And Uncle Penn too."

"Yes." Julia secured the bandage and then sat back on her heels to return everything to the basket. "What else can I do for you?"

Sadie looked down at the awful state of her attire and then removed Jefferson's hat and allowed her battered braid to fall down on her shoulder. "A long hot soak with some of Mama's soap from Paris would be heavenly, but I don't suppose that's possible, so a pitcher and basin will have to do."

The maid rose and smiled as she gathered up

the basket. "While I cannot promise a long hot soak as I do not yet know what sort of bathing facilities this vessel can provide, your mama did insist I add several round soaps in silk pleated paper to the things she sent for you. Would that be what you are wanting?"

"Yes," Sadie said with a sigh. "I do believe it is."

"I'll see what I can do then." Julia moved toward the door and then stopped. "May I ask you just one thing, miss?"

"Of course."

"Do you mind much that your mama sent me? I know you said I wasn't to come along this time, but we had discussed that perhaps someday . . ."

Her words trailed off, though her concentration did not. Rather, she seemed keenly interested in watching Sadie in anticipation of a response.

"I only told you what I was told. That I was going alone and you could not accompany me." She sat up straighter and began untangling her braid. "You brought Mama's soap. For that alone I am grateful."

Sadie smiled and Julia joined her. "Yes, miss. All right then. I'm very glad to be coming along after all. If there's nothing else, I'll see about a bath."

Julia returned a short while later with several of the schooner's crew in tow. A short while later, a tub had been filled with clean hot water.

Fingering the last of the tangles from her hair, Sadie found the temperature of the water just right. "Thank you, Julia. That will be all."

"Would you like me to ready your things to dress for supper in town, miss?"

Supper. Of course. She should have anticipated that Daddy and Uncle Penn would wish her to dine with them.

"The blue, then."

Opening the linen press that served as an armoire, the maid retrieved the dress, shook out the wrinkles, and then moved over to the bed to lay it flat. "With the sapphires?"

"I didn't bring them."

"No, miss, but I did. Your mother thought it might be nice to have certain accessories to go along with the gowns you had brought. I was able to tell her which were missing, and we determined from that what you would need. There is also a nice emerald set and your grand mother's pearls."

"That was very nice. Thank you."

"My pleasure," she said with a smile.

Sadie slipped out of her ruined dress and into the tub, submerging herself completely beneath the water. It was heavenly.

When her lungs could stand no more, she bobbed up and swiped at her eyes. Julia handed her a cake of perfumed soap and then placed a towel and wrapper within reach.

"I'll leave you to your scrub, then."

Murmuring agreement, Sadie sank back against the tub's raised edge. The water was just warm enough to cause her to want to linger well after she had bathed and shampooed her hair. It was Julia's insistent knocking that drew her out of her thoughts and into first the towel and then her wrapper.

A half hour later, Julia had her dressed and sitting in front of the mirror, her hair nicely pinned and the bottle of Lavande in her hand.

"Just a touch," she told the maid as someone knocked at the door. "Never more than that."

Julia set the bottle back on the table and went to answer the door. "Tell her she has five minutes," Sadie heard her father say.

"I'm coming now, Daddy," she called as she rose to join him.

"Is that a sunburn?" He chuckled as he linked arms with her. "Your mama would be—"

"Beside herself. Yes, I know, but we're not going to tell her, are we?"

"No, I don't suppose that would be a good idea." He slowed his pace. "But I would like you to promise me something."

"Of course. If I can, that is."

"Would you write your mama a letter I can take back with me tomorrow? Just tell her you're fine, something of that sort. I promised her I'd ask you when I saw you."

"I can do that."

Daddy leaned down to kiss her cheek. "She'll be most pleased to hear from you. And I'll be out of the doghouse."

"You're in the doghouse?" She gave him a sideways look and then punctuated it with a grin. "You know Mama can't stay mad at you long."

"This time she might. You left on my watch."

"You know, Daddy, there's something bothering me."

Her father stopped short. "What's that?"

"Please tell me the truth. Did you truly expect to find me or were you just humoring Mama when you promised her a letter from me?"

"I don't know what you mean," he said as if he were truly puzzled, though his expression told her otherwise.

"I mean, how did you know we would stop here in Key West? Jefferson and I certainly didn't. In fact, Captain Tucker made it seem as though it was all very much a last-minute decision."

"Now, Sadie, I truly don't know what you're—"

"There you are." Captain Tucker met them at the door to the salon. "Do come in. Penn and I were just discussing our evening plans."

Sadie reluctantly joined her father as he caught up with Captain Tucker. Their discussion might have ended abruptly, but she would be certain to get an answer before he left. Or, failing that, she would at least question Daddy again and then make her own decision as to what he was thinking.

She analyzed nonanswers all the time in the course of carrying out her Pinkerton duties. All she had to do was forget that Seamus Callum was her father and treat his responses in the same way she would treat a witness.

Now to pray that was possible.

Uncle Penn moved toward her and enveloped her in a hug. "My dear, you look lovely. Is that a sunburn?"

"We're not mentioning that to her mama," Daddy said.

Sadie let out a long breath and then adjusted her smile. As a Pinkerton agent, there were many things that were considered worthy of concern. A sunburn was not among them. The fact that her father appeared to be hiding something, however, certainly was. "I can see I should have allowed Julia to apply the powder she was insisting upon."

"Speaking of the maid, I do hope you're not upset with us for bringing her along," Uncle Penn said. "It seemed the most expedient way to make an exit."

"She's been most helpful." Not an actual answer to his question, and yet the truth.

"I hope our visitors don't mind, but I have arranged for us to dine in town tonight." The captain turned his focus on Sadie. "Did my son mention he would be otherwise occupied this evening?"

She opened her mouth to respond, only to see the man in question out in the corridor. He pressed his finger to his lips and then motioned for her to join him.

"I see. Oh, my. I've forgotten something in my room. Excuse me just a moment while I go fetch it," she said as she hurried out into the corridor.

When she reached Jefferson, he grasped her by the waist and hauled her behind the nearest unlocked door. As he shut the door to what appeared to be an empty stateroom, he breathed into her ear, "We need to be quiet, Sadie. I don't want anyone to hear me. Nod if you understand."

When she complied, he continued. "Your maid. I have my doubts she is who she says she is."

Sadie maneuvered herself around to face him and wriggled out of his grasp. In the dim light she could just barely make out the contours of his face.

The irrational thought that this man was far too handsome arose, momentarily distracting her. She pressed the thought away. "I'm listening," she whispered.

"I've been thinking about your description of the events at Valletta's shop. You said he called your maid by her last name, even though you had not used her name in his presence."

The intoxicatingly male scent of patchouli and soap rose when he shifted positions to lean closer. Focus became difficult, and yet she managed.

"Originally, that is what I thought happened. But later I wondered if that was what really happened."

"Why? I would think you would normally have a good grasp of the details of any situation, even one as highly charged as that was."

She paused to think. "I was talking to Julia about it, and she said . . . Oh, no."

"What?"

"I thought I was confused because I had hit my head when I fell, but . . ." She froze. "*She* was the one to suggest that when I questioned her about it. Oh, Jefferson, how could I miss such an elementary piece of police work as to let someone I suspected misdirect me?"

He was silent a moment. "It doesn't matter now. But before we can go any further, you and I need to find the answer."

"How?"

"I have an idea. I've already made my excuses for the evening. What I need you to do is keep my father and the others busy for a while. See that dinner is prolonged rather than quickly finished. Can you do that?"

"I'll try."

"I know. Tell him I have changed my mind and will be along later for dessert and coffee. That way I will come to you rather than having you and the men return early."

"I can see how that would work, but what

possible excuse can I offer for this sudden change in your plans?"

"You're good at what you do, Sadie. I'm sure you'll think of something."

Thirty-seven

Jefferson watched from the galley as his father escorted Sadie and the others down the gangplank and into a waiting carriage. Unless he missed his guess, the maid would either be in Sadie's stateroom readying her things for bed or she would be in one of the smaller quarters on the lower level.

Because Sadie's room was closest, he went there first, slipping down the darkened corridor and into her chambers without encountering anyone. Once inside the room, he turned the key to lock the door and then reached into his pocket to retrieve another gadget Kyle had loaned him.

Though the spectacles appeared as if they were merely normal eyeglasses, they were indeed, a miraculous way to see in the dark. What might appear in shadow, if at all, showed up in greater detail when viewed through these lenses. It was a marvel, this invention, and something he would be loath to return when the time came.

Scanning the room, Jefferson spied nothing out of the ordinary other than the oversized bathtub that the crew had emptied but not yet retrieved. He moved toward the dresser and found a hairbrush and a bottle of perfume. Even now he could detect the faint scent that was uniquely Sadie.

He smiled and moved on, unwilling to allow even a moment of distraction, however pleasant. On the table next to the bunk was a book and a glass of something, water from the looks of it.

Leaving everything as he found it, Jefferson returned to the door to unlock it and then slid the eyeglasses back into his pocket. Just as he was about to open the door, he heard footsteps in the corridor. When they stopped in the hall in front of him, he dove into the shadows.

Julia Oakman, if that was truly her name, entered the room. Light from the corridor spilled in but thankfully did not reach his hiding place.

She opened the linen press and appeared to be putting items inside. Or perhaps she was taking things out. Jefferson couldn't tell from his vantage point. He waited until she completed her work and left before he moved back toward the door.

Following her without being detected was impossible given the layout of the vessel, so he allowed her to escape the corridor before he pursued her. Keeping to the shadows once he spied her scurrying down the stairs to the lower level, Jefferson was able to see which of the quarters belonged to the maid.

He then doubled back to Sadie's stateroom and once again locked the door. This time he lit the lamps and made a thorough inspection, checking to see if anything appeared to be tampered with.

Finding nothing out of order in the linen press, at least as far as he could determine, Jefferson returned the room to its darkened state and headed back down to the lower level. Arriving at the maid's bedchamber, he knocked twice with no answer either time.

"Looking for the pretty redhead?"

Jefferson turned around to see one of the crew, a man young enough to still have splotches on his face, watching him from the door across the hall. "The maid, yes."

"She's gone out."

"Out? Are you certain?"

"Her lady gave her the evening free. That's what she told me as I passed her just now on the gangplank."

"Thank you."

Jefferson waited until the lad once again disappeared behind his closed door before testing the knob and finding that Miss Oakman had left her chamber unlocked. With another glance behind him, Jefferson slipped inside.

As there was no porthole on this level, the room was dark as night. He donned the glasses and had a look around.

The maid had only one nice gown, the green one

he'd seen her in earlier. Two other dresses were folded neatly at the bottom of a small trunk along with several other items of women's clothing and an empty carpetbag. A serviceable pair of ladies' boots were situated next to the trunk, and a wrapper and nightgown were hanging on a peg beside the pitcher and washbasin. A garment lay on the bunk. Jefferson reached out to touch it. Silk. Likely one of Sadie's dresses brought down to be cleaned or mended.

He stepped away from the bunk and gave the tiny space one more sweeping glance. With nothing to indicate anything suspicious, he could only conclude that either there was a logical explanation for Valletta's knowledge of the maid's last name or Sadie's recollection of the event was faulty.

Given the fact that the pretty Pinkerton agent had taken a nasty blow to her head and required assistance—by John, he was loath to recall—to reach the carriage, the latter was the more likely scenario. Jefferson left the room as he found it and went into town to join his father and their guests.

"Well, look who's here," Captain Tucker said when Jefferson took the empty seat at the table.

The music was lively, as was the conversation between Sadie and the two members of her family, but the look on his father's face told him he had best not ignore the warning there. "Perhaps we could speak outside?"

After making their excuses, the men found a quiet spot on the restaurant's easternmost side. "All right," his father said, "where were you?"

"I was making certain the maid was who she claimed to be."

"Jefferson, haven't I warned you about dallying with the staff—"

"That is *not* what I said." He took a deep breath and let it out slowly. "I said I was investigating Miss Callum's employee, Dad. Don't you find it interesting that she just happened to come along with Callum and his brother-in-law?"

"I do not." His father crossed his arms over his chest in what was surely a defensive posture. "Apparently, Mrs. Callum's opinions are highly valued, and she wished the girl to go. So she went. And truly, son, if I am wrong, then why did all three members of that family feel the need to discuss whether Mary Callum would hear about a sunburn?" He shook his head. "I assure you that would not be a cause for concern in our family."

"There are no daughters in our family," Jefferson reminded him. "I warrant there are other things Mother concerns herself with that these people might find strange. But that is not what we're discussing here."

"I am at a loss, then. What *are* we discussing?"

Jefferson thought a moment. "Coincidences. We are talking about coincidences. How do you think those men found us? Did you tell anyone you were planning to stop in Key West? Because I certainly was not aware of it."

His father shrugged. "I might have. Why does it matter?"

Why indeed.

"Because I do not like it when my plans are changed."

His father laughed. "Oh, so now we're at the heart of it. You're in charge here, and blast anyone who doesn't let you know when something's going to deviate from the schedule?"

Jefferson stepped back and copied his father's stance. "Actually, yes. The plan was to get Sadie and me to Newport in the fastest manner possible. An overnight jaunt in the Keys is not the fastest way, is it? And if you did not tell me ahead of time, then why would you tell Sadie's father?"

"I beg to differ, son. There's a wind blowing out in the Atlantic that's going to move out of my way come morning. But right now the charts aren't looking too friendly. And so I decided I'd make a stop and let the blow head away rather than take a chance and plow through it."

The answer sounded logical, and yet it was all too convenient. Too much of a coincidence.

"So you're swearing to me that you did not plan to stop here in Key West so that Seamus Callum and his entourage could join us?"

"That is ridiculous." The captain shook his head and then pressed past him. "You can stand out here all night for all I care, but we have guests in there, and I do not intend to cause them to believe that I am a poor host." He walked a few steps and then stopped to look back at Jefferson. "We were just about to order dessert. Are you coming?"

He nodded, though there was much more he wanted to say. His father always said the measure of a man was in knowing when to speak and when to remain silent.

So Jefferson said nothing as he followed his father back inside. Something was not right. His gut told him there was more to the situation. And his gut never steered him wrong. Therefore, he would investigate. Just not tonight.

Sadie met his eyes as he settled back into his place at the table. Her questioning look told him she was wondering what he had discovered. Not until their carriage ride back to the schooner was he able to respond.

"You recall the question I had earlier," he said when the three older men were sufficiently distracted in a conversation of their own.

"Yes." She glanced at her father and then back at Jefferson. "Was it resolved to your satisfaction?"

"For now. But the item must be returned. It cannot remain."

"I see." She worried with the trim on her sleeve and then lifted her gaze to meet his. "Should I practice vigilance or consider the matter settled? Once the item is no longer with me, I mean."

"Vigilance is always best when practiced regularly, don't you think?"

She did, of course. No one with a career such as hers would disagree.

"And in the meantime, so shall I." He smiled. "Though the likelihood of any concern is esteemed to be slight."

"What are you two discussing?" his father asked.

Jefferson affected a casual expression. "Matters of mutual interest," he said as Sadie looked away with a smile.

Later that night, after breaking the news to her maid that she would be returning to Callum Plantation with Daddy and Uncle Penn, Sadie lay in bed trying to sleep but failing miserably. If she were back home in River Pointe, she might have rung for Julia to fetch her a glass of warm milk. Or perhaps she would have donned a wrapper and stepped out onto the balcony to take in the night air.

Because neither was possible on the vessel, Sadie tried again to fall asleep but could barely keep her eyes closed. Giving up, she lit the lamp, reached for her valise, and retrieved the first notebook her fingers touched.

As was her habit, she started at the beginning and read every line as if it were the first time she'd seen it, studying each statement to find connections between facts or persons. She had been at the exercise for almost an hour when she despaired of it and returned the notebook to its place and then shut off the light.

Because of the moonlight shimmering through the porthole, the room dimmed but did not darken completely. Sadie went to the porthole and opened it, hoping the sea breeze might coax her into a sound sleep.

Deep voices and deeper laughter drifted toward her from somewhere outside. Crewmen going about the disposition of their duties, she decided as the watch bells rang out.

The voices soon fell silent and then footsteps rang out in the passageway. A door closed somewhere nearby. And then she heard snatches of conversation again. Though the words were not clear, the origin of the voice was.

Daddy?

Sadie donned her wrapper and tiptoed to the door. Easing it open, she peered out into the darkened hallway and found it empty. The latch on the door next to hers moved, and she darted back inside, leaving just enough space open to spy on whoever might walk past.

Uncle Penn?

He moved swiftly down the corridor and then a door shut again. Braving a look in the direction in which her uncle had gone, she saw a light burning in the salon.

With a glance down at her wrapper, a decision

was made. Sadie hurried back to her stateroom and did the best she could to tame her hair and then slip into a simple dress that would be suitable for a walk in the night air.

Not that she planned to go any farther than the end of the passageway. But when she reached the salon, she found it empty.

"This is odd," she said under her breath.

"What's odd?"

Sadie stifled a scream as she whirled and found Jefferson standing an arm's length away. "You scared me," she said as she gave him a playful swat on the arm.

He caught her wrist and held it. "Sadie," he said softly, "what are you doing walking about at this time of night?"

"I couldn't sleep." The warmth of his palm against her arm distracted her, rendering her unwilling to continue the conversation.

"I have just the remedy." He gestured to a chair near the starboard porthole. "Make yourself comfortable. I'll be right back."

He returned a few minutes later with a tray containing a teapot and two mugs as well as a plate of what appeared to be cookies and a sugar bowl. "I didn't find milk, but I think we can manage without it."

She smiled. "You Brits think tea is the remedy for everything."

He looked up at her, seemingly astonished.

"Isn't it?" A moment later, he had skillfully poured a tasty cup of tea. "I am only half British, but I manage."

"Duly noted. This is very good. What's in it?"

"I have no idea. Something my mother discovered on one of her trips to India. It should have you wanting slumber in no time."

She sipped at the tea and Jefferson did the same. After a moment, he set his cup aside and regarded her with a serious look.

"Did you deliver the news?"

"To my maid?" Sadie nodded. "She took it quite well, although I'm sure she was disappointed. She's keen to travel, and I cannot blame her for that."

"I suppose." His eyes became thoughtful. "When I came in you were talking to yourself. Something you found odd? What was that?"

"Oh." Sadie returned her cup to the tray. "I'm certain I heard my father talking in here, and I saw my uncle walk this way. But by the time I dressed and came in here, the room was empty."

"So perhaps they went to bed?"

"It's possible." She sat back against the cushions. "But I never heard anyone go past my door, so I doubt it."

Jefferson leaned forward and rested his elbows on his knees. "Then they're probably out on the deck. Shall we go and look for them, or are you more interested in finishing your tea?"

She shrugged. "I think I'd like to look for them. I have a feeling that something's not right. I can't exactly put my finger on it, but I would feel better if I investigated this just a little further."

"I understand."

Sadie studied him a moment. "Yes, I believe you do. You haven't changed your mind about the person you investigated earlier, have you?"

"No." He stood to reach across the distance between them and offer her his hand. "Shall we?"

Her fingers touched his palm, felt his hand envelope hers. And she smiled.

"I like that," he said when they reached the corridor.

She slanted him a look. "Like what?"

"Your smile."

Two words and yet she held them close to her heart as she followed him through the corridors and out into the evening air. Overhead the stars were a canopy of sparkling light that punctuated a clear black sky.

Though the lights of Key West blurred their brilliance at the edges, they lost none of their beauty above. And as they strolled to the opposite end of the schooner where the shadows were deep and the ocean lay vast and dark before them, the stars danced in tiny pinpricks on the rolling waves.

Sadie breathed in the warm salty air and let it out slowly as she looked around and found they were alone. Whether it was the tea or the beauty of her surroundings or merely the presence of the man beside her, she felt herself relax.

"I do so love the ocean," she whispered.

He threaded her fingers with his and together they stood very still. "Sadie, look. A falling star."

She saw the flash of light before it disappeared. "Just like the last time."

They were quiet for a while. How long, Sadie couldn't say.

And then Jefferson squeezed her hand. "We're professionals, you and I."

"Yes. Why?"

"I needed the reminder." He turned to face her, his fingers still holding hers. "Because all I can think about is you." He paused to allow his gaze to meet hers. "And not professionally."

Nervousness caused her to smile when what she really wanted to do was flee. For she also felt the same way in his presence. Less like a seasoned detective and more like a giggling debutante.

She thought of the afternoon and the kiss under the mangroves. Of how his closeness in the darkened stateroom distracted her. Yes, that was why her face burned now, and not because of the sun.

"Sadie." He released his grip to rest his palm on the small of her back, his free hand now tracing the curve of her jaw. "I don't know what to do about you. About us."

"Us?" she managed.

"Us."

"There cannot be an 'us,' Jefferson," she insisted, even as she looked into blue eyes that dared her to entertain the idea, even briefly. "Not while you and I are working on this case together."

"So you're saying you don't feel this connection that has grown between us?"

Connection. Yes, that was a good word for it. For the beginning of what was a deep well of emotion she preferred not to acknowledge.

"There's something there." She paused. Where were the proper words? The witty statements she made with ease on a regular basis.

They had flown away, soared on the wings of her nerves as she stood too close to Jefferson Tucker.

"Yes, there is something there." He sighed, and she almost did the same.

"We are two professionals with a case to solve. There cannot be an *us*."

"Of course there can," he whispered against her ear. "Eventually."

And then he kissed her.

Thirty-eight

The next morning, Sadie said goodbye to Uncle Penn and Daddy and tried not to think about the kiss she had shared with Jefferson the night before. In the letter her father carried in his pocket, she had promised Mama she was traveling for the purposes of bringing to a close the case that the Pinkerton Agency was paying her to solve and for no other reason.

She emphasized this as the reason for sending Julia back. The truth, of course.

If Mama didn't believe she was a Pinkerton agent, then perhaps Daddy or Uncle Penn could convince her. Failing that, she'd just let the woman stew until she could come home and have a proper discussion on the topic. After all, she had tried to tell her.

"Do take care, miss," Julia said as she paused beside her. "Perhaps next time I can accompany you."

Sadie took note of the girl's mournful expression and offered what she hoped would be a reassuring smile. "I would like that very much, Julia. You're quite a help, and I do appreciate you."

"Thank you," she said in a more hopeful tone as the captain beckoned her. "I look forward to that, then."

Sadie watched the maid go and then offered her uncle a hug one more time before he set off in the same direction. After that it was Daddy's turn.

"Take care of yourself, sunshine."

"Good luck with Mama," she whispered along with a reminder of how very much she loved him.

"The good Lord will take care of that," he said as he stepped from her embrace.

"Yes, I believe He will."

Sadie stood at the railing and waved as Daddy followed Uncle Penn and Captain Tucker and Julia down the gangplank and across the docks to the steamship *Montmartre*, which would be leaving shortly for Mobile and New Orleans. For, according to Daddy, Aunt Pearl had changed her mind about traveling to River Pointe and instead had asked that Penn would cease his journeys and return home.

Only when both men were completely out of sight did Sadie realize she never did figure out where they went last night. For that matter, she hadn't even completed her search of the schooner.

It was a lapse in judgment that might have extracted a heavy cost had she made it while on an official investigation. The knowledge of this chilled her even as the thought of Jefferson's kiss warmed her.

The reason for that mistake stepped up beside her and leaned his elbows on the rail, offering her a wide grin in the process. "Good morning."

It was just a kiss.

She spared him a brief glance. "Good morning."

A kiss stolen under the stars.

"Sleep well?"

She nodded. "Yes, thank you. The tea worked wonders."

His smile was quick, warm. Her thoughts strayed to his lips. The stars. *Us.*

Captain Tucker emerged from the crowd at the docks and waved in their direction. Jefferson responded in kind while Sadie offered a polite nod. Neither spoke until he had crossed the gangplank.

"Safely aboard the *Montmartre*," he said to Sadie.

"Thank you."

"It was my pleasure." He turned to summon the crew. "And now unless either of you object, I say we weigh anchor and point this schooner toward Newport."

Sadie watched Jefferson's father walk toward the loose knot of sailors awaiting their captain's orders and then turned to the man beside her. "There can be no us," she said gently. "You do understand."

"A statement, not a question." He smiled. "And I beg to differ. When this case is solved, there will be an *us*."

She let out a long breath. "If you will excuse me, I have case notes to go over."

"As do I." He snagged her wrist and turned her toward him. "When this began, I wanted the case solved so I could go back to Scotland Yard and rub their noses in my victory. I don't like admitting that, but that's the truth."

"You wanted your job back." She paused to search his face. "A job you should never have lost."

"I cannot disagree. But revenge was my motive first and foremost." He looked out across the water and then returned his attention to Sadie. "Now I have another reason."

"Oh?"

Jefferson leaned close, his lips grazing her ear. "Us."

"Then would you do me a favor?" She stepped back just far enough to see his face.

"Anything, Sadie."

"Would you hurry?"

"Hurry?"

"Hurry up and solve this case. Because until then, we need to promise one another that we will be completely professional."

Oh, but his smile was dazzling. And those blue eyes sparkled as he leaned closer. "I have a question."

"And what is that?"

"Do professionals share the occasional kiss?"

She shook her head. "You are impossible."

His laughter chased her down the stairs and

along the passageway into her stateroom. And yet each time she was drawn to think of his kisses, she pressed the thought away and doubled her efforts to make a connection between the disparate pieces of the puzzle.

For days his smile met her at each meal, at each meeting of the minds as they put together the framework of the means for solving their case. And there were no more kisses. No more mentions of *us*.

But even as the schooner neared Newport, the facts of the case refused to fall into place. There were too many unanswered questions. Too many reasons why each solution one proposed could be refuted by the other.

When the anchor dropped in Newport Harbor, Sadie was on deck to watch. She had been standing at the rail for an hour or more, watching the stately mansions—known by those who held the keys to the massive front doors as "cottages" —slip past one by one. A redbrick Victorian home with gardens sloping to the sea was Beaulieu, the home of William and Mamie Astor, and Sadie's destination for tomorrow.

Jefferson came to stand beside her, his attention focused on the docks below. Gone was the casually dressed man who had rowed a leaky boat beneath the mangroves. In his place was a man whose wealth was obvious from the cut of his suit to the gold in his cufflinks and watch

461

chain. A man who would fit in nicely with the Newport crowd.

Though they would arrive together, she would not see him again until he called for her tomorrow morning to escort her to Mamie Astor's home for an inspection of the Rembrandt. By prior arrangement, Henry had secured rooms for Sadie at the nearby Hampstead Farms estate.

The Hampstead family, apparently old friends of Henry's, were more than willing to allow a Pinkerton agent use of their home, even though they would not be in residence themselves. She would be introduced as a Louisiana cousin. Given the fact that Sadie's upbringing and education mirrored most of the ladies with whom she would interact while in Newport, the ruse was not far-fetched.

She cast a sideways glance at Jefferson, and he caught her looking. "What will you do until tomorrow?" she asked, more to fill the silence than to actually inquire as to how he would spend his time.

"I've a few things to check on," was his cryptic response. "I've taken a room at an inn on Pelham Street should you have need to contact me."

"I'm sure I won't."

He nodded. "All right, then. Shall we?"

Jefferson procured a carriage and escorted her as far as the grand front entrance to the three-story mansion known as Hampstead Farms. "Odd, but I see no farming going on here," he quipped as he helped her down from the carriage.

The door opened and a line of servants filed out, no doubt expecting a wagonload of luggage to accompany the Hampstead cousin. An elderly butler with brows like great gray caterpillars stepped forward.

"Miss Callum, may we assist you?"

Jefferson nodded toward Sadie's luggage, and two young men hurried forward to carry her trunk inside. Another came to retrieve her bag. The other servants filed back inside, leaving the butler standing sentry beside the door.

"Until tomorrow at nine thirty, then," she said as she left Jefferson standing beside the carriage.

The following morning they walked up to the house together.

"I'm sorry, sir, but the lady of the house is not expected today."

Jefferson fixed the butler with a look that rarely failed to accomplish his purpose. "Then we will see her representative. This is a matter of the greatest urgency. I'm sure you understand."

"Of course, sir. And to that end, Mrs. Astor has asked that you meet with Mr. Astor's attorney. Mr. Montfort will be here shortly. Won't you come this way?"

They were ushered into a parlor just off the front entrance. After declining the servant's offer of refreshment, Sadie seated herself on a settee and appeared to be studying her surroundings. Jefferson's attention went to a massive painting hung on the opposite wall from the door.

At least ten feet high and some sixteen feet across, *The Coronation of Napoleon* by Jacques-Louis David was a stellar example of paintings of the Napoleonic period. Had Jefferson not known that the original of this painting was twice this size and moved just last year from Versailles to be hung in a prominent place in the Louvre, he would have assumed he was now standing before the actual piece.

Sadie moved to stand beside him. "Apparently, Mrs. Astor doesn't always mind owning a reproduction."

Of course the woman whose background included years of instruction in the arts would recognize the piece and know its provenance. "Unless it is a favored Rembrandt."

The door opened behind them. But before the butler could speak, a gentleman dressed in a black morning coat and gray-striped trousers handed him his hat and then pressed past.

"Louis Montfort, Esquire, at your service." He stretched out his hand toward Jefferson but his attention was on Sadie. "Oh, my, but they are making Pinkerton agents much prettier these days. Mrs. Astor warned me you were one of her more lovely classmates in school, but I was not fully prepared as to the truth of her statement."

The man went on about Sadie's beauty until Jefferson had his fill. "So," he interrupted midway through the fellow's comparison of Sadie's fair hair and the midsummer sun, "perhaps you might show us the Rembrandt?"

When he had gained the lawyer's attention, Jefferson introduced himself properly, making certain to squeeze the man's hand slightly harder than he should just to make his point. Mr. Montfort's smile faltered slightly before he once again offered it to Sadie.

"Won't you come with me?"

She linked arms with the fool and fell into step beside him, leaving Jefferson to follow. As they walked through the foyer toward the grand staircase, Sadie let out a most unladylike squeal.

"The Durer," she exclaimed as she set off around a corner.

Jefferson and the lawyer hurried to catch up, but there was already a man standing beside Sadie. Montfort hurried to apologize while Jefferson watched with interest.

"Will Astor," the man in question said when he noticed Jefferson.

He reached to reciprocate a firm handshake. "Jefferson Tucker of . . ."

"Scotland Yard," Astor supplied. "Yes, I am aware of who you are. Sir Edward Thompson, our mutual friend at the British Museum, speaks highly of you. I understand you've been working with them on a case of some merit. And this must be Miss Callum."

Mutual friend at the British Museum? The museum's director? Hardly. And yet it gave Jefferson pause to wonder exactly what was going on at Scotland Yard. And at the British Museum.

There was only one way to find out. Today, however, he had another discovery to make.

"The Pinkerton agent," the lawyer added. "I was just taking them up to see the Rembrandt, sir. I was led to believe you and Mrs. Astor were not in residence."

"Officially, I am not." He winked at Sadie. "However, as this is a matter of great importance . . ."

"Yes, of course," Montfort said. "So perhaps you will join us up in the drawing room where the painting now hangs?"

"First, I would like to ask about this painting," Sadie interjected. "I wonder if you recall where and when it was purchased. And did you happen to get it authenticated?"

"The Durer?" Mr. Astor paused a moment. "I believe this was in a crate that arrived in New York at Christmastime. Mamie had it sent out here in anticipation of her next redo of the place."

Jefferson declined to comment. His mother

busied herself with the same sort of endeavors. He always suspected that was why his father continued to sell and purchase homes. Not only did it keep Lizzie Tucker busy, but it also allowed him to slip away to the solace of the sea while his wife was otherwise occupied.

"If you'll step into my library, I can tell you for certain. I keep copies of my invoices in here." He gestured to a room behind him, presumably the room where he had been when Sadie's squeal announced their presence.

While Astor settled behind his desk and consulted his books, Jefferson noted the room's features. Paneling and a marble fireplace, flanked by shelves filled with leather-bound books arranged according to size, gave the impression that they were standing in a regular English library. On one wall was a portrait of what had to have been a relative, while over the mantel he spied a painting of a clergyman.

"*Bartolomé Bermejo St. Dominic Enthroned in Glory*," Sadie said as she wandered to his side. "Late fourteen hundreds, I believe."

"Is it real?"

She shrugged. "Possibly."

"Here it is."

Jefferson turned to see Mr. Astor leaning over a journal, his finger on one line of what appeared to be a ledger. "The Durer was purchased . . ." He paused and lifted his attention to focus on

Sadie. "You asked if my Durer was real because you assumed the original was still hanging elsewhere."

"Yes, that's right."

"Perhaps the Pinkertons could assist me in confirming this, because the price I paid for that painting indicates that I have the original."

"I wonder if I might look at it more carefully," Sadie asked.

"Yes, of course." He nodded to Montfort, who returned a moment later with the painting and offered it to Sadie.

She carried the piece to a window, carefully holding it up to the light. First she examined the painting itself as Jefferson had seen her do with the one that arrived in brown paper to Callum Plantation. Then she turned it over and looked at the back.

"Interesting." She walked over to the desk, set the painting down, and pointed to the frame's construction. "See how the pieces are fitted together? That indicates the age, as do these marks here." She continued to point out nuances of the back of the painting before turning it over. Then she looked up. "Please understand that I am not an expert."

"I would beg to differ," Astor said, "but go on."

"Let me preface this by saying that there is nothing wrong with an exact copy of any painting. They are perfectly legal to own, just as it is perfectly legal for a painter to create. In fact, there was a time when a painter learned his craft by doing exactly this, copying the original."

"So, you are saying this Durer is a copy?"

"A very good one, but yes. And it is not the first exceptional copy I have seen recently. Where did you get it?"

Astor sank down in his chair and pointed to the ledger. "It was purchased as part of a lot being quietly auctioned off last fall. A Spanish nobleman with losses that needed to be covered by the discreet sale of a few family pieces."

"Who brokered the auction?" Jefferson asked.

"That would be me," Montfort said, the color now fading from his face. "Are you saying my European counterpart on the purchase was not truthful with me?"

"Did he represent this painting as an original?"

At Montfort's nod, Jefferson shook his head. "Then he was not truthful."

"What else was in that lot?" Sadie asked him.

Montfort looked to his employer to supply the details. Mr. Astor found the note in the ledger.

"In addition to the Durer, there were several pieces of various antiquities and one other painting." He lifted his gaze. "The Rembrandt."

"Before we see it," Sadie said, "I wonder if you could show me the invoices and any other documentation for the purchase."

"Yes, of course. I have photographs of the

entire lot in my files. I can have a courier bring them down from New York immediately."

"That would be most helpful." Sadie offered Mr. Astor a brilliant smile. "Actually, would it be possible for your courier to bring all of the files related to Mr. Montfort's purchases? And the photographs, of course."

"Easily done." Astor pulled the bell for a servant, and his butler arrived a heartbeat later. "Ring New York and have everything Montfort sent me gathered up and delivered. I want them here tonight."

The butler nodded and hurried off.

"Montfort was quite thorough in documenting the pieces in order to help me decide on whether to finalize the purchase." Astor offered the man in question a smile. "He always is."

Jefferson's attention went to the attorney, who was now perspiring profusely despite the cool temperature in the room. "As a point of clarification, Mr. Montfort, are you on retainer to Mr. Astor alone?"

"Oh, no," Astor said. "A man of his caliber cannot be held to one man." He smiled again at the attorney. "I heard of Montfort from my friend Commodore Luckenbach, who convinced him to take me on as his client."

"And an honor it has been," Montfort managed.

"He has quite a stellar client list," Astor continued. "Although, as I am sure you understand, these men would not wish to be included in any discussion that would bring them notoriety."

Sadie exchanged a look with him. "Of course."

"And he facilitates discreet purchases, such as this lot from the Italian nobleman?" Jefferson asked.

"Spanish," Montfort corrected. "And yes, I do act to discreetly protect my clients from anyone who might take advantage of their wealth. When one finds that an Astor or a Vanderbilt is bidding, one often raises the prices."

"Yes, I am sure one would," Jefferson said. "I wonder if I could trouble you to show Agent Callum the Rembrandt, Mr. Astor. Mr. Montfort looks as if he needs to sit down."

"Absolutely." Astor came around the desk to study the lawyer. "Are you ill, Montfort?"

"I'm afraid I . . . I am, sir."

"Then do sit. It would be my pleasure to escort the lady up to the drawing room."

Jefferson waited until he was alone with Montfort before closing the door and turning to face him. "Tell me everything. And you can start with Sergio Valletta."

The attorney removed a handkerchief from his vest pocket and dabbed at his forehead. "You understand that I am under no obligation to tell you anything."

"And yet you will," Jefferson said as he took a seat across from him. "Because I do not believe you are the only one who should be arrested."

"Arrested!"

"A man who was an unwilling pawn just might find a judge who would offer leniency." He paused to allow that statement to sink in. "And trust me when I tell you that there are courts in Great Britain that will want to hear testimony from you as well. Are you acquainted with this Sir Edward that Mr. Astor has spoken of?"

"No. He is not a man I know personally."

"I see. And have you made trips to Egypt or perhaps Iraq in the past? Or are you merely the man who sees that antiquities reach the London black market?"

It was supposition, and yet the moment Jefferson asked the question, he knew he was right. Montfort blanched, and he looked as if he might faint dead away.

Thirty-nine

Louis Montfort crumpled his handkerchief in his fist and sighed. "Valletta is not the man you want."

"You are mistaken." Jefferson leaned forward and rested his elbows on his knees. "Valletta is the name that everything goes back to. The invoices, the ship's manifest. And a particularly nasty blow to the head that Agent Callum took when Valletta threw a bag of supposed antiquities at her."

The attorney gasped. "That he would do such a thing seems impossible. The man I know is . . ."

"Is a fraud. Incidentally, he attacked Miss Callum after she announced herself as a Pinkerton agent."

Jefferson had not yet decided the depth of this man's involvement in Valletta's schemes, but he was beginning to suspect that the lawyer's worst crime was greed and nothing more.

"But he offered up papers. Documentation. He allowed photographs, which I then delivered to my clients who wished to have them." He shook his head. "I cannot believe that a man who swore on the head of his son that he was dealing in good faith would be doing exactly the opposite."

"His son?" Jefferson shook his head. "Sergio Valletta has no son." Nor did he have any other family, at least none that were known to authorities.

Montfort looked up sharply. "Indeed he does, sir. A young man of good manners and quite well educated. It is my understanding that he has been assisting his father in Europe for several years and has only just returned to the United States to take up some sort of enterprise here."

"He's likely enlarging the business to bring the black market goods he's stealing out of Egypt and Iraq to the American marketplace."

"Truly sir, if you were to meet the young man, I believe you would have a different opinion."

Jefferson's laughter held no humor. "And how do you propose I do this?"

"I can easily arrange that. Mrs. Valletta has family here in Newport."

"You are claiming Sergio is hiding a wife too?"

"Not Sergio. His son."

The door opened and Sadie stepped inside ahead of Mr. Astor. Jefferson rose but Montfort stayed where he was.

"Just as I suspected, the painting is not an original. A clever forgery, but still a forgery," she said, looking at Jefferson.

"Forgive me," Astor said to him, "but I must leave now. Use my library as long as you need, and when you're ready to go, please take my carriage. I will let the driver know to be at the ready."

"I appreciate that, sir."

He waved away Jefferson's thanks. "It's a small thing compared to the work you are doing to resolve this issue of ours. Rest assured that the moment the files arrive I will see that they are delivered. Where are you staying?"

"Hampstead Farms," Sadie said.

"Very well." He turned his attention to Montfort, moving toward the attorney to place his hand on the man's shoulder. "Are you still unwell?"

"I am recovering, sir."

"Good. Then you won't mind coming back the

day after tomorrow? Let's say after lunch. Mamie will be here by then, and I'm sure she will be giving you a list of items she must have for her redo."

Montfort mustered a smile. "I shall look forward to it, sir."

Astor held the lawyer's attention. "And this time perhaps we will use a different supplier." He paused. "Someone that our friends Mr. Tucker and Miss Callum will not have to return to discuss."

Relief flooded Montfort's face. "Yes. Absolutely, sir."

Jefferson reached to shake Mr. Astor's hand. "Thank you, sir."

His handshake was firm. "My pleasure. And do tell our mutual friend at the museum hello if you have occasion to speak with him."

"I will."

"You know, this business is unfortunate," Astor continued. "It makes me wonder if living here so far from the museums and collectors in Europe is the best choice." He paused to regard Jefferson with an appraising look. "Perhaps I should make England my home. You like it there, don't you? There is nothing like the culture and arts a man can experience in that part of the world."

"I do highly recommend it, sir," Jefferson said.

"Yes, well, it is something to consider." He turned to Sadie and offered her a smile. "It has been a pleasure, Agent Callum. You are every bit as charming as Mamie said you would be. Do please return when we can entertain you socially rather than have to do this sort of thing."

"I would like that very much."

He glanced past her to Jefferson. "And bring your friend Mr. Tucker." With that, Mr. Astor said his goodbyes and went on his way.

Jefferson leaned toward Sadie, his voice low. "Have the butler summon a police officer immediately. We may have a situation here." When Sadie's brows gathered in an expression of confusion, he continued. "He can take us to Valletta."

She nodded and hurried away. Jefferson returned to his seat.

"I believe we were discussing Mrs. Valletta's family. You said they are local to Newport?"

"Oh, yes." He nodded vigorously. "I found it particularly convenient to have a representative of Mr. Valletta's nearby, what with a good concentration of my clientele spending their summers here and owning these lovely cottages that are in need of decorating with beautiful art."

"All right." Jefferson stood. "I am going to give you a chance to prove that you're telling the truth."

"I don't follow."

"If Mrs. Valletta is in Newport, then you will take me to meet her."

"Right now?" Montfort rose on unsteady legs. "Yes, I can take you to her home. I know it well.

But as to whether she has returned, I cannot say."

"Returned? From where?"

"I believe she had some sort of travels planned that would take her away from the city for a few months. At least, that is what she told me upon the occasion of our last conversation."

"Which was when?"

"That would have been in late December of last year when the crate came for the Astors and a few other New York clients. Mrs. Valletta traveled to the city to see that all was in order. Because Mr. Astor wished his crate to come here, I had the pleasure of returning to Newport in her company."

"Excuse me." The butler now stood in the doorway. "There are Officers Barker and Crowley to see you, sir."

"Thank you. We will be right out," Jefferson told him.

"Officers?" Montfort fell back onto his chair. "You're having me arrested?"

Jefferson shook his head. "I am having you placed in protective custody. To keep you safe."

Sadie held her tongue and allowed Jefferson to continue conversing with Mr. Montfort. In her experience, men like the attorney might not listen quite as closely to a woman as they did to a man. And right now, Jefferson had Montfort's full attention.

"That is preposterous. I suppose they will come with us to the Valletta home?"

"They will keep a discreet distance, but yes, I think it prudent, don't you, Agent Callum?"

"Absolutely." She nodded to the door. "Shall we go, then?"

They emerged into the warm May morning to find a pair of Newport's finest waiting. Jefferson went to speak to them while Sadie allowed the driver to help her and the attorney into Mr. Astor's carriage.

The men rode along behind the carriage until they turned onto a street filled with modest homes bordered with tidy gardens. They paused at the corner while the carriage deposited Sadie and her companions at a home midway down the block.

After a moment's discussion, it was decided that the lawyer would approach the door while Sadie and Jefferson stood just out of sight. Mr. Montfort looked as if he might tumble forward, but somehow he managed to lift his hand and knock.

The door opened almost immediately, and a man stepped outside to envelop the lawyer in an embrace. "Welcome, Louis. To what do we owe this honor? Is Mr. Vanderbilt in need of another sarcophagus?"

At the sound of the familiar voice, Sadie gasped and stepped out of her hiding place. "Gabriel?"

Her childhood friend froze. Slowly he stepped

away from the lawyer and looked over in Sadie's direction.

His mouth opened and then slammed shut. A moment later, so did the front door.

Jefferson pushed Montfort aside and signaled to the police officers. Trying the door, he found it locked. After giving it two swift kicks, the door gave way.

Sadie held her gun at the ready as Jefferson raced inside. The house was small—tiny, really—and filled with all sorts of mismatched but well-kept furniture. Lace curtains covered the windows, and the smell of something delicious filled the air.

A woman's scream urged Sadie forward. In the kitchen, she found an elderly lady huddled in the corner, a pot of what appeared to be some sort of stew bubbling on the stove.

"I am a Pinkerton agent. We mean you no harm."

"Well, I doubt that," she said in a thick Irish brogue. "Your man's done chased my son-in-law right out the back door and into the yard, and an innocent man, he is."

"Gabriel is your son-in-law? But that isn't possible."

"Isn't it?" The woman moved past Sadie to retrieve a frame containing a tintype portrait of a couple on their wedding day from the wall. "What do you say to that, then?"

Sadie took the portrait and held it up to the

light. Indeed, there was the man she knew as Gabriel Trahan standing beside his bride.

"Julia?" She looked over at the woman. "Julia Oakman is your daughter?"

"She is, only her name's Valletta now. Mrs. Julia Valletta."

Sadie leaned against the chair as Jefferson hauled Gabriel back into the kitchen. "So you're acquainted with this man?"

"I am, but he is not a Valletta," she said. "I don't care what he's told you, Jefferson. That man is Gabriel Trahan."

Her childhood friend laughed. "For a Pinkerton agent, Sadie, you certainly are naive. My mother was married to a Trahan, but that man was not my father."

She pulled out the chair and sat down in a most unladylike fashion. "I don't understand."

"Well, of course you wouldn't." He swiped at a trickle of blood that escaped his nose.

"Get him a handkerchief, would you?" Jefferson asked the older woman.

"Here," Montfort said from his place at the door. "He can have mine." He moved toward Gabriel and handed him the handkerchief. And then he made to leave. A second later, he turned around and punched the man in the stomach, doubling him over. "That is for ruining my reputation, Valletta. And when I see your father, there's one coming for him too. You *promised* the purchases were valid. You gave me receipts and assurances of provenance. You took photographs and—"

"I think that's enough, Montfort," Jefferson said. "Why don't you let the officers get you settled? I'm sure something can be worked out, but you will need to stay in their custody until all of this is finished."

"The protection will be welcome, Mr. Tucker. Without officers in tow, I might have to come back and show this boy how I feel again."

Gabriel remained mute, the handkerchief held against his nose. One of the police officers stepped into the kitchen. "I have transport here, sir. We can take him and the old lady over to the jail now."

At the sound of the word jail, the woman began to cry. She made no move to interfere, however, as the policeman assisted Gabriel in standing.

Sadie, however, could not let her friend leave so easily. "Could I have a moment?"

Jefferson nodded to the officer, who escorted the woman outside. He turned off the fire under the stew and then regarded Gabriel with a look that told Sadie that Montfort wasn't the only one who wanted a piece of this man.

When they were alone, Sadie let out a long breath and said one word. "Why?"

He looked down at her, impassive at first and then, slowly a smile emerged. "You wouldn't know, would you?"

"Tell me."

"You had it all, you and your brothers. The big house, all you ever wanted, and more. But those of us down in those shacks your daddy called workers' cottages—"

"Those weren't shacks, Gabriel. They were nice, comfortable homes with—"

"Stop it, Sadie. You know nothing of any life but the one you've lived. My mother, she knew about that life. She was a lady before Trahan married her. He didn't deserve her and he knew it."

She wanted to speak but didn't. Instead, Sadie waited to see if he would continue.

"I didn't know until I was grown that the man I thought of as my father wasn't my father at all. I am royalty, Sadie. Descended from Spanish aristocracy, and I was left to rot on a miserable sugarcane plantation in River Pointe, Louisiana."

"You weren't rotting. You went off to Tulane. You studied to become a doctor."

He laughed. "I did nothing of the sort. I went to London and found my father, an exile living on money he made in a most inventive way."

"By stealing artifacts and selling them on the black market."

He shrugged. "It was commerce. I will make no excuses for people who cared nothing for where their precious baubles came from."

"You're a bitter man, Gabriel. And to think you pretended an interest in marrying me when all the while you were married to my maid."

"Oh, Sadie. Julia is no maid. She's an actress with no small measure of talent. I would wager a guess that pretending to be your maid was one of her best performances." He paused. "But yes, I would have married you. Gladly. I would have given you a baby or two just to see that the bloodline continued. I liked the idea of a child of mine inheriting Callum Plantation someday."

"And your *wife* didn't mind?"

He looked her in the eyes, any trace of amusement now gone. "My wife was the one who gave me the idea."

Jefferson stepped into the room and placed his hand on her shoulder. "It's time we allow the officer to take him."

She handed the tintype to Jefferson. "Gladly."

After the officer had taken Gabriel away, Sadie noticed that Jefferson was still studying the picture. "You were right about Julia," she said. "She wasn't what she seemed."

He set the picture aside and reached for her. She went to him and rested her head against his chest as he wrapped his arms around her. A thought occurred and she looked up.

"You didn't want Julia to come with us because you suspected her all along, didn't you?"

"I had a suspicion, but nothing I could prove."

"Based on the fact that she and your brother interacted at Valletta's shop."

"Yes. And Valletta knew her last name."

"What about the Durer? Do you think that was meant for you or was it sent there for Julia to intercept?"

"I suppose that's something she will have to answer when she's caught. But if I were to guess, I would think that even though the parcel had my name on it, it was meant for Julia. Your uncle just happened to stumble on it—literally—before she could find it."

"That makes sense." She rested her palms on his chest as she fitted another piece of the puzzle into place in her mind. "It seems as though we have everyone but Valletta."

"We will get him," Jefferson said.

She looked up into his eyes and mustered a smile. "We have to."

Forty

That evening a courier arrived at Hampstead Farms with a stack of files containing all of the photographic evidence Jefferson needed to prove that Sergio Valletta was accepting stolen artifacts from the British Museum dig site in Iraq and combining them with forged paintings to dupe wealthy Americans. What wasn't purchased in America went on to be sold in shops in London, Paris, and other European cities.

Though the possibility of Valletta somehow getting word of today's arrest was slim, Jefferson had determined he would take no chances. An officer was on guard at Hampstead Farms, and the staff had been instructed to allow no one to enter or leave the property without Jefferson's express permission.

Sadie was upstairs with a maid in attendance and a houseboy was stationed in the hall to watch over them both. And though he was sorely tempted to allow himself a few hours of sleep before morning, Jefferson did not dare.

He settled behind the desk in Mr. Hampstead's library and stared down at the blank page that had been defying him for the past hour. How could a letter be so difficult to write?

Finally, he stacked the stationery neatly and put it away, and then he returned the pen and ink to the drawer where he found them. He would write to his superiors at Scotland Yard eventually. But not tonight.

Threading his fingers together, he rested his head in his hands and dared to rest his eyes only a moment.

"Jefferson?"

Startled, his eyes flew open. The first thing he saw was the identical image of himself. "John."

His brother held up both hands. "I come unarmed."

Jefferson scrubbed at his face to wipe away the

last vestiges of the sleep he should never have allowed. "How did you get in here?"

John laughed as he made himself comfortable on the striped settee beside the fireplace. "Think. What did you tell the officer out front? And the staff?"

"That no one gets in or out without my permission." He shook his head. "And they all thought you were me."

He shrugged. "A common mistake."

"What do you want?"

Leaning back, John let out a long breath. "I'm tired of running."

Jefferson laughed, an involuntary response to an absurd statement. "Then by all means, do take a nap. Or perhaps you prefer a more comfortable chamber with a nice feather bed? I have it on good authority that there are a half dozen of those upstairs. Please feel free to find one and make yourself at home."

"Sarcasm." He shook his head. "That's my manner of speaking, not yours."

"It's been a long day."

"And a busy one." He shrugged. "Congratulations on putting two of the members of the Valletta gang away."

"The old lady doesn't know much," Jefferson said. "My guess is she's innocent of all but believing in the wrong person. Julia's mother will be back home and reheating her stew by morning."

"It wasn't the Oakman woman to whom I referred." He shrugged. "You've brought in Gabriel Trahan, although he prefers Gabriel Valletta now. Not his legal name that I am aware of, but he prefers it all the same. Then there is his lovely wife, Julia. She ought to be on her way to the Cabildo about now."

"The Cabildo? You're referring to the New Orleans jail of the same name, I assume?" At John's nod, he continued. "And just how do you figure that?"

"You sent a telegram to the chief of the New Orleans police around midday today, letting them know that a jewel thief would be returning to Callum Plantation by way of the *Montmartre*. It docked in New Orleans at five this afternoon."

"A jewel thief." He let out a long breath. "You do have a sense of humor."

"Yes, I do." His expression sobered. "But lately I have also been burdened by a ridiculous sense of right and wrong. It's extremely bothersome." John paused. "Or long past time."

Jefferson elected not to reply.

"In any case, you can check for yourself, but Miss Oakman, or rather Mrs. Trahan . . . or is it Mrs. Valletta?" He shook his head. "Anyway, the woman who acted her way into a position as Sadie Callum's maid would have been taken into custody the moment she stepped off the ship."

"At my word?"

"You are a detective at Scotland Yard working in conjunction with a Pinkerton agent on a case of mutual concern. Why wouldn't they take your word for it?"

"No, John, I am not. Thanks to you I lost my job."

He shook his head. "Actually, thanks to me, you got your job back." The fool paused to grin, and it took everything Jefferson had not to vault over the desk and knock the smile off his face. "You're welcome."

A wave of weariness passed over Jefferson as hard as the surf that had pounded him back in Key West. "I assume there's a story to go with this."

"A good one." He shrugged. "It starts with a Dickens tale and ends with a dare."

"Dickens and a dare?" He rested his hands in his lap to hide the fists that still wanted to punch his brother. "Go on."

"The last time I spoke to Granny, after she stopped throwing things at me, she insisted I read to her."

Jefferson nodded. "I got a Stevenson book, so I'm assuming you must have read the Dickens novel to her."

"I did, all the way through from beginning to end in just over a week's time." He shifted positions. "*A Tale of Two Cities*. Do you know it?"

" 'It was the best of times, it was the worst of times, it was the age of wisdom,' " he quoted.

"Yes, that's the one. There's a reference in it. Let me see if I can recall . . . 'Greater love hath no man than this, that a man lay down his life for his friends.' "

"John 15:13."

"I thought on that sentiment for a great while, Jeff. Even debated its meaning with Granny on more than one occasion."

An image rose of John and their formidable grandmother locked in debate. Jefferson smiled.

"Then there was another. This quote I do remember: 'Do you particularly like the man?' he muttered, at his own image; 'why should you particularly like a man who resembles you? There is nothing in you to like; you know that . . . Change places with him, and would you have been looked at by those blue eyes as he was . . . ?' "

"Quite a recollection," Jefferson managed through the lump growing in his throat. Though his brother stated the words, they might just as well apply to him too.

"Like you, I recall everything I read." He looked away. "Total recollection. It is both a gift and a curse."

Jefferson had never found the odd talent to be anything other than a gift, though he declined to argue the point. "And what came of those debates?"

John returned his attention to Jefferson. "After lively discussion, we came to an agreement."

"And that was?"

"Like the characters in the book, our lives and how they end come down to our own choices. To what we believe and in whom we believe."

Jefferson almost believed that John was affected by the tale he was telling. "Granny must have hit you on the head."

"No," he said softly. "In the heart."

"What? I don't believe you."

Jefferson's smile faded when he saw John swipe at a tear. An actual tear. John Tucker did not cry. Never.

"You can believe me or not, but it's true. She said plenty, but when she was done, she dared me to change. Dared me to change my spots and make a difference. To fix what I'd done wrong."

The next time I see that fool brother of yours, I am going to dare that leopard to change his spots. His grandmother's words. But then she had also told him she intended to pray that John would.

Silence fell as Jefferson waited for John to speak again. Finally, he said, "And?"

"And so I did." His fingers drummed on the arm of the chair, a nervous gesture characteristic of John Tucker.

"How?"

"Well, there was no small measure of prayer involved. And then I bought a ticket to London. I walked into your office at Scotland Yard and asked to speak to the man in charge. I told him everything. Of course, they thought I was you and you were explaining the devious deeds of your devious twin brother."

"You did? And why would he listen to you?"

"It helped that Mother came along with me to verify my story." He paused as if recalling the event. "Thanks to her glowing praise of her long-lost elder son, you'll probably go back to a raise and a promotion. She made you sound like the saint you are."

"I am no saint," he managed. "You really did this?"

"Send Mother a telegram and ask."

"I will. And I'll be sending one to the Yard as well."

"Be sure to tell them when you're returning to report for duty. They were keen to know."

Jefferson shook his head. "You really did this, didn't you?"

"I did." John sighed. "I also taught Julia Oakman how to steal jewelry." A smile began. "She was an apt pupil."

"All right," Jefferson said on an exhale of breath. "Explain that."

"She's a lovely girl, that Julia. I had occasion to meet her when your Mr. Valletta sought me out." He held up his arm and showed a scar several inches long. "He mistook me for you. It wasn't a pleasant visit. Of course, he was most apologetic when he realized the mistake."

"So Valletta tried to kill you?"

"I think he was trying to warn me, or rather you, off his trail. Scare me into deciding to go back to England, as it were. However, when he discovered I had a history of incarceration and several skills he might exploit, he was much kinder during our second visit."

"And that is when you taught Julia to steal jewelry?"

He nodded. "She contacted me when she learned she would be accompanying the men to follow you. I suggested she take a few things along and then see how many of them she might get away with stealing. It was to be an experiment to see how well she did."

"Some experiment."

"From what I understand, she left the *Lizzie* with Sadie's sapphires in her carpetbag. And, if I recall correctly, an emerald set as well as Sadie's grandmother's pearls. Those are the things you reported as stolen to the New Orleans authorities."

"Who arrested her this evening."

"Exactly."

Jefferson would know for certain in the morning, but his gut told him John wasn't lying. And his gut was never wrong.

"So you've apologized to Granny, got my job back for me, and seen to the arrest of one of the suspects in the Valletta case. Am I missing anything?"

"Actually, you are."

"Enlighten me, then."

"The Durer?" John shrugged. "Have you figured out yet that I sent it? I had hoped you would recognize it as a clue. And if Julia saw it, maybe she would get scared and confess her part. I assume, however, she did not see it?"

"No, she did not. However, what you've said makes sense."

"Of course it does. There's something else. I've written a few letters. I wonder if you would mail them for me." He set a stack of envelopes on the table in front of him. "Letters of apology."

"I see. Anything else?"

"Yes. I'm going back to Angola. I need to turn myself in." He rose and swiped at his eyes with the back of his hand. "Would you come with me to speak to the officer outside? I doubt he will believe there are two of us unless he sees us both."

Jefferson stood but found he could not move beyond the edge of the desk. So John came to him, clasping his hand on his shoulder.

"Come on, brother. Let's go."

Reaching around to gather his twin in the first embrace he ever could recall, Jefferson found he was fighting tears of his own. Together they walked out of the library toward the front door and the officer stationed there.

John stopped and turned to face Jefferson. "One more thing."

"What's that?"

"I'm sorry, Jeff. So very sorry."

And then he turned to open the door and walk out into the night. When the officer saw John, he rose. Looking past him to Jefferson, he froze.

"What's going on here?" he asked, seemingly unsure as to which of the brothers he should address.

"We're righting a wrong," John said. "I belong at Angola Prison in Louisiana. If you'll let them know where I am, I'm sure they will come and fetch me."

It was exactly what Jefferson had hoped for, and yet the knowledge that his brother was returning to his cell did not make him happy. The old leopard belonged there. This new one with different spots did not.

It was a conundrum and he hated it.

"He's telling the truth, officer," Jefferson finally said. "William John Tucker is his name. He's my brother."

The policeman checked his watch. "You want I should take him now, sir? My replacement should be along any minute."

Even as he knew what was right, Jefferson felt torn. One word from him, and the officer would look the other way.

"Yes. Go ahead and take him."

Unable to watch his brother leave, Jefferson turned around to face the house.

Before the man could open the gate, a scream split the night.

Sadie.

Jefferson raced inside and took the stairs two at a time until he found the room where she was supposed to be asleep. The boy who had been standing guard had been knocked senseless. He lay still with his eyes closed, a pool of blood spilling onto the carpet.

"See to him," he called to the officer who was a step behind. "Sadie!" he shouted. "Sadie, are you in there?"

Silence.

The door was locked, so he kicked it open. The lamps blazed to life overhead and revealed that the room was empty. Jefferson went to the open window and looked out.

"The maid. She's injured," John said.

Jefferson glanced back over his shoulder. "See if you can help her. I'm going after Sadie."

He stepped out onto the ledge and looked both directions. To the left was a wall that prevented any escape. To the right a narrow path led to what appeared to be some sort of balcony.

Following the path, he noticed a spatter of blood in the moonlight. His heart slammed against his chest when he saw Sadie's crumpled form.

Jefferson rushed to her side, knelt, and felt for a pulse. Yes, there it was. She was alive. A shot rang out, and Jefferson crouched down further to gather the woman he loved to his chest and try to shield her.

He eased to his feet with her in his arms and kept to the shadows. A moment later he moved toward the bank of windows nearby. Sadie groaned, her eyes still shut.

"Stay with me, sweetheart," he whispered against her ear. "You're going to be fine."

She wasn't, though. Not with the amount of blood now staining his shirt. He reached out to grasp the window and found it locked tight.

Another bullet shattered the wooden shutter just beyond where he stood, and Jefferson knew he had to get off that balcony. He knelt down again and settled Sadie safely away from the window. Then he pulled out his revolver and used it to break the glass.

Reaching inside, he slid open the latch and lifted the sash. A pane broke inches from his head, sending a shower of glass over both of them. He maneuvered Sadie back into his arms and then eased her inside. He climbed in with her and waited just long enough for his eyes to adjust to the dimness of the room.

He saw a bed and moved toward it. Settling her there, he situated her as comfortably as he could manage and then turned back toward the window.

"Jefferson."

Her voice was soft, barely there. He dropped to

his knees beside the bed. "Sadie? You're going to be fine. Remember what I told you in the mangroves?"

"You said nothing is certain," she whispered.

He had. Jefferson winced. "I also said we should live a little. And we will. But you need to stay right here while I handle a situation."

"Valletta."

"Could be. Or someone else who isn't keen on us arresting your old friend Gabriel."

"No," she whispered. "It is Valletta. He was in the hallway. I heard it when he hurt the boy. Went out to investigate."

"And he shot you."

She shook her head. "He ran into my bed-chamber and pushed away the maid . . . then . . ." She paused. "Then he went out the window. I followed."

"And then he shot you."

"Yes."

An ache began in Jefferson's chest that had nothing to do with bullets or broken glass. "I'm going to settle this, Sadie. I promise."

Reaching into his pocket, Jefferson retrieved Kyle's eyeglasses and put them on. The first thing he saw was her smile. The second was the blood.

Retrieving his handkerchief, he pressed it against the wound and watched the white cloth turn crimson. Casting about for something else, he tugged at the bed sheet until he could tear off several wide strips. From these he fashioned a bandage and folded it on top of the handkerchief. Then he wrapped several strips around her and knotted them tight, and the bandage held.

If only he could remain to see to her safety. Or better yet, to remove her from the place and into a doctor's care. Neither could happen at this moment. Not with the gunman still outside.

He leaned down to kiss her softly. "I love you, Sadie Callum. When I get back I'm going to marry you. Then we will live a little."

She did not answer. And he did not have the courage to check her pulse.

Instead, he stood and found his weapon. Then he went to the window. There was nothing to lose if Sadie was no longer drawing a breath. And if she was, then he must ensure she never had another moment's fear.

Stepping out onto the balcony, Jefferson heard another bullet hit the house just to his right. A figure down on the lawn moved between the trees. He took aim and pressed the trigger.

The figure fell, but not before he raised his gun one more time and fired a shot.

A lamp blazed to life down on the lawn, and a uniformed officer raced toward the shooter. "We have him," the officer called up to Jefferson.

He waved in response and then hurried back inside to Sadie. When he found her pulse, he let out a whoop. A moment later, the door flew open and the lamps lit the room.

"They're in here," one of the Hampstead servants called. "It's Mr. Tucker and the Pinkerton lady, and they've both been hurt."

Jefferson gathered Sadie against him again. Her nightgown was stained a bright red, but the blood seemed to be coming from her shoulder or perhaps her arm.

"Jefferson?" she said weakly. "Was it Valletta?"

"It was," the officer at the door said.

"The maid and the boy?"

"Both will be fine, ma'am." The officer fixed Jefferson with a look. "Your brother, sir?"

"Yes, what about him?"

"Well, he was a hero, sir." He looked down at his boots and then back up at Jefferson. "According to that man there . . ." He gestured to the butler. "While you were fetching Miss Callum from the balcony, your brother . . . well, he stood in her bedroom window and drew the shooter's attention away from you. On purpose."

The meaning of the man's words sank in slowly. Deeply. He said the first thing that came to his mind. "I need to thank him."

"I'm afraid that isn't going to be possible, sir." Again the man studied his boots. "He didn't . . . that is . . ."

Jefferson knew what he was unable to say. He slanted a look down at Sadie, who was watching him with her beautiful dark eyes. She smiled.

Her expression told Jefferson that she hadn't understood. Didn't know what John Tucker, the man she and the Pinkerton Agency knew as Will Tucker, had done for her.

"We are us now, aren't we?" she whispered.

He returned her smile, though it took all he had to manage it. "Yes, sweetheart, we are us now."

Forty-one

Three days later, Sadie walked out of Newport Hospital and into Jefferson Tucker's arms. She still didn't know about John.

He would tell her. Soon. Just not today.

Sadie held him tight as they walked to Mr. Astor's carriage and then refused to let him go until they arrived at the docks. When she spied the *Lizzie*, she smiled.

"How wonderful," she exclaimed. And then she saw her family.

All five brothers fought one another to be the first to run down the gangplank. While the other four were arguing, Donovan pressed past them to reach his sister. "Ready to go home now?" he asked.

"Yes, I believe I am." Jefferson helped her out of the carriage, and Donovan assisted in getting her situated in the main salon.

The captain captured Jefferson in a gentle embrace. "It's fine, Dad," he told him. "I've got a stitch or two where the glass cut me, but otherwise I'm unharmed." He leaned close. "John was a hero. You would have been so proud of him."

His father held him tighter then. "I know. I'll be taking a medal home to your mother. The mayor thought it appropriate, considering."

"Yes," Jefferson managed.

Dad put on the beginnings of a smile. "I have collected a stack of letters and telegrams for you. Several from Scotland Yard and at least one from a Sir Edward Maunde Thompson of the British Museum."

"Thank you. I will read through them later."

"There's something else." The captain nodded to the passageway, where his mother stood. "Guess I ought to have said *someone* else." He turned to Sadie's family as Jefferson went to embrace his mother. "Looks like the gang's all here."

Penn Monroe was the first to notice. "Lizzie Tucker, it has been far too long."

Jefferson held his mother against him. "Mother, how do you know Sadie's uncle?"

She laughed. "Well, now. That is an interesting story, isn't it, Mary?" she said, looking at Sadie's mother.

"Is there room for one more?"

Sadie looked up and shook her head. "Henry?" Her attention went to Jefferson. "Have you met

Henry Smith of the Pinkerton Agency? He's the man I work for."

Jefferson released his mother and laughed. "Uncle Hank?"

"Wait!" Sadie exclaimed. "Henry Smith is your uncle?"

"It's a long story," Uncle Penn said.

"And one that can wait until later." Seamus Callum clapped his hands. When that did not quiet the chattering crowd, he resorted to the whistle that he used to call the boys home for supper.

"I suppose it's time to get this started. Jefferson, I believe you're up. Unless you want me to handle this for you."

Sadie shook her head. "Daddy, what's going on here?"

Her father winked but said nothing.

"I can handle this just fine, sir," Jefferson said as he moved across the room to stand before Sadie. And then he dropped to one knee. "In front of God and everyone gathered here, I have a question I need to ask of you. Sadie Callum, will you marry me?"

"Marry you?"

The breath went out of her, and it had nothing to do with the bullet that had lodged dangerously close to her lungs. She looked into those blue eyes and found that words were impossible. So she nodded.

"That's a yes," Ethan said. "I saw it, and this time she can't change her mind."

"I saw it too," Aaron agreed as the other three Callum brothers nodded in agreement.

"Then it's official. There's going to be a wedding," Mama said.

"And right now," Daddy added.

"Right now?" Sadie shook her head. "But that's impossible. I don't have a dress or a preacher or . . ." She looked to Jefferson for help. "Where will we live?"

"Your mother brought a dress and my father is a ship's captain. He can marry us legally. I need to pay a visit to Scotland Yard to settle things, but we can discuss all that later. If you want a church wedding back in Louisiana, we can do that. Make it big and fancy with all the trimmings."

"No. I would rather marry you today." She attempted to stand, and Jefferson hurried to help her. "I can do this. I'm not completely helpless."

He smiled. "I know, but humor me. I like taking care of you."

She leaned up to press her lips to his ear. "We have a lifetime of that ahead, Jefferson."

Though she ached, Sadie straightened her spine and walked to her stateroom without help. The three other ladies followed after her. Mama fussed and worried about her bandages while she helped her only daughter into her wedding dress. Jefferson's mother and Aunt Pearl sat quietly and watched.

Mama paused to look past Sadie. "Do you approve, Lizzie?"

"You know I do."

Sadie shook her head. "All right. I refuse to leave this room until you two tell me what is going on here. How do you know one another? And why does Jefferson call my boss Uncle Hank?"

The three older women exchanged smiles. "You first," Lizzie said.

Mama settled Sadie on the chair nearest the bed and then sat down across from her. "Your daddy and Harrison Tucker are old friends. They have known each other since the war. Penn too."

"But Uncle Penn was in the Union Army."

"Technically, yes, but once he met up with Pearl here, his loyalties were a bit divided." Mama paused. "Those three decided they would join together and they did. Daddy was raising cane and Penn, he had a little money coming in from who knows where. He bought Harrison a boat, and the three of them started shipping cane and cotton to England."

"Harrison and I were already married," Lizzie said, "and my father had connections in the business world that provided our men with the buyers for their products."

"So Daddy, Uncle Penn, and Jefferson's father were business partners?"

"Yes," Mama said. "And there was a fourth." She looked over at Lizzie.

"Henry?"

"Goodness, no," Mama said. "Henry and Penn were roommates at Amherst."

"As was Harrison. Henry Smith spent enough time at Harrison's house in Mobile that the judge and his wife started calling him son." Lizzie chuckled. "I always did like those two. I mean to go and visit Harrison's mother before I return to London."

Sadie already knew that Henry Smith had a lasting friendship with Uncle Penn. But he was also well acquainted with Daddy? And Jefferson's father?

"I can see you're surprised," Aunt Pearl said. "But think, dear. Why do you believe Penn didn't try to talk you out of that secretarial job with the Pinkertons?"

"Because he trusted Henry?"

Mama nodded. "Same reason he allowed you to go on those assignments. And no, I did *not* know you were anything other than a secretary. I plan to speak to Seamus about that. Eventually."

A thought occurred. "But Henry was in charge of the Will Tucker case. Or, rather, I suppose it should have been the John Tucker case."

At the mention of Jefferson's brother's name, the women in the room fell silent. Sadie had the strangest feeling they were keeping something from her.

Mama touched her hand, and Sadie turned her attention in that direction. "Who better to right the wrong and see that John was stopped than the man who knew his family well?"

"I don't know," she said. "It just seemed as though he was so impartial. As though Henry wanted him captured more than any of us."

"He did," Eliza Tucker said. "It was his belief, and ours, that should John be brought to justice, he might have time to consider the error of his ways. We had all hoped that once he was released, things would be different. That he would be different."

Again Sadie felt as though she was the only person in the room who wasn't in on a secret of some sort. What that secret might be, she couldn't quite figure out. Nor did she want to ask. Not when a more important question loomed.

"You said there were four men in this partnership. Who was the fourth?"

Again the women shared a look. "Well," Aunt Pearl said. "He was a clever boy, really. He had charm, money, and a head for business."

"Another friend from Amherst?" Sadie guessed.

"No, dear." Lizzie rose and joined Mama. "He was a cousin of mine. He had done quite well for himself in London and was using Harrison's ships to transport cargo regularly. I will admit that his business kept the shipping company afloat in those early years." She giggled. "Oh, my. No pun intended, you understand."

Mama pressed her hand atop Lizzie's. "It's all right. We need a smile today."

"Well, anyway, when he expressed an interest in adding to his business with a location in Louisiana, Harrison contacted Seamus."

"Your daddy knew everyone back then." She paused to smile. "Still does."

"That's the truth," Lizzie continued. "Of course, he wanted Harrison to transport his goods, which meant he needed more vessels. That brought Penn in."

"And the business expanded," Sadie said. "But who was this man?"

Mama shifted to sit beside Sadie and then wrapped her arm around her. "Sergio Valletta."

The breath went out of her again. "But he . . ."

"Was a crook." Lizzie nodded. "Yes, we found that out. Penn and our husbands disbanded the company immediately and thought they were done with him."

"Until Key West." Aunt Pearl sighed. "There was money to be made in wrecking."

"So I've heard," Sadie said.

"Legal money," Lizzie said. "Although legalities never stopped Sergio."

"By then he'd run off with Caroline Trahan." Mama looked aggrieved. "I warned her, but she always did have notions she was meant for more than she had. And we all wondered whether her husband died a natural death or Sergio helped him along." She paused only a moment before drawing a deep breath and continuing. "The two of them set up housekeeping in Key West and Sergio, he made a point of seeing that Harrison's ships were lured onto the reefs."

"Lured?"

Aunt Pearl nodded. "False lights. He and his men knew when one of the ships was coming through the pass, and they would set up men in boats to look as if they were being warned off the reef but instead they would head them right onto it."

"That's terrible."

"Oh, he got caught soon enough. Ran off to parts unknown, he did," Lizzie said. "When Jefferson's investigation uncovered his name, we all knew something had to be done."

Mama leaned in. "And that's when the three of them—Harrison, Penn, and your daddy—they all got together and went to Henry to hire the Pinkertons to find him. And to get Jefferson out of jail."

"If only I had known sooner that Jefferson's brother was . . ." Lizzie dabbed at her eyes with her handkerchief. "Well, that is all something to consider another day, isn't it?"

Sadie was still puzzled about one thing. "But now Jefferson's father is considering the purchase of a home in Key West. Why?"

Lizzie smiled. "So that we might have a home near our friends the Monroes and the Callums."

"Oh."

"You sound disappointed."

Sadie shook her head. "Not at all. It's just that I have no idea where Jefferson and I will live. We haven't discussed it. Or anything else, really."

"Are you having second thoughts, dear?" Mama asked. "You don't have to go through with this today. Not if you need more time."

The other two ladies nodded. Sadie offered each one a smile.

"No, I want very much to marry Jefferson. The rest of it . . . the details? They will take care of themselves, won't they?"

"They always do," Aunt Pearl said.

Someone knocked. "Is the bride ready yet?"

Daddy.

"Almost," Mama called before returning her attention to Sadie. "Just one more thing, Sadie. Didn't you ever wonder who hired you to solve that case?"

"I don't suppose I thought of it. Henry only mentioned Mamie Astor. I guess I just assumed . . ."

"Hers was the first complaint he could connect to Sergio. Your father, Penn, and Harrison decided it was long past time that they do something about Sergio, so they went to Henry."

"Who chose me."

"I must say your father and Penn weren't keen on the idea," Mama said. "But Henry asked for their trust. You were the one for the job, he said. And he was right."

Sadie thought of Henry's demand that she go home and make peace with her father before setting off on the Astor case. "He always is," she said as she let out a long breath. "Does Jefferson know any of this?"

"I believe his father will tell him eventually," Lizzie said. "He could be telling him now. I don't know."

Sadie nodded. "But one thing I don't understand. Why didn't any of you say something before now?"

Mama shook her head. "I think we all just hoped things would never come to this."

Another knock. "Ladies, you're going to have to let loose of the bride before the groom comes and kicks down the door. Apparently he's had some recent experience utilizing that skill."

Sadie rose and kissed her mother on the cheek and then embraced Lizzie Tucker and Aunt Pearl before opening the door. Daddy reached to link arms with her and then led her down the passageway and into the salon, where her groom waited.

Jefferson met her at the door and escorted her to stand in front of his father. "Sadie Callum, you bought me a watch once. Do you remember?"

She nodded. "I do, although I will say that it was worth much more than what I paid for it."

He smiled. "Well, in any case, I don't have a wedding ring ready, although once we send our families back where they belong and have ourselves a proper honeymoon, I intend to remedy that."

"Can we just get to the marrying part?" Ethan called.

Harrison nodded. "Yes, we can. Are you two ready?"

"We've been ready for some time," Jefferson told his father before reaching to embrace Sadie. "We're us now."

And then he kissed her.

Author's Note

I hope you enjoyed reading the story of lady Pinkerton Sadie Callum as much as I enjoyed writing about her. During the course of my research for the Secret Lives of Will Tucker series, I was surprised to learn that female agents had contributed much to the lore of the Pinkerton Agency. For example, thanks to the detective work of Agent Kate Warne and others, Abraham Lincoln survived an attempt on his life and arrived in Washington, DC, to safely be inaugurated as president. Now *that* is girl power!

While planning the background of Sadie Callum and Jefferson Tucker, much thought went into what their homes were to look like. In my opinion, you can tell much about a person—or in this case, a character—by examining the place where he or she was raised. I chose to use the stunning Oak Alley Plantation as a model for my privileged Louisiana girl, Sadie Callum. I took a few liberties with adding and subtracting outbuildings, but in general the Callum home almost exactly resembles the grand mansion still standing on the River Road in River Pointe, Louisiana. To learn more about Oak Alley Plantation, visit their website at www.oakalleyplantation.com.

Though Jefferson Tucker hails from London, his roots are planted firmly in the South, where his father saw to it that the Tucker twins were brought yearly to visit their grandparents in Mobile, Alabama. While in Mobile researching the three books in the Secret Lives of Will Tucker series, I was privileged to visit the Bragg-Mitchell Mansion, a lovely antebellum home maintained by the Mobile chapter of the Daughters of the American Revolution. Surrounded by lush gardens and yet just minutes away from downtown Mobile, this home is the perfect backdrop for Judge Tucker and his wife to welcome their expatriate son, his British wife, and the twin boys. For more information on the Bragg-Mitchell home, visit their website at www.braggmitchellmansion.com.

Research on the Astor family provided many interesting facts that have added depth to this novel. The ongoing war between the two Mrs. Astors (egged on by William Waldorf Astor) was fascinating, as was William Astor's choice to move his family to England a short time later. The case of antiquities fraud that Sadie and Jefferson investigate is based on an actual case presented to Scotland Yard by the British Museum. Between 1886 and 1891, cuneiform tablets and other antiquities were disappearing from museum sites in Iraq and showing up in the shops of London dealers. I decided it would be interesting to explore the possibility that those stolen antiquities as well as other valuable pieces of art might also reach the United States.

And as an interesting aside, the visit that the couple pays to Key West on their journey to Newport is taken, in part, from a historical search for a buyer for businessman Asa Tift's home on Whitehead Street. The home, completed in 1851 in the shadow of the Key West lighthouse, was built of white pine shipped down from Georgia and boasted the only basement in the city. Later it would claim the first private swimming pool, but at the time that Jefferson's father goes to visit the property in consideration of purchasing it, the home had been sitting empty since Mr. Tift's death the previous year. Eventually, the Tift heirs would find an owner, but not until 1903 when Pauline Hemmingway and her husband Ernest purchased the property.

Also, while writing the scene set out in the flats beyond Key West's main harbor, I took liberties with the distance the mangroves are from shore. While Jefferson easily rowed the leaky rowboat out using only oars, it was a lengthy sail under wind power when I traveled there on a much larger sailboat. And while Sadie sees dozens of crabs skittering about, the truth of the matter is that the number was more like hundreds when I saw them. However, I found it difficult to write a romantic scene with that many crustaceans climbing overhead, and so the number was reduced.

As with any project, an author never writes a book alone. Thus, I must give credit to those who helped in this endeavor. Many thanks to:

Wendy Lawton, my amazing agent, friend, and writing Sherpa from Books & Such Literary Agency. I cannot imagine writing without you.

Kim Moore, my Harvest House editor, and the rest of the Harvest House team for your invaluable input and assistance. I also owe a huge debt of thanks to the entire Harvest House team for your support in bringing this series to print. Without you, Will Tucker would never have stolen his first jewels.

Laurie Alice Eakes (www.lauriealiceeakes.com), award-winning author of the Midwives series and The Daughters of Bainbridge House series for her assistance in matters of historical accuracy. Your ability to ferret out the facts astounds me. Thank you for your willingness to help and to read through the manuscript. Any errors are mine alone.

Malcolm Steiner, author of Old Mobile Restaurants, whose knowledge of the history of Mobile, Alabama's, dining scene proved invaluable in choosing the restaurant where Jefferson and Kyle would order their oysters. I urge you to visit Malcolm's website at www.oldmobilerestaurants.com to learn more about his fascinating book on this unique area of Mobile history.

Jeane Wynn of WynnWynn Media who went over and above the call of duty to see that the world knew about Will Tucker and the Pinkerton agents who chased him.

As always, to my husband, **Robert Turner**, who was invaluable in planning and executing the great writing research trip of 2012 where I was privileged to see firsthand many of the locations I went on to write about in this series. Not only did he play chauffeur, photographer, and tour guide, he has since given me great advice on plot and characters and has even read through the manuscript on a mission to seek out those nasty typos and mistakes authors are known to make. Bless you, Bobby T!

Finally, to my readers. You are the reason I write! I am always looking to hear what you like and what you would like to see next. Who knows? You might even find yourself in a book someday.

If you have enjoyed the Secret Lives of Will Tucker series, I hope that you will connect with me on Facebook (www.facebook.com /kathleen.ybarbo) or Twitter (www.twitter.com /KathleenYBarbo) to let me know. Also, check out my website at www.kathleenybarbo.com to see what's next!

Discussion Questions

1. Sadie Callum is good at what she does because her job as a Pinkerton agent requires her to pretend to be someone else. It is only when she is forced to answer to her father that she becomes herself. Sometimes we react to God in a similar way. Have you been hiding from your Father? Is there something you need to tell Him, and if so, why have you been putting it off? Sadie needed to go home and make things right. Is there an area in your life you need to do the same?

2. Jefferson Tucker is an innocent man who was locked up for the crimes of his twin brother. For almost a year he sought justice and yet found none. Through it all, he never gave up. Is there something in your life for which you've been seeking justice? Perhaps something you've been requesting of the Lord to which He has not yet responded? If so, persevere. We serve a God who hears our cries even when it feels as if He does not.

3. The men in Sadie's life love her enough to seek her out in an attempt to protect her. This protection, however, has been the cause of

more than one situation that did not end well. Have you been overprotecting someone in your life? If so, how can you take steps now to release that person and allow him or her to take responsibility? Or perhaps there is a situation you have been trying hard to control. Is there something you need to turn over to God and allow Him to handle? What can you do today to allow that to happen?

4. Sadie is trying so hard to get her way that she is willing to deceive those she loves in order to do as she wishes. It is only when the results of that deception come to light that she realizes what she has done. Is there something you want to do so badly—or are already doing—that you would be willing to hurt others in order to continue doing it? If so, what is God telling you about this? How can you take steps to make right choices in this area?

5. Jefferson's loyalty to his profession puts him at odds not only with Sadie, but also with his brother, John. For as a man sworn to uphold the law, John's claims should not carry any weight when compared to the arrest warrant sworn out against him. Why, then, do you think that Jefferson entertained the thought, however briefly, of helping his brother? Have

you ever been tempted to do something you knew was wrong because the outcome was something you wished to see happen? If so, what was it and why did you feel this way? Did you go through with it? Why or why not?

6. Sadie has been given all the benefits of being a wealthy sugar planter's daughter, complete with a beautiful home and a family who loves her. And yet as a girl she envied the children of the employees whose lives seemed far more interesting than her own. As an adult, she finds herself restless when languishing at home, almost as if she's missing something by being where she is. In short, Sadie suffers from an inability to find peace and joy in her surroundings. Are you always looking for the next thing? Perhaps believing that you would be happier if your circumstances were to change? Do you recognize the fallacy in that expectation? What can you do today to change that type of thinking and, in the process, put yourself on the road to finding peace and joy right where you are?

7. Sadie has five older brothers, each of them very different in looks and temperament, and yet all raised by the same set of parents. Each of the men has his strengths and weaknesses, and together the five Callums support one

another. The church is made of people very much like the Callum family. Each member has strengths and weaknesses that are complimented by others in their congregation. What are some of your strengths and weaknesses? How do you use these strengths to serve?

8. John and Jefferson Tucker look so much alike that their resemblance causes many to believe that one is the other. This similarity causes doubts to surface as to Jefferson's ability to do his job and eventually leads to his dismissal. Have you or someone you know ever been wrongfully accused of something, or has someone made incorrect assumptions about you due to the company you keep? What could have been done differently to avoid this?

9. Sadie's and Jefferson's cases intersect at a point where neither is certain of the other and yet they are forced to work together. Have you ever had an issue of trust with someone? What caused that issue and how did you remedy it? Or, did you find that trust could not be regained? If so, then why and what did you do about that?

10. Sadie's parents believe the solution to her problems is marriage, and so they take steps

to try to arrange a happily-ever-after for her. However, things do not work out as they planned. Has that ever happened to you? Have you taken action to make something happen only to find that God had another plan you never expected? If so, what did you try to accomplish? What did God do instead?

11. Sometimes people are not what—or who—they seem. While we may think we know someone, in truth, that person could be hiding deep and possibly dangerous secrets they wish would never come to light. Perhaps you have secrets you hope are never revealed. Do you know that God sees past whatever exterior facades we erect to peer deeply into our hearts? Is there something you need to admit to Him? Perhaps some secret has been burdening you. Unburden. Go to God and talk to Him. If you've done this, there is no need to share your secret with others. However, would you consider sharing how you felt after you came clean with God? Perhaps you might save someone else from carrying needless burdens with your testimony.

12. Sadie devised a plan to investigate a man she believed to be an art thief, only to find the plan had disastrous results. Have you ever

made plans without praying over them sufficiently? Perhaps you felt as if you needed to help God along? What happened? What might have happened if you had waited? What will you do the next time you are tempted to do the same thing?

13. Part of Sadie's job is keeping secrets. While she is good at what she does, the life she is living is not the one she wishes she had. Have you been in Sadie's place? Is there a life you wish you were living? Are you keeping secrets? What can you do to change this? Is this something you want to change? Why or why not?

14. Sadie and Jefferson must learn to trust one another before they can cooperate to solve the cases they have been entrusted with. The pair finds that the process of learning to work together is not easy. Has God ever put you in a position where you were required to cooperate with someone with whom you did not get along? How did you handle this? What was the result? If given the chance, what would you have done differently?

15. "Nothing is certain, Sadie. Live a little." With those words, Jefferson convinces her to get into the boat and sail off on an adventure.

Those same words, spoken by his grandmother a few weeks prior, had given Jefferson the confidence he needed to set off on his own adventure. Has there ever been a time when you felt that God was calling you to take a chance, perhaps to set off on an adventure with Him? What did you do? How did it turn out? If given the chance to do it again, would you? Why or why not?

About the Author

Bestselling author **Kathleen Y'Barbo** is a RITA and Carol Award nominee of more than forty-five novels with almost two million copies of her books in print in the United States and abroad. She was recently nominated for a Career Achievement Award by *Romantic Times* magazine. A tenth-generation Texan, Kathleen Y'Barbo has four grown children, seven bonus children, and her very own hero in combat boots.

Find out more about Kathleen at
www.kathleenybarbo.com.

Center Point Large Print
600 Brooks Road / PO Box 1
Thorndike, ME 04986-0001 USA

(207) 568-3717

US & Canada:
1 800 929-9108
www.centerpointlargeprint.com